WIND OF CHOICE

A SECONDARY WORLD FANTASY

UNEXPECTED HEROES
BOOK 1

MARTY C. LEE

Bookaholics Press

BOOKS BY MARTY C. LEE

Unexpected Heroes series

Wind of Choice

Seed of War

Wave of Dreams

Spark of Intrigue

Tales of Kaiatan

Legends of Kaiatan

Nobody's Revenge (novella 0.9)

The Cat's Fortune (a Legends novella)

Unexpected Heroes: The Complete Series

Unexpected Tales: Four Short Stories of Kaiatan

(an excerpt of Tales of Kaiatan)

Return of the Fae series

The Coming of the Fae

The Peril of the Fae

The Academy of the Fae

The War of the Fae

The King of the Fae

The Heirs of the Fae

The Escape of the Fae (novella 0.5)

Spotting the Fae (novella 0.8)

AS M. CATE LEE

Relatively Haunted series (2026)

Book design and publication by Bookaholics Press LLC, Provo Utah
Edited by Anna King
Front cover design by Brenda Camp Walter
Back cover and chapter heading illustrations by Naomi Rasmussen
Map illustrated by Michelle Allan and Naomi Rasmussen
Author photograph by Melissa C. Baxter
Back cover photo "White-rumped swift, Apus caffer, at Suikerbosrand Nature Reserve, Gauteng, South Africa" by Derek Keats CC BY 2.0, modified.

ISBN-13: 978-1-950230-00-6 (epub)
978-1-950230-01-3 (mobi)
978-1-950230-02-0 (paperback)
978-1-950230-03-7 (large print)
978-1-950230-26-6 (hardback)
978-1-950230-60-0 (audio)

Published by Bookaholics Press LLC
Provo, Utah bookaholicspress@gmail.com

Contact the author at MCLeeBooks.com

For Becky, who first asked me for bedtime stories,
and for Kylia, who begged for this one.

CONTENTS

Map of Kaiatan

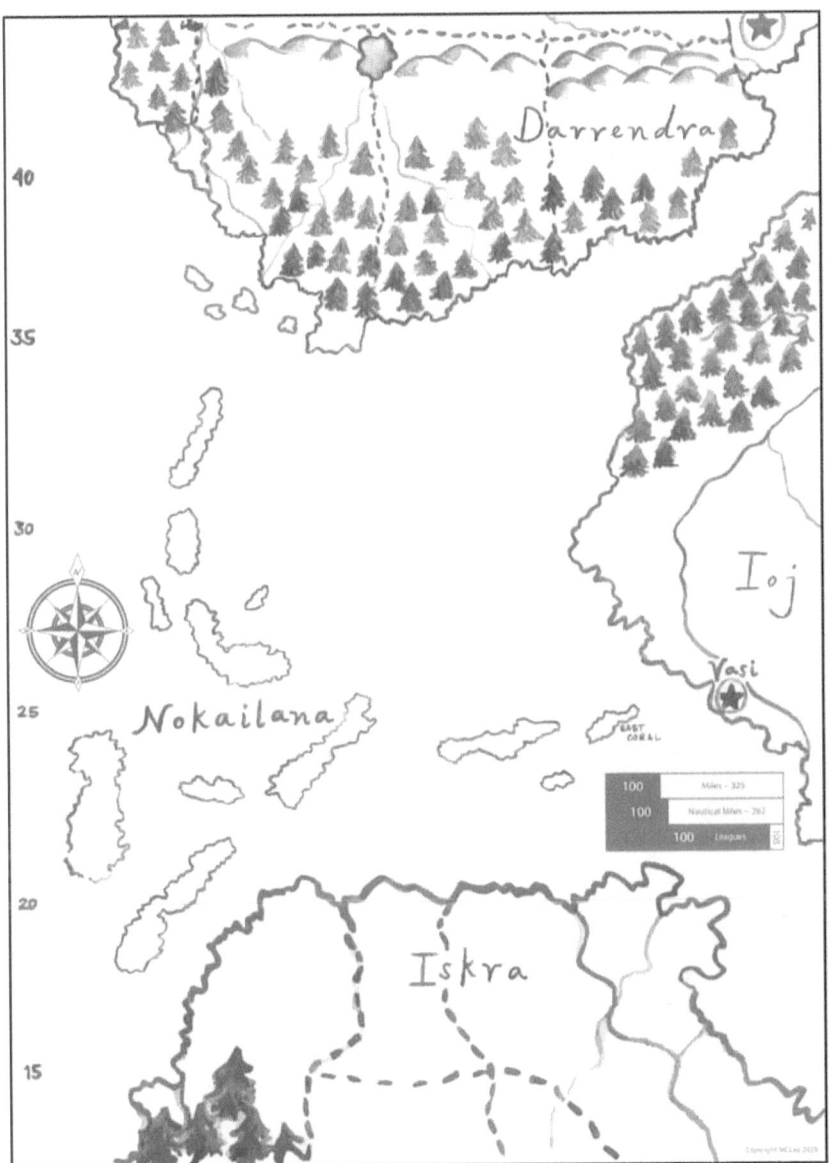

1. AHJIN
(VASI, IOJ)

Vasi: Capital city of Ioj. The view from the towering cliffs is awe-inspiring. The main temple of Irajahan, where the sixteen-year-old winged youths present themselves at adulthood, is one of the architectural wonders of the modern world.

The Visitor's Guide to Ioj, 5th edition

Ahjin's feathers whispered in the perfect updrafts. The air was sweet today, and escape was even sweeter. He shoved back his worries about meddling priests and flew higher in the pale orange sky.

When the city on the cliff below was almost too small to see, Ahjin tightened the tie restraining his curls. He stretched his arms and somersaulted into a dive. The wind whistled in his ears as he fell.

After one breathtaking minute, he tucked his arms and legs, spread his wings, and snapped into the roll that started his aerobatic routine. He ran through his old stunts, then added the new tricks he'd learned from spying on the advanced class. Father trained him daily after school and would teach him the rest of the techniques when he became a sky-dancer.

Ahjin spun into a deliberate spiral. He flew well, and hard work would make him even better. He'd be an asset to his parents and their troupe while he made a living doing what he loved best. All he had to do was stay away from the temple long enough to be forgotten in the vocational assignments, then follow his own skydancing goals without interference.

He ran through his routine three times. If he judged the height of the sun correctly, it would be too late for the priests to ruin his plans now.

To celebrate, he should buy something delicious for Mother. He flew lower and scanned the flying lanes in the market. There wasn't much produce available this early in spring, though, only some fruit and fresh greens.

As he removed his goggles and spiraled for a better look, Father glided from behind a group of shoppers. Oh, no. The market was busy today, with heavy traffic both on the ground and in the air, but not enough to hide Ahjin. He should have flown a little longer. Or a lot.

Father dodged through the airborne crowd with crossed arms and an impressive frown. "You're late. On purpose, I dare say."

Father had been more easy-going before Ahjin's birthday brought the possibility of change to their lives. He had trained Ahjin since his first flight so he could join the troupe at adulthood. Now it was time to follow their long-held plan, and Father still insisted he go to the temple. Why was the priests' approval so important?

"Father, I told you I wasn't going. We already have plans." Ahjin dodged a little girl chasing her pet bird. That had been one of his favorite childhood games, too, when he was younger and carefree.

Father sighed. "I felt the same way when I was your age. Don't roll your eyes — I was young once."

Ahjin snorted. Father's hair had been white from birth, and his body was as strong as ever. Ahjin had seen no evidence his attitudes had ever been young, though.

"Unfortunately for you," Father continued, "the only choice you have left is whether you want to arrive by wing or tied in a carpet. Don't shame our House by making me call the temple guard."

He motioned to the black marble road among the ordinary cobblestone roads made for the convenience of wagons and wingless visitors.

The cobblestone led everywhere, from the market to the Great Library, and between the older houses and the new, three-story towers with landing platforms on every level.

The black marble went only from the market to Ahjin's doom.

"Well, given those charming options," Ahjin scoffed, "I'll go. It won't make any difference. I don't need anyone telling me what to do with my life."

Ahjin slowed to an insulting speed, but whenever he meandered, Father was at his back, too experienced to be shaken. They traveled without wasting their breath on the same futile discussion they'd had every day for the last month.

Vasi was the largest city in the country, but Ahjin could cross it in half an hour at his slowest flying pace. He normally enjoyed the flight and visiting with people. Today, he only had time to wave and smile, hoping to annoy Father and slow the trip.

"Hurry," Father said. "Many of your friends are already there. You can talk to the rest after your interview." When Ahjin waved at a pretty girl, Father tried again. "The Winds won't be happy if you're late. If you cooperate more, they'll have no reason not to give you what you want."

Cooperate. Ahjin snorted. "If I avoid the temple altogether, dear Father, there's *no* chance for them to tell me what to do." He didn't care if Irajahan's priestly Winds were unhappy. The whole tradition was ridiculous. He was an adult now and could choose a vocation himself.

"That never works," Father said. "They'd just assign you something unpleasant later. Do you want to work in the sewers?"

Ahjin clenched his jaw and narrowed his eyes. "Why would they care about one person?"

Father sighed and didn't reply.

Even at Ahjin's best dawdle, they approached the temple too quickly. The grandiose stained-glass windows sat in gray-and-white marble traced with gold, but he didn't appreciate the splendor today. His normal schemes for flying through the high arches and between the towers were replaced with bitter musing.

Ahjin's pretty mother waited for them in front of the temple, her flyaway blonde hair pinned into place. Her pale golden wings were one shade darker than her hair, and her flowing dress hid muscles as toned as the ones displayed by Father's sleeveless vest.

Ahjin and Father swooped down to land by her. Worry eased from her face as she pulled Ahjin into a hug before he folded his wings.

"You're just in time." She smiled at him, but her look to Father was almost a wince.

As they entered the gilded temple, the long line of monthly petitioners waned to the last boy and girl, probably latecomers from the country. The priests gave Ahjin and his parents impatient looks and hurried them to the front of the antechamber.

He had been within minutes of being too late.

It wouldn't matter that Father dragged him here. Ahjin had no intention of cooperating against his own desires. If the official word coincided with his plans, he'd be the model of obedience. He might agree with something only a bit different from what he wanted, if it took advantage of his talents. Messengers, for instance, came from the ranks of talented fliers. Never let it be said he was *completely* unreasonable.

The dark-haired novice at the desk, wearing the empty-circle badge of the lowest priestly rank, had been a year ahead of Ahjin in school. While the novice wrote Ahjin's name in a massive book, his parents went outside to wait in the courtyard.

The novice walked Ahjin to the left-hand room and ushered him in with a scowl and a casual wave. Ahjin hid his own scoff; the incompetent novice hadn't advanced past Doldrums in almost a year.

Inside the room, colorful murals on the high walls detailed the great deeds of Irajahan, God of Air, guardian of their country. Ahjin had glimpsed them before, during required services and his rapid flyovers. If there weren't a row of plainly dressed priests staring at him from behind a long table, he'd examine them now. It would be more fun than this dreary interview. Only the Wind on the far end had even a hint of a smile.

"Come in, boy, and hurry," said the closest priest. "We don't have all day."

Ahjin stomped over and introduced himself — Ahjin Machol, son of Jayan and Aria — followed by his House and the names of his grandparents. Then the inquest began, with the priests taking turns asking arbitrary questions.

"How well did you do in school?" asked a Wind holding Ahjin's record, which made it a trick question.

Ahjin smirked. "I pay attention to things that are worth my while. School qualifies sometimes."

"What were your favorite subjects?"

"I liked flying, gymnastics, meteorology, and geography," Ahjin replied.

"Do you have any siblings?"

"One little sister, who's still too young to fly."

"What profession would you like?" asked the almost-smiling priest.

"I want to be a professional skydancer." Finally, a good question.

"Do you have any special skills or talents?"

"Well, obviously, I'm great at flying." Ahjin was in fair currents here. "I practice daily."

"If you're that good, why didn't you take the advanced aerobatics classes in school?"

Ahjin rolled his eyes and stared at the murals, but one of the other priests pointed to his school record.

"They have academic prerequisites for those classes."

Ahjin ignored that, too. It was stupid to need good scores in math for a flight class. Flying was unrelated and more important.

"Do you have any job prospects?"

Yes, a better question. "My parents want me to join their aerobatic troupe."

Then the questions came faster and more complicated. "Explain the political significance of the recent trade treaty." "Given a right triangle with one side the length..." "What are the major exports..." "Name the last three potentates and their policy differences." "If the barometer falls and the temperature rises..."

Ahjin got at least half of them correct.

"What's your favorite color?"

Ahjin blinked at the change of subject. "Blue." Flirting girls said it looked good on him, but what difference did it make?

The Winds glanced at each other and dismissed him to join his parents outside. At least the stupid question ended the obsolete ritual.

When Mother tried to get him to stand still in the courtyard, Ahjin dodged her grasp. When Father threatened to ground him if he even hovered, he walked back and forth in the corner. Ten steps left, turn, ten steps right, turn. The afternoon sun sank lower as he paced behind the other petitioners and their families.

It seemed forever before the stuck-up novice climbed the outer steps of the temple to the gilded marble podium used for public announcements. He unrolled a scroll and, in a bored voice, read the names of the new adults and their assigned jobs, in the order they arrived that morning. When he got to the end, he sneered at Ahjin.

"Wind." He snapped shut the scroll and swaggered back inside the temple.

Father gasped. "Really?"

No, that had to be wrong. Ahjin wasn't a priest. But thanks to the temple guard, he couldn't ignore it. Ahjin evaded Father's grasp to run after the novice.

"Wait, there's been a mistake," he yelled as he ran into the echoing antechamber. "I'm to be a skydancer with my parents."

He skidded to a stop when he realized the room was filled with priests and priestesses glaring at him.

Ahjin stammered an apology, then gulped and repeated his explanation with shaking knees. If he didn't find the courage to convince the Winds, he'd be trapped as a priest for the rest of his life. His skydancing training would be wasted and his talents ignored. That was unacceptable.

The nearly-smiling priest from his interview stepped forward, without a rank pin, but now dressed in lavish garb that overshadowed his plain gray wings. "Do you remember being asked your favorite color during your examination?"

"Yes," Ahjin said, "but many people like blue." Perhaps it was proof something had gone wrong in the interview or the entire flawed system.

"Hmm, true," the priest said. "There's only one issue. None of us asked you that question."

"I heard you." Why would they lie about something so obvious and irrelevant?

"No. Irajahan asked you." The Wind folded his hands together as he made that outrageous claim.

Ahjin flared his wings and jerked his head around to stare at the large stained-glass window above the temple door. It depicted the god in his ostentatious glory, summoning the winds from all directions. The caption said "Irajahan the Omnipotent." The artist had drawn the powerful god with a sulky face.

"A god has no better question to ask me than my favorite color? What's the point?" He folded his wings and edged away. Perhaps it was time to end the conversation and leave.

The priest grasped Ahjin's shoulder. "The point is that you heard him. Telepathy is an automatic qualifier for the priesthood. Other skills become inconsequential. Your personal desires and your family's needs are irrelevant. You have until tonight to say farewell to your family and bring your things to the temple dorms. Initiation starts tomorrow morning, so don't be late."

He waved his hand at the other Winds, who bowed to Ahjin's captor and filed out of the room. The novice from school scoffed at Ahjin, then simpered at the Wind on his way out.

Ahjin was left alone with the old priest. He had telepathy? When had that happened? Never mind, it didn't matter. "No thanks, I have other plans." Ahjin tried to pull away.

For an old man, the Wind had a strong grip.

"Let me explain. When a new adult is assigned a job, he or she may petition for a change if they truly feel the assignment is unsuitable for them." That blithe half-smile stayed annoyingly on his face.

"I appeal!" It wasn't smart to *tell* him the way out.

"The exception is the priesthood," the Wind continued. "There is no release for telepaths. They are too rare and too badly needed. I'm sorry. Go say your farewells." His hand tightened until Ahjin's shoulder ached. "Please don't make us get you in the morning." He released Ahjin and followed the other priests into the inner temple.

Ahjin's groan echoed in the empty room. He couldn't return to his parents yet. They wouldn't understand why he wasn't happy, but he had dreams he'd worked hard to reach. Did he have no choice but to give up skydancing? Tradition was strict and the priesthood apparently stricter.

How could he fight a god?

2. CHANGES

(VASI, IOJ)

While priests' many duties include administering rites, preaching, and caring for the temple, their most important task is to relay Irajahan's will for his people.

Handbook for Winds

Ahjin held his breath as he glared at the colorful temple window and thought nasty things he hoped were overheard. When he ran out of insults and could pretend to be happy, he set his shoulders and left.

The courtyard was empty. Even Ahjin's parents had gone to collect his little sister from their cousin's house. He flew home slowly, thankful for the chance to think.

How could the priests be so cruel? He had worked hard for his dreams, and he wanted to stay with his family. Father was wrong — Ahjin should have hidden longer. His telepathy wasn't in any record; even *he* hadn't known about it. If he hadn't heard that question, they would have let him be a skydancer. Now everything was ruined. Even if his assignment was a mistake, the Winds didn't care.

His life was over. As a priest, he wouldn't learn any more aerobatics and might not have time to fly for more than transportation. Wonderful flying would be replaced by boring duties. What a waste of his constant practice. Someone would always tell him what to do and where to go, even after Doldrums. He wouldn't be able to live with his family, and might barely have time to visit.

He clenched his fists. How dare Irajahan and the priests destroy his life!

If only his parents would help him fight this. Ahjin snorted. Father would think this great honor was worth changing their dreams. Mother was too gentle to oppose either the authorities or Father. Even if his parents wanted to back Ahjin, they couldn't win against the law of the Winds or the temple guard that enforced the holy dictates throughout Ioj. This was his last evening as a civilian.

Ahjin watched the children play carefree tag above the gardens. He admired the view from the cliffs and waved to an acquaintance among the city guards who operated the pulley platforms used for freight and visitors.

Lee beckoned from his post at the top of the cliff until Ahjin landed by the guards. "Fair winds, Ahjin. How many new soldiers were called today?"

Ahjin had anticipated that question, and the number was high enough to satisfy.

"So, congratulations on your big day. What's your new job?" Lee asked.

"Priest," Ahjin muttered.

Some of the soldiers whistled, but others flinched. Lee glanced at the temple and ended the conversation as quickly as good manners allowed.

Ahjin cringed and turned for home again. Would people always be wary of him now, afraid of his connections? He couldn't read their minds, after all. Could he? If he didn't know, how could they? When his friends and neighbors called to him, he waved and kept going, afraid they'd also pull away.

His stomach cramped as he turned the corner before his parents' modest, one-story cottage. He was out of time, and he'd never live with his family again unless he beat this dilemma.

Did he have to pretend he was happy about his life turned upside down? It could be worse. Garbage collector was worse, wasn't it?

And priests could still marry — in fact, they were encouraged to — if he found a girl who didn't mind sharing him with Irajahan. Some girls thought the prestige was worth the hassle and long hours. It was no consolation.

When he shuffled through the door, his parents jerked their chairs back from the table. His baby sister smiled and reached for him, fluttering her downy wings. Maili's wispy hair was as yellow as Mother's, but she had Father's blue eyes. Ahjin forced a smile and hugged them all.

"There is no appeal," he croaked. He swallowed and tried again. "I have until curfew to report."

Mother handed him the baby and headed to the pantry. "It will be fine. You'll see." Her voice wavered. "Tonight we'll have a feast; tomorrow will be a new day. Do you want to invite friends to dinner?"

"No, I'd rather be alone with you." He spent more time flying than with his friends, anyway. He tickled Maili and listened to her giggle.

Father reached for a traveling basket. "Should I help you pack?"

Ahjin shrugged and carried Maili to his tiny room at the back of the house. She sat on the bed while Father helped Ahjin choose clothes for his days off. The temple uniforms were ugly for the first couple of ranks, but that was the least of his worries.

"Why did you make me do it, Father?" Ahjin hunched his shoulders. "You said it would be better, but look what happened. This is your fault. I should have done it my way."

Father stopped folding clothes and bowed his head. "I had a friend who skipped his ceremony and became a miserable sewer worker. I didn't want that to happen to you."

He smoothed a shirt and folded it slowly, matching every edge. When finished, he handed it to Ahjin, eyes downcast.

Ahjin tucked the shirt into his pack silently. Father was still ruining his life. He glanced at the map he had painted on his wall, with a different color for each country and each direction of wind and current. There was a whole world he'd never see now.

Hmm.

How did this telepathy nonsense work? Could anyone eavesdrop on his thoughts? Until he knew, he should think quietly. He wrapped a small family portrait in the silk scarf Mother had embroidered last winter.

Father picked up Ahjin's surujin and swung the weighted ends for Maili to grab. "Do you suppose they'll let you hunt or continue your practice?" He coiled the rope.

"I'll find a way." Ahjin was good with a bow for a boy — no, he was a man now — and better with his weighted throwing rope. He could take down a goose on the wing or stop a horse in its tracks, although that stunt had almost gotten him arrested when the irate farmer called the city guard. The horse was uninjured, but Ahjin practiced on wild animals after that.

He tucked the weapon inside his pack with his wrist guards and bowstring, and strapped his recurve bow to the outside, looking around his room with regret. There was so much he couldn't take, and he didn't know when he'd return for the rest. Now that he was leaving, Maili would move from their parents' room to his.

He looked again at his wall map. Though it wasn't as splendid as the temple's murals, it was more useful, especially now.

Shh, think quietly.

Dinner smelled ready, so he lifted his sister and his pack and left the room behind Father. Ahjin glared at his parents' House crests hanging on the wall with his ancestor's triple-curled Wind badge between them. Perhaps his great-grandfather was responsible for the "gift" of telepathy. He had been a mid-ranked Squall who married late in life and had only one child, a girl who did not follow him into the priesthood. Ahjin would happily blame him if no better prospect appeared.

He fastened Maili in her baby seat, then sat between his parents. They ate slowly and in silence. Maili pounded her spoon on the table and burbled at Ahjin. These memories of home would be a treasure when he was gone.

When Mother served dessert, Ahjin took a deep breath. "I've heard novices don't get time away for a while."

Every new adult went through an initiation. The soldiers trained before a mock battle. Most entertainers and athletes had a similar display. Farmers grew a garden in summer or wrote a report in winter. Teachers taught a class in public. Whatever Wind novices did at first was a secret.

"I'll miss you so much," he continued. That was true. "Don't worry about me. I'll see you soon." That was the possible lie that made his chest ache.

Father ran his fingers through his short, curly hair. Ahjin regretted, a little, growing out his own hair to look different. Mother's purple eyes, mirrors of his own, filled with silent tears. Both parents tried to smile.

"Do you want us to fly you to the temple?" Father asked.

"This is hard enough," Ahjin said. "Please let me go alone." He pressed his feet against the floor to distract him from his own tears.

Mother squeezed Father's hand. "I know they'll feed you, but I packed treats. Is there anything else you'd like?"

She tipped the small basket to show the contents. Perhaps it was her mother's heart that thought he'd starve without her cooking, but it was handy.

"Do we have any of your dried fruit? Or jerky from our last hunting trip?" Bread would spoil quickly, but she had packed enough cheese and fresh fruit for a week.

"We have both." She wiped her eyes and added his requests to the basket.

It was time. Ahjin shoved away his unfinished dessert. He hugged Maili, tickled her until she squealed, and handed her to Mother. After kissing his parents, he slid his long jacket over his arms. Father straightened the back section of Ahjin's jacket between his wings and laced the sides.

Ahjin slid Mother's treats into his pack and slung it on one shoulder. He took one last look at his family and trudged out the door, hurrying to leave before he cried.

Mother's trembling voice followed him. "Good flight."

Ahjin held his breath until his eyes stopped burning.

This wasn't fair. Perhaps he wasn't even a telepath. The priest claimed nobody in the room had asked that question, but it might be the charlatans' elaborate trick to draft him into servitude. He trudged toward the center of town without bothering to keep *that* thought quiet.

The priests said the god of air was vital to the existence of the world, but Ahjin suspected the Windbag told them that story to justify his extravagant vanity and continued reign. Ahjin didn't like encouraging the fable, especially when it demolished his own ambitions.

Ahjin was *good* at flying. Why didn't the Winds realize that? He had often complained to his parents about life being unfair, but his earlier concerns seemed childish now. The only choice left was not much choice at all.

When Ahjin reached the market, he bought a compass and waved to some girls, then buckled his narrow pack between his wings and jumped into the air. He flew toward the temple with his heart pinched and palms damp. Could he really change his life in so many ways?

He spiraled higher and higher until he saw hints of other towns and villages near the horizon. Below him lay the city on the tall cliffs. Most of the businesses were in the center of town, with the residences along the outskirts. The farms were farther from the cliff, where the ground was less rocky. He waved farewell to his house, then flew west toward the temple. It was beautiful, gleaming in the sunset like an immense opal, more fantastic than the library or the palace.

He kept flying until he passed the cliffs and the lavender ocean was below him, then looked toward the far borders. Stories claimed the northwest forest was infested with giant spiders that trapped foolish explorers in vast webs. Discounting the ridiculous legends, any part of Ioj was within Irajahan's range and thus not safe.

According to the map on his wall, farther out of sight to the north lay deeply forested Darrendra, the land of the shape-shifting tribes. The few people who had visited those territorial folks and returned to tell about it had not gone past the narrow shore allowed to foreigners. There were no stories of how to survive inland.

Ahjin spiraled around and looked to the south, toward the immense desert continent. There were a few semi-permanent camps along the coast of Iskra, but much of the interior was inhospitable. Only the desert nomads knew where to find water in the sand, and a green oasis didn't guarantee a surface spring.

He stretched his wings with pleasure and made a long dive. The night breeze ruffled his unruly curls and cooled his angry flush. He flipped into a series of rolls and ended with an exhilarating loop. Flight was a distraction, but the sport soon palled under the weight of his errand.

Was he far away enough to think openly now? While in the city, he had tried to use his rage and loathing to hide his initial plans from any telepathic snooping. It was too bad he couldn't tell his parents what he was doing, but they would have stopped him. There was no way he'd be a priest, no chance he'd ruin his life.

Besides, he was an adult now. It was time to show he could take care of himself. Once he found how to get around Irajahan's selfish decrees, he'd fly with his family again. He already yearned for that day.

The Nokailana Islands to the west were a garden paradise full of clean springs, fruit trees, lush greenery, and easy-going natives. With wings to reach them and a net to catch fish or birds, the islands seemed his best opportunity for a successful escape. It should be easy to find land with fresh water and shelter until he found a long-term solution. He wouldn't give up his ambitions or his family for foolish priests and a stupider god.

Ahjin flew steadily away from Vasi until the three moons rose. The large, golden moon lit the clear sky with a mellow glow, while its tiny, pale blue companion chased its lavender twin across the heavens.

After three hours, he was tired and far enough from the city that nobody was likely to find him, if they bothered looking before morning. Any searchers would waste their time checking his house and the city before they looked farther. Even if Irajahan found him, Ahjin was out of his territory. The gods barely talked to each other and didn't cooperate for anything, much less the retrieval of one young man.

He searched the dark ocean for somewhere to rest.

A storm blew out of nowhere, with none of the usual warning signs. Clouds drizzled cold rain down his collar. Wind battered his jacket and plastered hair in his eyes. Stronger blasts bent his feathers and scrambled his steering control. His wings wrenched sideways. The drizzle turned into a waterfall. If he didn't land, the wind could blow him off course or snap his wings.

He shoved dripping curls out of his face. Green islands shone on the horizon under the moons, too far away. The only place close enough was a small, rocky islet below him. At least he'd be less at the mercy of the increasingly violent wind and could continue his trip after the storm passed.

He tried to land, but the gusts pushed him back into the air. In desperation, he waited until he was right above the rocks, then furled his wings and fell.

Ahjin missed the islet and fumbled for a hold in the ocean. The wave-splashed rocks were too slippery, and he slid off again and again until the water soaked his wings into worthlessness. He gasped for breath and grabbed a dead branch caught in the rocks.

A horrible scream echoed around him.

He forgot about holding on and covered his ears. It didn't help; the wailing was inside his head and didn't stop. The noise of the tempest rose to compete with the clamor in his head.

Now that he had no handhold, the storm grabbed him again and slammed him into the rocks headfirst.

Everything went dark.

3. NIA

(EAST CORAL ISLAND, NOKAILANA)

Holy Days: First Day of Spring; Summer's Return; Wave-Riding Festival; Festival of Rainbows; Dolphin Races; Makana's Day; Festival of Song; Festival of Clean Water; Day of Ocean Calming
Incomplete list, from Hail, Makanavailea

Waves lapped sweetly at the island shore, and birds sang sleepily. Niamolenulanami raised her head above the water to watch the rising sun turn the sky from black to blue to day's pale orange. She pulled her hair away from the gills on her neck and braided a foot or two of it. The morning light made the lavender waves sparkle. The coral reef was a busy, colorful backdrop to the houses under the surface. Life was good.

Life was good, but she was bored.

Ya'eel swam circles around her. "Come play hide-and-tag," the dolphin squealed. Nia swam almost as quickly as he, even without a tail, and it was one of their favorite games.

"Sorry, Ya'eel." Nia yawned. "Kala and Kamea are going to the big market today. Mom told their mom I'd go along." At least it was something to do.

The large market was on the next island west. Though Kala was an adult, it was a bit far for her to watch Kamea, her younger sister and Nia's only far-sister, by herself. Nia had actually woken early, but now the girls were late. She should have stayed in her hammock longer. Nia yawned again and relaxed in the warm water. Her eyelids weighed as much as a sunken ship. The waves rocked her.

"Good news, Nia," Kala said.

Nia jumped and opened her eyes again. The sun was higher than she remembered. Had she fallen asleep? Ya'eel laughed his dolphin laugh and sprayed water over her.

"The twin boys are fishing with Dad." Kamea waved at Nia and Ya'eel and somersaulted in the water. Her hair swirled behind her until she was a blurred, purple circle.

"And they'll drop us halfway," Kala continued, "so we'll make it home for the festival tonight."

Ya'eel towed Kamea while the older girls swam beside until they reached the boat and climbed aboard.

They sailed past the island's fruit trees and gardens to the fishing ground between the islands, where the twins let the girls jump overboard. It took only a couple of hours to swim the rest of the way. The girls reached the island market while there were still plenty of goods available in the booths.

As she looked around, Nia's shoulders slumped. She thought this would be better than their local market, but it was mostly more of the same old boring stuff. Where was the color, the originality, the excitement?

Most of the vendors were Nokai who laughed and sang and importuned buyers as usual. The few pale Iskrin stood out as much for their serious demeanor and boring clothes as for their plain black hair and long eyelashes. One of them had beautiful silk scarves hung in rows, and Kamea ran one finger above the fabric while Kala asked about prices. The Iskrin smiled and jabbered in trade tongue, holding up different scarves. Kala's grasp of the language was minimal, and she wrinkled her face as she listened.

"Ooh, how lovely." Nia slid beside Kala. "Let me help." She switched to Iskrit to question the seller about prices, then back to Noki for Kala. "I don't think you can afford more than one from this row."

When she repeated the price, Kala swallowed hard and shook her head. "Kamea, which is your favorite?"

Kamea pointed to a violet-streaked blue, and Nia bargained at top speed, glad for her birth gift of translating. With the addition of a string of shells that Kala pulled from her pocket, and the trader's appreciation for hearing her native language, Nia got the scarf for less than asked. After that, it was a quick matter to shop for the rest of their list and head for the ocean. The little fun available was over.

A rollicking music called to her. "Do you hear that?" Nia hummed along, trying to hear the words. "Let's find it."

She wandered to the docks with the other girls trailing behind. The music grew louder until she found Nokai sailors bellowing the song as they unloaded their cargo.

The words echoed across the waves. *"Oh, where are the ladies?"*

Kala skidded to a halt and adjusted her string bag of purchases. "I think that's close enough, Nia."

"Fish guts." Nia rolled her eyes. "It will be fine. I want to learn the song." She hummed, memorizing the tune. Finally, some entertainment.

Kamea cowered behind Kala. "I want to go home."

"We're going home," Kala assured her. "Come on, Nia."

"In a while." Nia danced down the rough, wooden pier.

"You're supposed to stay with us," Kala said.

Nia waved them off. "Tell my mom I'll be home soon." They'd be fine, and she needed a little excitement running through her gills.

By the time Nia reached the ship, the other girls had left. She wove up the gangplank between the busy sailors, greeted the captain, and talked her way into a perch on the railing. From there, she could hear the songs and smell the zesty spices as the sailors carried the barrels and sacks off the ship. She stayed while they reloaded with baskets of sweet pineapples and mangoes and casks of salted fish.

Before the captain approached her again, she had memorized three of the songs.

"It's time for us to leave," he said. "You'd better get off, unless you're heading southeast to Iskra." He winked at her.

"Could I catch a ride toward East Coral?" she asked. "I haven't learned all the verses of the last song yet."

The sailors bellowed approval, the captain laughed and nodded, and the ship was off with the tide. Nia stayed on the bulwark with a handy line for support. The ship swayed in the current, and the wind ruffled Nia's hair with the promise of adventure.

She spent two delightful hours practicing the new songs before a sailor sidled next to her and grinned.

"Are you traveling all the way with us?" he asked.

Nia smiled back. He was handsome, but far too old and weathered by sun and storm. "I'll leave soon."

"Not too soon, I hope."

Nia stood on the railing and squinted at a fishing fleet to the north. "Actually, I recognize the patterns on those sails. Thanks for the ride, but this is my stop."

She dove into the sea and swam home, arriving not long after Kala and Kamea and just in time to dress. This was a regular sixth-day festival, not one of the goddess' holy days, but she still shouldn't be late. If nothing else, this was her only chance to avoid boredom a little longer.

She swam past the coral reef and dove to her house on the sea floor, grabbing her jar of plankton light from its sun-feeding station as she passed through the door. On days she wasn't assigned to toil in the garden, she had enough demand for her singing to afford her own little house with two tiny rooms. The tidier room for visitors was on the upper level, with a hatch leading to the sleeping-and-storage room on the bottom.

Nia was close enough to adulthood to live alone, and near enough to her families' houses that everyone knew if she needed help. She had learned reading, sailing, and other life skills years ago, and even at her preferred lazy pace, she was already competent in her music. Now it was a matter of practice and increasing her repertoire.

She hung her glowing jar above her mirror. Since she didn't have time to search for it, she was lucky she had remembered to lock her costume in her hammock with the strap that tethered her while she slept. Her rich purple divided skirt looked like sweeping trousers with a foot of sturdy lace on the bottom. The long-sleeved top was plain white, but covered in Mom's best embroidery in a lovely range of colors.

Nia needed to braid her hair in an intricate pattern for her performance, instead of her casual plait. She grabbed her ribbons and turned back to the mirror, then squealed at someone else in the reflection. When the apparition laughed, Nia turned with her hands on her hips.

"Kalalamoanani, if I die of fright, who will sing your favorite songs tonight?"

Kala stuck out her tongue. "So you don't want help with your hair?" She swam through currents of clothes and unfinished projects the window mesh kept inside the house while it kept sharks outside. "You're lucky you don't have a roommate to drive insane with this chaos."

Nia ignored the comment and fluttered her eyelashes. "Please, I'll owe you forever."

"You still owe me for abandoning me at the market. And for the last time I helped you. And the time before that, and—"

Nia covered Kala's mouth to muffle her voice.

Kala rolled her eyes instead and reached for half of Nia's hair. "I'm so excited about tonight," she said as soon as Nia freed her. "Kua should be there."

"I'm sure he wouldn't miss a chance to see you." Nia envied Kala's excitement. "Did you see him get in trouble for pulling up the wrong plants in the garden yesterday?"

"No, really?" Kala backed up to maintain tension as she moved down each plait.

Nia looped her half-finished section around a hook on the wall to do the same. "He was watching you instead of paying attention to the plants."

She giggled and batted a floating braid out of the way. When she nudged her near-sister, Kala's golden skin turned a bright red that clashed with her persimmon hair.

"Amakualena..." Kala drew out the name lovingly. "He's so cute. And strong." She sighed. "And smart. And..." She stopped when Nia kicked her ankle.

"Seaweed, Kala, I know he's perfect," Nia said. "I don't need to hear it again." When Kala's face fell, Nia relented. "You can tell me tomorrow, I suppose. But no more tonight!"

"What's wrong with you, fish breath?"

Nia sighed. "Nothing."

"Hmm." Kala bumped her shoulder against Nia. "So you say. What project will you abandon this time?" She pulled hard on the braid to tie it off before switching to a new one.

Nia winced. "If you don't want to help, at least leave my hair attached."

"I'm sorry," Kala murmured, sounding more contrite than Nia deserved. "Let's change the subject. Tell me what you'll sing tonight."

"I thought I'd sing the island garden song in honor of spring. And Awa wants the one about the fish that swam so far north he turned into an iceberg. He thinks it's the funniest song ever." Nia giggled.

She finished the last of the braids on her side right after Kala finished her half. Now it was time to weave the plaits together with the ribbons to hold it into place and add color to the lavender braids. Nia let Kala do most of the work while she kept everything from drifting into knots. This *was* easier with help.

"We'll sing plenty of dolphin songs," Nia continued, "including a new whistle one. Ya'eel tells me I'm getting much better. The ocean songs are popular. I have several love songs. Oh, and some new ditties from those sailors this morning." She grinned and wiggled her eyebrows.

"Nia, you can't sing those today," Kala groaned. "There will be children there."

Nia kicked a heap of clothes. So much for the fun of the new songs. "I'll try to behave myself." She wrinkled her nose at Kala until her near-sister smiled.

Her hair looked perfect in the mirror, so she gave Kala a hug, threw a cover over her light, and swam to sit on the edge of her domed roof while Kala left to get her younger brothers.

To Nia's left was the festival, at the end of a stone-marked pathway currently lit by nets of blinking atolla jellyfish. She loved approaching from the surface and seeing all the roads form a colored picture of fish jumping through waves and coral. At the edge of the coral reef to her right were the homes of most of her family. She stretched her neck for a wistful look at the wide ocean beyond, but her family swept around her, chatting and threatening to sabotage hairstyles and costumes, and blocking her view.

"Shipwreck," Nia swore. "If you mess up my braids, I'll sing in your ears to wake you before sunrise tomorrow." She shot them one of the ferocious looks she practiced to compensate for her height.

They cheerfully surrendered, and she linked elbows with two of her siblings, who grabbed the others until all seventeen staggered across the road. The festival started as Nia's family arrived for their work shifts. They split to their various stations while the theater was empty. Mom left with the weavers, and Nia and her musicians set up next to a jewelry booth she wanted to browse later. As she sang, the busy crowd rotated between entertainment venues so she had only a small audience at a time.

Nia got as much praise from the crowd as ever, but instead of her usual happiness at the end of her shift, everything was duller today. Even the jewelry wasn't as pretty as it had looked from a distance. Who had thrown boring-juice in the ocean?

On her way to her family's prearranged meeting place, she found Kala and Kua flirting with each other. Nia dragged them along with her, one on each side.

"Come join us," she said. "We can't have you getting lost."

Kala glared at Nia. "We were fine alone."

"I'm sure you thought you were." Nia winked at Kua, who blushed and shrugged at Kala.

Once the rest of Nia's family arrived, everyone swam around, bargaining for pretty things and teasing each other. The still-blushing Kua was a popular target for jests, but no one was safe. When it was time for the presentation, the clan hurried to finish negotiations, then gathered at the theater.

Kala and Kua made fish eyes at each other while Nia and several other siblings squirmed together like a swarm of eels and made their multi-seater hammock sway. Nia elbowed her way through the heap until she had a good view of the stage. The dolphins swam through their newest routine in honor of Makanavailea, Goddess of Water. Nia waved madly when she saw Ya'eel in his debut performance. The tumblers swam off to wild cheers, and the night's officiator began the mundane part of the meeting.

Nia smothered a yawn and nudged Awakakama, the far-brother unlucky enough to be by her elbow. "Can't they post the information?" she whined.

When his mom glared at them, Awa closed his mouth, shrugged, and covered his own yawn. There were unsurprisingly no marriages this month, and Nia let her eyes glaze while the pod leader recited the names and parentage of the new babies. When the dignitary got to the stodgy announcements, the yawns she alternated with Awa spread through the audience.

Then Makanavailea swam in for one of her occasional visits and gave birth gifts to the clan's babies. The clan sang a hymn or three to her, praising the beauty of her luminous eyes and her rainbow fall of silken hair. She had no need of the gills her people used to breathe underwater, but she shared their golden skin and webbed digits. The Nokai included a hymn to her compassion, reminding her how the islanders depended on her loving protection. Makana was kind, intelligent, and generous, but if riled, could cause substantial damage until she calmed to her usual indolence. Nia loved the goddess' insistence on holding a party every six days.

After the goddess zipped away, the party continued with songs, games, and dancing. Some people — the very old or parents with small children — swam home early. A few stalwarts kept up the merriment until they fell asleep and drifted in the morning current.

Nia bounced between the different activities, desperate for something to hold her attention. She spent most of the festival with family, bothering Kala often to make sure her near-sister didn't have much time alone with Kua.

Kala tried to chase her away with increasingly less subtle excuses. After the fifth time, Kala drew her aside. "Will you go pester someone else, please? I'm *busy*." She simpered over her shoulder at Kua.

"You may continue for now, but I'll be back." Nia waved and swam off.

She headed for the singing, then changed her mind and swam toward the market stalls. Halfway there, she stopped and tread water, letting the ocean flow around her. Everyone else was having fun at the festival. Something must be wrong with her. When had her life become dull? Why wasn't she happy the way things were?

Shark fins! She needed a challenge. Ooh, she needed an adventure, more exciting than a mere ship ride. That was a great idea!

She didn't know where to find one. Maybe she should have stayed on the ship. Nia sighed again and headed back to the games.

She glanced up as a colossal storm suddenly raged above the ocean.

No, she did have an idea.

4. SALVAGE

(EASTERN EDGE OF NOKAILANA)

Nokailana consists of about a dozen larger islands and hundreds of small ones that support a loose assortment of Nokai clans. Many of the world's intercultural traders are Nokai.

Everything You Ever Wanted to Know about the Nokailana Islands but Were Too Lazy to Ask

Nia dragged herself from bed an hour or two before midday. It was adventure time.

She dumped her regular clothes into her closet and let her thermal swim outfits drift to her bedroom floor. After eliminating the cooler knee-length outfits and the unnecessary camouflage, she was left with three spongy, wrist-to-ankle suits in her favorite wild patterns. Mom's whimsical printing experiment of bright pink and purple fish swimming on a teal background fit her mood, and her canteen, medical kit, and a waterproof pouch of food hung nicely on the matching belt. The hook on the wall was enough help to put her hair in two plain braids, wrapped around her head and fastened with ribbons.

Nia whistled for Ya'eel, who planned to swim with her, then play while she explored. The dolphin arrived so quickly he must have been lurking between the houses.

The sun shimmered in ripples on the bottom of the warm lagoon.

Schools of colorful fish chased each other through the coral. Some were playing, some hunting, and all were beautiful. Though the noise from the upper world was muffled, the scraping of the beakfish feeding on the coral algae was so loud that Nia waved to any Nokai she saw rather than talk to them.

The two friends floated around the twisting coral reef and into the wide ocean, then swam east for two hours at moderate speed. Today was a good day to explore. The storm the night before had been horizon-to-horizon, and storms often left interesting flotsam on the rocks.

At the first islet she approached, she saw flashes of white and blue on the rocks. The potential treasure was unlikely to be part of a wooden ship. Ya'eel swam in search of fish while she pulled herself on land and walked through the storm-blown white gull feathers to the rubble. First, she saw a crushed basket and its scattered contents, then a crumpled pile of bright blue fabric stuck between the biggest rocks on shore. The cloth could make a carrying case for her salvage.

Nia pulled on it, and the pile moaned and twitched. She squealed and jumped backward, grabbing for a rock to throw. When the movement stopped, she crept closer, rock still in hand.

This wasn't a remnant of a ship's cargo, but a filthy survivor. How exciting! Curly white hair shone through the mud. Oh, flood waters, how could she get an old man away from here? He'd need water, food, shelter, and medical help first. She propped the broken basket over a few sticks to make spotty shade.

"Hey, are you awake? Can you sit?" Nia prodded his shoulder.

When he didn't answer, she pulled his arm. He groaned and batted at her hands, so she tugged again.

He curled onto his side as much as the rocks allowed. "In a few minutes, Father," he whispered.

Nia stared at his now-exposed back. Wings trailed off the island into the water! There had been no gull. No wonder he hadn't liked being pulled across the rocks. And his wings looked injured from the — shipwreck? — no, crash landing. Of course that storm had smashed him from the air. He was lucky to find land instead of miles of empty ocean.

"Hey, you, are you okay?" She poked him again.

He blinked open plum-colored eyes. "Am I dreaming?" he slurred. "I thought I was miles from pretty girls. Waz your name?" He closed his eyes again.

"No, no, stay awake. You have to move before the tide rises." Nia pointed to the feeble shade of the basket and adjusted her language to match his. "Come on, sit. Now put your arm over my shoulders, and... stand."

The old man staggered upright and stumbled a few feet, then collapsed when she let go of him. She knelt beside him and held her canteen of fresh island water to his lips. He sipped at first, then gulped. When the canteen was empty, he stretched his wings and flinched.

He didn't seem coherent enough to answer questions, so while he ate the fruit from her waterproof pouch, Nia tended his scratches with her tiny medical kit. To keep his damaged wing still, she untied the sides of his clever jacket and carefully refastened it with his wings inside. His hands were raw and bruised, but unbroken. The shallow cut on his head was already scabbing.

She had seldom seen a foreigner up close, besides the occasional Iskrin at the big market. His wings labeled him an Iojif, and his skin was much closer to peach than her own golden tone. On closer inspection, he didn't seem old, so maybe white hair was as typical for an Iojif as black was for Iskrins.

"I've fixed you as much as I can," Nia said. "You should let our healer see to the rest of your injuries." Then her curiosity overflowed. "What's your name? How old are you? What are you doing here? Can we send a message to your people? Is your wing broken? What's it like to fly?"

"So many questions." He smiled. "I'm Ahjin Machol; I just turned sixteen. No message is needed and flying is wonderful. I think I sprained my wing. Who are you, and where do you live?"

"I'm Niamolenulanami of the East Coral Clan, so we wouldn't have to swim too far." At his blank stare, she tried again. "Call me Nia. I'm 5668 days old."

"Five thousand — How old is that in years?"

Nia quickly calculated. "About fifteen-and-a-half. I live about twenty miles west of here."

"I guess I can ride in a boat for that long."

"I don't have a boat, silly," she laughed. "I'm not a fisherman or trader."

"No boat? How did you get here?" Ahjin looked behind her back. "You don't have wings." His eyebrows crept up his forehead. "I'm sure you can't walk on water, although that'd be a trick I'd like to see."

"I swam, of course."

"Swam. Twenty miles. This morning." Ahjin looked her over from head to foot. His eyes widened when his gaze reached her webbed fingers and toes, and his eyebrows shot higher at the sight of her gills. "I can't breathe underwater. I think my wings will get waterlogged and pull me to the bottom of the sea, even if I weren't injured."

"I'll ask Ya'eel to give you a ride," Nia said. "It'll be fun. The water makes you weightless. Maybe it will feel like flying."

She ran to the shore and trilled the dolphin's summoning whistle. When she heard Ahjin whimper, she turned.

Ahjin clutched his head, and his voice rose to a yell. "Shut up, shut up, shut up!"

The wind blew his broken feathers around the islet. His pitiful shelter collapsed.

Nia ran back. "What's wrong? I'm sorry about the whistle. I was calling for your ride."

"Not you. Someone is screaming in my head again. Make him stop! This shouldn't be real."

The wind shrieked harder and stung her eyes.

"Stop yelling," Ahjin said. "What do you want?"

He sounded frantic, though Nia didn't see or hear anything. Had he damaged his head when he hit it on the rocks? That would make everything more difficult.

Ahjin stopped talking, although his hands pulled so tightly on his curls, Nia thought he'd pluck himself bald. After a minute, he staggered to his feet and tied his few surviving belongings into a beautiful, soggy scarf.

"If you need to do anything before we leave, do it *now*," he said, "and hope my ride arrives soon. This island will flood any minute." He gave this absurd prediction with a serious expression.

Nia laughed in his face. "The bad weather was yesterday. That's why I picked today to explore. Now sit down and rest before you collapse." She tried to help him sit, but he lurched away.

"Unnatural weather is coming," Ahjin said, "like yesterday's. The god of air is throwing a tantrum in my head. There *will* be a major storm. This island is not high enough to survive the waves caused by this wind. Now, do we have a way to escape or not?" He stuffed his bundle inside his jacket and stared at the horizon.

When she followed his gaze, the rapidly darkening sky startled her. Ya'eel whistled, and Nia turned to see him cavorting in the surf, despite the choppy waves roaring out of nowhere. "There's your ride," she pointed.

The wind gusted. Ahjin staggered to the water. "How do I ride it?"

"You ride *him* by sitting on his back and holding his dorsal fin." Nia demonstrated, then gave Ahjin a second look and pulled off her belt. "Let me wrap this around you, please, Ya'eel," she whistle-clicked, "or Ahjin will fall off when you dive."

It took a moment to arrange the makeshift harness and tie Ahjin to the belt with her hair ribbons. Torrential rain started by the time he was ready. They dove into the water, and an unexpected hurricane blew the rain and hail sideways above them.

Ya'eel couldn't breathe underwater like Nia, but he could hold his breath longer than most of his kin, thanks to his adventures with her. They swam until Nia noticed Ahjin turn an unflattering blue. She motioned Ya'eel upward. When they surfaced, it was almost too windy to breathe. Nia apologized to Ahjin while he gulped air.

They dove again below the churning waves and swam against the turbulent current for another minute before resurfacing. This became the pattern for their frantic escape. The dark sky made the water as black as octopus ink. Nia relied mostly on Ya'eel's sense of direction, but they took over twice as long as usual to get home in the storm. Even with the help of the ribbons, Ahjin clutched Ya'eel to stay on and gasped for breath every time they surfaced.

As they approached the island, the rain and wind calmed to the level of a normal spring storm. Nia blew bubbles of relief. Safely home.

The massive waves had broken trees and flooded the lowest gardens on the island before receding. It would take a dismal amount of work to clean.

The explosive cracks of thunder-shrimp made Ahjin flinch. Nia untied him and helped him stagger past the storm-raised water line on the beach. When she let go of him, he fell at the base of a sturdy tree.

Ahjin dug his fingers into the wet sand and pressed his cheek against the earth, coughing up water. "Never again," he gasped. "What a nightmare." He coughed again. "*Like flying*, she says, but no control. *Fun*, she says. No air to hold me." He hacked again. "No air to breathe. Twice Windbag's tantrum-storms have ruined things. I hate him."

He closed his eyes and lay still except for the violent shivers that wracked him from head to foot.

Poor man. The shock excused his rudeness. Nia piled broken palm fronds over Ahjin for warmth and sent Ya'eel home to rest. She swam down through the debris-clogged water to find the healer, who left for the island. The underwater village had sheltered her family and the rest of the clan from the storm, as designed.

Nia stayed to collect food and get advice. "He can't swim," she explained to Mom, "he can't fly now, and I don't know what to do with him."

She left out the possibility of him being crazy. Maybe he heard a real voice in his head, maybe not, but he didn't seem dangerous.

"I'm too busy to help right now, but I'm sure you'll figure out something, dear." Mom dropped a kiss on Nia's head and returned to her list of repairs.

Nia glared at her. A little help would be nice, even from her easygoing mom. She kissed her cheek anyway and swam to the beach.

Ahjin was still on the shore, with new bandages on his injuries. Nia handed him food and sprawled on the warm sand. "It looks like I have no way to get you home again."

Ahjin laughed. "I'm happy to solve your problem for you. I have no intention of going home."

Nia gaped at him. "You don't want to go home? Why not? What will you do?"

"I thought I'd find a nice deserted island while I made plans. Do you know anywhere like that?"

"Sure, but they have food *or* water, or neither, but not both. That's why nobody lives there. Do you know how to farm? How about fish?"

Ahjin threw a mango into the tide. "You can't make me go home.

When my wing heals, I'll figure it out. May I stay here for a few days? Then you won't have to worry about me anymore."

Nia rolled to her back. "Oh, we don't make people do things. I suppose I could add you to my collection. You *are* what I salvaged today." She laughed at the scowl on his face and pulled one of her braids over her shoulder. "I have a better idea. You tell me your story, and I'll help you find a boat. Then we can explore together. What do you think?"

"Why would you do that? You don't even know me."

"Oh, I've been looking for an adventure! Say yes." She grinned at him until he laughed.

"It's a deal." While he finished his fruit and Nia cooked the fish over a fire in the sand, Ahjin described some of his city's famous buildings for her amusement and told her about his unexpected telepathy and unwanted duty. He assured her he'd be a much better aerobat than a priest. His descriptions of his aerial feats seemed unlikely, but he promised to prove his skill when his wing healed.

When her siblings and friends drifted in with more food, drawn by the smell to an impromptu party, Nia translated for them. Everyone protested the unfairness of his experience. Nia contrasted the carefree attitudes the Nokai had toward adulthood, and the big party she'd have when she became an adult at six thousand days old (six being Makana's favorite number).

After Ahjin found out half the audience was Nia's family, she drew in the sand to illustrate the connections between her three degrees of siblings and a collection of mostly unmarried parents who biologically belonged to someone but legally and emotionally belonged to them all. Although Nia's dad died when she was a baby, she still had two fathers from her siblings to care for her. It was nearly as good, or so she told herself.

The crowd flooded Ahjin with questions and answered his own until darkness fell. When they got bored and wandered away, Ahjin carefully stretched out his bandaged wing and lay on the sand with a sigh.

"What are you thinking?" Nia asked.

Ahjin took so long to answer, she thought he had fallen asleep.

"My family," he finally whispered into the night. "I miss them, even Father, but I can't go home yet." There was another long pause. "They'll be disappointed in me."

Of course his parents would always love him. Hers did, no matter what sort of trouble she got into. She searched for reassuring words, but he spoke again.

"I have to find a way home without giving up my ambitions and freedom. I can't let Irajahan take it away, Nia. Being a skydancer is all I've wanted since I was a child. I practice for hours every day so I can fly with my parents. I won't change my plans; I won't waste my talent and hard work. I *will* fly."

Nia wrapped her arms around herself and rocked on the sand. How awful to have such a pitiless god! Makana was much kinder. Then she smiled in the dark. "I'll help you find a way."

It would make the adventure even more worthwhile.

5. BARGAINS

(EAST CORAL ISLAND, NOKAILANA)

First eliminate your enemy's communication system.
Beginning Battle Strategy

The next morning, Ahjin relaxed in his new hammock, soaking in the warm sun and planning for when his wing healed. It seemed he was too far away to hear Irajahan, but would the temple guard come after him when they discovered where he'd gone? Or was too-far-to-hear also too far to catch? He couldn't take the chance. Once he decided where, he'd go farther until he found a way to stay out of the temple.

Ahjin let Nia run around in another attempt to find a boat not being used by fishermen. She had also taken his belongings to see if any of them could be fixed. He wouldn't count on it, though his heart twinged at the loss of his miniature family portrait and the scarf from Mother.

"I found a boat, a beautiful boat." Nia ran and tipped him from the hammock, her round green eyes wider than usual. "Come and see."

Ahjin barely stood before she tugged him to the beach at a jog. He admired the sleek shape and colorful sails of the large boat anchored near sailors mending nets.

"You're right, Nia, it's beautiful. When can we get started?"

"No, no. Not that boat. *This* boat." She pointed to a boat half-buried in the sand, about twenty feet long, with several holes in the side and no sails, mast, or tiller.

Ahjin stared at her. "You want to go to sea in *that*? You can swim home, but what about me?"

"Don't be silly; we'll fix it. It's perfect: small enough for us to handle, big enough for our supplies."

"Well, you're the expert."

"What do you have to bargain for the boat?" Nia rubbed her hands in anticipation.

"Nothing, so that plan crash-landed."

"Nonsense." She grinned. "How do you feel about physical labor?"

Ahjin shrugged. "I can do anything but fly or swim, I guess."

Her enthusiastic debate with the sailors involved dramatic gestures and the same cannily desperate looks he used to see in Vasi's market. He sat and let her barter in her native language to her heart's content.

After half an hour, Nia turned to him in triumph, catching him in the middle of a yawn. "You'll work each morning at various jobs, like gardening and fishing." She looked around the storm-damaged isle. "Cleaning first. Afternoons, we'll work together on the boat while I teach you trade tongue. The fishermen will provide tools and supplies. Is that acceptable?"

"It is." Ahjin stood and held out his hand for her to shake.

Nia shook her head with a grin. She stood on tiptoe and pulled him down to kiss each cheek, then tilted her head toward the fishermen.

Ahjin swallowed, then kissed each burly fisherman's cheeks to seal the deal.

Each morning, the Nokai children eagerly demonstrated every job he was assigned, from weeding to gutting fish, and let him practice his trade vocabulary on them. They snuck touches on his wings when they thought he wasn't looking. That was also a fair deal, so as his wings healed through the weeks, he stretched them when the children were nearby and pretended he didn't see their reaching fingers.

Each afternoon, Nia bossed him through the long list of boat repairs. Some of his mistakes left scars on the boat. After a week, the fishermen and women stopped laughing enough to offer suggestions and a helping hand on the trickiest parts.

Ahjin spent two of the almost-weekly festival times alone. While he watched lights flash underwater and listened to the music bubble to the surface, he thought of his family. The water was busy, but the sky was empty.

For the next party, Nia and Kala brought their friends and most of their siblings to the island after the official announcements in the underwater village. With a natural swimmer on each side, Ahjin felt safe enough for a surface tour of the beautiful coral. When he ducked his head under the water, he was amazed at the change in the color spectrum and sounds.

While his life was in their hands, he avoided comparing the colorful reef fishes to the wide range of brightly colored hair among the Nokai, including Nia's ankle-length lavender and the sapphire blue of her brother, Awa.

Ahjin didn't tell Nia swimming was indeed like flying, but he added swim lessons to his schedule each evening.

After a month, both the boat and Ahjin's wing were mended. To celebrate, he put on an aerial show for the entire clan during the next festival. He started with basic flying and gradually increased the difficulty of his techniques until he heard the amazed exclamations of the Nokai. That was his cue to pretend to fall from the sky. The islanders screamed, and he swooped up at the last minute and moved into his really impressive tricks. Squeals and cheers echoed over the waves until he landed with a bow half an hour later.

"Sparkling seashells, Ahjin, that was amazing!" Nia applauded wildly with the rest of the Nokai. "You're even better than you said you were."

The villagers slowly dispersed. Ahjin laughed and tugged one of Nia's braids.

She swatted his hand and pulled him toward their boat. "Fortunately for your ego, you still need to learn to sail."

She ran him through theory on the beached ship, then they pushed it into the water for anchored practice. As the most experienced crew member, Nia claimed the helm.

"Let out the sail, please," Nia said, after she declared him adequately trained for a real trip around the island. "Are you ready to tell me what telepathy's like? Can you hear my thoughts?" She scrunched her face and put her hands on her temples.

The girl never ran out of questions. "Stop that; I can't hear you." Ahjin fumbled with the lines. "I've only ever heard Irajahan, and I left to avoid listening to him, remember?"

He still needed a permanent way to escape, and the sooner they left, the sooner he could find a way to reclaim his life.

Nia shrugged. "Our goddess talks to us through dreams and her dolphins. It seems easier."

"You don't have priests, then?"

"We don't need them, and it doesn't sound like a fun job." Nia wrinkled her nose. "I have the boat under control, if you want to try fishing."

"Do you use a line or a net?" Ahjin looked around for either.

"My hands when I'm not sailing." She wiggled her webbed fingers at him and winked. "But there's net and line under the seat."

Ahjin found dragging the net worked better than casting it as for birds. Fishing gave him time to observe Nia. He was getting used to the webbing that ran halfway up her fingers and toes, but her golden skin looked sallow next to his own. Her gills were as amazing to him as his wings were to her, and her sunny humor was better than her knowledge of the islands and boating skill. Though she abandoned tasks half-finished when bored, she usually laughed at his pranks, even the spiny sea urchin he put in her seat.

As he pulled in the net, Irajahan screamed in his head again.

Ahjin recoiled and fell overboard, splashing by the escaping fish. His next wing sweep dragged the net around him. He struggled to keep his head above water, but barely held his breath before sinking.

The ocean sucked him down until the only hint of the surface was the sunlight sparkling through the waves. Ahjin yanked against the net, but couldn't free any of his limbs. His lungs burned for air.

Nia arrived with a second splash. She pulled him up enough to breathe, then shoved him into the anchored boat one net-entangled section at a time.

"You're the funniest fish I ever caught." She giggled, climbed in, and raised the anchor, using only the smallest sail to turn them toward shore. "Next time you should swim *away* from the net."

"Old Blowhard is back in my head. He found me!"

"Oh, he is? What's he saying this time?" Her eyes crinkled in a silent laugh.

"He's yelling; I'm still not listening." He pretended not to listen, anyway. Irajahan was loud and hard to ignore.

Ahjin tried to cross his arms in frustration and found himself too tightly bound to move. That was sheer insult added to the injury of the mental intrusion. "Can we get out of here, please?"

"How's not-listening working for you?" Nia beached the boat and unwound him from the net.

"What do you suggest? Seaweed earplugs?"

"I don't think earplugs will block voices in your brain unless you shoved them in much too far." She laughed and collapsed over the side of the boat onto the sand.

"Listen, fishbreath... ow, fine, I'll ask what he wants." Ahjin sat next to her and rested his head on his fists. He didn't know how to direct his thoughts to the god, but perhaps it would work if he spoke aloud.

"Hey, Irajahan. Can you hear me?" There was sudden mental silence. "Um, O great and powerful one? God of hot air — I mean, all air." Still nothing. "I guess he's gone, Nia. What a relief. What's next?"

"Who are you?" Irajahan's voice was back.

Ahjin swallowed. "My name is Ahjin." After a month of silence, this was disappointing.

"Finally! I've spent weeks trying to contact my Winds," Irajahan snapped. "I've tried every one. You're the first to respond. When I get back, they'll be in trouble."

"I'm not your priest." Perhaps it wasn't wise to contradict Irajahan, but Ahjin was too angry to care.

"But you are an Iojif telepath. Are you not yet an adult?"

"I've been sixteen for a while." Oh, to be a carefree fifteen again.

Nia stared at Ahjin with wide eyes. She leaned her ear toward him, then shrugged.

"Then you should be a Wind."

"And if I were a priest, you apparently wouldn't be able to talk to me." Ahjin crossed his arms. Irajahan didn't recognize his name and didn't seem to care. Did he know the names of *any* of his priests? Did that mean Ahjin could still escape?

"I suppose I must make do with you," Irajahan sulked, as if Ahjin were a second-best dessert.

"Then what can I do for you?" Ahjin asked Irajahan. "Better yet, how can I get you out of my head?"

"Have more respect, you impertinent fledgling! I am your god!"

"So I've been told." Ahjin yawned for effect.

"Shouldn't you be more respectful?" Nia whispered.

Ahjin sniffed. How dare the god wreck his life and then expect him to cater to his whims. While Irajahan ranted, Ahjin whistled. If he made him angry enough, could he get dismissed from service?

"I've been kidnapped, dolt! Raise an army! Get me out of here!" Irajahan's volume was impressive even if his manners weren't.

"Irajahan the Omnipotent can't rescue himself? How disappointing." Ahjin clicked his tongue in mock dismay while he secretly cheered. "Where are you? Who's holding you?" Could he send a thankyou gift?

There was a confused and angry silence.

"Where should I get an army?" Ahjin said. "How do I convince them to follow me? How do we get you out?"

"Don't bother me with details. Get me out of here before I go insane!" Omnipotent or not, Irajahan sounded on the verge of tears.

Ahjin's heart softened a little. Curiosity grew along with the speck of sympathy. "What *can* you tell me? Can you see or hear anything? What do you remember?"

"I don't know how I got here. I've heard someone else nearby recently, but he rudely ignores my shouts."

"Have you tried whispering?" It seemed like a logical question, but Irajahan raved again.

Ahjin's sympathy died, and he updated Nia while he waited for Irajahan to calm. "Now most of what I hear is tantrums," Ahjin finished. "He's screaming 'no fair,' and 'let me go,' and 'you'll pay for this' and threatening tornadoes and such." He rubbed his head. "It hurts."

Nia smiled. "I think we should help him. It will be exciting."

"I ran away, remember? If I rescue him, I'll get dragged back to the priesthood. Sorry, can't do it. If I let him stay wherever he is, I can go home to my family."

Nia pouted. "You're no fun. Take advantage of a perfectly good opportunity! And what will you do if he frees himself and comes after you? You'll be lucky if he only drags you back to Ioj instead of ripping off your wings with a tornado. And if he doesn't get out, do you want him screaming in your head for the rest of your life?"

"You're right." Ahjin slumped in despair until her first words sank in. He narrowed his eyes. "Take advantage — you're brilliant, Nia."

"Thank you." Nia grinned.

"Oh, Irajahan," Ahjin nearly sang in triumph. "I have a deal for you." A wordless roar acknowledged him. "I'm trapped in your priesthood, but you're just trapped. I'll rescue you, if you release me from your Winds."

That triggered another fit of rage.

"I'll wait until he stops yelling." Ahjin winked at Nia and whistled again. This was fun, and if the bargain worked, it might be the answer he needed.

"Waves," Nia swore, "again? My goddess doesn't act like that. Maybe when a party goes badly, but how often does that happen?"

"Irajahan's notorious for his bad temper, as Resef is famed for his pranks, Darravani for her reclusiveness, and your Makana for her parties." Ahjin preferred any of the nice gods.

Irajahan kept shouting, but Ahjin started planning. If Irajahan wouldn't cooperate, Ahjin hadn't lost anything.

"If he doesn't know where he is, where should we look?" Ahjin asked.

Nia bounced on the sand. "Makana isn't called Omniscient for her looks. We should ask her."

After a while, Irajahan agreed he had no choice. Ahjin indulged in a silent cheer, then explained the plan and asked him to investigate at his end. At least every other day, they would speak (quietly). That would be more than enough for Ahjin.

Irajahan's increasingly familiar presence faded. "I can't wait until I'm free of him," Ahjin told Nia.

"I understand why." Nia swam off to leave a message with the dolphins at the underwater theater.

N ia and Ahjin practiced their sailing and gathered supplies for two days, until three dolphins came to the beach. One of them swam forward to squeal and whistle. Nia provided a running translation.

"It's normal for Makanavailea to visit the other islands, but she's been gone longer than usual and isn't responding. If she's still playing, she'll be angry if we send someone after her. Since you have an excuse to be out there, we'd appreciate you watching for her. If nothing is wrong, don't bother her. If she returns while you're gone, we'll send word." The dolphins bowed their heads and swam away.

Nia frowned. "I was sure Makana would help."

"Do you think something happened to her?" Ahjin asked.

"I really think she's playing," Nia said. "It's not the first time. But what do we do now?"

"We look for help in Iskra or Darrendra," Ahjin said. "The desert is dangerous but a lot closer, and Resef is friendlier. The Darrendrakar share Darravani's dislike of strangers. They keep a constant watch and might kill us on sight." He paused. "Perhaps that would be good."

"To be killed on sight?" Nia smacked his shoulder. "I don't like the idea much."

"No, to be found quickly," Ahjin explained. "The Iskrins wander; it might be hard to find anyone. In the forest, they'll at least watch for us. Besides, I thought you'd like to travel farther. Is there any way to prevent the shapeshifters from killing us before we can explain?"

"We can ask the traders for ideas, but shouldn't we take the shortest path first?"

"I'm not worried about time," Ahjin said. "I expect Irajahan to rescue himself before we find him, and it sounds like Makana will come back on her own. So, is there anyone we can take north to interpret?"

Nia laughed. "I thought you knew. I don't just speak *your* language, I speak all of them. It was my birth gift from Makana."

"Oh, that's handy," Ahjin said. "And we've learned to sail, so we're almost ready to go."

They spent the next day packing their food, water, and tools. The Nokai didn't have a bow to replace Ahjin's shattered one, and there wasn't much choice in dried meat besides endless varieties of fish. His new compass had not survived its encounter with a rock, so a sturdy replacement was nailed by the tiller. The armbands that would let them safely approach the Darrendrakar were folded in a hidden compartment.

Nia let her family load supplies while she shyly opened his possessions to show how much had been saved from his crash. The family portrait was ruined, but Mother's scarf was expertly mended. His spoiled clothing was replaced with new shirts and pants copied from his old ones, although in Nokai colors. He stammered out his thanks to Nia, but she raised her hands for silence.

"You haven't seen it all." She pulled out a copy of his favorite jacket and bit her lip. "We know your taste in colors is more subdued, but..." Nia held up the jacket.

It *was* his old one, mended with many shades of blue embroidery. Waves bounced around the hem, while birds, dolphins, and fish danced across the rips. Satin ribbons replaced the broken laces. Ahjin gaped wordlessly.

Nia lowered her eyes and folded the jacket. "Shark teeth. We ruined it."

"I've never seen anything so amazing." Ahjin grabbed her hand. "It's better than festival garb in the city. Aren't you afraid I'll ruin it during travel?"

She looked up and smiled. "It's harder to tear or stain than before. Mom used all her tricks on it for you."

"Please, tell everyone I'm grateful for their generosity and talent." He repacked the rest of his clothes, except for his scarf, which he slipped into his pocket.

As soon as he tossed his bag into the boat, Nia's family overran him with warm hugs. They told him to drop Nia anywhere in Nokailana whenever she tired of the trip, and called "pleasant journey" as Ahjin and Nia sailed north for Darrendra.

That night, they anchored on a small island, and Ahjin called to Irajahan. There had been no response two days before, but this time he answered almost immediately.

"I have news and a surprise," Irajahan said. "I spoke quietly to the other person here, and it worked. I don't know why she wouldn't answer when I yelled. She had to hear me."

Ahjin got the impression of a mental shrug.

"Anyway, Makanavailea is here, and she has a gift for Niamolenulan-ami. I have one for you, too."

This time, Ahjin was sure he felt a smirk right before a blinding pain darkened his mind.

He awoke early in the morning with a headache, covered by a blanket.

"Good morning." Nia smiled, setting out fruit for breakfast. "Guess what happened to me last night!"

"I hope it was better than my night." Ahjin rubbed his head.

"Makana came to me in a dream and told me I'll be able to scry in water. Think how much help it will be when I figure out how it works! She said Irajahan gave you something, too. What is it?"

"Irajahan didn't tell me." He rubbed his head again. Since Makana had not merely lost track of time, their carefree adventure was now urgent.

"We should guess." Nia dipped a cloth in the ocean and handed it to Ahjin. "Put this on your head. Can you breathe water now? Can you swim faster than a shark? Can you see through stone? Can you *walk* through stone? Can we try it?"

6. LUDIK
(MAON, DARRENDRA)

Dandelion: faithfulness, happiness. Forsythia: anticipation. Jasmine, yellow: grace and elegance. Tulip, yellow: there is sunshine in your smile; hopeless love. Zinnia, yellow: daily remembrance.

Flowers and Their Meanings: A Guide for Darrendrakar

Forest blossoms filled the air with sweet fragrance. Ludik let the hammer dangle and named the many varieties he recognized from his seat on the roof. If he ever had a reason to petition his goddess, he wanted to personally interpret the meanings of the flowers she would bloom in reply, rather than rely on the shamans.

More importantly, he could pick significant flowers for Nemerra. Maybe in yellow.

Haider's voice floated up to him. "Here you go."

It had been at least two days since Ludik had brought his sweetheart flowers. He was lucky the most beautiful woman in the village loved him. His brothers always laughed and claimed there were prettier women, but their eyesight was obviously poor. Nobody compared to his tall and slender sweetheart.

"Ludik," Haider said.

Ludik's heart beat faster. Nemerra was the kindest, happiest, most loyal woman, as well as the prettiest. Love made her honey-brown eyes glow, and her russet hair shone in the sun like fire.

"Ludik!" Haider shouted. A rope hit Ludik's head.

Ludik blinked. The rope slithered off the roof. He leaned over the edge. "What was that for?"

His littermate coiled the rope and hopped on his good foot to throw it again. "Do you want more nails or not? You know I can't climb up there, so catch that, will you? The storm is getting closer."

Haider preferred working on Papa's farm, but a reckless climb too high in the trees left him with a broken leg. Until it healed, he was restricted to household chores. Working with Ludik was a break from keeping their little sister out of the catmint.

Ludik grabbed the rope and hauled up the bucket of nails. He hammered the next cedar shingle to the roof, making sure there would be no leaks. Last week, he had laid out the interior walls for the bedroom downstairs with the bath and the gathering room, and a loft in the attic for the many children he hoped they'd have as quickly as possible. Nemerra would be pleased at the progress, but there was still a lot to do in the next seven weeks.

As long as he finished the basic construction before the wedding, he could paint it and carve decorations in the woodwork later. Nemerra would understand. Though the windows and doors were still open to the warm spring air, he lived in it already, rather than his parents' crowded home. Maybe it wasn't the best idea, since it made him more impatient for the end of his betrothal year.

Ludik looked at the cloudy sky and hammered faster. It would be a worse idea if he didn't get the roof finished before the rain came.

He hadn't paid much attention to girls when he was younger. He'd thought he'd look around for a while after his all-important seventeenth birthday, but Nemerra had her own plans. She convinced him to notice her, not that it was a hardship. After that, one thing led quickly to another until he was blissfully walking her around the fire in front of the village.

"Ludik," Haider called again. "I have to go watch Hiranya. Do you need more nails?"

Ludik put down his hammer and checked his bucket. Only a few nails rattled at the bottom. "Yes, but you can head back. I'll come get them. I need a drink anyway."

He slid off the roof with the bucket and brought Haider his crutch. "I'll see you this evening."

"I'll tell Mama you're coming." Haider limped away.

Ludik cleaned the tools his brother had used and stowed the half-finished furniture inside the house. He removed the last few nails and lowered the bucket into the well.

He had the bucket winched almost back to the top when a lion bounded into the yard and threw him head over heels.

The bucket splashed in the well as the lion landed on top of him. Ludik's breath gushed from his lungs. Large paws weighed down his shoulders and legs. The lion bared his teeth.

Ludik struggled to inhale and free an arm, but couldn't move.

The lion's hot breath blew in Ludik's face as he leaned closer and closer to his face.

A long, wet tongue licked him from chin to ear.

Ludik howled, jerked an arm free, and hit the lion on the nose. "Furballs," he swore. "I told you that's disgusting."

Gurryon stepped off him, shifted form, and gingerly felt his nose. It was still his normal brown, without a hint of black or blue. "If my nose swells, that will ruin our plans."

"You're fine. I didn't hit you that hard. Your pretty face is undamaged," Ludik taunted his littermate. "Besides, I don't have time to play today."

The look-alike brothers switched places regularly, partly for variety, partly for the sheer fun of tricking their elders.

"But you promised," Gurryon whined.

"I have to finish the roof before the storm arrives." Ludik pulled up the bucket for a long drink, then dumped the water and reloaded the bucket with nails.

Gurryon looked at the sky. "It won't rain for hours. You have time. Please. I've been stuck inside all day." He bounced on his toes like a child.

Ludik sighed. "Only one lesson, and you owe me time on the house."

"Agreed."

Gurryon retrieved his tunic and boots from behind the house, and they switched clothes. Gurryon straightened his shaman's badge on Ludik's shoulder, then grabbed the bow and ran into the forest.

Ludik shook his head. If Gurryon broke arrows again, Ludik would take the price of new ones from his scruffy hide. He wound through the gardens and orchards between the scattered village houses and arrived in time for Gurryon's healing lesson. He sometimes subbed for his brother's botanical lessons, too, but never the boring religious ones. Their village was currently without a healer, but shamans were trained in healing for this reason.

Shaman Akamu looked up from the medical kit he refilled. "I'm glad you're here. We're running short of your famous salve. I've gathered the ingredients for you already."

Ludik had noticed he somehow made the salve about twice as often as Gurryon. "You want me to do that instead of a lesson?"

"Oh, no worries. I'll quiz you while you work," Akamu promised impishly.

While Ludik simmered the herbs in oil, the shaman asked about medicinal plants, anatomy, and first response treatments. Ludik was surprised he passed the test easily. There should have been questions from lessons he hadn't attended, but he couldn't ask Akamu why not without giving away his escapades.

Ludik added beeswax and poured the cooling salve into jars, then returned to the forest. Gurryon had broken no arrows this time, but he hadn't shot anything, either. They walked together to the family home. Mama always cooked a delicious meal, claiming it was easier than pulling weeds on the farm.

After he finished eating, Papa ran his hands through his unruly, tawny hair and gathered the dishes. "While you're both here, Haider and Gurryon, let's talk about marriage prospects. You have less than three weeks before you reach eighteen. Do you have someone special in mind, or will you let the council choose for you?"

Gurryon shrugged. "It worked for you and Mama."

He snagged the last chicken leg before Mama removed the platter. Hiranya glared at him until he gave her half the meat.

"Kalli and Narrasiman and I liked choosing our own mates." Ludik really liked his selection.

"I have plenty of choices, Papa," Haider argued, copying Papa's nervous gesture with his own nearly identical hair. Gurryon and Ludik had cropped their brighter gold hair almost as short as possible.

"We know," Mama said, "but have you narrowed the field to one?" On her way from the table, she bent her dark head to kiss his hair.

"You're having problems picking because I took the best woman," Ludik gloated.

"That isn't helping, Ludik, and isn't true," Haider said. "*She* chose *you*, and I have no idea why. Papa, I don't want to talk about marriage, either. It will be fine."

Papa sat at the table and gave him an unrelenting look.

Haider groaned. "So, Ludik, what is your next project on the house? Is it anything I can help with?"

Ludik chuckled at the attempt to change the subject. "Sorry, it's getting late, and I still have work to do tonight. But Gurryon owes me some work time when you finish."

He stood to leave, then jerked to a halt. Haider held his arm while Gurryon blocked the door.

"There is no way you're abandoning us to this torture." Haider clutched him so desperately with both strong hands that Ludik's arm went numb.

"Don't think you can walk out of here," Gurryon threatened. "You have to help us." He grimaced. "Talk to us about Nemerra, if you want; just don't leave."

Papa laughed. He caught Ludik's gaze and tilted his head toward the window, then slammed Gurryon merrily against the door.

Ludik jerked his arm from Haider's grasp and took Papa's hint, jumping out the open window accompanied by his brothers' howls of dismay.

Mama leaned out the window and cheerfully called, "Keep well."

In a moment, she was replaced by two younger heads yelling words that were neither cheerful nor good wishes. Ludik waved and wished them luck, then laughed all the way home. If he hurried, he could finish the roof.

Early the next morning, Ludik yawned as he passed the large farms on the outskirts of the village and made his way past the sentries. Now that the air was warm enough to go without fur, every other guard wore their two-legged shape for long-distance vision, while the others stayed four-legged for keener scent and hearing.

Ludik had drawn duty in one of the farther hunting grounds today, not far from Canid territory. Once out of sight, he wrapped his bow and knife in his long tunic, then stuffed them and his worn boots into the leather bag Nemerra had specially made. He leaned it strategically against a rock while his bones reshaped in seconds to his jaguar form and his claws extended. Though he was the only black jaguar in the village, there were spotted ones and another panther of the leopard variety.

His head and one foreleg fit through the strap of the bag, and a wriggle settled it in place on his back. Even at an easy jog out and walking back on two legs to carry the game, he'd get home sooner than if he stayed two-legged the entire time. Ludik stretched, then bounded off with the sun warm on his black fur.

The green, growing scents of spring were potent after the overnight rain. The flowers were so numerous, their fragrance almost overwhelmed the year-round aroma of pine and cedar. He missed the brighter colors he saw in his two-legged shape, but the improvements in his hearing and sense of smell almost made up for it.

Ludik loved the outdoors, and hunting was more fun than endless weeding with Papa and Haider. There had been talk almost five years ago of both him and Gurryon being healers or shamans. Poor Gurryon hadn't thought of an acceptable alternative for the council fast enough. The few minutes Ludik gained by being second for consideration had allowed him to suggest hunting, instead.

"Good to see you, handsome," someone purred.

Ludik jerked back to reality and missed a step. Nemerra giggled. It was an odd sound from a leopard. Ludik looked up until he found her perched on a high tree branch. It was a more precarious roost than he dared, but not unusual for her.

"What are you doing here?"

She put her head on her paws. "I thought I'd run with you for a bit, if you don't mind?"

"My pleasure," he said. "But only for a while."

Nemerra jumped down, one branch at a time, until she reached the ground. She rubbed her head along his ears, then took off with a teasing look over her shoulder.

Ludik caught up easily with his faster sprint, and they loped through the forest side by side.

Nemerra looked around the forest. "I wish we had more golden suvarna trees nearby. The leaves are so pretty in rose, violet, and silver."

"Not as pretty as you," he blurted. Nothing was as pretty.

"Thank you, dear," she purred. "How far are you going today?"

"I'll return tonight."

Nemerra jerked to a halt. "You're going to the border?" Her ears flattened with fear.

Ludik stopped beside her. "I'll be fine. I don't have to go quite that far. The wolves won't have any reason to come near me."

Darravani's children, normally allies, could be terrible enemies. The last interkindred war was two generations ago, when the hyenas temporarily conquered part of Felid territory.

"You'll be fine," Nemerra echoed firmly. She flicked her ears forward and changed the subject. "Do you suppose we'll ever make it to the Great Fair after the harvest? We can travel with Kalliona and Chalon when they accompany his papa to the council."

"Anything you'd like," he said.

Nemerra nudged his ears again. "I think I'll turn back here. You be careful. I'll see you tonight."

Ludik nuzzled her farewell and loped along, pausing only to drink at streams. After a couple of hours, he stopped, hoping to stay far enough from the border that the keen noses of the wolves and wild dogs that patrolled the other side wouldn't smell him.

There was no game in sight. He inhaled deeply and tilted his head to listen. Still nothing. He dug his claws into the bark of a tall tree and pulled himself to the lowest golden branch. After tucking his pack in a fork, he climbed higher for a better view to the north and south, since west was Canid territory.

He leapt quietly from tree to tree in the dense forest, hoping for a nice, plump deer. After a while, the shrubbery rustled, and Ludik froze. The rustle came again, along with a pungent whiff. There — a wild pig sniffing the ground for roots and nuts. It was so intent on its search, it didn't notice the predator above.

Ludik crouched. He sprang with a snarl, pinning the boar to the ground. Before it could free itself, he slit its throat with his claws. It was over before the boar had a chance to fight.

There was no sound or scent of other predators, so he shifted back and dragged the boar through the trees toward his pack. The biggest disadvantage to hunting as a jaguar was the distance he ended from his knife. Ludik's claws were sharp but not handy for dressing game.

When he reached his base tree, he dumped the carcass and retrieved his pack. He gutted the pig and cut off its head but left the meat in its hide for easier transport. After a bath in the stream, another snack, and a long drink, he dressed and put on his pack, hefted the boar onto his shoulders, and started walking. It would take him hours to get home, but if he hurried, there might be a little time to work on the house.

If he finished the house early, could he convince the council to move up the wedding?

7. FOREST

(MAON, DARRENDRA)

There are eleven Darrendrakar kindreds in strict territories. They mingle warily at trade fairs and in Kanshi, the holy capital in the east.

A Brief Sketch of Mysterious Darrendra

As Ludik arrived home, armed sentries escorted two people into the village at spearpoint.

The visitors had washed-out skin unlike any kindred he knew, nor even tones like each other. Each of them wore an embroidered armband that meant they had come from the Nokailana Islands as a trader or ambassador and were guaranteed safe passage and help. The sentries still watched them with ready weapons.

Ludik dropped the boar at his parents' house before joining his siblings in the middle of the village to gossip.

"Who are the strangers?" he asked his older sister, Kalliona, who was married to the headman's son. "Do they both come from the Islands?"

"She's Nokai, but he's Iojif," she whispered.

The girl's nearly skintight outfit clung to her curves and barely missed being scandalous by at least covering her from wrists to ankles. It was in many shades of such bright red and yellow he could probably enjoy the colors even with cat vision.

Only the man's jacket had more than a paltry two hues. He had attached immense feathered wings to the back of his jacket. What sort of bird had he killed, or had he made them himself from loose feathers on a frame? Ludik hoped for the second rather than a trophy killing. He didn't know of any birds that large, either. The wings must be seven or eight yards wide if spread.

"What do they want? Are they traders?" What else did he and Nemerra need for their home?

"No. They say they need information and help to find two missing gods. Have you ever heard such a crazy story in your life?" Kalli chuckled. "I'm waiting for Papa Asad to throw them back into the ocean."

Ludik's older brother, Narrasiman, said, "They will tell their story again at the council meeting tonight. It's great entertainment. I can save you a place."

"I'll bring Nemerra." Ludik kissed his sister's cheek and went to frame walls.

After the evening meal, he and Nemerra walked his parents to the council clearing. Haider was on Hiranya-watch again. The strangers sat with Asad and the elders. The woman was more respectable in a borrowed dress, and the man had removed his jacket and moved the wings to his shirt.

"Are those wings ceremonial or purely decorative?" Ludik whispered to Gurryon, trying to see how they were attached.

Gurryon shook his head sadly. "Don't you know anything? They *fly* in Ioj. With their own wings." He snickered and slapped Ludik on the back, then turned his attention to the strangers, still chuckling.

Asad called the meeting to order, and the girl told their story in trade tongue. It was as fantastical as his siblings said. It was good the little ones were in bed, or the village would lose face when they laughed.

The men and women of the council expressed sympathy for the visitors, but tactfully denied their requests. When the strangers protested, Asad looked up. "Honored guests, I have a solution. You must leave our territory, but to honor our agreements with Nokailana, we will send someone with you to help with protection, provision, and healing." He beckoned Ludik. The council murmured approval.

Ludik turned around in his seat. No, nobody was behind him. He grabbed Nemerra's hand and stalked into the circle. "What?" he growled at the headman.

Asad switched to Darrendran. "You thought we can't tell you and Gurryon apart, didn't you? Not only do you not look *quite* identical, as Nemerra could tell you, you smell different." He laughed, and the rest of the council left with muffled chuckles.

Nemerra nodded guiltily. "We didn't want to ruin the fun you two were having."

"I'll go." Gurryon bounced on his heels and grinned.

Asad ignored him. "You're trained as a hunter and partly as a healer. You have no injuries and aren't the shaman's apprentice. Can you think of anyone better for this fool's errand?"

The pale woman frowned, though Asad still spoke in Darrendran.

"How about someone older, more experienced? Or anyone who wants to go," Ludik hissed back. "Someone who isn't getting married soon and doesn't have a house to finish before then." He turned to leave with Nemerra, despite the blatant disrespect.

Asad continued with merciless cheer. "We can't send a child and won't separate a man from his wife and children. There are only three unmarried adult men in the village besides you and your littermates, and none of the others have your skills. You even speak a smattering of trade tongue. Our visitors will give up in time for your wedding. If they prove more persistent than I think, the village will help with your house."

"No." Ludik again turned to leave.

"We are required to help these ambassadors," Asad said. "If you don't cooperate, I'll talk to the council about annulling your betrothal."

Ludik gasped. Asad turned and introduced Niamolenulanami, who had fish gills on her neck, and Ahjin, whose twitching wings were obviously real. Ludik ignored his brother's grin.

"Well met, Ludik," Nia said in flawless Darrendran. "We're happy to have you join us. When can you be ready to leave?"

Ahjin only waved.

Ludik glared at his headman. Asad had him cornered. "I can leave after the morning meal."

The foreigners left for the guest house, and Ludik walked Nemerra home in raging silence.

"I'm sorry I didn't tell you earlier," she whispered. "This is my fault."

"No, it isn't," he growled. "I don't want to talk about it any more."

She glanced at his face and then looked away, but put her hand on his arm, as comforting as always.

He packed most of what he needed before he went to sleep. Did he need weapons besides his knife and composite hunting bow? All he could add was his ax and the old banded breastplate Grandpapa had passed down last year. He kept his mind busy listing names for Asad that he wouldn't dare use to his face.

The next morning, he ate with his family. Hiranya blinked back tears. Gurryon once again volunteered to go in his place and grumbled when Papa said it would be as the headman had decreed. The family agreed to work on Ludik's house in their spare time, and he returned home to finish packing.

Nemerra tapped on his door frame before entering. "I have something for you." She pulled calf-high leather boots from behind her back. They were unornamented and undyed, but sturdy.

"I made them for your wedding gift. I planned to have them decorated by then, but I'd like you to take them now." She swallowed. "I'll miss you. Please hurry back." Tears ran down her face.

Ludik took her in his arms and tucked her head against his shoulder. "I won't be gone long. You'll barely miss me."

Her hair smelled of leather and flowers, with a hint of the dyes she used on her leatherwork. He pulled the boots from her hand and dropped them on the floor, then tightened their embrace and stroked her hair. If they were already married, he'd be exempt from this mission. He inhaled again, locking her scent into his memory.

Nemerra continued to weep. "I know what Asad said, but it will still be too long. I'm being silly. Don't mind me." She sniffed against his shoulder.

"I'll be back for our wedding," Ludik said. "Don't worry."

After a kiss, he forced himself to let her go, and she walked him to the tiny guest huts around the council fire. Both of the visitors were outside for the farewell ceremony with the shaman, Gurryon, and Asad.

"I have petitioned Darravani the Omnifarious, Goddess of Earth," Shaman Akamu said, "and she had no suggestions except to hurry out of her territory."

Ludik waited until the proper moment to accept responsibility for the strangers' welfare. When they had arrived, they had blindly wandered north until found by a patrol. With his guidance, the trip back to the shore would be more direct. If only that were all they needed.

The girl gave the borrowed dress to Asad, tied in an embroidered ribbon. "Thank you, Asad. Ludik, call me Nia."

Ahjin accepted a sheath of arrows and a recurve bow of plain wood with only a nod.

Ludik clasped Gurryon's arm and gave Nemerra a long hug and one last kiss, then picked up his pack and hurried off without looking toward home.

Nemerra called "Keep well," and his stomach cramped.

Nia and Ahjin walked down the faint path silently. If nobody talked to him, maybe he could pretend he hadn't been abandoned to outkindred.

The winged man strapped his new bow outside his pack, then asked a question. In his own language. This would be a long trip.

Nia relayed, "He wants to know if the young man who looks like you is your twin."

"What is a twin?" Ludik asked. She hadn't translated that word.

"Twins are two siblings born at the same time."

Ludik shook his head. "No, Kalliona and Narrasiman, my older siblings, are twins. There were three in my litter. Our other littermate, Haider, does not look so much like us, though."

When Nia translated, Ahjin whistled and raised an eyebrow. Nia relayed another question. "Who's the girl you were with?"

Ludik narrowed his eyes. "She is my betrothed. Why do you ask?"

"Betrothed? To be married? How old are you?" Nia's eyes widened.

"I have nearly eighteen years. How many years do *you* have?" If they asked rude questions, he might as well get his own answered.

"Ahjin is a bit past sixteen years old, and I'm about half a year younger."

"Then neither of you is an adult. This is worse than I thought," Ludik said. "I have to tend two children with ridiculous imaginations." These were no ambassadors; he had been sent away for no reason. These kittens should go home for schooling in proper behavior.

When Nia translated for Ahjin, he drew himself to his full height and spit gibberish. Ludik tried not to grin at the boy's pitiful attempt to equal his own height and broad shoulders.

Nia exhaled deeply, then translated. "Tell him I am an adult in my society. I can take care of myself."

Ludik lost his battle for self-control and laughed in Ahjin's face.

When Ahjin clenched his fists, Nia stepped between them. "Settle down, or I'll stop translating a word you say."

She glared at them and said presumably the same thing in the boy's language. It was as well she had an imposing scowl, since she was short enough for them to throw punches over her head.

Ludik growled. Ahjin spread his wings impressively wide and glowered. Nia shoved them both and stomped toward the southern border. After a minute, both men shrugged and followed her. When they caught up, she pretended nothing had happened.

"So, Ludik, you were telling us about your pretty wife-to-be. What's her name? When are you getting married? Why did your tribe send you with us instead of someone else? I heard what your chief said, but it didn't make a lot of sense." Nia skipped, and Ahjin laughed.

Ludik scowled, then started with Nemerra, and his favorite subject made him forget to be silent. He talked until Ahjin yawned, then explained his trick with his brother and Asad's reasons for sending him. Nia and Ahjin made sympathetic faces and fell silent.

After a while, Nia giggled and lifted her face to the bright sun. "Turtle shells, how about language practice?"

Ahjin nodded, and Ludik shrugged. Ludik knew the basics of trade tongue in case he ever made it to the fair, while Ahjin had been learning intensely for only a few weeks.

When they tired of practicing, the two explained more of the situation to Ludik. Supposedly, Ahjin heard voices in his head and claimed an undiscovered magical gift.

"You know there are names for people like you. 'Crazy,' for instance." Ludik laughed so hard he fell when Ahjin shoved him.

They ate at midday in a small clearing. The sunlight filtered through the colored leaves of a tall suvarna tree and danced rainbows on the ground. Nia sat on a golden tree root and tossed fruit to Ahjin, who eyed Ludik from his perch on a large branch. Ludik basked in the sunlight in the middle of the long grass and gobbled the meal Nemerra had packed for him.

They set off after the meal. Now they had sized up everyone's abilities, they agreed Ludik would obviously serve as hunter and healer, Nia as translator and navigator, and Ahjin as scout and, in Ludik's words, 'mouth of the gods.' That earned Ludik a bruised cheekbone and respect for how much power one strong wing flap added to a punch. If the little pest weren't a child, Ludik would thrash him.

Ludik waited until he was unobserved, then shifted into jaguar. When Ahjin turned around, Ludik grinned widely to reveal his fangs mere inches from the boy's face. Ahjin jumped into flight, and Ludik grinned again.

When Ludik tired of carrying his heavy pack as a jaguar and changed back behind a convenient bush, Ahjin landed to walk in comparative safety and silence on the other side of Nia.

Nia ignored them. She hummed randomly and meandered down the path in bare feet, stepping from one grassy spot to another. When Ahjin asked for a vocabulary review an hour or so later, she jumped at the sound of his voice before continuing the lessons.

They crossed into a thinly wooded section with none of the tri-colored suvarna trees, and Ludik smelled fewer large prey. Birds sang, and squirrels darted across the tree limbs. He was used to walking for a long time, and Nemerra's boots were comfortable, but he no longer heard or smelled the village guards following them. His distance from Nemerra and his family nagged like a broken claw.

The strangers offered to explain their plans, but Ludik didn't care. None of this was his idea, anyway. They shrugged and chattered in another language. The unfamiliar sounds grated on his heart.

As evening fell, salt air tickled Ludik's nose, guiding him as accurately as his eyes in the dim light. Ahjin and Nia stumbled along, half-blind beneath two crescent moons, until they crossed the beach to an anchored sailboat. The small craft bobbed in rippling shimmers of reflected moonlight.

Ahjin hung a hammock in the pine tree closest to the shore, high enough nobody could reach him from the ground, and Nia swam to the far side of the boat.

Ludik changed back into his fur in his chosen tree, out of range of any pine cones Ahjin might send from his slingshot. He had a direct line of sight to the avian's hammock and could keep an eye on any mischief. From his own high post, Ludik saw Nia floating in the water with a peaceful look on her face. He waited until Ahjin slept and then let the sound of the lapping waves lull him into slumber. The scent of pine brought memories of home, and his last thoughts were of Nemerra.

8. ZEFRA

(HOTARU SUMMER CAMP, ISKRA)

Guide for Desert Survival: Never travel without adequate provisions and maps. Carry at least a gallon of water per day and when the water is half gone, turn back. Travel with others. Stay on the road.

Iskrin Culture and History, appendix 1

Zefra took a long drink of the sweet well water. The first step of her plan was simple — be out of sight by sunrise and walk due south for a day. She wrapped her scarf securely around her head and strode toward the true desert of sand and rock instead of the baked earth of the coastal camp.

She could not take a sword, if she had one, but had grabbed her knife and iron-bound staff on the way from her family's tent. It would be easier with a blanket, food, tools, medicine, or even a water bag, but those restrictions were almost the whole point. If she survived for one month without help or supplies, she would be an adult and allowed to begin the profession of her choice. If she gave up, she would be a child forever — forbidden to marry, have children, or take any but the most menial jobs.

Candidates could try twice between the ages of fifteen and eighteen, with attempts spaced at least one year apart, but she would not fail even once. She had studied and practiced for two years to take this chance at the first opportunity.

As the sun rose, Zefra did not see the camp or smell the ocean. Good progress, then. She faced south and trekked across endless sand. When a desert rat or lizard crossed her path, she killed it quickly or quit rather than waste energy on the hunt.

At midday, the scorching heat drove her to a stop near a large cactus. While she chewed out the water from a piece of cactus, she skinned the gutted carcasses of her successful hunts, re-wrapped them in their skins, and buried them in the sand on the sunnier side of her refuge. Thirst eased, she curled under the shade of her scarf stretched from cactus to staff and longed for her familiar bed.

Zefra awoke a few hours later and donned her scarf. After digging out the now-cooked meat, she walked between the sand dunes while she ate. Her trek continued through the afternoon and half the night. When the air finally chilled, she dug a hole in the sand at the base of a large rock, then crawled into the still-warm hole. She collapsed the walls around her body for warmth and camouflage. With the sand as her pillow, she slept the dreamless sleep of the exhausted.

Sunrise woke her to dawdle over prayers and a scanty breakfast of lizard before moving to stage two of her plan. She scraped the inside of yesterday's animal skins and used some of the hide to make snares. After catching a few rats for her next meal, she found a spiky Resef's-needle shrub.

Zefra sat in the meager shade of the rock and carefully pounded the bases of the needle-tipped leaves between two stones until they separated into fibers. Twisted together, they became a forearm's length of strong thread already attached to a needle. When the skins were tanned, she would use the needles and thread to make bags. The largest was for her supplies, and she would waterproof the smaller ones for when she found a real source of water.

Zefra spent a week eating rats, chewing cactus and drinking dew, and spending every spare moment building her supplies. At the end, she had three empty water bags; watery cactus flesh for particularly dry stretches; a handful of precious xaffac berries; a few useful herbs; some leather remnants; the last two unbroken needles; two paces of twine to turn her scarf into a scanty tent; a primitive pack; a painstakingly detailed map of the scouting she had done during hunts, drawn on a tanned lizard hide; and a moderate supply of dried meat for the next, hungry part of her trek.

North, toward home, was out. Straight west or northeast led to established caravan routes to be avoided. Historically, most of the children from her clan had gone southwest, far enough from the caravans to avoid being seen. They had better access to water and green food, and fewer encounters with large animals and other dangers. Some of them still never returned. Sometimes their bodies were found later. Sometimes they were not.

Zefra understood their logic. Candidates were required only to survive, not to go anywhere in particular or bring back anything but an answer. Her brother had succeeded two years ago, at seventeen. Izo had returned with nothing but a sand rash and his predictable decision to be a blacksmith. Perhaps she was foolish to think she could succeed at barely fifteen years old, but she preferred to think she was prepared.

She had spent the last year poring over her clan's extensive map collection and talking to any caravan leaders brave enough to travel off the established routes. By combining their stories, she had eliminated remarkably barren areas and had a few clues that might lead to hidden treasures. Some caravans had seen signs of a possible undiscovered oasis due south. They could not investigate with so many animals and people to keep fed and watered that far off the paths.

Zefra, however, had only herself. Returning with information of another oasis would enrich her clan and prove her worth as an explorer.

The sun would set in about an hour. Zefra loaded her supplies, then turned so the low sun shone on her right shoulder. It was just cool enough to enjoy a brisk walk. She hiked until she was too tired, then lay for a few hours of sleep under the midnight stars.

When the cold woke her, she checked the stars and headed south again, deviating only enough to walk around hills instead of over them. She stopped at sunrise long enough for prayers, then continued her trek. As the sun grew white-hot, her pace slowed. Before she sweated enough to waste water, she stretched the twine from her new pack to her staff and turned her scarf into scant shade. If she slept now, she could walk through the cooler evening and late into the night. Her eyelids fluttered closed, and a lazy yawn stretched her face.

She was asleep when something touched her arm. Zefra rolled and grabbed for her knife. The harmless sand snake raised its head and hissed. Before she woke enough to kill it, the large snake tunneled into the sand and disappeared.

The sun was several hours lower in the sky. Since she was awake, she might as well walk. Zefra repinned her midnight-dark hair, then disassembled her makeshift tent and slung her supplies on her back, including a week of slim rations. With her next meal in one hand and staff in the other, she strode south again.

Z efra kept this pattern for more than a week. The desert provided her with many opportunities to fight boredom by pondering. She missed her family, and she often reviewed her botany, cartography, and survival skills, but most of her time was spent on her choice of profession. Besides survival, that was the point of this trek. Her decision was entirely up to her, but she must make the right one. She knew what she wanted, of course, but she had to be sure.

Her feet were tough, but her muscles ached from walking on the shifting sands. She missed Father's horses. She could breed or train horses, but that would compete with her parents, since they did not need her help.

When she hid from the midday sun, she thought of her brother's forge. He had offered to make her his apprentice, then ruined it by calling her puny. As if she would ever be as hulking as Izo.

After fighting a jackal for a desert hare, she considered being a warrior. She had practiced well with the guards. But her clan was small, so perhaps that was not saying much. And she was still on the 'puny' side.

She sucked a bone clean and licked her fingers. Zefra was a decent cook if mere edibility was enough. The hare tasted fine, though she could not save the fur. But she would not cook for others for the rest of her life. Then she stopped thinking until every trace of juicy hare was devoured.

Zefra updated her map twice a day so she could find her way home again. She could follow her grandparents and make maps like Mother did before marriage. Mapmaking was the clan's speciality, but she preferred more variety and being outside. She would not complain about boredom in her prayers. There were too many stories about Resef spicing up someone's boring life.

A caravan master did many of the things she could do. That was a good backup idea. But she did not have the supplies, animals, contacts, or funding for a caravan, and her family could not afford to help her. Her entire clan did not have enough resources to maintain more than the caravans they already had.

Zefra thought about all the jobs in her clan to make sure she had not forgotten better possibilities. Then she considered neighboring clans and rare jobs from districts so far away she had only heard about them.

She considered her favorite for days. It was a good idea, and no one would tell her she could not do it, but people dared not put their lives in her hands without proof, either. If that oasis existed, if she found it, then she had hope.

The white sand sparkled in the harsh sunlight and crunched under each footstep. Sweat pooled under her scarf and dampened her hair. Shadows rippled across the landscape from the ever-changing dunes. Scrubby plants gave welcome color even when they were not edible. The desert was stark and deadly, but she loved her home.

Scorpions, bandits, and poisonous snakes had been fortunately scarce this trip, but sandstorms came more frequently than usual for the season. Zefra's only strategy was to huddle in the lee of a cactus or a rock, clamp both sets of eyelids closed, and wait. The most savvy desert dweller could be caught in a storm too big or too erratic, but only one of her storms lasted longer than an hour. By the time that one ended, and she dug herself free, she lost half a day of walking and had to restock her cactus supply.

It had been ten days since she left her first camp. The trip south was taking longer than she had hoped. Even the sandstorms were not as bad as hunger, thirst, and fatigue. Her stomach growled, and she licked her dry lips. Where was prey? Nothing but a sudden flock of birds in the distance. Forget hunting! There were birds in the desert, but this far in the sand dunes, they were usually seen only one or two at a time. An entire flock probably meant there was open water in the area.

Zefra noted the direction — barely east of true south — and quickened her pace. When midday came, she slept as usual, but at midnight, she napped only briefly.

By noon, trees spiked the horizon. That meant a relatively large source of water, perhaps on the surface. Desert distances fooled the careless; she hoped it was no farther than it seemed. She skipped her nap and trudged on, saving her last pitiful remnants of food and wishing she had caught the snake.

A few hours later, she stumbled into a beautiful oasis. The third and hardest step of her plan was a success.

A narrow spring bubbled from the ground and through the tall grass into a small pond. A dozen short trees clustered in thin groves, and rabbits hid in the scrubby bushes.

Zefra threw herself by the pool and scooped water into her dry mouth until her stomach rebelled. There were several hours till sundown, so she staggered to a nearby tree and fell asleep.

Zefra awoke. The birds chirped sleepily in their nests, and the sky grew darker. It was the most rest she had gotten for days. She rubbed her eyes and stretched, then drank more water. Time for the next stage. She would fast all night while meditating on her life goals, then pray for confirmation from Resef, the desert God of Fire. When morning came, she would watch for a sign her choice was correct. If there was none, as usual, she would assume there were no godly objections. She would not need to cast runes and hope for clearer directions.

She sat cross-legged with her back against the tree, runes in her lap and hands on her knees, and counted the stars as they appeared. When there were too many to count, she pondered her options again.

Her mind was blank by the time the stars disappeared from the brightening sky. It was time to pray, before day completely arrived. She took a deep breath and closed her eyes.

"O Resef the Omnificent." Zefra tried for a reverent tone. It was an ironic title, considering Resef frequently used his creative powers for mere practical jokes rather than 'all things.' "I am here in thy desert, meditating according to tradition. I traveled on foot and alone." She flexed her tired feet. "I have proved my worthiness as an adult." And then some, since she not only survived but found this oasis. She did not smile, lest she be given a lesson in humility.

"I have given my choices for a profession considerable thought and made a decision that will not waste my talents. Not horse breeding or training." *You're welcome, Father.* "Not a blacksmith's apprentice." *Puny.* Zefra sniffed. "I suppose a guard is possible." *Do not mention cooking.* "Mapmaking *is* traditional." *Do not even think about boring.* "Caravan master does not seem possible."

Cactus spines. The sky was growing lighter. The sun would rise soon, and she still did not have the courage to ask for what she wanted.

"Ah, Most Holy Flame, I know most people guide themselves, but I know where this lovely oasis is and nobody else does. I would love to guide people here, if you approve. Better yet, I want to be an explorer." She had already proven she was good at that. "I think it will benefit our people if I looked for east-west routes to connect the north-south roads." She held her breath.

A rush of joy swept through her, and she opened her eyes in triumph.

The sun rose in front of her, greener than the trees. In a moment, it flickered back to white.

That was odd. Zefra eyed the sun and walked to the pool to wash the sand from her face. She removed her scarf and bent over the water with her eyes closed. As much as Resef loved pranks, she had never heard of him joking during a trial. Odd signs always meant something important, at least to the person who saw them. She reached for her scarf to dry her face.

If she told her family, would they believe her? The sun had been green so briefly, it was possible nobody else had seen it.

Zefra dragged her comb through her hair, looking at her watery reflection to see if she had removed the dirt. Oh!

She dropped her comb and stared with wide eyes as she touched her hair with shaking fingers. Perhaps they would believe, since Resef had left proof.

9. OCEAN
(OCEAN, NEAR DARRENDRA)

Target possible leaders early.
Beginning Battle Strategy

Ahjin finished his breakfast before Nia finally awoke. While she ate, he loaded the boat with Ludik's help, watching him carefully. Why had no one trained Ludik to favor his right hand? Didn't they know left-handers were clumsy and unlucky?

Ludik wrapped his boots in a waterproof tarp and tucked them into his pack. Nia rolled her eyes behind his back and wiggled her bare toes. Ahjin knew her opinion of shoes, but his own soft ankle boots kept his feet warm while flying.

"You have many supplies," Ludik said in rough trade tongue, lashing a barrel of water in place.

"We need them to reach Iskra," Nia said. "We'll petition Resef since Darravani won't help us."

"You not say we go around world." Ludik scowled as he fumbled through the sentence. "You children give up; I go home."

Ahjin whirled to face him. How dare he! "You—"

"Your headman, Asad, said you had to come," Nia interrupted. "Do you want to lose Nemerra?"

"Some adventure," Ahjin muttered in Iojo. "I'm not giving up." He wanted his life back.

While Nia repeated his words in Darrendran, he raised the anchor. Ludik grumbled something.

"I do not like adventure," Nia translated. "Asad should declaw himself."

Ahjin knew someone else who should be declawed. The stupid cat should have listened when they explained their plans.

"Adventures are fun." Nia took the helm while Ahjin ran up the sail.

"How long this take?" Ludik asked.

"We sailed about a month from Nokailana," Nia said. "Iskra is a few days farther."

As they left the shore, Ludik mumbled and ran his finger along the line gouged into the closest plank.

Ahjin glared at him. They should leave the sourpuss here and spare themselves his griping. He and Nia were fine by themselves. When Resef told them where Irajahan was, they'd finish this quest and go home.

"Ludik, please help me trim the sail." Nia asked.

Ahjin glanced at the perfectly set sail. She was making excuses.

Ludik stomped to his feet. Ahjin flicked his wings and shoved him overboard. Perhaps a swim would cool the cat's temper.

"Sorry," Ahjin hollered over the side of the boat. "I tripped on rope."

Nia glanced at the empty deck, then glared at him. "Fried fish, Ahjin, grow up. Help him back in."

She swung the tiller around. Ahjin offered a hand to Ludik. When the cursing shapeshifter threw his right arm over the bulwark and shook his left in his face, Ahjin flew off with a wave and a laugh. Even from the air, Ludik's angry posture was easy to read. It served him right.

When night fell, Ludik and Ahjin sprawled in the anchored boat while Nia took the first watch.

When Ahjin woke for the third shift, he heard Ludik whispering. Teasing jabs about talking to oneself sprang to his tongue, but before he said them, two words came to his ears.

"Darravani," Ludik pleaded. "Nemerra."

Ahjin couldn't translate the rest, but that was enough. He swallowed his teasing and closed his eyes. When Ludik fell silent, Ahjin yawned loudly and stretched, then struggled through trade tongue. "Is time? Sleep now."

He leaned against the mast while Ludik lay down. When he was sure Ludik's purring meant he slept, Ahjin pulled his scarf from his pocket and traced the birds Mother had embroidered. He'd been gone ten weeks and wasn't sure if he was more used to his family's absence or less.

Unlike Ludik, Ahjin had at least chosen to leave home. He frowned. No one had asked his opinion, either, or he'd have let the cat stay. He ran his finger over the birds again and folded the scarf back into his pocket.

During his watch, he tried to discover what magic Irajahan had given him. It might have worked better if he had any idea what to try. If he needed words or gestures, he didn't know them. Perhaps it was strictly internal, but that didn't give him any hints, either.

In the morning, Nia started Ludik on sailing lessons. He steered better than Ahjin but was not as good at trimming the sail. It might be the left-handedness, although he was surprisingly deft otherwise. When Ludik's eyes glazed during Nia's lecture, Ahjin took pity on him, adjusting the lines after a look at the sky.

Ludik turned the tiller to compensate. "How you tell wind so easy?"

Ahjin shrugged. "I see it."

Nia winked at Ludik. "It's a bird thing. I asked if he was a bird man or just a birdbrain, and he gave me the nastiest look." She clicked her tongue in mock dismay.

"Is fair question." Ludik grinned.

Ahjin rolled his eyes. Nia always thought she was funny.

They continued their language and sailing lessons until the boat's movement grew too bothersome. Ahjin put his hand on his stomach and groaned.

"You sick?" Ludik reached for his medical kit.

Ahjin didn't need help, only control over his motion. He spread his wings and launched into the air, flying steadily for a bit, then climbing high. He swooped up and down, flew in loops, and dropped in a rotating spiral. Then he flipped head over heels and pulled back into a climb.

Voices from the boat reached his ears.

"He fly like that," Ludik said, "but seasick on calm ocean?"

Nia didn't quite giggle. "He says if men were meant to travel on water, they'd have sails. When I compared his wings to the shape of our sail, he sprinkled sand in my pack."

She probably wouldn't tell that story if she knew he could hear her.

Ludik burst into laughter. Nia's laugh was followed by a splash and a shout from Ludik.

Oh, what now? Ahjin flew closer. "What is wrong?"

"Nia fell over." Ludik pretended to laugh to illustrate. "How long she hold breath? She need help?"

Ahjin scoffed. "That girl swim like fish and breathe like one." He paused. "Why boat go wrong way?"

"You both left, seasick idiot. Wind shifted. Not sail alone."

"Ask help, wrong-hand freak." Ahjin dropped on deck. "You steer, I do sails." They had to work together sometime, after all.

Nia came back with raw fish for lunch. Ahjin settled for bread and vegetables. Nia placed her half and vegetables between bread. Ludik nearly purred, tearing into his fish whole while the juices dripped down his chin.

Ahjin swallowed hard and looked away. Watching them was almost as bad as eating raw fish himself.

After lunch, they sailed on. Nia fished again a few hours later, but climbed back in the boat with blood streaming down her half-bare leg.

Ahjin pressed a cloth to her skin.

"Sand and sun, I should have stayed in my long suit," she hissed. "Under the sea is not as safe as it seems."

"Show me." Ludik grabbed his medical kit. "Not deep." He opened his jar of salve. "Wash, use this."

Nia followed his instructions and shoved back the jar. "Here's your goop."

"*And* cover." Ludik carefully wound a bandage around her leg.

"See, we need you." Nia smiled charmingly.

Ludik shook his head. "I go home, not waste time here."

"We not waste time," Ahjin muttered.

"That your opinion, idiot bird." Ludik tied Nia's bandage and repacked his salve.

"That opinion of god," Ahjin retorted. Irajahan had begged for help, even if Ahjin had agreed for his own reasons.

But during their scheduled conversation that night, Irajahan asked what was taking so long. He dismissed their excuses and refused to reveal his gift to Ahjin. And when Ahjin asked why the gods couldn't help with their own rescue, Irajahan said whatever held Makanavailea and him captive was also damping their abilities. He still couldn't break out. She had only discovered they must bring the cat.

"Whatever that means," Irajahan whined.

Ahjin thought of grinning fangs and grouchy silver eyes and felt like whining himself. He'd rather kick the cat overboard again and let him swim home.

When he recited the conversation to Nia and Ludik, they both frowned.

"I sorry gods agree with Asad." Ahjin was sorry for Ludik, and sorry for himself, stuck with a sourpuss.

"Same," Ludik said. "Irajahan always speak to you like that?"

"Yes," Nia said. "He's rude, thinking power makes right, and as All-Powerful, he can do what he likes."

Ludik snorted. "Not so powerful now, hmm?"

"I not think he believes yet, despite..." Ahjin waved his hand. "That."

Ludik snorted again and lay to sleep.

The next day, the slowly increasing wind brought a gentle rain. Ahjin occupied himself with aerial stunts and tag-the-seagulls. At least it gave him practice time.

Nia saved the last of the salted fish for him. "Look how generously we sacrifice for you."

She winked at Ludik as the two of them bit into their fresh, oozing fish. Ludik licked his fingers and grinned.

Ahjin gagged and planned revenge.

On the fourth day, Ahjin got seasick again. Ludik offered medicinal tea, speaking in much-improved trade tongue.

"You should try it," Nia said. "His goop scabbed my leg, and it's already healing well."

Ahjin pressed his hands to his stomach, shook his head, and flew away. He wouldn't risk Ludik's swill, even if the cat was trying to help.

Ahjin flew half an hour before he noticed a tiny island with a tall fruit tree in the middle. He flew back to describe its black bark and sweet-scented white flowers.

"Black pudding matasano," Nia said. "They're delicious." She swung the tiller to match Ahjin's directions, and they quickly arrived at the island.

"I'll meet you there," Ahjin said. "You should go barefoot, Ludik."

He launched himself into the air and flew backwards to see if Ludik took his advice, a little sorry for his prank-in-progress.

"He's right; you don't want to wade in your boots." Nia's voice drifted on the wind.

"I can jump to shore." Ludik shoved his feet in his boots. "Youch! Furballs!"

He yanked off one boot and turned it upside-down. A broken fish skeleton tumbled to the deck.

"Are you hurt?" Nia asked.

"No." Ludik's denial held more than a hint of a growl as he shoved his boots under the seat.

"Then let it go. I think he changed his mind and tried to warn you." Nia tossed the bones overboard and dove into the water. "You pick fruit while I fish."

Ludik cursed as he jumped from the boat.

He was lucky it hadn't been a raw fish to make his stupid boots slimy. Ahjin flew to the highest branch big enough to carry his weight and dropped matasanos in his bag.

"You are annoying mongrel!" Ludik said. A fruit hit the back of Ahjin's head.

"Ow." Ahjin flinched but didn't turn around.

From the corner of his eye, he watched until Ludik's bag was almost full. When Ludik stretched for the last fruit, Ahjin aimed his first juicy missile.

The shapeshifter fell from the tree, turning at the last moment to land on hands and feet. The bag squished into the dirt, and the fabric slowly darkened at the bottom.

"You are such child," Ludik shouted, followed by a chain of insults.

Ahjin hovered in the air and yelled "have another" with every fruit he threw at the jammy shapeshifter.

"Stop," Nia yelled, running to them. "What do you think you're doing?"

"He started it." Ahjin flicked a piece of rind off his sleeve.

"You deserved for stupid pranks." Ludik's attempt to wipe off the fruit smeared it down his tunic. "And you knocked me from tree."

Ahjin laughed. "Looks like you got what you deserve."

"Apparently you both deserve a steady diet of fish, since you destroyed the fruit." Nia stomped back to gut the fish she had caught.

The men slowly followed her.

"Sorry, Nia." Ahjin was more sorry about the fish.

"Sorry," Ludik growled, glaring at Ahjin.

Ahjin cooked the fish and took them to the boat while Ludik tried to wash the black stains from his tunic. Then they let Nia lecture them until her anger faded.

"Don't do it again, please," she finished with a sigh. "And Ahjin, quit pestering Ludik. He's cranky because he misses Nemerra and his family. You should be nice. Ludik, try to enjoy yourself a little."

Ludik crossed his arms.

"We get it, Nia." Ahjin fingered the scarf in his pocket. "Ludik, when we reach Iskra, we'll send messages to your family and Nemerra." He didn't have to make the trip more miserable for the curmudgeon.

Ludik nodded without turning around. Nia opened her mouth for a final comment, but Ahjin silenced her with a glare.

After they set sail, Nia grabbed an unraveling braid and cursed. She reached into her bag and tied a blue ribbon around her braid before noticing it was knotted to a pink one. And a green one. And a yellow. And—

She dropped her braid and peered into her bag. "Ahjin, you barracuda! What did you do to my ribbons?" She shook out a long line of ribbons in a rainbow of colors.

Ludik snorted behind his hand.

"Sorry, Nia, I have to go scout now." Ahjin was already in the air, shoulders shaking with amusement.

"You come back here and untie these," Nia yelled. "I hate it when you fly away from me."

"I can't hear you," he called back.

Nia's curses and Ludik's laughter trailed on the wind behind him.

Ahjin hadn't flown far when his conscience twinged. Oh, not the ribbons. Nia deserved that for the oozing fish, and the ribbons were unharmed. No, he shouldn't have let Ludik bait him into the food fight. It was his own fault after those fish bones.

His stomach cramped. It was no wonder Ludik wouldn't believe he was an adult. Ahjin hadn't been mature about Ludik joining them, and it wasn't the Darrendrakar's fault. Ludik couldn't be expected to end his betrothal just to stay out of Ahjin's way.

Ahjin sighed and circled back to the island at racing speed. He hovered above the top branch to pluck the last two matasano, then hurried back to the boat before Nia got suspicious.

Ahjin landed on the deck, hidden behind the sail, and quietly set one matasano on Nia's lumpy pack and the other on Ludik's tidy bag. There was a shadow on top of his own bag. He warily poked it, then drew out a slightly squished matasano. He ran a thumb across the flattened side and put it back.

When Nia laid out dinner, she gasped, then put one matasano next to each person's fish. Ludik stared, then nodded at Ahjin and ate the fruit in three bites, licking the juice from his fingers.

E arly the fifth day, a small bat flew from the north, dangling a beaded cord. Ludik whistled loudly and furled the sail. To Ahjin's surprise, the bat landed on Ludik's outstretched arm and held its leg for him to untie a tiny scroll. Ludik tucked the bat under the bench, then unrolled the scroll, read it, and threw it on the floor. Nia picked it up and stared at it.

After a minute, she passed it to Ahjin, who looked at the seven tiny symbols for even less time. "You need to translate the code, Ludik," he said. At least they had both improved in trade tongue.

"I do not think I am meant to tell you," Ludik growled, taking back the note, "but there must be mistake. It says, 'Goddess Darravani garden empty. Suspect treachery from strangers. Hold position for arrest.'"

"What does 'garden empty' mean?" Ahjin asked.

"For us, flowers have meanings. You can send an entire letter with a bouquet." Ludik's voice trailed off before he shook himself. "Darravani answers our prayers with flowers. I have never seen her garden empty. She must be gone." His eyes widened, and his fingers twitched.

Nia sucked in her breath and flopped onto the seat.

Ahjin sank beside her. Darravani was gone. What would they do if Resef couldn't help them, either? How could he find the missing gods and keep his deal with Irajahan? Or would he automatically be free if all the gods disappeared? Some might miss them, but he wouldn't care if they were gone. The world would be better without the parasitic feather mites.

Ludik waved the message. "Worse, my people think you did something to her."

"How could we do anything?" Nia asked. "Darravani was fine when we left, and we've been on the boat since."

"I do not think you are that kind of people," Ludik admitted. "How could you do anything to a goddess, anyway? If you tried, she would annihilate you. The timing must be coincidence."

Ahjin hunched his shoulders. "I promise we didn't harm her." He didn't even want to harm Irajahan, just avoid him.

Ludik narrowed his eyes. "Did you lead the enemy to Darravani?"

"I think the timing is a coincidence," Ahjin said. "Though Makana disappeared while we were still in Nokailana, your goddess vanished *after* we left Darrendra."

"How do you explain it, then?"

"There's an obvious reason for taking Irajahan first and Makana second." Nia said. "Irajahan is communications, and Makana is the brains. Whoever-he-is wants to prevent anyone opposing him. Or her."

"Darravani is smart," Ludik protested.

"Oh, yes, of course she is," Nia said, "but Makana is the smartest and Omniscient. I'm sure if we think about it, we can find lots of reasons Darravani was next on the list. She's a wonderful goddess." She patted Ludik on the side of his knee as he towered above them. "What will you do with us horrible criminals?"

Ludik sighed and crouched. "The council only cares about Darravani. They might rescue the other gods if it is convenient, but they will not care about Ahjin's bargain, even if they do not throw you in prison. They will not spare a boat to take me home. I will be gone as long, and for nothing." His eyes narrowed to angry cat-slits, and he clenched his fists.

"That's not fair," Ahjin said. "We can handle it ourselves. And do we dare wait a week for them to catch up? How long before Resef disappears? We need to do something *now*." He tried to stand, but Nia grabbed his arm.

"Makana said we need to take you with us, Ludik," she said. "What do you want to do?"

"I will help you. When we rescue the gods, my people will forgive me. Nemerra will understand." Ludik took a deep breath. "I hope."

He added four small symbols to the back of the note while the bat ate. After he retied it to her leg, he whistled a short tune and lofted her into the air. "That code means to take her time going home."

"What did you put in the message?" Ahjin glanced at the wind and adjusted the sail.

"Innocent. Will return when successful." Ludik's voice was almost calm.

Nia swung the tiller, and the wind caught the sail. "Time to leave."

As they sped southwest, they kept a constant watch behind them.

"Don't worry, Ludik," Nia said, "we'll return you to Nemerra as fast as we can. Until then, it will be an adventure."

Ahjin glowered at her. She never took anything seriously. He still wasn't convinced the world still needed the gods, but it might be possible — barely possible. Even if not, didn't she realize his whole life depended on this? Irajahan had promised to free him from the priesthood only if he rescued him. Ahjin had to keep that bargain to be a skydancer with his family.

10. BATTLE
(MIDDLE OF THE OCEAN)

To avoid discovery, eliminate your enemy's closest outpost first.
Beginning Battle Strategy

Ludik jerked awake and blinked. Someone had yelped. He squinted in the faint dawn light. Did Nemerra need him? No, he was in the boat, and Ahjin was squalling and clutching his head.

"What's wrong?" Ahjin said. "Stop yelling, or I can't understand you."

That didn't sound good. Ludik leaned over the hull to wake Nia. It took a while, and he pulled her aboard just in time to hear Ahjin's explanation.

"Nia, I need you to scry," Ahjin said. "Darravani just showed up with Irajahan and Makana."

Nia gasped, and Ludik clenched his fists.

"Their captor overheard them talking," Ahjin continued, "and he's sending something after us. If you can get a hint of what or where, we might have a better chance. Ludik, get our weapons. Strap everything down in case we can run."

Nia filled a bowl with water and settled on the bench to stare into it.

Ludik peered over her shoulder. "Can you actually see anything in that?"

"Not if you're bothering me and sloshing the water. Go away and let me concentrate."

Ludik headed for the packs, and Ahjin flew for a higher viewpoint. When Nia called them, both men came to hear her report.

"I have good and bad news." Nia drank the water and stashed the bowl. "I saw which directions we should watch, but everything else was blurry, almost like I was blocked."

Ludik patted her shoulder and laid out their weapons. "It is more than we had before."

"There's something underwater to the west," Nia continued, "and something flying in from the north. I don't think we can outrun them."

Ahjin strung his bow and strapped his quiver to his left hip. "I'll cover the aerial attack. Nia gets underwater, and you defend the boat, Ludik."

He stuck his slingshot and knife in his belt and wrapped his weighted rope loosely around his waist. Despite his brave face, he wiped his hands on his trousers and shifted from foot to foot.

Defend the boat. Ludik wanted to help Ahjin and Nia fight. He cursed his uselessness.

Nia sheathed her knife, then wrapped short pieces of wire around cords of her net. When Ludik pointed at them, she said, "My net is meant for fishing. Pokey bits will make it better for fighting."

Pokey bits. That was creative if not eloquent.

Ludik's razor-sharp knife was sheathed at his waist, and his bow lay next to him. He donned his breastplate, but left his boots packed. "Is there anything else we can do? Nia, how long do we have?"

Nia shrugged and nibbled on her lip. Ahjin sighed and returned to his aerial post, flying in jerky spirals.

Ludik pulled his medical kit from his pack and tucked it under the seat. Maybe they'd be lucky enough to not use it. That wasn't likely. He silently cursed again and wished to be home with Nemerra.

Nia hung her net over the rail and sat next to Ludik, dunking into the water every few minutes to spy. Ahjin varied his spirals with loops, dives, and twists, turning on a wingtip and defying the laws of nature.

"He really is superb, you know." Nia watched Ahjin with a smile. "After he finds Irajahan and returns to his family's troupe, it will be the best time of his life. And fun for me, too. He invited me to his first show.

You may come if you like. Imagine how amazing it will look with several fliers like that."

"I think I will be too busy with my new wife." Time with Nemerra was better than watching aerobatics, no matter how spectacular.

Nia rolled her eyes. "Oh, but you should come—"

Ahjin swooped lower and shouted. "There are swift-moving shadows on the horizon. They don't fly like birds. I think they're bats, but a lot bigger than the little messenger bat. Anything in the water yet?"

"Nothing," Nia said. "How many bats are there?" She and Ludik picked up their weapons.

Ahjin counted. "Five, ten, fifteen, tw— If I don't thin them, we'll have a real problem."

"Are you sure it's a good idea to go out there?" Ludik said. "Maybe you should wait until they get closer."

Ahjin ignored him. "As soon as they're in range, Ludik, try to shoot them, not me." He sped away.

Ludik watched him for a moment before Nia shouted.

She pulled her torso back over the bulwark and cursed inventively. "There are giant kraken coming! We fight the smaller ones in the islands sometimes. They're fierce but dumb, and they don't work as a team. Watch my back. If any surface, whack them with your ax or something. Stay out of their tentacles and don't let them eat you."

Ludik watched Nia dive overboard toward the huge shadows with a grace that would be fun to watch if she weren't heading toward monsters many times her size. Her harpoon looked like a scalpel in comparison.

Ahjin had reached the bats, who looked nearly the same size as the boy. How did bats grow that large?

Ludik punched the mast. He couldn't fight in the air and was almost as useless in the water. Somehow, those two had worked their way into his heart. If they died, he'd never forgive himself. How would he find their families? What would happen to their mission? Nemerra would be almost as disappointed in him as he was himself.

The boat jerked. Ludik staggered around and saw a large, gray-green tentacle crawling over the bulwark. He rushed it, yelling and swinging his ax. After a few strokes, the tentacle sheared off, leaving the edge of the hull a mess of splinters. A long list of his brothers' favorite insults rolled off his tongue.

He swore again when another tentacle appeared. The kraken was nearly as long as the boat and threatened to capsize it. The monster reached for a better grip, and waves splashed Ludik in the face. He blinked the salt water from his eyes and chopped, heart pounding. The tentacle dodged and swung back, knocking him to the deck.

Ludik rolled away and gasped for breath. The mast blocked the kraken from him for a moment, so he tightened his grip on the ax and sprang to his feet. He was getting a feel for the monster's rhythm. This time, as he lunged around the mast, he hacked with less damage to the boat. The tentacle broke, leaving bits of squirming kraken and slimy blue blood.

More dripping tentacles stretched over the hull and slapped the deck to find him. Then a monstrous head emerged, with a large, beak-like mouth and unblinking eyes that filled most of its face. The creature tried to pull itself into the boat.

Ludik settled his weight evenly and chopped. It was like cutting one of the big deadfall trees at home. Trees didn't writhe and try to catch him in their branches, but the pretense took his mind off his ugly task.

The monster seemed to have an endless number of tentacles. Ludik lied to himself again and chopped the entire oak into kindling. When the kraken's head finally rose above the bulwark, Ludik smashed it between the eyes. The broken head sank.

Ludik leaned against the railing and panted. He kicked the biggest chunks into the sea while he scanned the area. The clear water gave a good view of Nia's fight.

She had one twenty-foot kraken partly tangled in her net while she approached with her harpoon. Nia was more agile, but the kraken had a longer reach. If she didn't kill it before the second arrived, she wouldn't have a chance. At least he had killed the third.

He kicked more monster bits into the water and swore, then turned to shoot the bats that had gotten past Ahjin. They were much larger and nastier than the little fruit bats around his home, with red eyes, scabby fur, and notably longer teeth and claws. Their high-pitched cries hurt his ears. Ludik downed three of them before the rest flew back to swarm Ahjin.

"Come here, you mangy ratwings," he shouted after them. The

cowards kept flying, too far to shoot. If he chased them in the boat, Nia would be left alone.

Ahjin's amazing flying made good use of his weapons. He shot distant bats with arrows and struck nearer ones with his surujin. When they closed on him, he flipped from their path at the last second and let them collide.

The runt was surprisingly good.

Ahjin didn't always escape grazing the bats. Once, he even crashed right into two of them and barely escaped. Worse, the sheer number of bats was forcing him lower. A little more, and he'd fall into the ocean.

There was no way for Ludik to help from here, and he couldn't leave Nia. He prayed quickly to Darravani and turned back to the water.

The kraken had worked free of the net, just below the surface. This was Ludik's chance. He rapidly drew back on the bowstring, aimed, and fired. The arrow skimmed above the waves and hit the colossal eye!

The kraken thrashed into Nia's path, and she pinned it on her harpoon like an oversized butterfly. She swam out of the way while it thrashed the ocean into froth. When it stopped moving, she kicked it off her weapon and shook her fist in triumph.

Only one left. Where was the straggler? Ludik didn't see it anywhere.

The last monster shot from below and grabbed Nia in its tentacles. Before Ludik could do anything, it shoved her inside its cavernous mouth in one bite. Her harpoon sank.

"Plague fleas, no!" Ludik shot an arrow at the kraken, but it skidded off its head. He growled and shot another arrow, but it was deflected by the water.

The kraken dove deeper. Nia was gone.

Ludik drew another useless arrow on his bowstring and prayed for revenge. Before he fired, the monster convulsed. Its tentacles stilled, and its mouth cracked open. It slowly sank.

Ludik let his bow sag. What had happened?

A bedraggled Nia fought her way out of the gigantic beak.

Ludik dropped his bow and leaned over the bulwark, heart pounding.

She swam after her harpoon and surfaced with it a minute later.

Ludik jumped overboard to tow her in.

Nia smiled wearily and let him. "I told you kraken are stupid. He didn't chew before swallowing. And he obviously underestimated the reach of *my* tooth." She waved her dripping knife in feeble triumph, and a mix of red and blue blood trickled down her arm.

"Lucky for you." Ludik dunked her underwater again to wash off the gore, then shoved her into the boat and climbed in after.

He handed her a blanket and looked toward Ahjin's fight. A few bats wavered back the way they had come, but Ludik couldn't see Ahjin. He yanked the anchor and set the sails to go find him.

Nia stared wide-eyed at the splintered bulwark and shakily pressed a cloth to the three-inch cut on her arm. "You destroyed Ahjin's handiwork. That was the board he, um, decorated so well." She giggled a little hysterically.

"He never told me how he made that crooked gouge across the plank." Ludik tried to smile. "He is not here now. You tell me." Maybe the distraction would calm her while they sailed. Nemerra would know how to help Nia regain her composure.

"Well, I asked him if he knew how to use an adze." Nia's face twitched. "He said he could do anything I needed, so I asked him to smooth the board. But he," she choked, "he didn't, he didn't even know which tool to use, and he..." She doubled over, laughing too hard to breathe.

When she recovered, Ludik repeated his request. She howled and waved her hand, dissolving into tears.

They arrived at the other battle scene a few minutes later, sober again. The sky above them was empty, and the rest of the bats were a retreating smudge in the distance.

White feathers floated on the waves, but there was no other sign of Ahjin.

Nia threw off the blanket and dove underwater. Ludik searched the air and the top of the waves. They couldn't be too late! He wouldn't accept it. Ahjin had to be here somewhere.

But he wasn't. Ludik's gut clenched.

Nia surfaced. "Do you see him?"

Ludik shook his head, and she dove again. He scanned the sky while she swam around the area. Every few minutes, she repeated her question. His heart grew heavier each time he had to tell her no.

When she finally gave up, Ludik hauled her back in the boat and wrapped her in the blanket. She cried while he threw the last chunks of kraken overboard. His eyes burned with every splash.

He pulled up the anchor and loosed the sails.

"You're just in time." Ahjin's voice came from above.

They turned around, but ocean and sky were empty. Their joyous smiles faded.

Nia whispered, "Do you believe in ghosts?" She pulled the blanket tighter around her.

"Not before now," Ludik murmured, putting his hand on his knife.

The wash of waves and the calls of birds were the only sounds. A moment later, laughter burst out. The boat jiggled, and Ahjin appeared on the deck.

"I'm sorry," he said, "I forgot I was still invisible."

"Invisible?" Nia threw herself on him, blanket and all. "When did that happen?"

"And how?" Ludik lashed the tiller and joined them.

"I finally figured out Irajahan's mysterious gift. By the end, the few surviving bats were so disoriented they almost gave up. I was chasing them when you arrived. Thank you again. I'm exhausted, and invisibility gives me a headache."

Ludik clasped Ahjin's arm and eyed him for injuries. Under splashes of blood, Ahjin was covered in small bites and cuts. He should heal well.

Nia wasn't so lucky. Ahjin wrapped his arms around her shoulders while Ludik washed the gash on her arm. Nia kept silent until Ludik stitched, then she howled and called him names. She had worked her way from "son of a shark" and "lousy tailor" to "butcher" and "torturer" before Ahjin freed a hand to cover her mouth.

"Let the poor man help without insulting him, please."

Nia huffed and quieted to a whimper, but her eyes bored into Ludik.

He ignored the silent threat and finished his sewing. After adding ointment, he bandaged her arm.

"At least I can heal you, Nia. I will do better next time." While Ahjin still held her down, Ludik dropped a brotherly kiss on her forehead. Then he tousled Ahjin's curly hair and dodged the return swing. "My brothers are worse, Ahjin."

He deserved every curse for not protecting the younger ones. There must have been a way. Somehow. This wouldn't happen again.

It took a while to clean Ahjin's wounds, even with Nia's help. Rather than apply a small bandage to every wound, Ludik smeared him liberally with salve and wrapped each limb in one long bandage.

Ahjin endured his treatment quietly. When he winced, Nia took his hand. His mouth twitched at the corners, but he thanked her solemnly.

After cleaning, Ahjin and Nia sprawled on the floor and nibbled food. In moments, they were fast asleep, Ahjin with his head on his pack, and Nia resting her head on his shoulder.

Ludik ate while he steered. They still had weeks before reaching Iskra, and it looked like a storm was on the way. He rubbed his eyes — he was not crying — and murmured a prayer of thanks to Darravani for his friends' survival and his own erratic healer's training. At least he could tell Nemerra he had done some good.

11. SIGNS

(OASIS, ISKRA)

Use runes wisely. Be warned: Resef listens personally to all prayers addressed to him.
How to Read Runes: Introduction

Zefra must leave the oasis soon to reach home in ten days. Too early, she would fail. Too late, and her clan would think her dead and travel the planned migration they had postponed for her.

She set snares and gathered vegetables and herbs from the stream bank, then took another nap. When she woke, her snares held a bird and two desert hares. A ring of stones made a fire pit in the sand outside the oasis. There was no dry dung, and she would not cut wood, so she gathered fallen twigs to build a small fire. The wild-onion-stuffed bird would roast for dinner, while the herb-wrapped hares smoked on a tripod for the next day.

Zefra filled all three water bags and checked for leaks. The more water she carried, the less time she would spend looking for it on her trip. One with a slow seep would have to be used first. With the water and food, her pack would finally be half-full.

Her dinner smelled too delicious to wait for it to cool. Burned fingers were worth it. After she ate and drank her fill, she stowed the smoked hares in her pack. She tucked the leftover greens next to the leaky water bag, then drank again and left.

The trip home was uneventful although the wind was still rougher than normal. As Zefra traveled, she double-checked her map's accuracy, retracing her steps from the newly marked oasis. She also discovered further proof from Resef and practiced it often so she could demonstrate the gift when she arrived.

Zefra made such good time, she had to camp overnight to not arrive too early. She walked the final hour with every bit of her hair tucked under her scarf. It was hard to control her excitement, but she wanted to approach her family's tent with something resembling decorum. When she rounded the last dune and saw her youngest sister playing with a lizard, she abandoned the pretense.

"Haru," Zefra shouted, running through the outer rows of drab tents and swinging her sister in circles. "I'm so glad to see you."

Haru squealed and dropped the lizard, which scuttled for a rock. She threw her arms around Zefra's neck and shook her chubby finger. "Zeffa, I missed you. Why were you gone so long?"

She had obviously escaped both her minder and her scarf, and her black hair was plastered unevenly to her sweaty neck.

"I told you I would be gone for a long time. Risa promised to tell you how many days until I returned. Did she forget?" Zefra kissed Haru's cheek.

Haru tried to count the days on her tiny fingers. "No, Zeffa, but it was too long."

People ran from the dun tents, the corral, and her brother's smithy. Father passed Haru to Mother and hugged Zefra tightly, engulfing her in the familiar scent of horses. Mother passed Haru to someone else and threw her arms around both of them.

Zefra only had a second to enjoy the embrace before everyone called, "Bright day," and buried her in the middle of a seething mob of dark-haired parents, siblings, aunts and uncles, cousins, and neighbors. They all wanted a hug and a story, more or less in that order.

Father held up his hands and shouted for order. "She's home safe, and we will talk to her later. Right now, she needs food and sleep."

The babbling crowd trickled away, and her parents and siblings swept her into their tent. The handwoven carpets and tapestries were the same, well mended from generations of use, although someone had rearranged them while she was gone. It was still home.

Father took her pack; her brother removed her boots; Mother gave her fresh greens in flatbread; and her little sisters tackled her onto her narrow bed. Her parents kissed her forehead and promised to tell her all the news when she woke, and they and Izo wrestled the younger girls out of the tent. Zefra gobbled her bread and fell asleep smiling.

When she awoke a few hours later, she was alone. The familiar scent of kiziak fires, fueled by dried dung-and-desert-grasses, beckoned her to leave the tent. Zefra washed her face, fixed her scarf, and drained a water bag. Now, where was her family? Darkness approached, but few of the fires were lit. The chieftain's fire burned, and she followed it to find most of the clan, including her parents.

Father drew her under his arm. "I'm afraid your return has been overshadowed, my dear."

"What is going on?" Zefra asked.

"It seems we have strangers on a quest." He shrugged. "I do not think I understand their story yet, but Prathap called for a council. 'Tis almost time for it to start. Do you want to eat more first?"

Zefra laughed. "You must remember your own trek well. What do we have?"

"I made your favorite stew," Mother said.

Zefra hugged her, then ran back to the family tent. She filled a bowl with the luxuriously slow cooked, vegetable-laden stew and walked back to the fire while eating.

Chieftain Prathap came out of his tent with the priest. Behind them were three strangers in ill-fitting desert robes. Everyone settled around the fire. Prathap's wife gave him a basket of bread and a tiny bag of salt. He took a slab of bread and a pinch of salt and introduced himself to the visitors, then passed the basket and bag to Isvah, the priest, who did the same. As the basket traveled around the circle, Zefra memorized the names of the newcomers, whose coloring stood out among the Iskrins' white skin and dark hair and eyes.

Ludik Moriko was the lean, dark giant wearing a robe half a cubit too short. His close-cropped hair was the color of Mother's gold dowry bracelets, and his silver cat eyes watched the crowd warily.

The girl was Niamolenulanami. Everyone practiced her name in whispers and admired the lavender hair drying loose to her ankles after the guest-bath.

The other young man, Ahjin Machol, had white hair and a large hump on his back under the borrowed robe. His xaffac-colored eyes watched the chieftain almost constantly.

After the introductions, Prathap invited the guests to explain their visit. As the short young woman told their fantastic tale of missing gods and a mysterious enemy, Isvah tossed runes hand-to-hand. The girl explained about Irajahan's messages — which earned Ahjin some speculative looks — and laid out a time line.

"The gods have been taken every five weeks," she continued, "and we don't know if that's coincidence. Nine days ago, Irajahan stopped talking to Ahjin. He hadn't been more upset than usual, so we think his captor blocked the leak that allowed him to communicate. That's why we sailed day and night across the ocean, despite the bad weather from Makana and Irajahan's absences. We wanted to warn Resef, so he can fight back and help us. I saw how to get us to this coast, but no farther. Can someone please tell us how to contact him?"

Her round, green eyes fluttered with exhaustion. Her friends leaned to support her between their shoulders.

Zefra touched her hair to be sure every strand was hidden under her scarf. These strangers were unusual enough to be connected with the green sun at the oasis. Resef's approval of her vocation suddenly seemed part of a hidden agenda. What did he have planned? She wiped her sweaty hands on her robe.

Prathap glanced at Isvah, who nodded and returned his runes to his pocket.

The chieftain rose to his feet. "We're sure you have told us the truth as you know it," he said. "You're lucky you arrived before we moved our camp. Perhaps the gods are smiling on you. However, our council must meet to decide how we can help you, and 'tis too late to leave tonight. You may eat and sleep here. We will talk tomorrow."

He beckoned his wife, who led the strangers to the guest tents despite their feeble protests. When she returned alone a few minutes later, she kissed Prathap and went to their own tent to finish cooking dinner. Everyone else did the same, and Prathap extinguished the fire to save fuel.

Zefra walked to the borders of camp while she pondered. The tale might explain the unusual rate of sand storms she had experienced. Could the green sun have meant Resef wanted her to help the strangers? He could not force her. She made sure her hair was still tucked under her scarf. Nobody else even knew about her sign yet.

This might be a wonderful opportunity. If she did this, whatever Resef had in mind, it would make her reputation. Zefra wrapped her cloak to block the usual nighttime chill and watched the setting sun dye the white sand blue. The desert stretched to the horizon in deceptively gentle-looking dips and wrinkles, whipped by the wind into a frenzy around her feet. As the sand rose to waist level, she lowered her inner eyelids to protect her eyes and turned back to camp.

Isvah caught Zefra on the way to her family's tent. "Bright stars, Zefra. I'm sorry the commotion has darkened your time to shine. We will have your celebration tomorrow, but tell me about your experience now."

Zefra waved to her parents and followed the priest to his tent, which doubled as the clan's shrine. Asitha, the only girl among his apprentices, waited to chaperone. Zefra sat on a rug across from the priests while Asitha served tea in precious wooden cups. Zefra drained the cup and set it gently on the ground. This was her best chance to convince someone. The priests refilled their cups and politely watched her from the corners of their eyes.

Zefra explained how she had dealt with her daily needs and listed the supplies she had found and made. She described her basic route and her reasons for taking it. "I found an oasis, with greenery, water, and animals. I made a map, and I would like to be a guide. When I do not have a hired job, I can find new routes."

Isvah smiled and opened his mouth, but Zefra held up her hand. Her face grew hot, and she took a calming breath. "That is not all. The sun rose green in the morning." She looked up to offer a clear view of her face.

Asitha looked skeptical, but Isvah's face remained bland. "I do not doubt you, but others might. I do not suppose you have any proof of this sign?" The priest abandoned politeness and stared into her eyes.

Zefra swallowed hard and reached for her scarf. When she unwound it into her lap, bright red hair tumbled over her shoulders.

Asitha dropped her cup. The last of her hot tea spilled across her knees, and she yelped.

Isvah dumped cool water in her lap and passed a towel. He turned back to Zefra and examined her still-black eyebrows, then felt her hair.

"Is it just the color, or did it come with the traditional legacy?" His voice trembled.

Zefra reached toward the low-burning lamp. The little flame rose and nestled into her hand. She held it in front of Isvah until he nodded. After she dropped the fire into the lamp, he turned over her hand and drew his fingers across its unmarked palm.

"And what is it you think Resef wants you to do?" He signaled to Asitha, who left the tent at a run despite the wet robe clinging to her legs.

Zefra looked out the open tent flap. "I think he wants me to be the strangers' guide. And we should provision them and give them any information you can get from Resef."

She watched Asitha stumble to each council member's home and point toward Isvah's tent.

"I need to talk to the council after I talk to Resef. You may tell your parents what you told me. Please return with them in one hour."

Zefra donned her scarf and exited. Isvah dropped the tent flap so abruptly it smacked her in the back. She arrived home in the middle of dinner and sank to the floor. Father handed her more stew, water, and a piece of flatbread.

"I have an hour before I have to return," Zefra said between bites. "Mother, Father, you are to come with me. Let me tell you why."

With questions from the girls, it took most of the hour to finish her story. When she yet again removed her scarf, little Haru jumped to feel her hair. Everyone else stared. Then she demonstrated her flame-calling. Mother's lip quivered in distress until Izo laughed.

"Little sister, I should have asked you to be my apprentice. Think how easily I could keep my forge going." Izo stopped laughing when Mother slugged his shoulder, but his eyes still twinkled.

Zefra frowned. "I'm not a furnace, brother." She turned to her parents. "'Tis almost time to go. Do I have your approval? I do not know how long I will be gone."

Father put his arm around her shoulder. "You're an adult now; you make your own decisions. What can we do to help?"

"I have some gear, but if I may get a few items from the family...?" She knew resources were tight.

"If we have it, you may take it," Mother said. "Risa can check your list."

Risa rubbed her hands with delight.

"Put no metalwork on the council's list," Izo said. "I will give you anything not spoken for, or if I can make it before you leave."

"Is that all, then?" Father asked. "Is it time?"

"Oh, yes. We should hurry." She scrambled to her feet and grabbed a slate and a piece of chalk. "I will let you know what happens," she promised her siblings on her way out the door.

Inside the priest's tent, Prathap and Isvah sat at the head of a circle of ten mats. The other councilors, three women and two men, sat on either side. Zefra and her parents sat at the end and accepted cups of cool water.

Prathap called the meeting to order, and Isvah reported on Zefra's trek.

Zefra scribbled notes on her slate while she waited. She wrote her personal list of supplies and what the group might need. She doubted the strangers had adequate desert gear.

Mother nudged her shoulder. The councilors were staring. The priest grinned.

Chieftain Prathap sighed. "I said, show us your evidence, please."

Zefra flushed and scrambled to her feet. For the third time that day, she removed her scarf and let her hair spill down. Usri had offered to braid it for her, but it made more of an effect waving loose to her elbows. While the council gaped, she reached for the closest lamp to repeat the trick she had shown Isvah.

The shocked elders doused themselves as Asitha had, with the water wisely provided in place of the customary hot tea. Isvah passed around the stack of towels set at his knee.

Since everyone took her revelation so well, Zefra snapped her fingers and called fire from thin air. That rattled even the priest. She blew out her flame and showed her unburned hands to the slack-jawed crowd.

Since the rest of her story had already been told, it only took a few minutes to explain her requests. "And I asked Isvah to talk to Resef. I would like to hear what he learned."

She returned to her seat, and Mother put her arm around her shoulders. Father patted her knee and handed her the slate.

The priest shrugged. "Resef is not talking to us, and that is unusual. I assume whatever plague has taken the other gods hit him as well. All we get from the runes is a repeat of a cast from last week that said, 'Go to green earth.' That made no sense before, so we ignored it as a miscast." He shrugged again. "Sometimes we make mistakes. This time, I thought of Zefra. The world cannot afford to have the gods missing for long. Approve her requests and send the strangers to her oasis. Perhaps Resef left something there to help."

"The girl is not even officially an adult," one councilor protested. "She has little experience with life and none being fire-touched. This is too dangerous for her. She should stay and learn to control her power."

"Zefra will be an adult tomorrow," Prathap gently said, "and will gain life experience by living. None of us have experience with Resef's rare gift, so there is none to teach her. Though this quest *is* dangerous, is it safer to deny Resef's wish?"

He passed around the voting basket, and each of the seven elders placed a stone inside. When the chieftain dumped the stones, there were only two black negatives.

"Very well, the council has spoken," Prathap said. "I expect everyone to help supply the group regardless of your personal vote. I will choose a handful of warriors to send with them. 'Tis not that we do not trust you," he told Zefra, "but we want you as safe as possible."

He turned back to the council. "We will divide the tasks from Zefra's list after I talk to our crusaders in the morning. Please do not discuss this with anyone until tomorrow. Thank you."

The elders filed out of the tent. Zefra quickly copied the group's lists from her slate onto one of Prathap's, then went home with her parents. Risa took her personal list and disappeared into the back room with Izo while their parents put the two youngest girls to bed.

Zefra mentally rehearsed her plans. Pack tomorrow, leave the next day, find whatever Resef thought they needed at the oasis. This would be easier if she had better information, but she would trust Resef and handle her part. If only she were sure the strangers knew what they were doing.

12.SURPRISES

(HOTARU SUMMER CAMP
AND NORTHERN DESERT,
ISKRA)

**Each god created his or her own people and kept them with
private diligence. They spoke not to each other, neither meddled
in one another's affairs. Thus were maintained peace and order
throughout the world.**
A Comprehensive History of the Gods, vol. 2

After breakfast, Zefra walked through the whispering crowd to the
Hotaru guest tents. She fingered her uncovered hair as she
reviewed verb tenses in trade tongue. Although she would be favorite
gossip for a long time, her job today was to prepare the strangers for the
coming journey. Tomorrow would be harder, but it would also give her
the chance to learn about the outdwellers.

She passed Father leaning on the corral fence and talking to two
council elders. Though there were swift horses that crossed the desert
faster than anything but the wind, they took extra care. Her group would
surely use the little ponies instead. They were easy to handle, and could
walk long hours and eat desert shrubs.

Zefra reviewed the list of clothing for the strangers as she worked her
way past people sorting gear. The woman would fit a child's robe, and the
tailors could easily make a larger one for the tall man. It might be more

difficult to accommodate the other's hump, but there was already a tailor with Izo and his fellow blacksmith.

The strangers emerged from the guest tents in their own clothes. The deformed young man wore an impractical, feathered cloak. He shrugged his shoulders, spread his cloak, and jumped.

He did not come down.

Zefra looked up and up. She forced her open mouth closed. There was nothing wrong with his back, but his wings might indeed be a challenge for the tailor.

Izo chatted in trade tongue with the other two outdwellers. After the tall man whistled down the winged one, Izo hugged her and introduced the three interestingly named strangers.

"I expected you five minutes ago," Izo teased Zefra. "Did you get lost in your lists?"

Zefra ignored him. "What supplies are we discussing first?"

"I have everything but desert clothing," Ludik said. "Are there choices? I do not like scarves or belts."

"There is a hooded version, and belts are removable," Izo replied. "We can discuss it after we see your gear."

"I'll get our stuff," Ludik said. "And you can sew the hood onto my collar." He stalked toward the tents.

Zefra frowned. Would he be difficult about everything?

"Why is he so finicky?" Izo asked.

Ahjin grinned. "You've never met a Darrendrakar? He'll show you in a minute. I have weapons and arm bracers. Ludik has armor, including hidden greaves in his boots, but Nia needs something."

"You do not want armor?" Izo asked.

"I fly. I can't afford the weight," Ahjin said.

"He has a really hard head." Niamolenulanami giggled.

Ahjin stepped on her foot, and she shoved him.

"A laminated linen breastplate would work if we had time to make it." Izo tapped his chin. "Ah." He whispered in the younger apprentice's ear, and the boy ran off.

"Now what can we do for you, my dear?" Izo beamed at the short woman, who fluttered her eyelashes.

"Resef help me," Zefra muttered. "Focus, brother." They needed to prepare for the journey.

"I *was* focused." He winked at the pretty islander.

Ludik returned in time to hear the comment. He glared and dumped an armload of gear at Izo's feet. "Here are Nia's weapons. This net can catch fish or unwanted pests."

"Oh, Ludik." Niamolenulanami rolled her eyes.

Ludik continued. "She killed a kraken with this harpoon. Her knife can gut a shark in the ocean — or desert."

"Great tides of fish bubbles, Ludik. He's not a shark." She folded her arms and tapped her foot.

Ludik held the serrated blade under Izo's nose until Izo swallowed and nodded, then switched weapons. "This is my ax, equally good for trees or enemies, and my bow. I keep my knife sharp enough for surgery."

Izo, about to test the edge of the knife, yanked back his fingers. Zefra smothered her grin. No one had ever objected to her brother's flirting so aggressively.

"Are you finished, you overprotective clod?" Niamolenulanami tapped her fingers on her arm.

Ahjin snickered. "Relax, Ludik. Izo asked why you're choosy about clothes. Want to impress him more?"

Ludik grinned wickedly and slid his knife into a hidden boot sheath. He dropped his breastplate over his head, smoothed the banded segments, and clicked the odd buckles. Then he unbuckled the armor in one second and bent to yank both breastplate and knee-length tunic over his head.

Before Zefra could turn away modestly, he emerged from his clothing as a black panther. Her jaw dropped. She reached for her knife before remembering the giant cat was a person. She pressed her trembling hands together and bowed an apology as her clansmen sheathed their weapons and did the same.

Ludik ignored them. He sat on his haunches and rested his claws on Izo's shoulders.

When he growled at the islander, she sighed. "He wants you to count his natural weaponry."

Izo nodded rapidly. "Makes sense. Um, let me go now, please?"

Zefra took a breath to calm her thundering heart. This was more than she had anticipated learning.

The panther dragged his tunic to the tent. He emerged a moment later, two-legged, dressed, and smug.

"So," Izo cleared his throat, "we can reinforce your ax handle with metal strips, if you like. Niamolenulanami's weapons are good."

After examining Ahjin's weapons, he offered arrows, lead balls for the slingshot, and a long dagger. The apprentice returned with a bundle of tough leather and was sent off again.

Izo unfolded a large forge apron that hung neck to knee and wrapped around Ahjin's back. "Lightweight armor for you."

Ahjin took it for a test flight. When he landed, he shook his head. "Not enough leg movement."

The tailor cut the bottom half of the apron into wide strips, then stepped behind Ahjin to measure the placement of his wings.

The apprentice returned again, with a dubious look on his face. "You do know this armor is a sample? 'Tis not big enough for an adult."

Izo laughed. "She is not big enough for an adult, either." When the islander stuck out her tongue, he pretended to pout. "Such thanks I get for finding you the perfect armor."

"Prove it's perfect." She pulled herself to her full, unimpressive height.

Zefra felt unusually tall until she looked at the imposing shapeshifter, nearly a cubit taller than herself.

"This is kikko armor." Izo showed a tunic of padded silk, thigh-length on the girl and covered in overlapping scales of polished horn. "'Tis lightweight and flexible."

"And shiny." Her eyes gleamed.

"And," Izo grinned, "if you do not mind, I thought the scaled pattern is appropriate."

Ahjin chuckled and muttered something about fish in the desert.

"It's perfect, thank you." Niamolenulanami ignored her friend and wiggled it over her head.

"How many Hotaru are going with you?" Izo asked Zefra. "Does anyone else need armor or weapons?"

"Prathap said he's choosing a handful," Zefra said. "I am sure they will be prepared."

"You're going with us? And more?" Ahjin groaned.

Niamolenulanami smacked his shoulder and scolded him in a foreign language.

Zefra did not understand his disappointment. They did not know how to survive in the desert. "Did no one tell you what the council decided last night?" she said. "I will be your guide and guard."

"Why you?" Ahjin asked.

Zefra nodded. It was wise of him to check her credentials. "Resef only said I should take you to an oasis I found. The priest thinks Resef is gone, too, and cannot say more. At least we know the next step."

Ahjin ran his hands through his hair until it stuck out in all directions. "We thought we were early enough." He paced toward the tent. "We should've come here first, after all. What are we supposed to do at the oasis?"

"He's sneaky," Zefra said. "Perhaps he left a hint when he disappeared. We will find out."

Ahjin looked at his friends. Ludik frowned. The girl smiled and bounced on her toes.

After a minute, Ahjin said, "You can be our guide, but we don't need other people."

"A small group travels faster, but a larger group is safer," Zefra said.

"Just you," Ahjin repeated. "We don't want to be noticed. Fewer is better."

Izo chuckled, and Zefra shot him a fiery look. He warded it off and swaggered back to his forge after a last smile at Niamolenulanami. Ludik scowled at his back.

Zefra asked the three friends to cooperate with the other Hotaru, then left to speak to the chieftain about Ahjin's request. She spent the rest of the day packing and planning.

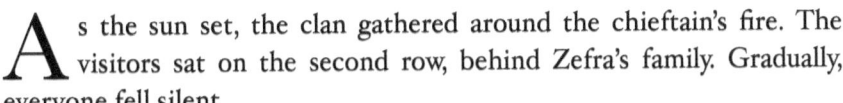

As the sun set, the clan gathered around the chieftain's fire. The visitors sat on the second row, behind Zefra's family. Gradually, everyone fell silent.

Isvah boomed her name. "Zefra Ashvakosha, come forth and be recognized."

Zefra brushed off her best robe and joined him at the front. She had waited a long time for this.

"Zefra, you have survived your ordeal and chosen your life's work. From this day forward, you are an adult of the Hotaru of Iskra. We have gifts for you. Zefra Ashvakosha, sister to Risa, Usri, and Haru."

Her little sisters came forward. Haru placed a lopsided circlet of flowers on Zefra's head while the others carefully tied an embroidered sash around her waist. One side showed Risa's beautiful stitches, while the other half was Usri's less-practiced work. The girls buried her in hugs and scampered to their parents.

"Zefra Ashvakosha, sister to Izo."

"I made you a saif and a kazagand jerkin, little sister." Izo unwrapped a curved sword, three-quarters the normal length, and a lacquered leather vest with a high collar, fastened in front to the waist and then hanging free to the knees. It was lined with padded silk and studded with metal rivets. "I used a lighter wire for the inner mail, to suit your weight."

Zefra lifted the perfectly balanced sword. "How did you finish in one night?"

"*One* night? I worked on these every day since you left. Would I turn you loose unprotected? Go conquer the world, Zefra. Just remember to come home." He kissed her cheek and returned to his seat.

"Zefra Ashvakosha, daughter of Hesketh and Shara."

Her parents presented her with a small tent. When she married, her husband's tent would be sewn to hers. "We taught you everything we know. Be true to your family, your people, and your God."

They kissed her on opposite cheeks, then braided her hair around her head to mark her as adult. Mother set Haru's flowers on the braids.

"Zefra Ashvakosha, daughter of the Hotaru of Iskra."

Chieftain Prathap and his wife approached. "We will spread the tale of your discovery, so when you return, you will have many opportunities for honor and prosperity." Prathap whispered, "I compromised on the caravan size." He gave her a long knife. His wife gave her a helmet and a warm hug.

"Zefra Ashvakosha, daughter of Resef the Omnificent."

Asitha approached with an unlit lantern. That was odd. Traditionally, it would be lit as a symbol of their God and passed on as a token of His favor.

Asitha faced the crowd. "Resef has already made His favor plain with Zefra's fiery hair. He also gave her the ancient power." She held out the lantern.

Zefra sighed and lit it with her outstretched finger, illuminating the amazed faces of the crowd.

"Boiling oceans," someone in the second row blurted.

"From this day, she shall be Zefra Ashvakosha Kezhekori!" Asitha handed the lantern to Zefra.

The crowd cheered. Zefra bowed, and everyone came to congratulate her before dinner.

Niamolenulanami skipped over, followed by the young men. "How did you dye your hair that color?"

"'Tis not dyed." Zefra tried not to blush at the attention.

"Then what were they talking about?" The girl leaned toward Zefra.

Ludik pressed a hand on her head. "We'll talk tomorrow," he said. "Let her eat with her family."

"Oh, but I want to know..."

Her friends picked her up under her arms and walked off with her still talking.

The next morning, Zefra went to the corral before sunrise. Father groomed three pack-ponies while his apprentices stowed gear into rolls and saddlebags.

"Your guards are ready." Father nodded at two of the clan's soldiers.

Sayaka was one of their tallest women, a little taller than lean Askari, who was merely average for a man. Both were middle-aged, tough, and experienced. They waved and continued loading their gear.

Zefra handed her pack to Father and kissed his cheek. "Where are the outdwellers?"

"I suspect they're asleep." He handed her a steaming plate. "Your mother made spice bread. Why not wake your new clients?"

Zefra ate a slice of aromatic bread and headed for the guest tents. Noises came from the men's tent. When she scratched on the tent flap,

Ahjin opened it. He was dressed but barefoot, and his curly hair was wild.

"Are you ready?" Zefra held out the plate of bread.

"We just need to wake Nia." The way he munched a slice would have been dainty if it were slower.

Ludik joined them while Ahjin took more bread. "That smells wonderful. It's your turn to wake Nia, Ahjin." He stuffed a slice of bread in his mouth and snagged another. "Mmm."

"You cannot go in her tent," Zefra said. "I will wake her."

There was no response to her scratch on the girl's tent, so she ducked inside and called softly. Still no response. The windows were shut, but Zefra's small lamp showed a rumpled heap of blankets. Zefra shook it gently. "Niamolenulanami. We must leave before it gets too hot." No reply. "Niamolenulan— Oh!" She ducked the fist that hurtled toward her face, then backed up with the blankets. "Niamolenulanami, wake."

The girl curled into a ball and mumbled.

Zefra thought, then slid the last of the warm bread toward her.

Soon the sleeper rose, tangled in her own braids, eyes half closed. She crawled to the plate and took slow bites. After half a slice, she opened her eyes. "When did you come in my tent?" she squeaked.

"Hurry, we need to go." Zefra bowed backwards out of the tent.

Despite her sleepiness, the girl soon met everyone at the corral to load their packs on the ponies. Niamolenulanami had wrapped her frizzy plaits around her head and tied them with a wild variety of colored ribbons. Her lumpy pack was strapped with more ribbons. The sleepy girl leaned on her staff, bareheaded, but both a hood and a scarf sat on her pack. Instead of adult tan or cream, her robe was a child's size and easily-seen bright turquoise.

Ahjin wore an unfamiliar scarf instead of a hood.

Zefra adjusted the folds. "That's pretty embroidery. Did you do it?"

"My mother," he mumbled.

Prathap handed Zefra a precious map with landmarks, trade routes, known oases, district boundaries, and star navigation marks. She ran her fingers across the fresh ink marking her own discovery before stowing it carefully in her belt pouch.

Isvah asked a brief blessing on the quest, and Zefra hugged her family. She and Sayaka took point while Askari fell in behind with the last pony.

They alternated a steady walking pace with short breaks. At each break, the Hotaru briefly taught a desert skill, including identifying a water-bearing cactus and finding fuel. Askari showed the island girl how to wrap her water-doused scarf around her gills to keep them from cracking, like the Iskrins used palm-pith and silk helmets to keep cool as well as protect them in battle.

At midday, they ate a cold meal and pitched two open tents for a long nap. Zefra settled for a short nap and a practice session with Resef's gift. Pulling a small flame from midair was a start, but the councilor was right; she needed to control her power. Only the gods knew what she might need to do in the future. By the time the air cooled to sweltering and the others woke, Zefra had doubled the size of the flame she could create and control.

As they walked again. Zefra mentally reviewed the route to the oasis. With so many depending on her, she must not make mistakes. Askari and Sayaka stayed watchful, but the newcomers chattered almost constantly.

Niamolenulanami skipped next to Zefra. "I haven't forgotten. What was that name stuff last night?"

"Among our people, names always mean something," Zefra said. "If a name is inadequate, it can be changed. Kezhekori means 'burning fire' and honors Resef's blessing."

"Or warns of it," muttered Sayaka.

"Do all your names mean something?" Niamolenulanami asked.

"Zefra means 'west wind in the morning.' My family name means 'sound of the horse,' implying our horses are so fast you will not even see them, just hear their pounding footsteps." It was an old family jest.

Sayaka went next. "My given name means 'good arrow of the sand.' 'Tis unusual for a woman, but my mother wanted to remember my recently deceased father. Ruchi means 'light or beauty.'"

"Askari means 'fighter.' I was the only survivor when my caravan died. I was too small to tell my rescuers anything, so they named me in honor of my continued existence. I never felt the need to add another name." He smiled at the newcomers. "Do your names mean something in your lands?"

"Yes," the islander said, "but we don't put much significance in them. My clan generally picks something pretty with lots of syllables and uses nicknames." She paused. "You should call me Nia, like these two fishbrains."

When the Hotaru hesitated, Ahjin spoke. "I suggest Fishbreath, or Wave Runner, or Voice-So-Loud." He kept a straight face until Nia's elbow collided with his ribs.

Zefra ignored Ahjin's absurdities. "Nia, thank you for this familiarity. What about you two?"

Ludik shrugged. "My name did not come from the traditional pool, so I do not know."

"Machol means 'dance,' also from a family profession." Ahjin smiled at Zefra. "My parents picked my first name because they liked it, but the Great Library of Vasi says it means 'fights for what is his.'"

"Oh-ho, they were smarter than they knew," Nia chortled, then danced out of Ahjin's range.

If they were so immature the whole way, the trip might be harder than Zefra thought. She hoped Resef's reason for involving her would be worth it.

13. DESERT
(NORTHERN DESERT, ISKRA)

Do not judge people before you have walked a day in their boots.
Iskrin Proverb

Ahjin's eyes flickered when Askari called. The tiny lavender moon settled to the desert horizon, but the sun wouldn't rise for a couple of hours. Ludik and the Iskrins never seemed to have trouble walking in the dark, but he and Nia stumbled on every wave of the sand when the moons were down.

Ahjin groaned and closed his eyes again until the smell of breakfast hit his nose. He dragged himself from his blankets and took a heaping plateful of warm flatbread from Askari. Ludik arrived a close second, followed by the others. Nia was the last to rise and the last to eat, with closed eyes.

When Zefra headed to Nia, Ahjin stopped her. "Don't bother reminding her of chores; she's not really awake yet. We," he included Ludik in his wave, "will take care of everything. She can make up for it later."

He and Ludik packed Nia's things as well as their own. Nia staggered into place in the caravan just in time.

"I hate these boots," she said. "Distract me, please. What was that red hair and fire stuff at your ceremony?" She tripped flat on the sand, and Ahjin helped her upright.

"What do you know about our culture?" Zefra asked.

"I've heard stories of your climate." Ahjin had been surprised to discover it was cold at night, but when the sun rose, the searing heat always returned. He pitied those without wings to flap for a breeze. Even the erratic wind blew hot.

"And your trickster god," Nia said.

Ludik shrugged.

"Oh. Well, Resef is a good place to start, I suppose," Zefra said. "Most Iskrins have black hair or sometimes dark brown like Sayaka's, brown eyes, and skin as white as our sand. Rarely, though, a baby is born with red hair. These infants are chosen of Resef and can call fire. It has been many generations since our clan had one." She looked at Sayaka. "Do you know any stories of adults becoming fire-haired?"

"There are legends." Sayaka grinned at Zefra. "Based on new evidence, they might be true."

Zefra frowned. "Resef uses those he favors. Sometimes they appreciate his blessing. Often, 'tis more trouble than 'tis worth. His sense of humor can be disturbing and his priorities odd."

"How does your power work?" Ahjin asked, "We should know the resources of our group."

"So far, I can create fire, touch it, and manipulate it in limited ways," Zefra said. "I cannot sustain it for long without fuel, though. I have only had the ability for two weeks and am still learning."

"That's amazing." Nia bounced on her toes. "I can understand all languages and water-scry on nearby places." She looked at the endless sand and wrinkled her nose, then patted her water jug. "The water is perfectly safe to drink after."

"Do you two have any talents?" Ahjin asked Askari and Sayaka.

"Just the ordinary sort. We're both good warriors, and Sayaka is our best archer," Askari said.

Sayaka tapped the unstrung longbow strapped to the pony she led. "I brought something with more power and range than your shorter bows."

Zefra looked at Ludik, who stared blandly back. "And you?"

"I regret to inform you I have no magic." Ludik's lip quivered.

She stretched to full height and bent her head back to look up and up to his dancing silver eyes. Ahjin smothered a chuckle. Ludik towered over her by more than a foot.

"I do not believe you." Zefra narrowed her lovely, tilted eyes at him until her long lashes hid all but a glint of brown.

"You're right; I lied." Ludik laughed. "I do *not* regret to inform you I have no magic."

"He makes a nice healing ointment," Ahjin said. "And you've seen his alternate form."

He smothered a chuckle. Her startled reaction had made Ludik's surprise shifting almost as good as one of his own pranks.

"Alternate form?" Askari said. "I did not hear about that."

"Do you never listen to the gossip?" Sayaka said.

"The Darrendrakar are shapeshifters," Nia explained. "He can turn into a big kitty-cat with fuzzy black fuuuurr." Her sentence ended in a squeal as Ludik swung her upside down by her ankles.

Ludik smiled politely at his thrashing victim. "Don't call me a kitty." He dropped her just above the sand.

She rolled to her feet at a safe distance and stuck out her tongue while she brushed off her robe.

"Shapeshifting is not magic?" Zefra asked.

"No magic," Ludik repeated.

"I can turn invisible for a few hours, if it's worth a headache." Ahjin frowned at Zefra. "Let's say I understand *the favor of the gods*." Their gifts had strings attached, usually hooked to snares.

"Can you hide anyone with you?" Zefra asked.

"No." After a minute, his smile faded. The favor of the gods. If Resef was gone, was this a fool's quest now?

Nia stuck her hands on her hips. "What are you thinking?"

"Resef was the last god available to help us. If the gods stay gone, is my bargain with Irajahan unneeded?"

"If our quest is useless now, I can make it back to the coast quickly by myself," Ludik muttered. "A fast ship and a faster wedding..."

"We have no ships," Askari murmured. Ludik sighed.

"Do you miss home, Ahjin?" Nia probed. "Are you ready to go back yet?"

"I'm fine," Ahjin growled. He wanted to go home, but not until he was free. And his feelings weren't any of his nosy friend's concern.

"What would happen if Irajahan escaped by himself?" Zefra asked. "What if he cannot?"

Ahjin twitched his wings. If the gods never got free — the weather wasn't really that bad, and surely it would eventually settle again. And people would be better off without the gods poking their noses in everybody's lives. But if Irajahan freed himself, or someone other than Ahjin did, the god would certainly not keep his side of the bargain. Ahjin would be trapped as a priest forever, and Irajahan would make his life as miserable as possible in revenge. No, he wouldn't take the chance.

Nia patted Ahjin on the shoulder. "There's still time. And Ludik, Nemerra loves you; she'll wait."

Ludik turned his face away from them.

Two days later, a mild sandstorm gave them a chance to practice their new survival skills. Ahjin flew above it and watched anxiously until it ended. Everyone survived without a fuss, though it took Nia a while to clean the sand from her gills.

Ahjin grinned. "Too bad I can't literally scare the sand from someone."

Sayaka had jumped quite far when Ahjin popped into visibility after scouting the day before. He edged away, in case she wanted to give another lecture about his joke.

The group had settled into a routine, except for Ahjin's pranks. Everyone took turns with the cooking, guard shifts, and other camp chores. Ahjin and Ludik served as the long-range scouts because of their speed and, in Ahjin's case, invisibility. Askari and Sayaka alternated front and rear guard. Zefra navigated, calculated their pace, and practiced her magic. Every evening, Ahjin tried and failed to contact Irajahan. He wasn't quite sorry.

Nia always woke once they started walking, but it was useless to give her early morning chores or the last guard shift. She was an excellent choice for first watch, though. She scried daily, with no more results than Ahjin, and spent several hours every day singing to the group and learning their songs. No one was allowed discouragement while she was awake.

Everyone carried at least one waterskin, with spares on the ponies. Most of their moisture came from chewing cactus, saving the water for the driest sections, cooking, and Nia's scarf. Ahjin tried to sneak an extra sip once and was stopped by Zefra's glare. After a painstaking explanation of the rationing needed to make it to the oasis in seven days, she handed him a sliver of moist cactus flesh. He recapped the water and wiped the sweat from his brow. The cactus might offer enough water to live, but the taste was less than ideal.

Askari gathered edible plants and set snares at night. Sayaka shot rats and lizards without breaking her stride. After his first meal of rat and lizard, Ahjin netted birds while he scouted. Ludik went on random feline trips for "a little peace," and once brought back a wild goat.

Each day, they trekked slowly from before dawn until after midnight, with a meal and a long nap at noon. Ahjin spent a fair amount of his time flying, practicing his tricks and routines. Father was the most intricate flier in the city, and Mother the most graceful. He would equal Father within a few years and prove he was right to decline the priesthood.

On the fifth morning, Ahjin was surprised when Nia woke quickly at his call. She packed her gear, ate breakfast, and trudged without a word or a note of song. He walked silently beside her, waiting for her to finish waking. But by the time Zefra sent him scouting, Nia still hadn't returned to her usual cheerful self.

When he returned after two hours of seeing nothing, he snuck up on Askari, who jumped as high as Sayaka had, but drew his sword and whirled immediately. Ahjin barely ducked a stroke that might have separated his head from his shoulders. Sayaka might be right about him needing to be more wary of guards with fast reflexes.

His report to Zefra took almost no time. Her reply took longer.

"I should not have sent Ludik hunting while you were gone," she complained, tugging on a pony's lead rope. "Nia whined the entire time. 'My feet hurt. When are we stopping? Why do we have to go so fast?' We are not walking quickly, and our next break is in two hours. I told her that." Zefra sighed. "I know she's a soft outdweller, but she will dehydrate if she does not stop crying."

Ahjin cast her an exasperated look and went to plod with Nia. "You're slower today. Are you tired?"

"My feet hurt," she whimpered.

"Mine, too," he sighed. "I'm not used to so much walking. I'd fly with you, but even you're too heavy."

She sniffed. "You should be jealous. If you were my size, you could fly forever without getting tired."

"You might be right." Ahjin took a drink from his water bag and handed it to her. "I'll have to make do with sheer athletic prowess." He winked, but she didn't laugh.

"What will you do when you get home again?" Nia asked thoughtfully.

"Besides hugging Mother?" Ahjin said. "Father promised to teach me his double-spiral triple-loop backwards-somersault." He explained the flying trick, demonstrating with his hands. "And when Maili is old enough, I'll teach her."

The three months he'd been gone from home suddenly felt like three years. At her age, Maili would be quite changed.

Nia walked slower and slower. Something must be wrong, but Ahjin didn't know how to fix it.

When Ludik returned, Ahjin excused himself. He explained the situation to Ludik, and they watched Nia limp.

They rejoined her, and Ludik asked, "How do you feel?"

"Apparently, I'm no worse than anyone else." She stumbled onward. "Zefra said to keep walking."

"You look like you're having problems walking," Ludik persisted, "and you smell like blisters." He inhaled again and frowned at Ahjin. "What did the others say?"

"I didn't tell the others," Nia muttered. "My feet do hurt, though."

"I believe that falls under my responsibility," Ludik said.

Ahjin pulled on Nia's elbow. "Let him help. You can't keep this up."

Nia wobbled to a seat on the sand and blinked back tears. "Go ahead."

"Sayaka, please call a brief halt and fetch my medical kit," Ludik called.

He knelt on the sand in front of Nia and started pulling off her first boot. When she gasped and clenched her fists in her robe, he glanced at her sharply and gentled his tugging. The boot finally came free to reveal her long stocking, sodden with blood.

Ahjin choked and dropped beside her. This was much worse than he'd expected.

"Teeth and claws, Nia!" Ludik carefully removed Nia's other boot and both stockings, revealing blisters on top of broken blisters.

Sayaka dropped Ludik's kit by him and ran for Zefra. She didn't have to go far; the others had heard Ludik's bellow.

"Why didn't you tell me before?" Ludik ranted as he tenderly cleaned one tattered foot. "I could have helped."

Tears welled in her eyes. "They weren't bleeding earlier," Nia protested, "just sore. I'm not used to shoes or so much walking. Last night, I was so tired, I didn't remove my stockings. If I had known my feet were this bad, I would have told you, I promise." She broke off in a sob.

Ahjin sat cross-legged and put Nia on his lap with her feet dangling above the sand. He wrapped his arms around her and nodded silently to Ludik to continue. This trip was already a disaster. His life was a ruin; nothing would go well until he was free from Irajahan.

"She told me," Zefra's voice quavered, "but I thought she was exaggerating a little footsoreness. We will rest now, for as long as she needs. We can ration the food if we have to travel slower. Please excuse me." She grabbed one of Nia's boots and dragged Askari to the ponies.

Ahjin glared as they hunted through the packs and made a pile of tools and supplies. Askari came back and pitched a tent over Nia. Zefra remained by the horses.

Ludik sent Sayaka to make medicinal tea from a packet from his kit while he dabbed at Nia's other foot.

Nia buried her head in Ahjin's shoulder. His shirt got damper and his mood darker.

Someone yelped. Ahjin glanced toward the Iskrins. A small fire burned on the sand, and Zefra was beating flames from her hem.

It served her right. This was Zefra's fault. She should have listened to Nia.

Nia shook again, and Ahjin tightened his arms around her.

Ludik paused. "I liked it better when you called me names."

"Ahjin didn't like it, and it didn't do any good." Her muffled voice was pained.

Ahjin stroked her back. "Go ahead and swear at him. Or I'll see how many insults I remember from our first lessons." If Nia didn't want them, he did.

Nia laughed shakily and shook her head. She wrapped her arms around him and squeezed while Ludik covered her feet in his salve and bandaged them loosely.

Sayaka brought a hot cup of tea while Zefra extinguished the fire.

Ludik stood to dispose of the bloody water. "The tea will make you sleepy. We'll move on when you wake." He smiled at her, then glanced over her head at Ahjin.

Ahjin nodded grimly. After she drank, he put the empty cup on the sand and Nia on her blanket. When he stood with the cup, she was already asleep. He headed toward Ludik and Zefra, rage burning in his veins.

Ludik took one look at his face and stepped in front of Zefra. "I already talked to her, Ahjin. She'll listen next time." Ahjin dodged, but Ludik blocked again. "Leave her alone until you calm down."

No stupid cat would stop him from teaching a lesson to the heartless desert brat. Ahjin threw the cup at Ludik's head and spread his wings.

Ludik rammed into Ahjin's chest, driving him to the ground. He dodged Ahjin's fists and grabbed his wrists, pinning them down. When Ahjin tried to buck him off, Ludik bounced until the air left Ahjin's body and his head banged on the ground.

"Will you listen before I damage your brain? I said leave her alone."

Ahjin nodded. His head ached too much to argue, and he couldn't breathe.

Ludik let him rise.

Ahjin inspected Zefra head-to-toe with a scathing glare, then hurled himself into his aerobatics.

There would be time later to finish this discussion.

14. TALES
(NORTHERN DESERT, ISKRA)

**Many legends surround the mystery of the creation of the earth.
Myths conflict, stories obscure, and the truths of its origin have
been lost to time.**
A Comprehensive History of the Gods, vol. 1

When Nia woke two hours later, everyone ate a hearty meal. She cheerfully insulted Ludik while he slathered more ointment on her feet. The tent was rolled, her boots were stowed, and half the packs from one pony were redistributed among the others. Ludik settled Nia into a makeshift nest of the remaining packs, with the tents as a backrest and her feet across convenient bedrolls. It was a comfy seat, and the best part was that she wouldn't have to walk. If she'd known this was possible, she would have told Ludik about her blisters earlier.

If only people were as easy to fix. Ahjin still hadn't landed. He hovered above Nia until she waved, then flew off without a word. He wouldn't answer hails and kept pace in simple flight instead of his typical athletics. Every wingbeat was dreary. His mood was contagious, and everyone walked with downcast eyes.

Ludik encouraged, cajoled, and teased the others, until the quiet conversations grew more enthusiastic. "If Ahjin won't behave by nightfall, I'll find out if a cat can catch a sulking bird," he whispered to Nia.

"Good idea," she whispered back.

It would serve Ahjin right. He was supposed to be an adult. Maturity was more about responsibility than privilege, which made Nia glad she was still a child.

She kept an eye on Ahjin until he flew away in the afternoon. Ludik sighed and took over sentry duty.

At twilight, Ahjin landed with a tired thump, his hair a mess of windblown curls. He untangled two large birds from his net and offered them silently to Zefra, folding his wings so tightly his feathers rustled.

"I apologize for my rude behavior." Ahjin flickered a glance at Ludik before looking back at Zefra. "Please forgive me." His hands trembled around the birds.

Nia sniffed. He should feel sorry; she had been told how he treated Zefra. She wasn't happy with how Zefra had handled things, either, but it was a misunderstanding. The girl would learn.

Zefra held her breath for a few seconds before exhaling raggedly. She bowed with her hand over her heart, then reached for Ahjin's hands, birds and all. "I accept your apology and beg pardon for my lack of consideration. If you have suggestions in the future, I promise to listen."

Ahjin threw one arm around her for a quick hug, and her wavering smile broke into a grin. He ran to the fire with the birds. Zefra looked at Ludik and Nia with wide eyes.

"That is Ahjin. Quick to anger, slow to cool, but when he forgives, he forgets." Ludik's mouth quirked. "I am impressed you escaped one of his famous revenge pranks, though."

"He loves surprising people with his invisibility," Zefra said.

Ludik whispered in her ear, and her inner eyelids flickered over her eyes as her mouth dropped open.

Nia grinned. Ahjin's pranks had been mild since they reached Iskra, but she'd bet Ludik was reciting memorable ones from earlier. Since she couldn't help with walking chores, she cooked supper while Askari brought her supplies. The soup turned out well, and the flatbread was so mildly scorched that no one mentioned it.

After supper, they walked for a couple of hours in moonlight, and then camped. Everyone gathered around the small fire Zefra kept burning with an absurdly small amount of fuel, and Nia crooned an old ocean lullaby.

"The bounding waves call me to roam.

The west wind blows the scent of home.

I feel at home upon the sea,

But true home's where I long to be."

Nia looked at Ahjin and put more feeling into the chorus. His stubborn face was showing again: tight lips, furrowed brows, firm chin. Could she make him admit he missed his family?

"I can sail a year and day,

But I can never stay away.

Home again, go home again,

Remember everywhere I've been.

I can sail a year and day,

But I can never stay away."

Ahjin frowned. As the wistful melody rose and fell like the waves, he tightened his scarf and turned away his face. At the start of the next verse, he folded his arms across his chest and glared at her with glistening eyes.

"The sunlight brings new lands to view.

The moonlight sends me dreams of you.

My ship is like a sweetheart dear,

But I would rather have you here."

Ludik purred, swaying with the music, a smile hovering on his lips. He must be thinking of his sweetheart, who was nothing like a ship.

Nia smiled and continued.

"I can sail a year and day,

But I can never stay away.

Home again, go home again,

Remember everywhere I've been.

I can sail a year and day,

But I can never stay away."

Nia drew out the last line with a mournful flourish.

Everyone applauded, though Ahjin's measured claps sounded like an executioner's drum. Any revenge he took would be worth it. It would do him good to admit he missed his family.

Meanwhile, she'd love to indulge herself with that amusing sailor ditty, but the last time she sang it, Zefra turned as red as her hair, and Ahjin smacked her with his wings. Some mangy seagulls were too prim to be believed!

Nia rubbed her hands across her face. The song wasn't worth embarrassing their hosts again. "Maybe that's enough singing. How about stories, instead? Or are you ready for sleep now?"

Sayaka smiled. "I know the story of how Resef bleached the sand to white."

They took turns reciting legends of the gods' and goddesses' adventures, from the scary to the hilarious to the romantic. Before they tired of divine exploits, Nia started them on a cycle of creation legends.

"Long ago, before the easy days of now and then, Makanavailea came to the dry clay of our world." Nia nearly sang the words, illustrating her tale with gestures. "In sorrow at its barren state, she gave birth to the bountiful seas and covered the earth in vital waters. When life was abundant in the ocean depths, she drew back the waves and bared the land. She formed her people to go forth upon the land and spread life from shore to shore. Then all was beautiful, and she and her people returned to the sea to live in peace and joy and song. May it continue so until the seas dry and the world ends. Hail, Makana."

Nia spread her hands in the traditional signal of a story ended.

"That explains why you have legs instead of a tail." Ahjin smirked at Nia.

Nia rolled her eyes. "I'm not a fish, birdbrain."

"Something about your tail — er, story — seems fishy." His grin grew to phenomenal proportions.

"I agree," added Ludik, "but not the way he means." He smacked Ahjin's head. "Who made the dry clay? Or the sun?"

"We know who made the sun," Zefra said. "Let me see if I can remember the customary words." She thought for a moment, then stood.

"Resef was bored. It was a common state, alas, but he had a solution. 'Perhaps,' he thought, 'I can create an everlasting amusement. I shall make life to provide variety and entertainment.' He grew a fire to colossal size and set the blazing ball in the sky, then melted the elements together to form a dismal lump of stone. The new sun gave heat and light to the world of his scheming, and life to plants and animals. Most promising, it drew forth peoples with the fire of life, to amuse their god as they acted and were acted upon. 'Now life is good,' said Resef, planning diversions with his beautiful new world. And thus it has been from that day to this."

Zefra bowed and sat.

"Still no mention of the other gods," Nia said, "but there are hints they helped behind the scenes. Resef didn't mention water, for instance, or explain how the sun gave life to plants and animals."

"We already know Makanavailea claims credit for the water," Ludik said, "and the Darrendrakar honor Darravani for creating life."

"Ooh, tell it in the classic way, if you know it," Nia said. "I enjoy the different styles."

Ludik frowned. "I don't have the usual flowers, but you don't know their meanings, anyway. This will look stupid."

He reached out and picked a nonexistent flower. "Darravani looked at the empty world and knew herself to be alone. She embraced the bare earth and warmed it with her love." He picked another pretend blossom. "Flowers, trees, and grasses multiplied across the face of the land. When all was green and growing, she looked for movement, but there was none. Now Darravani formed animals of many kinds." With each sentence, he gathered make-believe flowers.

"The earth became lively and beautiful, but still there was no one to love her. Darravani took the best of her animals and changed them into people with the powers of speech and affection." Ludik continued to add to his imaginary bouquet. "Those she favored kept the strengths and abilities of those animals from which they came. As her chosen people, we must remember the blessings of our goddess and give her honor and glory." He threw his armful of invisible blossoms to cascade over the heads of his listeners.

"Normally, the flower you catch is considered a message from Darravani," he explained. "Under the circumstances, you have no way to know what you got, so make up whatever blessing you like." Ludik smelled the imaginary flower he had kept for himself and smiled.

"That story leaves out even more," Ahjin protested. "Although it seems like a more reasonable portion of creation for one goddess."

"You have not told us your people's version," Zefra said.

Ahjin raised an eyebrow. "You won't like it."

"Let us be the judge of that," Askari said.

Ahjin raised a skeptical eyebrow again, but sat upright and spread his wings and arms. "Irajahan the Omnipotent," he intoned dramatically, "created a world to reflect his own glory. His commanding winds blew the stardust together into a sphere in the heavens. Mighty cyclones carried water across the new earth. Thunderous tornadoes pounded the continents into place. Magnificent hurricanes swept the waters to make dry land. The fiery south wind dragged a star into orbit to give light and heat. A forceful east wind circled the globe to provide air for his creations. Gentle west winds warmed the earth and spread seeds to bring forth plants in every land. The north wind formed dust into many shapes and breathed life into people and animals. All hail the All-Powerful."

Everyone stared in disbelief except Nia, who fell over laughing. Irajahan's ego was as swollen as a puffer fish.

"Are you serious?" Ludik exclaimed. "Not a hint of the other gods? He's taking credit for every single bit of creation?"

"Even the sun?" asked Zefra.

"Is he crazy?" blurted Sayaka, then slapped her hand over her mouth.

Ahjin shrugged. "He tells us many things. We aren't encouraged to question them."

"I'm sure you aren't," Nia chuckled, "because his teachings are full of hot air."

Ahjin carried her to her bed to spare her feet, mock-seriously lecturing her on the esteemed dignity of his god. As he walked to his own blankets, his wings shook with silent laughter.

Nia giggled while she watched Zefra play with the fire, making it blaze and die and dance under her hands. Eventually, the wavering light soothed Nia to sleep.

In the morning, Nia washed her face and limped to breakfast. She ate the squishy fruit and dry bread without comment, then sat with a pile of ribbons to fix her hair while everyone else packed. It was too much trouble to rebraid her hair every day, but she had to arrange the plaits. Yawns cracked her face as she randomly wrapped hair on top of her head and tied it in place. She grabbed the last piece to tuck in the ends, then stopped.

A hand-length of her lavender tresses were pitch black.

The remnants of sleep vanished under a tidal wave of anger.

"You lice-ridden, bumble-footed, molting plague! I'll break your poxy wings!"

Everyone flinched and looked in her direction, except for Ahjin, who industriously tied the rolled tents.

Nia jumped up to express her displeasure more emphatically. When her feet hit the ground, agony flared up her legs. Every grain of sand felt like a jagged stone under her feet. She flopped down again and wailed.

"I can't believe you forgot." Ludik brought fresh bandages and salve. "You still have to stay off your feet today and probably tomorrow, too."

"Did you see what he did to me?" Anger had the extra benefit of keeping her mind off what Ludik did.

"No, who did what?" Ludik paid more attention to her feet than her protests.

"Look at my HAIR!" She shoved the offending section under his nose. "Ahjin did it. I know he did!"

"Why would I do that, hmm?" Ahjin dropped the tents in the pile to be loaded and sauntered over to inspect Nia's hair. "That's quite the adornment you have there. Are you making a statement about something in particular or just being more unique than usual?"

"*Did* you do this?" Ludik's voice was serious but his mouth twitched. He kept his eyes firmly on Nia's feet.

"How would I? And when?" Ahjin looked particularly innocent as he protested.

Nia clenched her fists and wished for healthy feet and an extra half-ell of height. If she had Ludik's fathom-and-beyond, she'd pound Ahjin into the ground like a tent pole.

"You had the middle watch alone last night, and we sleep without walls. You could manage even without your stupid invisibility."

"Why would I want to do something like that?" Ahjin's voice oozed smugness.

He was so stupid. If he'd admit his homesickness, Nia wouldn't have to manipulate his emotions with her song. She was only helping. She narrowed her eyes and pressed her lips together.

He patted the top of her head and strolled away whistling.

Ludik smelled the black tip of her braid and rolled it in his fingers. "It's a mild vegetable dye. It will wear off without damaging your hair."

He pried the last ribbon from her fist and tied the end of her braid next to the other coils. After dropping her on the pony, he grabbed the lead rope, and the caravan departed.

Nia glowered, arms crossed, and watched Ahjin fly loops. What a pain! He shouldn't be afraid to admit he missed his home. And anyway, this would be over soon, and he'd go back with his family.

There was no reason to ruin her hair! Her song wasn't *that* devious. Was it?

15. OASIS

(ZEFRA'S OASIS, ISKRA)

Actions speak louder than tongues.
Darrendrakar Proverb

Zefra had made a mistake with Nia's feet. Remorse beat on her like the desert sun. She needed to apologize, and she knew how. When the group stopped at midday, she volunteered to take the watch. After everyone ate and the others fell asleep, she pulled out the project she had cut out while Nia slept off Ludik's first treatment. She glanced at the high sun. If she hurried, she might finish before it was time to leave.

At least she had proper tools now. She placed an oval of short fur upside-down on each leather oval, then punched holes around the edges and sewed the end of one set together.

Zefra checked the sun again while she flexed her fingers. There was still time, and a nap was less important than making amends. She tucked another fold of her robe between her legs and the burning sand. Now came the tricky part. She arranged one strap between and above the layers, with a low arc over the front of the oval, higher crossed curves in the middle, and straps at the opposite end, then sewed it into place.

The sun had passed its highest point, and the others were waking. She stuffed her materials into her pack before anyone saw them. Tomorrow, it would go faster with the sewing holes pre-punched.

T he rest of the day's travel proceeded unremarkably. After dinner, they sang and told stories. It was entertaining, but Zefra needed to work on her project. She pulled her crossed legs closer to her body to still herself. Ahjin and Nia had even reconciled from their latest quarrel.

It had been amusing, actually. She grinned, remembering the way Nia had whistled Ahjin down from the air. He bowed theatrically in mid-air, just out of her reach. "You summoned me, my lady?"

"Can you do any other colors?" Nia fingered the blackened end of her braid.

"What do you have in mind?"

"Come down and let's have a little chat," she had exclaimed, then talked about colors at breakneck speed as Ahjin walked beside her.

Zefra brushed a wayward strand of oh-so-red hair out of her face. Perhaps it was more fun if you got to choose the colors yourself. And if no bonuses came with it. The new fire-calling was useful when she lit their daily fires, but that was not enough for Resef to give it to her. The real reason was likely to drop her in scorching dunes of trouble.

Which reminded her, it was time to practice. She let the stories fade into the background as she reached for the fire. First, feed it. She sent energy from her fingers to the fire until the flames soared knee-high despite the mere handful of fuel beneath. Good. Next, she pulled back the energy until the flames dwindled to hot coals. Her face flushed with the extra heat, so she let some of it back out. The fire returned to its previous low sparkle.

Zefra took a deep breath and started again. Feed the flames. Retract the energy. Feed. Absorb. Feed. She knelt high and raised her hands above her head. The fire blazed as high as the ponies.

Ahjin stopped Nia's story in the middle of a sentence. "Zefra, that's enough for now."

Zefra's hands shook, but she kept them up. Just a little longer. Her legs trembled, and the flames wavered. Almost there. She could do it.

Faintly, she heard Ahjin's voice continue, but the words were muffled. The flames flickered. She gulped for air and pushed harder.

Sand showered over the fire, and someone tackled her to the ground. The flames burst into a thousand bits of starlight and vanished.

Zefra lay on the warm sand and shook in the dark. Someone removed arms from around her and stood. Feathers brushed her arm, and then someone knelt beside her.

"Zefra," Ludik said, "can you hear me?"

"Yes," Zefra whispered.

Ludik shook her. "Zefra."

Zefra coughed. "Yes," she repeated louder. "I am well."

Steel banged on flint, and a spark caught. Sayaka carried a small lamp to Zefra's side.

Ludik helped Zefra sit and examined her. The others watched, serious faces gleaming in the lamplight.

Finally, Ludik sat back. "She will be fine. It is merely a mild drain."

Ahjin brushed ash off his wingtips. "Good. And might I suggest you practice more moderately in the future?"

Zefra nodded.

"Do you need help getting up?" Ahjin asked.

Zefra shook her head. She had already made herself enough of a fool. She did not need more of an audience.

The others stared for a moment, then walked to the tents and silently went to bed. Zefra waited until she stopped shaking, then crawled to her own blankets and fell asleep.

The caravan continued its journey in the morning. While the others slept at midday, Zefra waved at Sayaka on watch, then hid to finish her project for Nia.

She made it back in time to cook a better meal than usual. With several hunters in the group, Zefra had never eaten so well while traveling.

While the others packed, Ludik checked Nia's feet again. Zefra watched from the corner of her eye. Nia babbled a stream of colorful expressions but barely winced when Ludik cleaned her healing blisters.

"Good news, Nia," Ludik said. "I'll use lighter bandages this time, and you can walk for a little at a time. But don't overdo it and don't put your feet in the sand. I'm sorry, but it's back in the boots for you."

Zefra was not used to male healers treating women, but he seemed competent and kind.

"I'm telling you, I hate these things." Nia waved her boots. She pulled on her stockings, shoulders drooping.

Zefra inhaled. "Wait," she said. "I'm truly sorry I did not believe you. I should have listened. To show my remorse, I made these for you." She knelt and slid one sandal over Nia's toes.

Nia's face brightened. She threw the boots to Ludik with a whoop of delight.

Zefra crossed the laces behind the girl's ankle and tied them in front.

Ahjin did the same with the other sandal, hampered by Nia running her hands over her new footwear.

"These are wonderful," Nia gushed, hugging Zefra. "Thank you, I love them."

She stood and squeezed Ahjin breathless, then hobbled to show Ludik. She tried to lift one foot before the other was back on the ground and almost fell. Ludik grabbed her arm to keep her upright and grinned at Zefra and Ahjin above her head. Nia babbled about the soft leather and the padded sole and the lack of confinement. Her exhilaration drew in Sayaka and Askari.

"Why didn't someone give her sandals before we left?" Ahjin asked.

"Boots give more protection from heat, sand, insects, and more," Zefra said. "Sandals are worn only around camp. None of us realized she had never worn shoes. We will have to keep her feet clean to avoid infection, but the sandals should prevent further blisters."

"Thank you." Ahjin watched Nia alternate her improving limp with an attempt at a skip, and his faint smile grew wide. He finally turned to Zefra and tried to replicate her formal bow from the day before, then walked to join in the merriment.

Zefra watched him with wide eyes. Her apology had worked better than she anticipated. She looked at the miles of barren sand stretching in all directions and smiled. It was a lovely day.

The next day, a hint of green on the horizon beckoned for hours before they finally reached Zefra's oasis. She sighed in relief. Her map was correct, of course, but anything could happen during travel.

Ahjin was already waiting when the others arrived. Sayaka dangled her fingers in the cool stream and watched the birds fly from branch to branch.

"Grass," whispered Nia. She slipped off her sandals and shuffle-skipped across the clearing.

"May we hunt here?" Ludik fingered the buckles on his breastplate. "We should save the rest of our supplies for the return trip." His nose flared at the long grass.

"Go ahead," Zefra said. There was nothing sacred or forbidden about her oasis. At least, she did not think there was.

She frowned. What did Resef have in mind?

Seconds later, the panther stalked toward the trees, tail and whiskers twitching. Small animals scurried for cover.

Ahjin looked toward the beckoning shade and yawned. "This is lovely, but do you know what Resef meant for us to find here? I'd like to get on with it."

"You won't get your life back today," Nia called over her shoulder, "no matter what we find. Try to enjoy yourself while you wait."

Zefra turned in a circle to eye the entire oasis. "I do not know where to look, but I will help after we set up camp."

By the time Ahjin returned from another search flight, the ponies were groomed and happily grazing. The tents were pitched with men and women on opposite sides of the oasis. Nia added to a small pile of hand-length fish on the stream bank while Sayaka gathered edible plants. Ludik had caught three desert hares and killed an impressive number of little scorpions, now piled in the sand at the edge of the oasis.

With a little bread, this would be a feast. Zefra put down the gear she and Askari were checking and left to hear Ahjin's report. "Did you find anything?" Everyone turned to listen.

"Nothing but green inside the oasis and white sand outside." Ahjin kicked a rock at a defenseless tree.

"Why not start cooking dinner before we search?" Askari said. "It will give us something to look forward to even if our search takes a while."

Ahjin drew his knife. "I'll help Nia gut her fish."

"Askari, would you help Ludik with his hares and scorpions?" Zefra asked.

"Help me do what with the scorpions?" Ludik said.

"We do not want to eat the stingers." Zefra shook her head. That was obvious.

"We don't want to eat any part of them," Ludik emphasized. "That is why I caught these lovely hares."

"You have plenty of scorpions," she protested. "You can share."

Ludik crossed his arms. "I only killed the scorpions to keep them away from us."

"I agree," Ahjin said. "Lizard was bad enough. Zefra, where should we cook the edible stuff?"

Zefra pointed. "I built a fire pit, that way. I will start a fire so we can have coals for the fish."

She gathered an armful of deadfall twigs and built a small fire and a spit for the hares. When she built the pit weeks ago, she had surrounded it with level stones to cook flatbread and contain the fire. There was room around the edges of the flames to bake the fish and vegetables in the coals. They would change their minds about scorpions when they got hungry tomorrow.

Ahjin wrapped two fish in greens and tucked them in the shade of the stones. When Zefra reached to add them to the others, Ahjin cleared his throat. "Not everyone likes properly cooked fish." He jerked his head toward Ludik and Nia.

Zefra withdrew her hand. Her nose wrinkled until she politely smoothed the disgust off her face.

Ahjin laughed. "You'll eat scorpions but not raw fish? That's interesting."

"I cook scorpions." Zefra raised her voice. "Are we ready to search?"

Zefra, Askari, and Sayaka divided the grass into three sections and examined it step by step. They checked under every rock and bush and looked between every tuft of grass. Askari cautiously searched rabbit holes, leaving snares behind.

Nia explored the spring, ducking underwater to check the bottom. As she wormed along the bank, her colorful language bubbled through the water to broadcast her lack of success. When she finally emerged, she tossed her sodden braids over her shoulders with more curses.

Ludik left his boots in the grass and climbed the stunted trees, walking every limb sturdy enough to hold him, and climbing high enough to make the branches creak. He probed knotholes and birds' nests, then growled and shook the trees until they rained leaves.

Ahjin flew over every bit of the oasis, circling again and again. His tuneless whistle grew higher with every pass, until Ludik threw an empty bird nest at him.

"Come down, you screeching seagull, before you break my ears," Ludik roared. He stomped back into his boots and stalked to the fire pit with the others.

Nia knelt to check the food and dry her robe, while Zefra set out the bowls, and Askari ferried fresh water in their cups.

"We have to find Resef's whatever-it-is," Ahjin demanded as soon as his feet touched the sand. "I didn't come this far to give up now."

"Settle down, Ahjin," Nia said. "We'll talk more when your empty stomach isn't souring your mood. We can eat the fish and vegetables now, and the hares will be ready soon."

She turned the spit, then filled six bowls with vegetables, adding cooked fish to four of them and raw fish for herself and Ludik.

Nia waved her hand at the fire stones. "Zefra, I'm impressed you decorated the stones for a fire pit you might never see again."

Zefra laughed. "'Tis good you're eating now, if you're hallucinating."

"I meant the designs you drew on them," Nia said.

Zefra stared at her. Why would anyone decorate fire stones? Even the outsides of tents were left plain, though the insides were beautifully embellished.

Ahjin looked at the rocks around the fire. "Zefra, we can't read these. Do you know what they mean?"

"Read what? You mean she's right? I did not put anything there." Zefra scrambled up to see for herself.

There were runes burned onto four of the stones, two next to each other on the top semicircle, and two spaced apart on the bottom. "The bottom two mean 'yes' and 'no,' and the top two are letters. I do not understand the pattern."

"I think we found Resef's message," Nia said.

Zefra stared again. "How is that a message? It does not say anything."

"It has to mean something," Nia said.

"The stones were blank before," Zefra insisted, staring at the row of dubious faces. "They were bare when I built the circle, and when I made the fire. I know they were."

"Did you do anything unusual today?" Ahjin asked.

"No. Well, not for me anymore," Zefra qualified.

"Not anymore? What do you mean?" Ludik asked.

"I did not use my flint and steel." Zefra waved a burning finger.

"You called fire near these stones." Sayaka nodded. "That must have brought out the runes, but I do not know what they *mean*."

"What happens if we touch them?" Nia reached for the stones.

Sayaka grabbed her wrist. "Resef has a twisted sense of humor sometimes. We should find what he wants us to do before we touch anything."

"Fine," Nia pouted. "Why can't he be clear?"

"There are only so many runes," Zefra said.

"And Resef likes to make us work for his gifts," Sayaka murmured.

Askari kicked her ankle. "It does not matter. The letters say A-N? An... enigma?"

Sayaka flicked his head.

"Maybe they're your initials." Nia grinned at him. "Askari No-Family-Name. *You* touch them."

"Very funny," he said. "But... perhaps they are initials and this message is meant for you and Ahjin. You can scry and Ahjin has telepathy. Perhaps you need a sort of mental power to translate the message."

"Why wouldn't he leave something his own people can interpret?" When Nia touched each rune one at a time, there was no reaction. She frowned and touched them in combinations of two or three, but still nothing. She stretched her hands to touch all four at once, then threw up her hands in defeat. "You try it, Ahjin."

Ahjin followed her example with the same results. They all stared at the fire pit in puzzlement.

"Perhaps the way they're arranged is important," Zefra guessed. There had to be some clue how to read them.

"Initials together, yes and no apart," Ludik said. "I still do not see an answer."

"Together," Nia blurted. She grabbed Ahjin's hand and touched the stone with the affirmative rune before anyone could stop her.

16. VISION
(ZEFRA'S OASIS, ISKRA)

Monsters roam the deep wilds. No god claims them; no myth tells of their creation.
A Comprehensive History of the Gods, vol. 2

Ahjin didn't have time to yank his hand from Nia's before a shadow rose and the oasis disappeared.

When his sight cleared, he was in a meadow surrounded by a forest. Some trees stretched to the orange sky; others were splintered across the landscape. Whiffs of sulfur fought the scent of pine. Glass shards and chunks of smoldering coal littered the grass between a stream and a smoking hill. Waves of thunder eclipsed the burble of water. The ground shook under his feet, and the sun flickered.

Silver wings disappeared behind turbulent clouds.

Bodies lay scattered around. Two had dark hair and one a red coronet of braids. A panther was half-buried under a pile of odd black and gray lumps. Nia still squeezed his hand, yet her lavender hair streamed from the smallest crumpled body in front of him. To the side were white feathers streaked with red and black.

Ahjin clutched Nia's hand tighter. This couldn't be true.

He turned to the real Nia. "You touched 'yes.' This happens if we go on?"

She bit her lip. Tears spilled down her face.

"How do we get out of this?" He shook her hands. "How do we stop this?"

"Together," she whimpered, "together." She stared at their clasped hands, then jerked hers free.

The world shook. They knelt outside the oasis while Nia's lip bled and the others stared at them.

"What happened?" Ludik asked.

"I think we saw what would happen if we continue," Ahjin said. "We die, but Irajahan, at least, is freed. Perhaps the other rune will show the results if we don't go."

He hoped there was a better answer.

Nia took back his hand and reached for the 'no' rune with shaking fingers.

The world suddenly lay far below them. Nia screamed and grabbed Ahjin.

"Relax. We can do this, since you apparently weigh nothing," Ahjin teased, spreading his wings into the wind.

This was his territory, even in a dream. He pulled Nia in front of him and wrapped his arms around her while she clutched them. Her feet bounced against him until he hooked his feet around her ankles.

Flight took little effort here. He swooped above the land at speeds he never achieved in real life. Nia soon relaxed and exclaimed at the beauty.

Ahjin let himself hope that 'no' was the right choice. He wanted to go home.

The wind rose as Ahjin headed north. A brisk breeze turned into chilly gusts and then a tempest that almost drowned out a dull rumble. Below them, the ocean quivered.

Nia patted his arms. "May we check on my family? Please."

Ahjin turned west. In only a few minutes, they saw Nokailana in the distance. A few minutes was too late. The rumble turned into a growling boom, and the ocean exploded.

A mighty wave rolled across the islands, followed by another and still more, until the boats sank and the lush gardens vanished.

"Mom," Nia moaned. She pressed her cheek against Ahjin's arm. Tears soaked through his sleeve.

Ahjin flew east toward home, against tumultuous gales. His wings burned with strain, but he couldn't reach the city on the cliffs. A tornado shattered the gleaming temple and blew apart the library, and he could only watch. The storm ripped through the countryside, scattering houses and fields and blowing bodies like loose straw.

The winds blew him and Nia back. He barely saw his house when the tornado cut it in half. Ahjin screamed for his family and almost dropped Nia. She pinched his arm until he shook himself and let the gusts direct his path.

They flew impossibly high. Below them, the earth shook, and fires sparked. On the beaches, the growing waves put out some flames, but the rest spread across the lands. The southern desert spilled into cracked ground like a broken hourglass. The Darrendran forests shattered into twigs amid anguished howls. Nia sobbed while the western islands crumbled. The tall cliff of Ioj tumbled to the sea, and Ahjin's heart broke with every splash.

The sun glowed brighter until it exploded in the sky. Ahjin threw up his arms to block the light.

Nia fell, and he grabbed hopelessly for her.

His arms were struck aside. He was back at the oasis, falling away from the fire, which blazed as high as a man. Askari crouched beside him, keeping him from the inferno.

Sayaka held Nia as the girl vomited into the sand.

Zefra poured two cups of water for Ludik. She heaved the rest of the jugful onto the fire, then held her hands above the flames. Askari left Ahjin and scooped sand on the dwindling blaze.

Ludik added herbs to both cups and gave one to Ahjin. "Just drink it without arguing," he said, heading to Nia with the other cup.

The flames died, and a stone in the fire pit cracked. The spit and hares had vaporized.

Ludik dabbed salve on Nia's lip. "Not good?"

Ahjin looked at Nia's haunted face. She closed her eyes and shivered as he recounted both visions. He got halfway through the second before faltering over his city's doom. His stomach clenched, and his throat closed around his sister's name.

Before his voice worked again, Nia nudged herself under his trembling arm and told about his destroyed home. They alternated the rest of the story, each speaking when the other couldn't.

"The whole world shattered," Nia finished. She buried her face in her hands, shoulders shaking.

"And then the sun blew up, and we were back here." Ahjin glanced at the blackened fire pit. The sand had melted into lumpy glass. He gagged down the last of his leafy water.

No one spoke. Zefra gave a smothered sob. Ludik brushed the sand off his boots. Sayaka glanced at the sun and exchanged grim looks with Askari.

"So our choices are to die rescuing the gods or let the world be destroyed?" Sayaka said.

Ahjin nodded. It didn't sound any better when she said it.

"What if Resef is wrong?" Nia asked. "Makana is the omniscient one."

"He might be," Ludik said. "The first vision was a little ambiguous."

Zefra wound a stray lock of hair around her finger, then glared at the red curl and stuffed it under her scarf. "Dare we risk it? The second vision was clear."

"Do we know where to go?" Ludik asked.

"No," Ahjin said, "but the vision-place had evergreen trees."

"That eliminates nearly all of Iskra," Askari said.

"All of Nokailana, too." Nia cleared her throat and wiped her eyes.

"It can easily be Darrendra," Ludik said.

"Or anywhere in the northern half of Ioj," Ahjin said. "That's too much for us to search."

"Are we really doing this, then?" Ludik looked at his boots.

"We must try," Zefra said.

Ahjin rewrapped his scarf. His dreams of flying with his parents seemed so petty now. On the other wing, it no longer mattered if Iraja-han canceled their deal. Die alone or die with the world.

"Yes," he said. Whatever it took to save his family.

Zefra dug a hole in the sand with her heel and stared as the grains rolled down the pit.

Ludik rubbed his hands across his face. "We'll need more supplies and a faster ship. Can the Hotaru help?"

"No," Askari said, "but we have signal flares. Nearby clans should arrive at camp by the time we do."

"Do you have bats around here?" Nia asked.

"Yes. Does it matter?" Sayaka asked.

"Maybe." Nia nibbled on her lip. "What if the flares attract the wrong attention?"

"We need to take the risk to get help quickly." Ahjin met each person's gaze. No one smiled until he got to Nia, and her attempt was wobbly. "We should hurry. Zefra, make sure the fire is cold, please. Everyone else, pack. Let's see how much distance we can cover today."

Everyone split up to clear camp and set off the signal. Zefra called Ahjin.

"What is it?" he asked. Nia and Ludik followed him to the fire.

"Look," Zefra pointed. "The 'yes' stone cracked in half. There is something underneath."

Ahjin grabbed the rock. Still hot! He hissed and stuck his fingers in his mouth.

Zefra pushed aside the stone and dug out a scroll.

"How did that survive the fire?" Ludik asked.

Everyone looked over Ahjin's shoulder as he unfurled the scroll. The rough map had no words, only outlines and two glowing dots. One blinked yellow in Iskra, the other shone red in northwest Ioj.

Ahjin heard a loud pop. Yellow and light blue fireworks rained from the sky, followed by more in red.

"'Tis our signal," Zefra said. "Red means urgent; yellow and turquoise are the Hotaru colors."

Ahjin touched the luminous spots on the map. "Like the signal. Red means urgent. Yellow is us. Too bad we didn't know this when we were across the strait in Darrendra. At least we're finally getting help." He slid the scroll into the back of his belt and stalked off to roll up the tents.

They took less than an hour to break camp and fill their water bags. After watering the ponies, they drank all they could stand themselves.

Nia dunked her scarf in the stream and tossed it soggily around her neck. "I'm ready to go."

Everyone trudged silently, and Zefra frowned.

"Don't worry about the future," Nia said. "It will come soon enough."

"It's not that," Zefra said. "I forgot to pack the scorpions."

Nia laughed and started singing. First one and then another joined, until everyone but Ahjin sang. After two songs, he left to scout. He'd rather be alone above the dreary sand that matched his dismal mood.

After two hours of boredom and despair, Ahjin came back, and Ludik left on four legs. He soon returned at a dead run with his fur standing on end. Ahjin threw Ludik's robe over his head and pulled it down so he could report immediately.

Ludik changed and stood in one motion, thrusting his arms into his sleeves. "Scorpions are coming!"

"We are wearing boots, you know." Zefra looked at Nia. "We will throw Nia on a pony."

Ludik turned Zefra's head toward a distant sand dune. "The dots on that hill are scorpions. Apparently, it wasn't bats we needed to worry about alerting."

Zefra jerked her chin back. "If we can see them at this distance, they would be huge. You're confused."

Ahjin grabbed the caravan's spyglass and turned invisible. It took only a few minutes to fly close enough to see that Ludik's dots were twelve giant scorpions, at least as big as the ponies.

Ahjin raced back, thumped to the ground, and turned visible. "He's right. Boots won't protect us, Zefra." He put away the spyglass with shaking hands.

"Can we run for it?" Ludik asked.

"The ponies are not much faster than our feet," Askari said, "and we only have three. You and Ahjin can outrun them and take the map to the Hotaru."

"I'm not leaving any of you," Ahjin said. "We'll have to fight."

If there was a chance to rescue the gods, they would need everyone's help. And if not, he still wouldn't abandon his friends.

Ludik looked at the endless sand. "Is there better terrain anywhere close?"

"No," Ahjin said.

"Nia, put on your helmet." Zefra's voice was determined. "Right now." She buckled her own helmet and checked her weapons.

"But I — Yes." Nia had worn her scaled tunic since they left the oasis and now dug through a random bag, surfacing with her helmet and new net. "I wish I still had pokey bits," she mourned.

Sayaka, already armed and armored, dumped the rest of the war gear and Ludik's healing kit on the ground. She tied the harnesses out of the way and smacked the ponies on their rumps.

Nia lunged after them. "Why did you do that?" she shrieked.

Sayaka grabbed her arm. "They cannot help us and will be safer away. If... if we do not call them back, they will go home later." She grabbed a quiver of her heavy war arrows and checked her bow string.

Ludik started to undress again, then stared at the scorpions. "Mongrel curs!" he growled. "The little ones are easy to kill, but those freaks are as big as I am."

Instead of shifting, he buckled his armor over his tunic and donned his boots. He strung his bow and slung his arrows on his right hip before grabbing his ax in his left hand.

Ludik had already proven himself dexterous, despite his left-handedness; perhaps he'd also be lucky. Ahjin looked at his own weapons, suited for aerial combat against enemies his size. He had no large blades and wasn't sure his arrows could punch through the scorpions' natural armor. Just in case, he grabbed his bow and quiver. He tied his scarf around his waist so he could wear his leather cap, then donned his apron-armor. He grabbed his surujin and net and bent his knees to spring in the air.

"Wait," Askari called, "let us discuss tactics. There are a dozen of them. Their claws will be bad enough even without poison. You," he pointed to Ahjin and Nia, "trap their stingers with your nets while we hack-and-bash."

"I will take Ludik and Nia on my team," Sayaka said.

"Just keep them off me while I burn them," Zefra said.

Ludik shrugged. "Try it. If we lose, Ahjin needs to fly with the map." He looked at the rapidly nearing line of a dozen scorpions and finished in a rush. "Tell me if anyone gets seriously injured."

Ahjin and Nia shook out their nets. He considered invisibility, but his allies needed to see him. The others spread out, weapons in hand, Nia enthusiastically inventing curses again.

The sky was a calm, pale orange, contrasting the danger below. Ahjin leapt in the air, missing his old, simple life. Even this quest had been simpler once. All he wanted was freedom to live his own life in his own way, without people telling him what to do or the fate of the world weighing him down.

He reached the top of his climb, and there was no more time. The scorpions had arrived. He hovered for a moment, pulled in his wings, and plummeted toward the earth. At the last moment, he uncoiled his net and threw it around the nearest scorpions, crawling side-by-side, and was lucky to catch both stingers at once. He flared his wings and pulled the tails backward while Askari split one head with his long, curved sword.

Zefra clapped her hands together and shot fire. When the shells didn't ignite, she drew her sword, but it had less reach and power than Askari's. She only wounded her target, and the behemoth tried to sting her.

"Again, Zefra!" Ahjin pulled harder on the net.

Zefra ducked under its claws and swung again. Two down.

Ahjin couldn't untangle his net until the scorpions stopped thrashing, so he shot at the others. Most of his arrows bounced. A few lucky shots punctured their eyes or spiracles.

Ahjin's aerial role let him see the entire battle. Nia had stabbed her harpoon into the sand, and as she crouched to swing her net, she looked like a doll next to the scorpions. Ahjin held his breath as she took a step and flung hard. She wasn't really a warrior, despite her experience with the krakens. Perhaps they should have sent her with the ponies. And the map.

Nia's net missed.

Ahjin shot more arrows as distractions. Ludik and Sayaka protected her while she gathered the net, each darting in to attack when the monster's attention was on the other. Ludik's agility was well-matched by Sayaka's speed. She cut off one claw, and when the enraged scorpion turned on her, Ludik cracked it in half. Sayaka danced back to avoid the carcass's waving legs and leaky innards.

The fourth scorpion, one of the largest, tried to circle them. Ahjin threw his surujin, and the weighted rope tangled the monster's tail against one of its claws. Ahjin whistled to Askari, who stabbed its eyes and free claw. Zefra ran behind and hacked off its head with more boldness than precision.

Ahjin untangled his net from the first two scorpions while he waited to collect his surujin. Alternating his weapons was frustrating, but he had no choice.

Nia tossed her net high, catching another beast's head and claws. When it rushed her, tail stabbing, she yelled and scurried backward. Two more scorpions headed for her. With one hand pulling the net, Nia reached for her harpoon.

Ahjin drew his bow and fired rapidly. The scorpion was twice Nia's size. If he couldn't penetrate its armor, he'd at least distract the scorpion.

"Hey, over here, ugly," he yelled.

Nia stretched her whole body to grasp her harpoon. She turned and desperately stabbed it between the scorpion's eyes. The scorpion thrashed, and she leaned backward to avoid its claws.

Ludik and Sayaka ran at the two closest monsters, followed by Askari and Zefra. The four soldiers fought back to back until they had killed their attackers.

Nia pulled her net free. She waved off Ludik and wiped her nose on her sleeve, then grabbed the harpoon.

Ahjin slung his bow on his back and threw his net at the next scorpion. He caught its tail-half, turned his back to the battle, and pulled hard to keep the beast confined. More than half the scorpions had died. Their tactics were working. Victory tasted sweet.

"Ahjin, they're coming for you," Nia yelled. "Everyone, help!"

Ahjin heard a sudden stream of rapid whistles and clicks behind him, followed by the scratch of claws on sand. He turned, and Askari and Zefra hacked his captured beast in half, along with his net.

The rest of the fighters raced to meet the other scorpions speeding toward Ahjin. Nia threw her net over the next scorpion's tail and whooped in triumph. It flipped its stinger and swung her screaming through the air. She smacked on its back, still holding the net.

Sayaka parried the claws while Ludik split the scorpion's shell with three hard blows of his ax. Nia untangled her net and slid down. The trio raced after the last three scorpions.

Ahjin used the respite to untangle his surujin. He almost had it free when Nia shouted again.

"Ahjin, watch out!"

He glanced up. One scorpion had evaded the others and was coming straight for him. His net was destroyed, his bow useless, and his slingshot too weak. He yanked desperately on his surujin, but the scorpion darted behind him and clawed at his back.

The first snatch brushed his feathers. Ahjin raised his wings to fly, but the monster's next pinch raked his waist.

Agony shot through his back and wings. He screamed and collapsed.

Blood and broken feathers rained on the sand. Ahjin felt the beast still pinching at him like fire.

He struggled to rise, but his blood turned the sand to mud under him. His legs didn't work, and when he grabbed his knife, it slipped from his hand.

He couldn't concentrate enough to turn invisible. He tried to roll away, but failed. Torment swept through him, carrying him into darkness.

17. BROKEN
(NORTHERN DESERT, ISKRA)

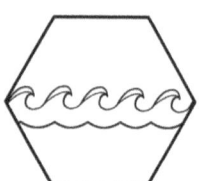

The afternoon knows what the morning never suspected.
Nokai Proverb

When Ahjin stopped moving at the scorpion's feet, Nia feared the worst. How dare that monster hurt her friend!

Everyone left the battle with the other two scorpions and ran for Ahjin. Nia's harpoon shook in her hands. She cursed the sand that gave under her feet. She had to reach Ahjin before the scorpion chopped him to bits.

She sobbed raggedly. Adventures were supposed to be fun. There shouldn't be giant scorpions as big as jaguars and as heartless as kraken. She wished she were back home, where bad things didn't happen.

Askari and Zefra reached Ahjin first, but trying to avoid stepping on him put them in an awkward position between the dead scorpion and the one that had wounded him.

Ludik ran faster than Nia in her sandals, even faster than Sayaka. He ran behind Ahjin's attacker while it was fighting the two Iskrins and cut off its poisonous tail with a wild swing of his ax. When the scorpion turned on him, he cracked its head and knocked it aside. He dropped to his knees and felt for Ahjin's pulse.

The visions shoved themselves back into Nia's mind, and she wiped at the tears. Ahjin still wasn't moving. Without him, was the adventure at an end? The others would go on, but could they succeed? They should have at least had more time to find the gods.

But that didn't matter right now. She could worry about it after she knew Ahjin would survive. He had to live.

The last two monsters sprinted toward the bloodstained sand. Askari and Zefra raced to help Sayaka fight them. Nia veered to join them. She'd kill those monsters for what they did.

"He's alive," Ludik shouted. He tossed the undamaged map from Ahjin's belt and pressed his hands against the avian's back.

Nia sobbed with relief. So much blood soaked the sand. How could Ahjin still be alive? For how long?

While Askari and Sayaka fought one of the scorpions, the other dodged Nia and knocked Zefra off her feet. It ran toward Ludik and Ahjin with claws outstretched.

Nia screamed a warning, but Ludik was too busy stanching the blood flow to pick up his weapon. But instead of killing the two men, the scorpion veered and tried to grab the discarded map with its awkward claws. The women left the other scorpion to Askari and hacked the distracted monster into little pieces.

"Sayaka," Ludik called. "If you can get away, grab my medical pack and come help me."

Through a red haze, Nia distantly heard him cursing. She slashed at the scorpion, ignoring Zefra when the younger girl called her name. Not until Zefra clashed her sword into Nia's harpoon did she shake the wildness from her head and retreat from the diced scorpion.

The final scorpion also reached toward Ahjin, but when Askari and the two girls charged, it gave up and scuttled out of range.

It drew in the sand and hissed, "You will still lose." With one last brandish of its claw, it burrowed into the side of a sand dune and disappeared.

Nia ran back and flung herself next to Ahjin. "Can you fix him?"

Ludik had to heal Ahjin. He had to. She didn't know how to help. She wasn't a warrior like Askari or Sayaka. Or a healer like Ludik, or a guide like Zefra. She didn't have wings or telepathy like Ahjin. Everyone spoke trade tongue now; they didn't need her on this quest. If Ahjin was dead, why should she stay? She reached for him uselessly.

Ludik blocked her with a bloodstained hand. He murmured a steady current of instructions, hands racing. "Sayaka, move his wings. Put your hands here and press hard. Nia, stay out of the way and get my sutures. They're in the red box in my kit. Also my ointment in the green jar and all the bandages you can find. And our water."

He slit Ahjin's desert robe from neck to hem, pausing only half a second before slicing through the remnants of Ahjin's beloved scarf. When he flipped back the edges of the robe, he cursed.

Chum, what a grisly mess. And what an unfortunate choice of curses. Nia ran for the supplies while Zefra grabbed the water jugs and Askari cut a blanket into strips. Ludik kept his kit organized, and it took only moments to find what he wanted. She staggered back over the lumpy sand and laid the equipment next to Ludik.

Ahjin didn't seem any better. The bleeding under Sayaka's hands had slowed, but there were still so many injuries. His robe was drenched in red, as were the trousers the silly man had worn under his robe. Tidal waves, he was modest. But it did make sense when he was flying overhead. When Ludik cut off Ahjin's trousers, Nia turned her head so she'd be able to tell Ahjin she didn't look.

"If you think there is any chance of the gods hearing us where they are now," Ludik said, "start praying."

Behind Nia, Zefra whispered.

Nia plotted recipes for scorpion stew and scorpion filet. If the gods couldn't help, she'd have to settle for revenge. Ahjin would approve. She closed her burning eyes.

"I don't have enough training for this," Ludik complained under his breath. "We should have a real healer. I don't know how to sew shredded muscles. I've never set hollow bones before. Teeth and claws," he shouted, "I'll ruin everything. Although, it won't matter if I can't stop this bleeding."

He continued to work and fret while Nia arranged his supplies. "Thank you. Now go away. I can't do this with you watching." Nobody moved until he looked up and growled. "Be gone, I said."

Sayaka stayed to assist him. Zefra, Nia, and Askari dragged themselves to the place the scorpion had etched before it left. It had left a rough sketch of a circle, hand-deep in the sand.

Zefra frowned and rifled through her rune bag. She laid an identical rune next to the sand picture. "'Tis a message, perhaps."

"But what does it mean?" Nia asked.

"Nothing." Zefra replaced her rune in her bag.

"What good is a message that doesn't mean anything?" Nia wrinkled her nose.

"It does mean something," Zefra said.

"That's not what you said." Nia threw out her arms. "What does it mean, then?"

"'Tis the rune that means 'nothing,'" Askari clarified.

Nia blinked. "And what should we understand from that?"

Zefra shrugged. "I have no idea."

They stared at the cryptic message and the barren landscape until it seemed likely the scorpion wouldn't return and they couldn't decipher the drawing. With nothing else to do, and not daring to bother Ludik, Nia limped around on aching feet to collect and clean weapons. Zefra and Askari dragged the scorpion carcasses into a pile.

By the time they finished, Sayaka was repacking Ludik's bag under his direction while he scrubbed his hands with soap. Ahjin lay still, wrapped in so many bandages he looked laid out for burial.

Nia sniffled. She should have warned him faster.

"This is my fault," Zefra said. "I should have helped sooner."

Ludik held out his hands for Askari to pour water over them. "I should have protected him. Do you want the good news or the bad first?"

He was using his inscrutable healer's voice. Not good. The front of his robe was soaked in Ahjin's blood from knees to hem. Even Nia's weak nose could identify the metallic tang.

Sayaka spoke without looking up from her packing. "Give them the good news."

"He's alive," Ludik said, "and likely to stay alive."

Nia sighed with relief. She didn't want to tell his mom she'd killed him.

"He isn't paralyzed." Ludik tightened his lips. "He hasn't lost any limbs yet."

"Hasn't lost any — yet?" Nia croaked, staring at the shocking red on Ludik's tan robe. Zefra tightened her arm around Nia but wavered. Was the grasp to comfort Nia or keep Zefra from falling?

"The scorpion seemed to be after that." Ludik pointed at Resef's seemingly indestructible map, now sticking from his own pack.

How unfair that it, godly gift though it was, survived better than a living being.

"Oh," Nia said. "That must have been what they were talking about." She had been more worried about Ahjin being their target.

"What were who talking about?" Ludik asked.

"The scorpions. During the battle? The whistling and clicking right before they attacked Ahjin?"

"You understood that?" Zefra asked. "What did they say?"

"Oh, 'Look what they have,' 'Let's get it,' 'Over here,' 'Hurry.' Nothing very specific." Nia shrugged. "Although the bit about 'He'll be pleased' was a bit strange."

"Why did you not tell us you understand animal speech?" Zefra asked.

"I told you I understand all languages," Nia said. "Doesn't that include animals?"

"Did you understand the krakens and bats back on the ocean?" Ludik asked.

Nia snorted. "Kraken are stupid. What they say isn't worth shark spit. And I was too far from the big bats. Your little messenger bat didn't say anything."

Ludik shook his head. "Anyway, because the scorpions were less focused on killing than... retrieval, most of Ahjin's injuries seem almost accidental, although they are severe. The map protected his spine from being severed, but the muscles in his back are shredded. We'll have to watch for infection, and he'll scar impressively. I don't know if he'll be able to walk normally."

He stopped and looked at Ahjin. Nia followed his gaze but there was no movement. There didn't seem to be much good news. And there was still bad news. How much worse could it get?

Ludik turned back. "Ahjin was lucky he didn't have his wings furled, or the scorpion would have shattered them. As it is," he choked, "his wingtips were still nipped. The feathers should grow back, but he might lose part of his wings. Even if he doesn't, I don't know if the broken bones can heal well enough for him to ever fly again. *I* don't have the skill to mend him." He swallowed hard.

Tears slid down Nia's cheeks, and her breath caught in her throat. Ahjin loved his beautiful, athletic aerobatics. If they saved the gods and Irajahan kept his half of the bargain, would Ahjin think it was enough?

"I'm not sure he'll thank me for saving his life," Ludik whispered. He collected his pack from Sayaka and turned to check on his patient again.

Sayaka whistled the ponies' return signal and left to hunt. Askari made a stretcher with Ahjin's and Nia's staffs. When the ponies arrived half an hour later, Nia and Zefra set up camp, pitching one of the tents over Ahjin. Morning was early enough to move him.

Before they went to bed, Ludik treated everyone else's wounds. The fragile skin on Nia's healing feet had cracked. She knew without looking at them, but Ahjin's wounds were more important. While Ludik replaced her bandages, she hummed tunelessly to Ahjin as he slept.

Ludik and Askari took turns watching Ahjin through the night while the girls shared guard duty.

Nia took a childish delight in the campfire Zefra finally managed to set. During her usual first watch, Nia carefully washed and mended Ahjin's shredded scarf by the bright light of the burning shells of their fallen enemies. She wanted to have it ready for Ahjin when he woke.

When she got bored, she threw rocks into the fire to crack the flaming shells. She imagined they were the scorpions' master and tallied each victory in the sand until Sayaka sent her to bed after her watch.

Nia hadn't understood why the others twitched so badly in their sleep until it was her turn. Nightmares woke her every hour.

As the sky lightened before sunrise, everyone but Ahjin was already awake, even Nia. They did their morning chores, covering for both Ahjin, who hadn't woken yet, and Ludik, who had to prepare his patient for transport. After a hot breakfast, Ludik treated everyone's injuries again and mixed a batch of his pain-killing tea.

Askari arranged the stretcher behind one of the ponies. He and Ludik carried Ahjin gently while Sayaka held the pony. They placed him on his stomach with his splinted wings carefully arranged over him. While the older Hotaru rolled the tents and put out the fire, Ludik strapped Ahjin in place and worked clean socks onto his feet. Zefra arranged Ahjin's mended scarf to shade his head and neck. Nia overlapped the edges of his cut robe and used cactus spines from Zefra's collection to pin the bloodied fabric shut. There was no point in putting him into his spare robe when they'd need to change the bandages that covered half his torso.

Ahjin stirred and mumbled. Ludik held him gently still and knelt to listen. Nia strategically slowed her pinning to eavesdrop.

Ahjin's whispered questions were no surprise. "How is everyone else? How badly am I hurt? Can you fix it?"

"The others only have minor injuries." Ludik took a deep breath and repeated Ahjin's diagnosis.

When he reached "probably never fly again," Ahjin shuddered under Nia's hands. Her stomach clenched, and she rubbed away her tears before they fell on Ahjin, then tried to still her quivering lip.

"But you'll live," Ludik continued, "and—"

"And you think that's good news?" Ahjin closed his eyes and clenched his fists.

Nia wiped at tears again. The adventure might be ruined, but she needed to be strong for Ahjin when he was ready to think about his situation. Ludik was concerned with his physical well-being, and the Iskrins didn't know him well enough to help with his emotional crisis. The others could worry about the quest; she'd take care of Ahjin.

Ludik made Ahjin swallow as much analgesic tea as possible, then rose and signaled the return home. He walked beside the stretcher and kept watch. Whenever Ahjin woke, he dosed him with more painkiller.

Nia guarded Ahjin's other side until her feet hurt too badly. It was a wasted effort. By the time Ludik forced her onto a pony, Ahjin still hadn't spoken.

Ahjin didn't make any sounds the first day, even during the horrific task of changing his bandages. Nia might have thought he was sleeping, particularly considering the amount of the drugged tea he drank, but Ahjin's clenched fists betrayed when he was awake. That was always her signal to sing to him. He didn't respond, but he didn't tell her to stop.

That was as good as permission. Someday he'd thank her. If he was still around to be thankful.

18.RETURN
(NORTHERN DESERT, ISKRA)

The hammer shatters glass but forges steel.
Iskrin Proverb

I t had been two days since the battle with the scorpions, and Ahjin wanted to gag Nia. That girl didn't know how to shut up and wouldn't recognize privacy if it hit her in the face. In self-defense, he finally talked about anything but his injuries or the future. If those forbidden subjects arose, he shot her a glare he hoped would strike her down, pulled his scarf over his face, and faked sleep on the stretcher. Real sleep came only with difficulty.

He could ignore Nia and the other walkers, but he couldn't ignore his own thoughts. The light filtered through his scarf, casting jagged lines of shadow from Nia's careful mends. It made him sick to see the uneven slashes, knowing his back must look the same. It certainly felt similar, with ragged streaks of pain burning from side to side. Even the ache in his broken wingtips paled in comparison. Every breath pulled muscles into agony.

Ludik's words echoed in his head. '*Shredded muscles and broken wings... Beyond my abilities... Might never heal properly... Probably never fly again. Might not even walk...*' Ahjin's stomach cramped. There had to be something to do. He couldn't live like this. How could he go home if he couldn't even fly with his family.

Never fly again.

Ahjin's belt and knife had been stowed by Ludik, who claimed his waist couldn't tolerate any pressure. It didn't escape Ahjin's notice that his weapons had ended in Ludik's pack rather than his own.

Retrieving his knife was only his first problem. Even without the relentless watch, Ahjin couldn't stand at all, much less long enough to search the packs and slip away from everyone else. He clenched his fists again. If the long-term outlook didn't improve in a few days, he'd find a way. It would only take a few minutes apart from his keeper.

And if he couldn't reach his knife? Worries buffeted him like a cold cross-draft. If Ahjin didn't help Irajahan himself, would the god accept his friends' help to fulfill his agreement with Ahjin, or would he use it as an excuse to cancel their deal? Ahjin didn't know if he could heal enough to do his part, whatever that was.

But if he rescued Irajahan and the god kept his bargain, would Ahjin heal enough to skydance with his family? What sort of life would he have if he never recovered? He'd be a burden on his family. But even if he was good for nothing else, he didn't want to be Irajahan's Wind.

Of course, if he and his friends died, that was the end of that dilemma.

If he couldn't reach his knife, perhaps he could find a way to spare his friends and die in their place, since he was already ruined.

Ahjin shifted on the stretcher, and pain shot through his back and wings. He bit back a groan to avoid anyone hovering over him. Ludik's analgesic tea helped a little with the agony, but the incessant spirals of worry wore on him as much as the pain. He wanted to get up and find answers, not lie here uselessly.

In the meantime, he still had to endure the return travel to the Hotaru camp. The fastest pace he tolerated was nearly a crawl. The three Hotaru took care of the ponies and scouting, since he was worthless and occupied Ludik with his care. Nia, prone to dehydration and still too footsore to scout, did much of the cooking and camp chores when not pestering Ahjin. Meals had dwindled to their simplest states. It was a blessing; simple was harder to ruin. Ahjin didn't have much appetite anyway. His stomach was permanently cramped with worry and nauseated from pain and medicine.

Ahjin ate only flatbread and drank copious amounts of Ludik's nasty brew. He still felt every bump and dip as the stretcher hissed across the sand. His wings ached with each jostle. Every curve of the desert mapped itself on his back. Lucky Nia got to ride a pony, but it wasn't an option for him until he could sit.

"So, Ahjin." Nia popped up by his litter and interrupted his fretting. "How do you feel?"

Ahjin grunted.

"That's what I thought," Nia said. "You should have more hope."

Ahjin snorted.

"Well, flashing jellyfish, I don't know where hope is, either, but it has to be somewhere, and we'll find it."

Ahjin glared at her.

"If you don't have hope for yourself," Nia said, "then I'll have it for you. Just remember, we need and love you. Irajahan is still waiting for you to rescue him, and I certainly won't tell your parents you gave up on going home. We'll talk more about this later." She rearranged the scarf over her gills and hummed a lullaby.

Perhaps she was right about hope. Perhaps not. Time would show which direction the wind blew. First, they had to decipher the map and what it might hold for their future. Could the Iskrin clans help? Assuming he and his friends arrived in time. There might be an unknown deadline. They didn't know what they'd find at the place on the map. How could they help the gods if the gods couldn't help themselves? And who could possibly be behind this?

Ahjin listened to Nia's music until he finally fell asleep.

He woke to a howling wind. From the corner of the eye not pressed against the stretcher, he saw a fierce storm in the distant sky. A soggy cloud-finger stretched toward them until rain misted the dry sand. Askari had told him about typical desert weather, and this wasn't it.

The three Iskrins stood in the sprinkle with faces lifted and hands raised. Despite their surprise at the unusual storm, their cries of joy celebrated the blessing.

Ahjin pondered hope.

Two days later, small tremors shook the earth, and the sand dunes nearly leveled themselves. The ponies knelt while the people sheltered next to them. They periodically struggled free of the shifting sand just enough to rise to the top again. The movements barely lifted Ahjin's stretcher enough to keep his head above the sand, but were more than enough to jolt his wounds to full agony. He closed his eyes and waited for the torture to kill him.

When the earthquakes ended, it took an hour to dig Ahjin free, brush off the sand, and rebandage his injuries. They shouldn't have bothered for a cripple.

Ahjin dreamed Resef's visions again that night. Die trying to save the world, or don't even try and let the whole world be destroyed. He woke sweating and tried to turn over. His muscles flared with agony but no movement, and his bad dreams turned into a living nightmare.

He smothered his gasps in his scarf, but Ludik still woke, gave him more tea, and resettled him. Nia left the girls' tent to curl by his head, tears creeping down her face. Ahjin didn't have the energy to comfort her. If he could only save the world first, dying would be a relief.

Ahjin improved a little each day, but even with the tea, it took five days before he sat upright with heavy support. He subtly exercised his back and wings for a few seconds whenever Ludik wasn't watching. He would look for an outcome that wasn't complete despair, but he couldn't hope for it. The pain and lack of muscle response in those seconds of exercise didn't encourage him, nor did the unrealistic good wishes of the others.

He refused to let anyone but Ludik see his injuries, and would have rejected his help if Ludik hadn't given him a gruesome lecture on infection and idiocy. Ahjin would accept the diagnosis of stubborn, but stupidity was a bit much. And if he ever found out who taught the healer to use that nauseatingly detailed lecture, he'd have something to say to him.

As the caravan got closer to the Hotaru camp, other Iskrins passed at a distance. Zefra suggested speeding their pace since no one at the camp understood why the signal had been sent. After a discussion, which Ahjin refused to join, everyone else agreed they couldn't risk it, even if the other clans left before they arrived.

Ahjin was in no hurry to let other people see his wrecked body. If the trip took long enough, perhaps he could sit by himself by the time they arrived. How dismal that his ambition had shrunk to mere sitting.

On the eighth day, Ahjin heard muffled thunder, but his limited view of the sky didn't show clouds, and he felt no shifts in air pressure. The mystery was solved when Iskrins on beautiful horses swept into their path.

Hesketh was the first to reach them, throwing himself from his horse to embrace his daughter. Other horsemen pounded in behind.

"Bright day. The clans told us they saw you. Are you well?" Hesketh stared at Ludik's blood-soaked robe and held Zefra at arm's length to examine her.

"We're alive and think we have discovered the gods' location." Zefra glanced at Nia and Ahjin. "We have wounded, though, and we're short on food and water."

"We have enough horses to carry you double," Hesketh said. "You can be home by tonight."

Ludik cleared his throat above Ahjin's head. "I cannot allow Ahjin to ride a horse or for his stretcher to be pulled at those speeds. It would cause him irreparable damage."

What difference would it make? It couldn't be worse than now. Ahjin's stomach clenched again.

The Hotaru stared at Ahjin before looking away. Ahjin closed his eyes and imagined he was somewhere else. Anywhere else. The conversation rang in his ears despite his efforts to ignore it.

"You take the others and leave Ahjin and me more food and water," Ludik said. "You know as much about the situation as we do. Ahjin has gotten no direct messages in weeks now. I'll give you the map. We should be there before you have to leave again."

There was a brief pause before Askari spoke. "Sayaka and I will not leave you here unprotected, but Nia should go on the horses, and Zefra may if she wishes. We know the way home from here."

"I think that is an excellent idea." Relief flooded Hesketh's voice.

It sounded like a good compromise to Ahjin. Anything to keep the other Hotaru from staring at him.

He cleared his throat. "Someone really ought to take the map as soon as possible."

No one acknowledged him.

"Nia," Zefra asked, "do you want to ride a horse back to camp?"

"Not at those speeds," Nia said, "and I won't abandon my friends."

Ahjin peeked through his eyelashes and saw her frowning ferociously at Askari. And she called *him* stubborn. He squelched his smile.

"And you can't make me, so I'll stay." Nia smiled sweetly at Hesketh, shoving wayward hair out of her face with both hands.

"There you have it, Father," Zefra said. "We are not going. But we will send you with the map, and we welcome supplies. Ludik can tell you what he needs prepared for our arrival. And keep the other clans there until we arrive." She smiled at him and stretched to kiss his cheek.

Hesketh sighed and hugged her again.

The other riders unloaded food, water, and a few medical supplies. One had a whetstone and sharpened the weapons dulled on scorpion shells. He kept his good humor when Ludik had him sharpen his knife for a third time to get what he considered a satisfactory edge.

Although Ahjin's knife was also honed, it went back in the shapeshifter's bag.

When Zefra started to repeat her instructions to her father, Ludik said, "My turn."

Zefra flushed and left to pack the new supplies on their ponies. Ludik went over a long list that Nia had translated into trade script. Hesketh promised to consult with any healer he found before they arrived.

A faint hope blew into Ahjin's heart. Perhaps a more experienced healer could help. If it wasn't too late already.

Ludik handed his list and the map to Hesketh.

"Yow!" Hesketh dropped the map. "It burns." He pressed his hand against his robe, and Zefra ran to him.

"No, it does not." Ludik furrowed his brow and picked up the map. He held it out to Hesketh again.

Hesketh turned one hand to show a red stripe of blisters. He tucked Ludik's list into his belt pouch with the unburned hand.

Zefra pushed the map back to Ludik. "I think Resef wants us to keep it. We will show it to everyone when we arrive." She dripped water on her father's hand while Ludik brought his ointment.

Ahjin sighed. Apparently, Irajahan wasn't the only god that insisted on having his own way.

"Too bad the scorpions didn't actually pick it up," Nia muttered. "We could have saved Zefra the trouble of broiling them."

Now that was a lovely picture. Ahjin grinned viciously.

Askari stripped their load to the bare minimum. The riders left with the rest of the gear, and their own caravan resumed walking.

Now that they were alone, Ahjin opened his eyes. "You should have gone with them," he told the boots nearest his stretcher. "There's no need for everyone to suffer with me, and you might need the extra time to save the gods. The way the weather and earth has been misbehaving, it might be the start of the catastrophes in Resef's vision. You must stop it before it gets worse."

"I'm ignoring you," came Zefra's calm voice. "Separating our group is senseless."

"Yeah, what she said," Nia smugly added from behind him. Her gait sounded odd. She might be limping, or still trying to skip in the sand. He hoped for the skipping.

"Don't be more of a birdbrain than you can help," growled Ludik. He kicked the stretcher ever so softly.

Ahjin thought he heard a chuckle from Sayaka in the lead and a suspicious cough from the tail end of the procession. It seemed all his friends agreed. Gratitude warred with annoyance.

"I surrender," he said. "You're all birdbrains. Nia, will you sing to me?"

She sang of a cheerful call to battle that ended in hilarious catastrophe. When Ahjin's uncontrollable laughter made his back throb, Ludik forced more tea into him. Nia apologized by singing a quiet lullaby until Ahjin fell asleep.

The next two days were filled with more walking, talking, and singing, but no more side-splitting ballads, on healer's orders. Their replenished supplies included enough travel rations that they didn't need to hunt or cook, allowing them to spend more time walking. Extra water spared them from chewing cactus and collecting dew.

The group rehearsed their information again and again, practicing for the presentation to the Iskrin clans. Ahjin replayed their discussions when he dreamed, but they all ended the same way. They still did not know what to do when they reached the spot on the map. How would they rescue the gods or save the world? If they didn't figure it out, the world was doomed.

He dreamed about that, too.

19. HEALING

(HOTARU SUMMER CAMP, ISKRA)

Ludik's salve: Chop calendula, comfrey, lavandula, honey myrtle, coneflower, woundwort, piperita, orangeroot, mallow, rosemary, snakeweed, and leopard's boon. Heat herbs in ipeku oil for one-half hour over low heat; strain. Melt honey and beeswax into infused oil. Pour into jars, cool.

Ludik was starving by the time they saw the dun Hotaru tents nestled like shadows between the white sand dunes, just before the evening meal. Their group had finished the last of their food at morning, but the Hotaru and representatives of the other clans swarmed them before they reached the closest tents. Eating would obviously be delayed.

Askari, Sayaka, and the ponies were swept off by Hesketh and the guard captains for an informal debriefing while they fed and groomed the mounts in the corral. The children of the camp collected the unloaded bags and started a contest to see who got his or her claimed pack put away first.

Shara welcomed her daughter home, then took charge of Ahjin and escorted him to a prepared tent. "I've sent for the healers," she said.

Ludik followed her, happy to hand Ahjin's care to someone more experienced.

"Not yet." Shara put a hand on Ludik's chest. "You go change your clothes while I settle Ahjin."

Ludik ran for the men's guest tent with equal measures of relief and disgust. The desert robe would smell anyway, after wearing it for more than two weeks, but the bottom half had been soaked in Ahjin's blood for over a week. Flies swarmed Ludik faster than he could swat them. At least Nemerra wasn't here to see this.

He changed into one of his own tunics and hurried back to summarize for the three Iskrin healers outside the tent. By the time Shara exited, Ludik was already deep into the conversation in trade tongue.

Ludik finished the long list of Ahjin's injuries and their original severity and healing progress. "I have done the best I can, but I am not skilled enough to fix the rest. I am grateful for any help you can offer."

He was ready to beg, but the healers raised their hands to stop him. They opened the tent flap and gasped.

"Where did he go?" asked the oldest one, tugging on his midnight blue belt and staring at the empty cot. All three turned and glared at Ludik.

"What? Ahjin cannot go anywhere. He cannot *sit* by himself." Ludik sniffed and turned his head to listen. Even as a man, he smelled Ahjin's distinctive feather-flecked scent and heard the rustle of his wings.

Ludik stepped inside the tent and stood by the seemingly abandoned bed. "How stupid do you think I am, Ahjin?"

Nobody answered, although he heard a puzzled murmur from the healers at the door. Ludik pinched an invisible ankle. Ahjin hissed and reappeared on the cot, twitching his leg from Ludik's fingers.

"If you wouldn't torment me, I might not hurt myself trying to escape you," he groaned. "Haven't I been poked and prodded enough? Can't you leave me alone?" He lifted his head to glare at Ludik.

"No, and if you don't behave, I'll arrange for healing sessions three times a day until we leave, whether you need them or not." Ludik glowered at his friend.

Ahjin growled in a reasonable imitation of a Darrendrakar and dropped his head back on the cot. Shara had stripped him of his equally blood-drenched robe and draped him with a blanket that covered everything lower than his wings.

Ludik suspected he'd have to guard against retribution once Ahjin recovered. It bothered him little when balanced against his friend being well again. Besides, he still weighed at least twice as much as the bird-man, so he'd be fine. He pushed away an inconvenient memory of fish bones.

The three healers entered the tent and rummaged through their bags for equipment, then descended on Ahjin like a clan of hyenas, muttering in their own language. Their examination took a long time, especially since Ahjin pretended he didn't understand any of the questions they asked in trade tongue. They finally resettled Ahjin and escorted Ludik from the tent.

"Except for his broken bones," their elder spokesman said, "I do not understand why you were so worried. His injuries are moderately serious but not critical, and they're healing well. Your own healing magic is obviously up to the task. We will be happy to reset his bones with the help of our animal healer." He motioned to the youngest Iskrin with the lavender belt.

"Moderately serious? Ahjin looked like chopped venison and almost bled to death before I stitched his wounds. He still cannot move, and I do not know if that is normal, or if I botched putting him back together." Ludik stared in shock as the rest of the message sank in. "And I have no magic."

"Gift, then." The animal healer with the lavender belt waved his hand to brush away the distinction. "Whatever you call it, it has done well. Very well indeed, if you're not mistaken about the original extent of his injuries." He looked both skeptical and impressed at the same time.

"No, you do not understand." Ludik tried again. "I have basic training for simple illnesses and emergency treatment for injuries. I *can* make an accurate assessment, though I do not know how to treat everything. And I have been told I make a good ointment, but I just snuck in on some of my brother's lessons. I have no magic, no gift."

He ran his hand through his hair. It had grown long since he left home. The ends stuck out between his fingers, threatening a proper mane like Papa's. "I thought he was healing faster because of his avian elements."

"Bird *bones* heal about twice as quickly as those of mammals. We expected his wings to be at most half-healed by now, not the three-quarters we see. We have little experience with his race, so I do not know if that explains the difference or not." The animal healer seemed torn between fascination and worry.

"*Muscles* do not heal that quickly, though you did put him back together correctly. I need to teach you how to stretch his injuries so he will have full movement when he heals. Birds should not be kept immobile for more than a few days." The apology on his open face softened the criticism.

The oldest healer fingered the crescent-moon badge on his blue belt. "Did you use the ointment on Ahjin? May I see it, please?"

Ludik's shoulders slumped. "If it will help convince you, I will get it now."

He ran for the salve, cursing the time wasted on a fool's errand. He didn't have magic, and the healers should be helping Ahjin. When he returned to the healing tent, he thrust the ointment at them.

The healers removed the lid and passed around the jar. The lavender-belted healer stuck a finger in the jar, rubbed the ointment onto the back of his hand, then smelled it. At his raised eyebrow, the other two healers copied his experiment.

"You see, it is an ordinary herbal salve." Ludik clasped his hands behind his back to keep from fidgeting. He was a second-rate healer taught with stolen lessons. Why wouldn't they just heal Ahjin?

"Hmm." The healers exchanged looks. The middle-aged one — probably from the Hotaru clan, judging by his turquoise belt and firefly badge — cleared his throat. "We can identify most of the herbs and assume the others are native to your land. We also recognize the strong magical component. If you made this yourself, the healing magic had to come from you." He paused for a minute. "I'm impressed, actually. We cannot get such powerful medicines, except from the Tukiko adepts. Such remedies are precious."

"Indeed." The blue-belted healer inspected Ludik. "If you want to trade your salve, contact a healer in any Iskrin clan. If you ever decide you want a real apprenticeship, send a message to the Tukiko asking for me, Shri Okechuku. I will teach you myself or see you get someone adequate to your talents."

The animal healer gasped slightly. When Ludik glanced his way, his face was pale, his lips clamped, and he gripped the ship badge on his lavender belt as if it were a lifeline. What had shocked him so badly?

The Hotaru healer put a hand on his younger cohort's shoulder and shook him casually as he listed their recommendations for Ahjin's treatment, starting with re-breaking and setting his wings. After a moment, the young one took a deep breath and joined the conversation.

Ludik carefully wrote their suggestions, including descriptions of herbs whose names he didn't recognize in trade tongue. Some he identified by the descriptions; others he'd need to investigate.

When they finished, he thanked them. They'd return after the council meeting to help with the treatments. They left with the young one whispering emphatically to his colleagues.

Ludik ducked inside to talk to Ahjin. His friend was already asleep with his scarf clenched in his fists and his wings sliding over the edges of the narrow cot. A frown shadowed his face.

Ludik pulled up the blanket and resettled Ahjin's wings where they wouldn't pull on his healing back. At least he was recovering. Ludik hadn't ruined everything. Maybe the other healers could restore Ahjin completely. Was it too much to hope? Maybe it was only reasonable for him to walk again. Did he dare dream to see him fly again?

Ludik crouched on a colorful rug to read his notes, but couldn't concentrate. Could he have magic? The possibility scrabbled in the back of his mind like a frantic squirrel. He couldn't kill it, ignore it, or chase it away. *No one else in his line had magic before,* muttered the squirrel.

His parents would puff with pride. His siblings would laugh and accuse him of delusions. He couldn't blame them. Despite the Iskrins' assurances, he still wasn't sure he believed. And, oh, what Gurryon would say! His annoying mental squirrel yipped with amusement and dismay.

There would be more lessons and fewer hunting trips in his future. Maybe Nemerra wouldn't mind the changes. He hoped *he* wouldn't mind.

Yes, he would mind. Could he hide the magic from his village? If he didn't tell them, maybe they wouldn't find out.

No, it wouldn't work. Ludik was suddenly sure Akamu knew already, at least a little. That must be why Gurryon said he didn't make the ointment as often as Ludik had. It was no coincidence. Not only had they not fooled the tribe when they switched places, the elders suspected things he never knew. He groaned. They were probably waiting for him to find out for himself.

Ludik idly admired a hanging on the tent wall and contemplated healing instead of hunting.

Furballs.

Then he remembered Ahjin and Nia's visions. If he never got home, his worries wouldn't matter. His family would never know; his village would never take advantage of his unexpected skills. If they were real.

Ludik narrowed his eyes as the intricate tapestry in front of him suddenly made sense. He rose and traced his finger along the calendar, ignoring the foreign names and numbers and merely counting the months and days until the firefly pin that marked the day.

It must be wrong. According to this, today was to have been his wedding day. Even taking care of Ahjin, he couldn't have lost track of time that badly. Ludik stared at the firefly until the message sank in.

He had missed his wedding.

His finger slipped from the calendar, and he dropped numbly to his knees. He had missed his wedding.

Nemerra would think he abandoned her. She'd think he didn't love her anymore, or maybe assume he died. Ludik didn't know which would be worse. His throat tightened. Could he send her a message to spare her the pain? What if he told her he was well and *then* he died? Maybe it was better to leave things the way they were. No, he couldn't let her think he stopped loving her.

She might wait a while for him to return. But if she was upset enough, she might not welcome him back. What if she decided he wasn't worth the wait? His eyes burned. She wouldn't do that.

Even if she waited for him, she couldn't wait forever. After a few months, the council would pressure her to marry another. If Ludik came back after she had promised herself to someone else, it would be difficult for her to break that betrothal. His breath wheezed in the silent tent.

He had missed his wedding. Ludik clamped a hand over his mouth, too late to hide the moan that squeezed through his fingers.

Ahjin's injuries were terrible, and Resef's visions foretold the end of the world. A simple wedding was nothing in comparison, but oh, he missed Nemerra. Ludik didn't want her in the middle of danger, and even if he could instantly get home, he couldn't abandon Ahjin and the others. And yet, he missed her warmth and joy and perpetual love. This should be the first day of their wedded happiness.

Ludik curled his head to his knees and wept, glad Ahjin was asleep and wouldn't hear him. His tears ran down his knees. By the time his eyes ran dry, the colorful rug under his feet was damp.

When he finally emerged from the tent, there was nobody in sight. A bowl of steaming stew held down a brief note for him. "Council at fire," Nia's scribble said. Ludik scooped the stew into his mouth as quickly as possible without burning his tongue. The ingredients were simple, but the unfamiliar spices were delicious, and the large bowl was very full.

When he finished, he looked around the unpopulated landscape, shrugged, and left the bowl in its original depression in the sand. Ludik put the note in his pocket next to his new medical lists.

There was only one fire at the edge of camp. The sound of many voices wafted in the breeze. He hoped they hadn't wasted time waiting for him.

As the flaming sun set above the endless sand, Ludik wished for a cool forest and the warmth of his dear ones. The dry desert air didn't smell properly of green growing things. This was not home, but he had no more tears.

Ludik stomped his feet to settle them in his boots before strolling toward the fire.

When — if — he got home, he'd beg Nemerra's forgiveness. She loved him and might think he had a good enough excuse for his tardiness. If she'd still take him, he'd do anything to make it up to her.

20. COUNCIL

(HOTARU SUMMER CAMP, ISKRA)

It is wise for strangers to have permission before wandering across the borders of the sixteen Iskrin districts. District colors are used in signals or to identify clans from a distance.

Iskrin Culture and History, vol. 2

Zefra watched Mother escort Ahjin and the healers. Nia had removed her scarf when they entered camp, and a tiny child dragged it after his older sister while she carried Nia's pack to her tent.

Home again, but only for awhile. Zefra must get used to that way of life if she was to be an explorer. If she succeeded in her first mission.

"Bright day, Zefra," Chieftain Prathap said. "Your sisters cooked for you at each meal in hopes of your arrival. Take your friend to bathe and eat while your injured companion is examined. We told our guests what you instructed, so they will be ready for you around the council fire." He strode toward the corral, arm-in-arm with his wife.

Izo sauntered to Nia and kissed her hand extravagantly. "My lady fair, I missed you. I know you cannot stay with me." He grinned. "Yet. So I brought a gift to remind you of me." With a grand flourish, he pulled a small faceted glass jar from behind his back.

Zefra shook her head. It seemed her brother was not satisfied with appreciative glances anymore.

"Thank you," Nia clapped her hands in delight. "It's a beautiful bottle! It sparkles like a jewel."

Izo blinked in confusion. "'Tis perfume," he said less dramatically. "I picked a basic floral scent. If you like something else better, I'm happy to look for it." When Nia just stared at him, his smile faded.

Zefra reached over Nia's shoulder for the bottle. She wiggled out the stopper and held the tiny jar under Nia's nose.

"Perfume smells pretty, Nia, and makes *you* smell pretty." She waved the jar to spread the scent.

Nia's jaw dropped. "I can smell like flowers?" She stretched on tiptoe and pulled Izo lower for a kiss on his cheek.

He puffed his chest. When she grabbed the bottle and ran for the bath tent, Izo watched her go in perplexed dismay.

Zefra patted him on the shoulder. "Sorry, brother. Perhaps next time she will stay and let you impress her." She headed for her own bath before she lost control of her hidden smile.

Zefra got her bath and a quick check from a female healer. Nia emerged from her side of the curtain in the bath tent, shining clean and smelling of a thousand roses, with her damp hair loose to her ankles.

Zefra breathed through her mouth. "You like the perfume. Do they have none in the islands?"

"It's wonderful," Nia said. "No, it would wash off, and the flowers are everywhere."

"I'm glad you're happy. Did you know you only need a drop or two?"

"Isn't more of a good thing better?" Nia twirled. "What are we doing next?"

"Food and then a council with the Iskrin clans."

Nia's shoulders slumped. "Another meeting? Can't they hold it without us? I want to check on Ahjin."

"We will after the healers finish."

They went to the family tent, where Nia charmed Zefra's sisters and parents with her cheerful banter. Izo came, claiming a need for family time before Zefra left again. Based on the lighthearted flirting crossing the table, Zefra doubted his motives.

After glutting themselves silly, or sillier in Nia's case, they left for the council fire with a bowl of stew for Ludik. In the twilight, Zefra barely saw Nia's frown. As she opened her mouth, Zefra rushed to speak first.

"I will tell you interesting things while they're talking. Take this bowl to Ludik, then save me a place, and I will be there in a minute." Zefra tried to wiggle her eyebrows like Nia.

Nia pursed her lips. "Offer accepted." She grabbed the bowl and zigzagged between the tents on her way to the edge of camp.

Izo followed Nia, and Zefra grabbed his arm. "I need to tell you something."

He tilted his head toward her, but he kept his gaze on the exotic islander.

Zefra pulled harder. "You need to be careful of the attention you pay to Nia. She's still a child."

That got his attention. "Do not be ridiculous. Nia might be short, but she is not a child. Look at her, um, her shape." When Zefra glared at him, he cringed. "Her figure? Sorry, I do not know how to say that politely."

"In her culture and her own eyes, she's not adult for another half year. Flirt, but nothing more serious, or not only will her friends bury you like a sandstorm, she might gut you herself. And since she's *my* friend now, you will deal with me, too." Zefra stared hard into her brother's eyes.

After a moment, Izo nodded and kissed her on the cheek, then walked into the tent city with diminished swagger.

The other clansmen settled on the ground in half-circle rows around the fire under the stars. Zefra sat cross-legged next to Nia in the front row and rubbed her sore feet while she kept her promise to entertain.

"We did not know who would come to our signal, but you can tell who is who by their clothing. Chieftains wear a colored sash across their chests, a dyed belt means a healer, and a headband indicates a priest. The colors and designs tell their clans. You have already met Isvah and Prathap. The Hotaru badge is a firefly." Zefra pointed to the yellow insignia on Prathap's turquoise sash. "Behind him, the pale-green tree on brown is the spice-growing Kazuki."

She paused while Prathap started the meeting. While he reviewed the situation with the gods and the strangers' arrival, Zefra whispered in Nia's ear. "The dark brown bee on the saffron field is the Devora. They grow most of our grain, in the territory just east."

A handsome young man standing behind the Devoran chieftain caught

Zefra pointing and grinned. When he kept staring, she turned away and checked that her braids were still hidden. "The Rikatsu use a bronze ship on a lavender background," she told Nia. "They have the ships we need."

Nia squinted at the badge. "I recognize that one. They trade with the islands sometimes. Mom bought some beautiful silk from them."

"The silk comes from the Ravisu over there." Zefra pointed more discreetly this time.

"That's confusing." Nia frowned. "Rikatsu and Ravisu sound alike. How do you keep them straight?"

Zefra shrugged. "The meanings of the names are different. Anyway, their emblem is a cream sun on a bright orange sky. You can remember that. They also make pottery." She scanned the crowd again. "Have I missed anyone? Oooh, the far-southern Chiharu must have been close already. Their name means 'thousand springtimes,' and their symbol is a dark green and pink flower because they make perfume."

Nia squealed under her breath.

"You can get more perfume later," Zefra hissed.

Prathap finished his summary. "Zefra was their guide and will continue the tale." He sat beside his wife.

Zefra swallowed, rubbed her hands on her knees, and stood between the crowd and the fire. Nia's cheerful smile calmed her. Ludik and Izo slipped through the crowd together and dropped on either side of Nia. Only Ahjin was missing. Her outdweller friends stood out against the fire-lit Iskrin expanse of white faces and dark hair, including Sayaka and Askari in the middle of the crowd.

Zefra took a breath and recited the facts, starting with the visions. When she mentioned the wind storms and earthshakes they encountered on the way home, the chieftains exchanged grim looks. The battle with the scorpions and the mysterious rune made the mob erupt in shouts of surprise and fear while the priests whispered in a huddle.

"The map from Resef says to go somewhere in north-western Ioj. Since the ocean is the fastest route, we lit the flares for help." Zefra raised her voice over the increasing roar of the crowd.

It was time to ask for transportation and supplies, but no one was listening. She looked at her friends and brother in dismay. Nia shrugged and made a funny face to break the tension. Zefra laughed before thinking, then frowned at Nia, who made another face. Izo looked at the chaos and whistled shrilly twice.

When the crowd settled, Zefra continued. "Their little boat is not fast enough. Will the Rikatsu take us in one of their ships? Can the other clans provision us?"

The crowd sat in motionless silence. Finally, someone from the back spoke without standing or introducing himself. "Who are you, and can you prove you are telling the truth?"

How rude; she never lied. For what she hoped was the last time, Zefra removed her scarf to expose her red hair. "They call me Zefra Kezhekori."

The crowd murmured in confusion. "Burning fire?"

Zefra tossed her scarf to Nia and snapped fire into her hand. While the crowd gasped, she blew out the flame and took the map from Ludik.

"Here is the map we told you about." Someone grabbed at it, so she held it above her head. "If you want to examine it, we will help you later."

"Still sounds like a hoax," someone shouted.

"There have been strange storms and shakes recently," a woman in the front row said, reaching for the map.

"Do not touch it," Father called, holding his burned hand toward the crowd. "Resef left it for them."

Sayaka worked her way through the crowd. "If you still need proof, then here."

She upended a bag and poured a cascade of scorpion stingers longer than her hand. Everyone in the front row scuttled backward.

Heti, the clan healer, stood. "You should listen to them. I already have one patient with scorpion wounds and do not have time to deal with more, so do not come to me when they catch you." He walked away, and most of the healers followed.

Chieftain Prathap stood and raised his voice without moving to the front of the crowd. "The Hotaru will provide you with maps. Furthermore, although we have little food until we move on, we will beggar ourselves to aid you if no one else will help. We will, however, remember those who refused you."

It was a valid threat. While the Hotaru were not wealthy, the Iskrins relied on them for safe routes and other trade information.

Zefra scanned the crowd. Most of them would not meet her eyes.

"What if we think we're better off without the gods?" a man in the back row shouted.

Isvah left the cluster of priests and worked his way to Zefra. "I must talk to you after this," he whispered. "'Tis urgent. I will wait for you and your friends in the healing tent."

He turned to the crowd and raised his hands for silence. When the chaos died to a murmur, he spoke firmly, making eye contact with each person.

"I vouch these brave people have been instructed by the gods themselves. It is no mere whim. How can you put your personal concerns above the safety of the entire world? If the end of civilization and the death of your little children is not enough to stir you to action, think of the future of your soul. If you do not help, I pray the gods will curse you for your apathy and abandon you to darkness forever. May your soul burn in Resef's fire until he has purged you of obstinance. May charity be seared on your conscience with the scorching brand of justice. If you would prefer the gentle light of mercy when you face our God, prove yourself worthy now." He pointed at the man in the back. "I will talk to *you* later." He walked away, leaving Zefra standing alone.

The handsome young Devoran had whispered to his chieftain during Isvah's call to repentance.

His leader waved him off and stood to speak. "We will supply food for the trip there and back. If you get a ship to take you, we will include food for the sailors." He sat again and patted his companion on the knee.

The young man glanced at Zefra. When their eyes met, he was the one who blushed.

A tall man with the Rikatsu badge stood. "We will provide one of our fastest ships for you."

"I have medicines and supplies from the Tukiko. I'm going with them." The speaker behind him was a slender young man wearing the lavender belt of a Rikatsu healer and the mulish look of someone expecting opposition.

"But, Koray," spluttered the tall sailor, "you cannot. I must get you home again. They're expecting you." When the healer ignored him, the sailor sat, muttering to himself.

"What can the rest of us do?" asked a woman in a bright orange robe.

Zefra blinked at the vibrancy and expense of an entire robe that hue. Most Iskrins wore only a dash of color. She looked at her friends for help. "I do not know."

Nia stood, merely head and shoulders above the seated crowd. "Do any of you plan trading journeys soon, close enough to our homes to carry messages to our families? We live in south-central Darrendra, far eastern Nokailana, and south-western Ioj."

Zefra watched until three hands rose. "If you will meet Nia in the morning, she will give you our letters and exact directions."

She cocked her head at Nia to confirm her assignment and had to stifle a giggle when the girl accidentally dropped onto Izo's lap.

Zefra was not sure whose expression was funnier: Nia's shock as she toppled sideways to regain her proper seat, or Izo's wishful embarrassment. Ludik's shoulders shook with muffled laughter. At least the shapeshifter had relaxed enough around them to also think it was funny.

The meeting ended quickly after that. The Rikatsu and Devora sent messenger birds to arrange for the ship and food to be delivered tomorrow. It was fortunate they were close neighbors.

Zefra walked with her friends to Ahjin's tent while she told them what the priest had said. Nia babbled one theory after another about what he would tell them.

Ludik watched the stars. "I was offered a healing apprenticeship," he blurted in the middle of Nia's fantastical hypotheses.

"That is nice," Zefra said. "From whom?"

"That old healer, um, Shri... Shri Okechuku."

Shock froze Zefra's feet. "Okechuku? Why? Will he teach you himself, or find you a teacher?"

"Either," Ludik shrugged, "depending on availability, I suppose." He cleared his throat. "He seems convinced I have healing magic."

Zefra still could not move. "Shri Okechuku thinks you have enough healing magic to teach you *himself*?"

"I know," Ludik nodded, "who knew?" His smile faltered when Zefra did not smile back. "What is wrong?"

"Shri is not his name; 'tis his title," Zefra explained. "It means he's a top-ranked healer with a lot of power. 'Tis a popular exaggeration that the Shri can bring the dead back to life. This false rumor persists because of the many miraculous healings they do perform. If one of them is impressed with you only when partly trained, you must be remarkable. As for Okechuku," she finished in a near whisper, "he's good even for the Shri, but he hardly ever takes an apprentice, even when begged."

Nia whistled and stretched to slap Ludik on the back. "Good work, kitty cat."

Ludik did not even flinch at the forbidden nickname. He and Zefra stood in overwhelmed silence until Nia pulled them toward Ahjin's tent.

Isvah waited inside the tent with an old scroll in his hands. Ahjin was awake and propped with many pillows on two side-by-side cots. Two lamps hung from the tent roof, and an unlit one sat by a collection of bandages and medicines on a low table. The herbal scent of Ludik's salve almost covered the aroma of the kiziak fires. Zefra sat cross-legged by Ludik and traced the colors in the textured weave of the rugs, while Nia curled at Ahjin's feet.

"Bright stars, all," Isvah said. "Thank you for coming. While you were gone, we priests searched our legends for help. Asitha found this." He delicately unrolled the fragile scroll and squinted at the worn writing, tilting it for the best light. "Nobody was jealous of the gods and left the world, vowing to return for revenge." He looked up from the scroll.

"I don't understand." Nia pulled a lock of hair over her shoulder and wrapped it around her arm and hand. "Why write a story about nobody at all? Where's the rest of it? What does it have to do with us?"

"There is only that fragment," Isvah said. "We kept it because it follows one of our oldest legends of creation, but we thought 'twas a mistake. I forgot it until you told us of the scorpion and its nothing rune. 'Tis hard to see," he turned the scroll in Zefra's direction, "but if you look closely, you can see Nobody is written as a proper name."

"You mean," Ludik said, "our mysterious kidnapper has plotted this since the beginning of the world?"

"And those scorpions work for him. Her? It?" Ahjin's feathers rustled.

Nia put a hand on his ankle. "The scorpions said 'him.' The krakens and bats are his, too. What else might he have in store?"

"Is there anything else you can tell us? Any ideas for help or defense?" Zefra asked.

Isvah shook his head sadly. "I'm sorry. I will keep looking until you leave, but that does not give me much time. Warmth to you." He bowed to them and left.

21. DEPARTURE

(HOTARU SUMMER CAMP, ISKRA; OCEAN)

May your journey be pleasant and your companions cheerful, and may the currents shield you from adversity as they carry you to your desire.

Traditional Nokai farewell, frequently shortened to "pleasant journey."

Nia didn't have time to discuss the new information about Nobody before three healers came to reset Ahjin's wings. They laid out various instruments and smelly herbs while Ludik set his half-empty jar of now-famous ointment next to the other medicines and hung a lamp above the cot.

The Hotaru healer escorted Zefra and Nia out. Nia failed to wiggle her way back inside, so she found a spot outside the tent, behind Ahjin's cot. A dip in the scratchy sand made a decent seat after she tucked her robe under her legs to protect from residual heat. Zefra sat beside her with a nervous look.

Koray's muffled voice came through the tent wall. "When this is over, his wings and muscles must be stretched every other day until they're healed. I will teach you how while we travel."

"I didn't know," Ludik mumbled. "My training didn't include birds. I'm sorry, Ahjin."

"Don't worry about it. I've been stretching behind your back." Ahjin's chuckle broke off in a pained gasp.

"I think we're ready," Okechuku said. "Ludik, you hold down his shoulders here, please, and try to think about him healing well. I wish I had time to teach you how to properly use your healing. Heti, hold his legs. Koray, break and reset while I hold his wings. Let me know when you have everything aligned. I will make sure they're partially healed before we leave. And... now."

Ahjin screamed, and the girls flinched.

"'Tis best to finish the breaks before we set anything," Koray panted. "Do not let him tense more."

The other healers must have agreed, for the next sound was another howl that ended in muffled sobs.

Nia buried her face against Zefra's shaking shoulder and cried. Hadn't Ahjin been hurt enough? When would this end? But if the torture meant he'd be able to fly again, he'd think it was worth it, stupid man.

Ahjin's whimpers continued for several minutes. When silence fell, the girls wiped their faces and scrambled to their feet. They tiptoed around the tent and fidgeted at the entrance until Ludik opened it.

He let the girls pass, but his face was ashen, and his hands trembled. "You can come in for a minute. I knew you'd want to check on him." He turned his face and muttered, "I hate this job. Forget the stupid apprenticeship."

Ahjin, with newly splinted wings, kept his face turned to the tent wall. He did squeeze Nia's hand and croak a brief good night. The bandages around his waist were speckled with fresh blood.

Ludik walked them from the tent, then turned back in, jerking the tent flap closed.

Nia wanted to follow the ocean smell that had tantalized her all day, but she was too tired. The girls' guest tent was full of visitors from other clans, sitting on low beds and layered rugs, but her pallet was empty except for her lumpy pack. She shoved it off and tumbled under the covers and into slumber.

The next morning, Nia dragged herself from bed before sunrise and lethargically sat by the open tent flap to write a letter to Mom. So many yawns interrupted her writing, she barely finished before Ludik arrived. He stood outside the tent and waited for her to take his letters and Ahjin's sealed note.

"Zefra is going over maps and stories with everyone in camp." Ludik rolled his eyes. "If you don't feel up to a crowd, don't go near them. I'm going back to help with Ahjin's next exam." He winced. "I saw the other tribes waiting for their morning meal. You decide who is taking which of those messages."

He turned Nia to face the correct direction and pushed gently until she got her legs working. Nia stumbled toward the tables of bread and fruit and cracked wheat, blinking in the faint light. Zefra's mom took the letters from her limp hands and replaced them with a bowl of cereal sprinkled with tart berries the color of Ahjin's eyes.

When Nia finished, she looked up to find three sets of eyes fixed on her face. She picked up the letters Shara had placed by her side.

"Farthest first? Who's going to Darrendra?" Nia asked.

"We are," volunteered a rotund man wearing pale green and brown accents. Kazuki, then.

Nia flipped through the letters. "Maon, Maon... Great smashing waves, is he writing to everyone in the village? That man has almost as much family as I do."

She handed all four letters with a simper at the thick missive for Nemerra. The Kazuki tucked the letters into his robe, struggled to his feet, and bowed before waddling to a guest tent.

"Who's going to Ioj?"

A Chiharu matron with a pink sash around her sedate green gown raised her hand.

Nia pouted. "Oh, I think you should go to the islands, instead." The lady could leave more perfume with Mom.

The hand turned and lowered, waiting.

"Fine, but I hope you're feeling brave," Nia said. "I'm sure Ahjin's parents will be thrilled to discover what their son is doing."

The hand didn't move until Nia dropped Ahjin's letter into it. The woman stood smoothly, bowed, and strode toward the corral.

"So, you're the lucky one." Nia smiled at the last woman's beautiful orange robe. "When you give my letter to my mom, be sure to tell her I love your silk."

The woman grinned. "Can I consider that a hint for a trade?"

"A splendid idea." The two laughed, and when the woman left a little while later, Nia had a new friend and a plan for a gorgeous new dress.

Nia packed her bags with her own outfits instead of desert robes, then fixed her hair into two long braids. She walked to Ahjin's tent and sidled through the tent flap. He was conveniently alone and unfortunately moping again. Ahjin's healers had impressive skills, but she still planned to monitor his emotional state of being herself.

"I've come to rescue you from boredom," she proclaimed. "Also to jam your stuff into your luggage." She shrugged and fluttered her eyelashes.

Ahjin snickered. He lay on his side with his wings stretched over the second cot. "Fortunately for my poor belongings, my most excellent slave, Ludik, has already packed for me this morning. With folding, no less."

Nia pretended to pout, then gave up and laughed. "I count myself lucky not to be your slave. Now I can pester you with impunity. So, how do you feel?"

Ahjin shrugged, and she bounced over and tickled his feet. "How. Do. You. Feel?"

Ahjin gasped, twitching like a fish on a hook. "Lousy, you stinking fish eater, and I'll feel worse if you keep doing that."

"Thank you." Nia released his feet. "Would it kill you to admit it when I asked nicely? Now, how shall I entertain you? Song, story, sheer silliness? Why, Nia," she congratulated herself, "what excellent alliteration."

Ahjin laughed until he had to clutch his injured sides. They passed the day in absurdity, interrupted only for meals and healing sessions.

By the time the ship arrived just after supper, Ahjin's mood seemed to have improved enough for the trip. Nia hoped Ludik and the healers did as well on his physical injuries. It would be better for him to stay here, but they might need his ability to speak to Irajahan. And think of his revenge for being left behind... She shuddered and grabbed his pack while Ludik and Koray transferred him to a stretcher.

All the Iskrins went to the shore to say farewells. Zefra spoke with her family, with hugs and teary kisses all around. The three visitors got a generous share of the farewells, to Nia's sheer enjoyment, Ludik's amusement, and Ahjin's great embarrassment.

Sayaka's family clung to her with dry-eyed somberness before releasing her. Askari said quiet farewells to his friends and then helped the Iskrins ferry the supplies to the ship under the direction of Captain Fathi, a middle-aged man barely taller than Zefra, but with muscled shoulders almost twice as wide. His Iskrin-white skin was as weathered as shark hide.

Nia watched Koray's tall friend lecture him in a whisper for a quarter hour before grudgingly letting him board. Koray rode in the dinghy with Ludik to hold Ahjin steady during transport.

Nia was disappointed the tall ship had plain white sails, but the sleek lines and sanded wood reminded her of home. She sniffed the salt air and watched the ship sway in the waves splashing against the beach.

"So, Zefra, what rules are we using onboard?" She coiled her braids around her head and tied them with her usual rainbow of ribbons.

"What do you mean?" Zefra asked.

"Are we going by Iskrin customs or reverting to our native ones?" Nia pulled the last ribbon tight and turned to her friend with a carefully straight face.

"I suppose it does not matter," Zefra said.

"Then I'm going swimming." Nia kicked off her sandals and pulled her robe over her head.

Izo blushed crimson at the skin-tight, knee-length Nokai attire she had hidden under her desert robe that morning, but he didn't turn away his wide-eyed gaze.

Nia handed everything to Zefra with yet another of Mom's embroidered ribbons. "Please return this with my thanks. And bring my sandals on board with you."

She winked at Izo and ran into the ocean. When the water became too deep for walking, she dove under the billows and circled the ship. The water caressed her skin and supported her in loving waves, and the fish here were nearly the same as the ones around her island. For the first time in weeks, she felt at home.

Zefra gave her family one last round of hugs and then climbed in the dinghy with Sayaka and the last of the sailors.

After the Iskrins had boarded the ship, Nia climbed a rope up the hull. "That was marvelous." She shook water on the deck. "Are we ready to leave?"

A sailor took them below deck and showed them the men's and women's quarters while the crew set sail. They would use the sailors' triple-high hammocks.

Nia snorted. "I'm finally on the ocean again, and you want me to sleep below where I can't see it? I don't think so."

She grabbed a hammock and climbed the ladder, followed by the flabbergasted sailor and most of her friends. She strapped her baggage in an odd corner on deck and strung the hammock above her packs.

"Come join me." She climbed into the hammock and folded her arms behind her head.

"Ahjin needs to keep his bandages dry," Ludik said. "I'll stay nearby to watch him."

Nia looked at Zefra.

"Thank you, but I think I will stay below." Zefra declined with a slight bow and a smile.

"Isn't anybody brave enough to stay up here with me?" Nia challenged.

Askari and Sayaka exchanged glances and then laughed. Askari shook his head and strolled to the ladder while Sayaka swayed Nia's hammock. "You can be brave for all of us, bantam," she teased.

Nia spent the rest of the day humming to herself while she swung in her hammock. Bad things were certainly coming, if Resef's vision was true, which made it more important to enjoy herself now.

The young people passed the slow days in a variety of ways. Zefra asked the sailors for lessons in sailing or knot-tying. Ludik and Koray continued Ahjin's healing, carefully stretching his wings and back while ignoring his complaints. Nia spent each meal asking Ahjin for stories about what she saw as they traveled northeast along the tall cliffs of the Ioj coast. Her favorite tale was about the annual diving competition the Iojif held from the steepest cliff. Ahjin had planned to compete as an adult this year. He looked sad until Nia suggested highly ludicrous dives to perform. At least Ahjin had healed enough that laughter no longer hurt.

The temperature flipped unnaturally each day, between tropically hot and near-freezing. Heaving clouds swelled in the clear sky and poured rain and hail and flung lightning with abandon, and then all would be sunny again. All the sailors greeted the faintest rumble of thunder with instant storm preparations.

The first terrible storm washed Nia overboard. She dove deeply under the tumultuous waves to smoother water and followed the ship until the storm ended. With every toss of the ship above her, she prayed her gill-less friends stayed aboard.

She climbed aboard after the storm. Retreating below decks during the tempests now seemed a measure of her intelligence, not her courage. After that, she held a bucket for Ahjin when his stomach rebelled. As the giant swells menaced them, thoughts of her family and their low island made her swear. When she saw bits of the distant cliffs crumble, she didn't tell Ahjin, but she prayed for her family on their fragile island.

Sudden wind storms gusted so hard the only way to survive them was to furl every sail, lash every person and piece of equipment, and wait for them to pass. The ship lost a small sail once, when the storm grew even faster than before. Worse, when the sail ripped loose, it took with it the sailor who had been trying to save it.

As the frequency and severity of the storms and waves increased, the sailors whispered about doom and the anger of the gods. When the sky burned across the night horizon, they muttered about the end of the world and looked at Ahjin's group with a desperate mix of hope and fear.

Nia shared their fears but couldn't convince herself their hope had a foundation in reality. The best she could do was pretend, so she pretended with all her might.

Ten days into the voyage, Nia cheered when Ahjin limped to the upper deck with a cane. The sailors strung a line of hammocks by Nia, and the seven landlubbers relaxed in the temporary sunshine despite the potential danger. Nia thought Zefra might purr like a kitten in the warm sun while they named cloud shapes.

"So, Ludik and Ahjin," Nia pretended it was an idle question, "what did you write in your letters home? Ooh, do you see the dolphin west of the sun?"

Ahjin looked at her reproachfully. "I see a hawk's head far to the east."

"You tell us about your letters first, minnow," Ludik said. "There is a squirrel above the horizon."

"Oh, you know, the usual things. The sights I've seen, the people I've met, my plans for when I get home, a suggestion to get to high ground." Nia's lip quivered. "And an order for a very special wedding gift for you." She batted her eyelashes. "Your turn."

"Hmm. I wrote something of the sort to my family." Ludik pursed his lips and narrowed his eyes at Nia. "Minus the wedding gift. I wrote something... different to Nemerra." A deep blush rose from his collarbone to his forehead.

Nia chortled in delight. "Your turn, birdbrain." She swung Ahjin's hammock with her foot.

"There's a ship with square sails." Ahjin slid his hand inside his pocket and stared at the clouds.

Nia recognized the stubborn look on his face, but the subtle wince was unfamiliar.

"There's a bird," Nia mimicked, "with a square head." She craned for a better look at his face.

"Leave me alone, you nosy piranha," Ahjin hissed.

"You know she'll drag it out of you anyway," Ludik said. "Don't let her embarrass you."

Nia rubbed her hands in glee. "That's what I think, but I can do it the other way. Let me see..."

Ahjin struggled to sit in his hammock, failed, and glared at her. "I told my parents I was sorry for running away, and I hope they'll still love me enough to tell my little sister nice stories about me after I'm dead. And since you're so snoopy, you can make sure they get the message."

He jerked his hand from his pocket and shook his scarf in her face. Tears glistened in his furious eyes.

Zefra looked at the sky and held her breath.

Nia's lip quivered as her pretense of hope crumbled. Before she could apologize, Ludik jumped out of his hammock. He put one hand on Ahjin and the other on Nia.

"Calm down," he choked. "It will be fine. I'm sure they'll forgive you, even if... um, I'm sure they'll forgive you."

He jiggled Nia's hammock. She blinked back tears. They would never see their families again, and Ahjin was the only one brave enough to admit it.

22.MESSAGES

(NORTH-WEST IOJ)

On the field of battle, the spoken word does not carry far enough, nor can ordinary objects be seen clearly: thus the use of drums and banners.
Beginning Battle Strategy

Nearly two weeks after leaving Iskra, the ship could go no farther. Though his home was long out of sight, Ahjin stood by the railing and watched Ioj creep by on the right and the distant shadow of Darrendra on the left. The Darrendran forest spilled across the strait onto Ioj, with trees clustered darkly up an unusually mild slope. Ahjin had last seen his home country in spring, and now summer was nearly gone.

The yellow light on Resef's map crept closer to the red until Ahjin nearly went insane. While he hadn't liked the finality of the life laid out at home, he didn't care for this much uncertainty, either. They still had no idea who Nobody was or how to free the gods, despite useless hours discussing possibilities. Only their deaths were certain, and that was no improvement now he was healing. But plan or no plan, they would go forward. And if he found a way to succeed *and* save his friends, he would do it, no matter what it cost himself.

Ludik interrupted his musings, looking toward Darrendra and

scuffing his boots on the deck. "Koray agrees you seem healed enough to try flight. Are you ready?"

"Now? Right now?" Ahjin blinked. "Before we land?"

"Do you *want* to wait?" Ludik asked.

Ahjin held his breath and nodded. Now was good. He climbed onto the ship's rail and stretched his wings. Another breath, and a hard flap into the air. The wind tickled his feathers as he reclaimed the sky one wing beat at a time. Joy swirled in his heart.

On the next downstroke, his wing stalled; he spiraled out of control and plummeted into the waves. Water rushed in his ears, and his last breath escaped his lungs.

Before he remembered how to swim, a small hand dragged on his collar.

Nia held him while he coughed. "Come on, breathe. Now, can you swim better than you fly, poor little duck?"

Ahjin had a response but not enough air to share it. He settled for a pointed look. They swam to the ship in silence while the ocean washed tears from his face. Nia scrambled up her usual knotted rope, and the sailors raised Ahjin. Ludik and Koray helped him over the bulwark and into his hammock.

"You knew that would happen." Ahjin squeezed water from his hair while he glared at Ludik. "That's why Nia was there so quickly, and why you said to try now."

"I'm sorry. We might have been wrong."

Ahjin slumped. "You weren't. I can't fly." Somehow, he still wasn't used to the death of his dreams.

Ludik shook him. "Birdbrain. Did you think this was the final test? This was only your *first* attempt."

Hope spiraled up in Ahjin's heart again.

Ludik flicked still-dripping curls out of Ahjin's face. "Based on your performance, we have some exercises for you. You can try again tomorrow."

Ahjin jumped up and hugged him. Koray snickered at the wet splotch left on Ludik's tunic, until Ahjin gave him the same treatment. He didn't mind Koray's fastidious grimace or Ludik's amused offer of another dunking. Ahjin spread his wings in his hammock to dry in the warm sun. All he needed was time and practice to regain his old skills.

By the time the sailors rowed them to the rocky beach, Ahjin and Nia were nearly dry.

"We have supplies for two weeks," the first mate called as the sailors rowed back to the ship. "After that, we will resupply in Darrendra and come back once to check for you."

"Are we ready?" Ahjin asked. "Does anyone want to swim back to the dinghy?"

Ludik looked toward Darrendra and then away. Nia yawned.

Zefra picked up her pack. "Who has the map? Which way do we go from here?"

"I do." Ahjin unrolled it. The red and yellow lights shone close together. "Southeast, not too far."

"You mean we have to go up that mountain?" Zefra complained.

"This is just a large hill, Zefra," Ahjin said. "We're lucky the terrain is so gentle here."

"This is gentle? Are you sure?" Zefra's exotically tilted, dark brown eyes widened under the long, thick lashes that were her first defense against sand.

"Well, ghastly eels, Zefra, terrain is irrelevant for fliers. For those of us stuck on two feet, it's different." Nia shot Ahjin a pointed look. "I'd rather climb a wall of water. But if Ahjin can climb it, so can you."

"We'll divide into teams. I'll take the weakest link." Ludik tousled Ahjin's curls, then stepped out of reach.

Askari paired with Nia, and Sayaka with Zefra. The first two hours were easy, even for Ahjin. Beach shrubbery gave way to tall, densely growing trees that blocked most of the cloud-filtered sunlight. Small animals scurried through the branches and underbrush. Insects buzzed happily in the meager clearings and even more happily when they discovered the fresh meat in their territory. Frequent slapping accompanied the rustle of leaves.

Ahjin amused himself by telling spooky tales of giant, man-killing spiders that legendarily infested this region. After describing their size and eerie demeanor, he lingered on their evil natures. His account of them ensnaring travelers in their invisible ground webs made Zefra shudder and probe the earth with her staff.

Nia laughed until he told how they immobilized their victims with a slow poison that prolonged a painful death for hours. He drawled the final touch. "There is no known antidote."

The pinch she gave his arm was almost as sharp as her glare, but not as pointed as her curses.

When Ahjin explained how the spiders used the bodies of their prey as living hatching grounds for their eggs, Ludik put him in a headlock while Sayaka and Askari firmly requested an end to the horrifying tales.

"Or we will pluck a feather for every word," Sayaka said. Askari stroked a long primary feather.

"They're just stories," Ahjin croaked. "I'll stop."

After that, he used his practice flights above the trees to stay out of range. His early coasts from branch to branch lengthened into flights of a few seconds, then a minute and more.

He didn't, of course, see any giant spiders. Although he reported their absence every hour, his friends still huddled closer together than usual during the night.

In the morning, Ahjin and the others climbed again. Green forest scents almost covered the whiff of the ocean, out of sight beyond the trees, past the western cliffs. The trees leaned closer; the forest grew darker. The slope increased, and the group began to sweat. Tree roots dipped in and out of the earth. Ludik was used to a forest floor and the desert dwellers to shifting sands, but Nia and Ahjin stumbled often. Every stagger jerked his healing muscles.

Nia sang a marching chant until she ran short of air in the rising altitude. The Iskrins' breathing was no steadier. Ahjin, used to flying even higher in the sky, breathed without difficulty and stubbornly ignored how much his back ached despite his lighter-than-normal pack. He carried only a change of clothes, a few personal items, and the small eating knife Ludik had finally returned. The group equipment, food, and the rest of Ahjin's things were divided among the others. When Ludik asked him yet again how he was doing, Ahjin said nothing.

At the next break, Ludik shook a powder into Ahjin's canteen. Ahjin silently drained the bitter tonic while Ludik strapped Ahjin's pack on top of his own. When the others stopped gasping for breath, they trudged uphill again. The incline leveled enough to give them hope of reaching the top.

After another hour of exhausted shambling, they stopped in a gap among the trees. It wasn't really a clearing, since the trees' overlapping branches blocked the sunlight, but it was level enough to use their tiny, twig-fed stove. The unexpected advantage to the heavy cover was the limited shelter offered when rain fell again. By the time the torrent worked through the foliage to the ground, it had thinned to a cold trickle.

After dinner, Nia sagged against a tree and closed her eyes. Ahjin pulled his knees to his chest to stretch his back. Sayaka sat cross-legged as if meditating, but a hint of snoring escaped. Zefra and Askari blinked hard, then leaned against trees to guard in opposite directions. Ludik shifted shape behind a large tree and crept off to scout.

When he returned, Ahjin was the only one awake.

"I guess we won't go farther tonight," Ahjin said.

Ludik walked to the closest pack and rifled through it. "Can you help me with the blankets? We're north enough to get cold at night, even with more reliable weather. I'll take first watch."

Ahjin helped Ludik cover the sleepers, took his own blanket and another dose of tonic, then stretched out and closed his eyes. The last he heard was the scratch of claws on bark and a sigh from a high branch.

Ahjin woke to Ludik's nudge with a groan and a shiver. The fallen leaves crunched with frost, and his breath hung in the air. He was so stiff, he barely rolled to his side to watch as Ludik slept.

When Ludik woke again at dawn, he helped Ahjin sit. While Ahjin stretched and drank a cup of vile-but-effective tea, Ludik tried to wake the others. Nia mumbled, swung a fist, and curled with her blanket over her head. Ahjin chuckled, glad it wasn't his turn to wake the sleeping fiend.

The Iskrins didn't move when shaken. "What's wrong with them?" Ahjin asked.

"I'm not sure," Ludik admitted. "Can you finish waking Nia, please, while I check them?"

Ahjin groaned and crawled to Nia. "Neeeee-ah, wake up." He dripped his medicine into her mouth and sat back on his heels.

She shot upright, spitting out the noxious residue. "Why, you!"

He muffled the rest of her choice commentary with one hand while he used the other to fend off her fists. "I'm sorry, but we need your help," he blurted.

Nia held her breath before exhaling. "What's wrong?" Her voice was sluggish, but her eyes were fiery.

"Ludik can't rouse the others. We don't know what happened."

"They're too cold, but there is no reason for it." Ludik felt Zefra's pulse. "They were fine last night. They ate nothing new. I haven't found any unusual insect bites. I don't see wounds beyond mild blisters. They're breathing, very slowly. Their heartbeats are strong. It gets almost this cold at night in the desert."

"Yes, but not for as long. Could that make a difference?" Nia shivered and yawned. "The desert isn't as dark, either." She looked up at the dim light through the tree branches. "This forest is depressing."

"What do you want us to do?" Ahjin drained his canteen and staggered to his feet with Nia's help.

Ludik felt Sayaka's cheek. "I don't understand."

"Perhaps Nia's right," Ahjin said. "Remember how the Iskrins meditate each morning in the sunrise? Perhaps that isn't only a spiritual thing. We haven't gotten a lot of sunlight for weeks. There wasn't much yesterday, and there isn't much now. When you scouted yesterday, did you see any real clearings nearby?"

"There is one two furlongs in the wrong direction." Ludik pointed and pulled Askari over his shoulders. "I suppose we must take the time. Can you two get Zefra?"

Nia slipped Zefra's arm over her shoulder. "You take right."

She was too short to make up for Ahjin's weakness, so they dragged Zefra's feet, reaching the clearing by the time Ludik came back with Sayaka.

They arranged the sleepers in the brightest sun. Ahjin guarded them while Ludik and Nia fetched the packs.

After an anxious hour, the Iskrins slowly woke. While they ate, Ludik explained what had happened.

Zefra held out one white hand. "Would not darker skin absorb more light? I thought this was camouflage."

"Do you feel better or worse when you tan?" Ahjin asked.

"Tan like leather?" Zefra asked.

Nia chattered in Iskrit, pulling her neckline sideways to show the different shades in her skin.

Zefra ran her finger over the line between the dark and pale golds on Nia's shoulder. "We do not tan."

"Or burn?" Ludik asked.

"You saw Father's hand when he touched the map," Zefra said.

"I mean sunburn."

Zefra shook her head. "Never. We cover ourselves to be modest and retain moisture. If you 'tan' in the sun, why did you not change color in the desert?"

"I live somewhere nearly as sunny," Nia said, "and Ahjin's been with me for a while. We already tanned as much as we're likely to do, and we kept covered in Iskra so we didn't burn."

"What about you?" Zefra asked Ludik.

He put his brown hand next to her white one. "I'm already dark."

"Why do you think we're so white, then?" Zefra persisted.

Askari shrugged. "I'm sure Resef made us correctly. No sense poking a dead fire. What are today's plans?"

"Walk that way," Ahjin indicated the map, "and see what's there."

"That's a lousy plan," Nia complained.

"What do *you* want to do?" Ahjin asked.

Nia sniffed. "Fine, we'll follow your lousy plan."

Ahjin rubbed his aching head. Another day of racing against an unknown deadline. When the earth shook again, he moved up his imaginary timetable. However much time was left before, it was less now.

The forest was still dense despite the shallower incline. After half an hour, the ridge leveled to nearly flat ground. Vines infested the higher branches, growing in tangled patterns that further blocked the sunlight.

The inside of Ahjin's head itched, and he scratched the outside uselessly.

Zefra had a hand on her rune pouch, and Ludik kept glaring at the plants.

"What's wrong with all of you?" Nia asked. "You look like someone spit in your tea this morning."

"Those flowers." Ludik waved his hand. "Did you see those yesterday?"

"No, but I was not looking," Zefra said. "I'm more worried about the wriggle in my pouch. I have checked three times. Nothing is there but my runes, but it jumps like there is a lizard inside."

"I think Irajahan is trying to talk to me again," Ahjin complained. "But all I get is an odd tickle in the back of my head, like someone snoring or shouting through water. It's annoying."

"These flowers," Ludik tried again, "have traditional meanings, and I don't like the combination."

He pointed at hip-high, reddish-pink flowers in the middle of a beautiful pink and purple arrangement. "The catchflies aptly mean snare, and the lavender rose means enchantment." He indicated spicy, pink flowers spiraling up knee-high, gold stems. "These stock mean promptness, or maybe, hurry. I'm confused about the cleome, though." He motioned to the tallest flowers that waved their spidery pink balls of unpleasantly musky blossoms near his shoulders. "They mean 'elope with me,' which doesn't make sense. Maybe Darravani meant 'take me away,' but I'd have picked a different plant."

Ludik frowned as he pointed to a low shrub with purple-black berries. "Those are a late crop of bilberries. They're edible and make a strong dye or ink. But they mean treachery, and—" He shoved Nia away when she knelt to pick them. "Sorry, Nia. They're growing through wolf's bane, which is a deadly poison. Don't touch the purple hooded flowers; the toxin will absorb through your skin."

Nia rubbed the elbow she had banged in her fall. "What does the poison one mean? I want to kill you?"

"Beware, deadly foe is near."

"Of course," Sayaka said. "Any idea who?"

"That is all these flowers say," Ludik said.

"None of that had anything to do with confined spaces or heat or suffocation." Ahjin complained. "I don't know if Irajahan will choke me or broil me first." He tugged his collar and unbuttoned his top button.

"Are you getting anything else from him?" Nia asked.

"Just panic, heat, and the need to get out." He fingered his next button, then glanced at Zefra and dropped his hand. It was only in his head, anyway.

"I wish you could actually talk to Irajahan," Sayaka said, "but if he can get any information to you now, we must be closer. Perhaps all the gods will help before 'tis too late."

"Why didn't I get a message then," Nia pouted. "Makana could send me a dream. I'll nap right now."

"No time," Askari said. "If she did not send one last night, we will do without."

"I had a nightmare last night." Nia crossed her arms and frowned. "Birds flew into a lightning storm and never came out. The clouds rained white feathers until I woke."

Ahjin folded his wings tightly and hoped it was only a nightmare, not a message. "Here, Ludik, does this mean anything?"

Ludik stared at two saplings tangled around each other in the middle of a patch of ferns and white lilies. "Why can't the gods be more clear?" he finally growled. "You are a flame in my heart, magic, maiden charms, and elevation. I don't understand. Is it another warning, or advice, or what?"

"We do have a charming maiden with magical flame," Nia said, "but she isn't tall, and her fire is in her hands, not her heart. Maybe 'elevation' has to do with us climbing the mountain?"

"Who knows," Ludik said. "Maybe Zefra has to climb a tree. This is useless."

"Perhaps our magical maiden can get a clearer message from Resef," Ahjin said. "Zefra, pour out your runes."

"That might explain the twitching." Zefra dumped her runes, which landed face down. "Nothing." She reached for them, and five turned upward by themselves.

She studied them for a minute. "If we assume Resef is using the simplest possible meanings, these two," she pointed to the symbols on either side, "say 'need' and 'earth.' This group of three in the center might spell 'dig.' Clear advice, if we knew where." She touched the rest of the runes. When none moved, she scooped them into her pouch.

As they continued up the hill, they looked unsuccessfully for recently disturbed ground. All they found was a sparkling cactus squatting at the foot of a white-blossomed shrub and two tall flowers in white and scarlet.

"Another goddess bouquet," Sayaka suggested. "She's color-coordinating her confusing messages."

Askari chuckled and murmured something about respect.

Ludik ran through another muttered analysis while he fingered the white flowers. When he stood to report, he broke the tall stalk. "I think 'bound' and 'eternal sleep' go together somehow." He sniffed the flower. "I don't know if our looks do 'freeze' her, or if they should, and I don't know how to 'come down.' It seems the opposite of 'elevation' from before." He inhaled again. "Any other ideas?"

"Perhaps I have to climb a tree and then come down?" Zefra said. "Should you snap off godly messages, Ludik? What if 'tis poisonous, or enchanted, or incredibly disrespectful?"

Ludik sniffed it with a smile. "It isn't toxic or enchanted, and it's just a flower. Creeping valerian fights fevers or makes a black hair dye."

Ahjin smothered a chuckle and made mental notes.

"You didn't take any of the other flowers," Nia asked. "Why this one?" She narrowed her eyes and covered her lavender braids with her hands. "Are you planning to dye someone's hair?"

Ludik blushed under their stares and clenched the stem until it bent. "It's like catmint," he finally said.

"I've never seen you so red," Ahjin teased.

Ludik walked off with the mangled flower still in his fist. The others followed, their laughter covering their anxiety while they looked for more messages from the gods.

23.FOUND
(NORTH-WEST IOJ)

Easier sung than done.
Nokai Proverb

Ahjin and the others found no more messages. Eventually, they stepped into a strange meadow. The far side held a rounded volcano-hill as large as Irajahan's temple. Lava bubbled from a rift in the peak and oozed to a depression at the base. Burning cracks hinted at the inferno under the crust. The fragrance of meadow blossoms and pine trees didn't cover the whiff of sulfur. A violent lightning storm raged at the volcano's summit. Rumbling thunder punctuated the lightning flashes.

A bubbling spring in the middle of the meadow kept the sluggish lava from the forest. The near stream bank bordered marshy sand and mosquitoes. Nia's feet twitched visibly as she stared at the soft grass in the rest of the clearing.

When Ahjin turned to hide his smile, his gaze rose to the sky. A second storm — this one a miniature hurricane no taller than the trees — swirled between the lightning and the woods where he stood. Although the wind fluttered the grass, the rain evaporated ten feet above the ground.

"What place is this?" Ludik asked. "Where do we go from here, Ahjin?"

"I — don't think we go anywhere." Ahjin showed the map. The red and yellow lights had merged to orange.

"But there is nobody here," Zefra wailed. "Is it broken?" She touched the map, and it burst into flames.

Ahjin dropped the map, which burned so ferociously it was gone before it reached the ground.

"Shark bait," Nia swore. "Now we have no help."

"We'll have to do it ourselves." Ahjin brushed ash from his fingers. "Let's start over there."

He pointed to a ridge of discolored bricks, half-concealed behind bushes at the edge of the forest. As they approached, they saw a row of enclosures so short even Nia had to duck to look inside. There were no windows or comforts, just bare stone and bars. The first cage looked scoured, with gouges circling the walls and sand on the floor. Bowed walls of the second were water-stained to the ceiling. The third had deep cracks through the walls and roof. The last was blackened and reeked of smoke.

"It looks like a prison break," Nia said.

"If the gods are free, why are we here?" Zefra slumped on one cage. "Why not send us home?"

"They're not free." Ahjin tugged his collar again. Irajahan still choked, somewhere.

"If they aren't free," Nia said, "then they're... moved to somewhere more secure?"

"Where do we look now?" Zefra asked. "We have no more map."

"Perhaps the messages will help," Sayaka said.

"Most of them are cryptic," Ludik said. "Perhaps the first one means 'Hurry, take me from the enchanted snare before the deadly foe betrays you'? Or perhaps the snare *is* the treachery of the deadly foe?"

"Brilliant, Ludik," Nia said.

Ludik grinned. "I've been thinking about it for a while."

"So what kinds of snares can hold our gods?" Ahjin asked.

"Something remarkable," Askari said. "Even with probable enchantments, those cages did not last."

"Remarkable like a suspended typhoon?" Zefra looked at the miniature storm.

"Perhaps exactly like that," Sayaka agreed. "Do any of our messages match?"

"Not heat or confined spaces," Ahjin said.

"It does not match 'earth' or 'dig' in any way," Zefra said, "but it could match 'elevation' or 'freeze.'"

"Do you think you can evaporate it with your fire?" Askari asked.

Zefra shook her head. "I do not have that much power."

Nia choked, pointing at the savage firestorm atop the volcano. "That looks exactly like my nightmare, except it isn't raining feathers. In the islands, we see volcanoes generate similar storms."

"I don't recall any inland volcanoes here," Ahjin said. "We should check it as well as both storms."

Nia looked at Ahjin's alabaster wings and tears ran down her face. "Stupid storms." She flung a rock at the hurricane, and it bounced off an invisible barrier.

Ahjin wrapped his arm around her shoulders. "If it's solid enough to deflect a stone, perhaps it's solid enough to 'come down.'"

"If the gods are in the storms, are they all there, or only two?" Nia scrubbed tears from her face. "Maybe we can rescue one and get help with the others."

"Let's find the easiest one to free," he said. "With godly help, perhaps we can change Resef's prediction."

"The hurricane is close to the trees," Ludik said. "I'll climb for a look. Ahjin, can you fly by the lightning?"

Nia linked arms with Zefra and Sayaka. "There were more clues. We'll search for hot, confined spaces and earth to dig."

Ahjin walked to the base of the volcano with Askari, then scooped up rocks and flew toward the storm until his hair stood on end. The clouds were too thick to see inside. He threw a rock at it, with the same bouncing results. When he turned invisible and tried again, the rock went through the storm and emerged smoking. That was interesting.

He landed, and Askari helped him stagger back to the others. When would mere flying not tire him? The pain was less, but he was exhausted even without his aerobatics. It would take a long time to regain his old skills.

As they approached, Ludik swung out of the trees. Zefra sat in the meadow with stockinged feet and a muddy robe, cleaning a remarkable amount of dirt off her boots. Nia and Sayaka were nearly as dirty.

"What happened to you, Zefra?" Ludik asked.

Ahjin's feathers crackled, and his wings dragged. Since he wasn't actually hurt, he ignored Ludik's glare.

"You wanted somewhere to dig. How about quicksand?" Zefra pointed toward a patch on the stream bank opposite the volcano. She rubbed her boots in the grass again before pulling them on her feet.

"Quicksand." Ludik groaned. "What about the lightning storm, Ahjin?"

Ahjin reported, ending with the problem he knew his friend was pondering. "No, Nia, I don't know how the storm could see me, but we shouldn't tackle that prison without help."

Nia glanced at his wings again and sighed with relief.

"I saw nothing useful," Ludik said. "Anyone else?"

"We think Irajahan is buried under that pile of lava at the base of the volcano," Sayaka said. "That is our guess for a small, hot place. I do not think a storm of any kind would panic him as badly as you say he is."

"We cannot dig through lava," Askari said, "but quicksand is not that dangerous, and 'tis only a small patch."

"I saw large, flat stones we can use to dig," Zefra said. "And we have a trowel."

"Ludik can use his paws," Nia suggested with wide eyes and a hint of a smile.

Ludik growled and stomped off. He returned as a panther and licked Nia's ear until she squealed and swatted him. While the others collected stones, he loped to the quicksand and began excavating.

"Wait." Askari tied a rope around the big cat's torso and gave it to Ahjin. "This is just a precaution, and you should not strain your back bending." He took a stone from Sayaka and joined the diggers at the edge of the quicksand.

The single trowel worked better than the stones, but Ludik's big paws worked best. He flung out a heap of wet sand, one pawful at a time. He was making good progress until he suddenly disappeared under the surface.

Ludik was gone!

Ahjin yanked on the rope. Instead of moving backward, it tugged him into the sand, which sucked at his feet almost like it was alive. He couldn't float on top without releasing the tension on Ludik's safety line. There wasn't enough purchase to rescue Ludik.

Ahjin couldn't get his own feet free. The farther he sank, the more he feared he'd be swallowed by the earth and never fly again. He screamed.

Hands grabbed his shoulders. Arms wrapped around his chest and yanked backward. Ahjin choked down his cries and held the rope while the others dragged him from the mud. Once his feet were on solid ground, everyone pulled the line.

Ludik's head and shoulders emerged a moment later. He struggled for purchase until the others pulled him close to the solid edge.

"You're fine, settle down," Nia told the snarling panther as he crawled out. "You're free. Let me help — stop cursing before I translate and embarrass you." She dug through her pack and threw soap at him. "If you're not ready to speak nicely, you can wash in the stream while we plan. No, by the waves, my soap will not make you smell like a *girl*. But if it did, it might be an improvement."

Ludik swatted the soap toward the bank and stalked after it. Ahjin settled for a clean pair of socks.

"It should have worked," Askari said. "Natural quicksand does not suck actively, but this would explain why that god has not surfaced."

"'Tis magic, of course." Sayaka wrapped bandages around her rope-burned hands.

"Hey," Nia murmured in Ahjin's ear while she finger-combed mud from his feathers. "Are you better now?"

Ahjin flushed. "I'm fine," he whispered. "It was only the thought of my head going under." He brushed at the line of mud that ended at his shoulders. "It was silly." If he was lucky, they'd think his scream was for Ludik.

"You stayed to help, and that's what matters." Nia raised her voice to a normal level. "That's all the mud I can remove. What do we do now?"

"I have an idea," Zefra said. "We should drag the hurricane to the lava, to evaporate the storm and freeze the molten rock. After the lava is cool, we can break it out. It matches the gods' clues, approximately. 'Come down and freeze' the 'flame in the heart' before we 'dig earth,' perhaps?"

Ahjin nodded. In theory, at least, it sounded reasonable. "Let's try it."

Zefra rolled up her sleeves and lay in the sun for an hour. After she energized her fire-calling, Askari and the girls jumped over the narrow stream, away from the quicksand, and spread out on either side of the lava pool. While Ludik climbed the tall tree closest to the hurricane, Ahjin flew up slowly. By the time he landed at the top, Ludik had used his claws to slice a large section of thin vines from the branches. The creepers grew in interconnected groups, as if they had been woven together.

Ludik shifted form and shrugged into his tunic. "I've never seen vines like this, Ahjin. I see no flowers or leaves." He pointed to an uncut creeper as he tied long vines to the corners of the makeshift net. "I can't tell how they get nutrients up here, unless this sap collects pollen or something. I wish we had enough rope to not use these." He gave the net to Ahjin with the dangling ends coiled.

"At least they aren't mythical, invisible ground webs," Ahjin said. "Are you ready?"

"As much as possible." Ludik picked up half the net and walked toward the end of his branch.

They spread the net between their two branches. On the ground, Zefra raised her hands. It was time. Ahjin jumped high, flapping hard in the warm updraft Zefra created. As he flew backward, the net tightened. Ludik took a few more steps until his branch bent. Ahjin beat his wings harder. He had to get high enough before the branch broke under Ludik.

Just in time, the vine net reached over the top of the hurricane. It caught as if the storm were solid instead of the indefinite mass of rotating air and water it should have been. Ludik fell from the branch, holding one of his ropes. He dropped the other for Askari to grab from below. Ahjin plunged from the third corner while Sayaka and Zefra grabbed the rope he dropped from the fourth.

"A little to the left." Nia called.

As Ahjin reached the ground, she ran to help him pull. With six of them pulling from both sides of the lava pit, the hurricane gradually sank toward the ground. It was the oddest thing Ahjin had ever seen. If he hadn't been convinced before that magic was involved, he was now. It didn't make him happier.

As the hurricane dropped, the wind and rain engulfed them. They were blinded, wrapped in freezing shrouds of clinging hair and clothing. Two more hard pulls, and the hurricane slammed on the pool of lava.

When the cold deluge hit the pool of steaming lava, the hurricane shrank and the hot rock exploded. The spinning winds flung the steaming rubble in all directions. Embers showered over them, and head-sized, spiky coals thudded across the ground. Spears of nearly molten glass shot through the air with utter disregard for fragile skin and flesh. The nearest trees splintered.

Everyone let go of the net and dove for cover. With the restraints on the storm released, the diminished typhoon rose again.

"Ashes, no," croaked Zefra.

She rolled across the volcanic glass to her knees and reached toward the rising hurricane. Flames shot from her bleeding hands to the whirling gusts. The rain steamed, and the wind evaporated.

As the storm finally dissolved, a figure dropped from the boiling cloud and crashed into the emptied lava pit. The steam kept Ahjin from seeing which god they had freed.

Zefra's fire vanished. She collapsed in the middle of the smoking debris.

Nia ran to Zefra. The other four raced across the hot ground for the lava pit, dodging the steaming rocks and shards of burning glass. Occasional exclamations marked when someone misjudged a step. Ahjin hit one of the large coals and felt the scorching heat through his boots, but he shook it off and kept going until he could see into the pit left from the exploded pool of lava.

The falling body had landed in the pit, on top of another person. The one from the sky was — scrambled. Ahjin thought he saw a cat's tail, and here a wolf's paw, and over there an elephant's trunk that shimmered into a boar's tusk. Size and shape changed without warning, and body parts did not come close to matching.

The one on the bottom had a fancy orange robe and scorch marks marring his very large, silver wings. He was gagged and wrapped from shoulder to ankle with rope.

"No wonder he was frantic." Ahjin shuddered. The quicksand had been bad enough.

Neither of the gods moved or spoke.

"You were right, Sayaka," Ludik said. "That must be Irajahan with the shiny wings. And I'm afraid my goddess is squashing him." He ran to fetch their rope.

"Can she stop doing that?" Ahjin looked away, nauseated by Darravani's fluctuations.

Ludik returned and climbed down the rope. He removed the bindings on Irajahan and determined both deities were breathing. Though Irajahan was smaller than Ludik, his wings were so oversized they could barely wrap the line around him. Getting him out of the jagged lava pit took two of them pulling from above while two pushed from below.

Darravani changed size and shape so erratically, each random shift slid her from the restraints. In the end, Sayaka tied the rope to her own waist and gripped the goddess in her arms while the other three dragged and pushed them out together.

They cleared a spot of ground by the pit and laid Zefra next to the two gods. Everyone else's minor cuts and burns would wait.

Ludik examined the gods and Zefra, then leaned back on his heels. "Zefra must rest until she regains her strength, if she can. Irajahan is drugged with something I don't know. Where do I even start with Darravani?"

"Please let there be good news, then." Nia pressed one of Zefra's hands between her own to staunch the bleeding cuts.

Ahjin crouched and did the same with her other hand while Ludik rummaged for bandages.

"We rescued two gods. I think they'll recover if they get the time, and hopefully Zefra will, too. Maybe the other gods will help if we can save them." Ludik wrapped Zefra's hands, then started on everyone else.

"We're lucky we had Zefra to destroy the hurricane," Nia said, "but there are two gods left to find. There's no way a lightning storm would hold Resef, so he has to be in the quicksand. Can't we wait for Darravani to recover? She can help us rescue him, and then he can free Makana from the lightning." She sniffled. "Look what happened to Zefra."

"Darravani said to hurry," Ludik said. The earth shook again, as if in emphasis, and the sun flared.

"Resef's advice didn't work." Ahjin's voice cracked. "We've used Darravani's hints. It's time to follow Makana's dream."

He took off his jacket, torn again by the flying glass, and laid it across Zefra for warmth. He wouldn't need it anymore. Nia could take it to his parents later, when she made sure the letter had arrived. Resef's vision and Makana's dream had made his fate clear. They had tried every alternative, and failure was sour in his dry mouth.

"No, Ahjin," Nia whispered. "We'll find another way. You can't do this." She burst into tears.

"We don't have time." He wrapped Nia in a tight hug. "There are still two gods left to save, and you and the others deserve a chance. If I rescue Makana, she can save Resef, and the gods can save the world together."

The earth shook again, and the sun flickered behind the roiling clouds. No, it didn't matter what befell him, he thought numbly. His parents would understand.

Ahjin shuffled toward his other friends and clasped their hands. When he took Ludik's left hand, he hoped the Iojif were as wrong about left-handers being unlucky as they were about them being clumsy. His friends needed luck now, though it was too late for him. One of the remaining gods must be able to help them.

He tied his mended scarf snugly around his waist and forced his heavy limbs toward the burning hill. The remaining mud on his feathers kept him from fine aerobatic control, even if his injuries didn't, but this would be a simpler task.

He turned invisible and flew high toward the volcano, then swung around to approach from the back. If he built enough speed, he might punch through the lightning storm. When he thought he was in the right position, he took a deep breath and dove as fast as his half-healed state allowed.

As he crossed into the storm, hot and cold winds pummeled him from all sides and stole his breath. His wings wrenched in ways they were not built to move, and the damaged muscles in his back tore again.

Lightning filled the air with the stinging scent of charred feathers. Even when he closed his eyes, the fiery bolts imprinted in his mind. His hair stood on end, and his burnt feathers crackled. He forced his eyes open and searched between the lightning strikes for the goddess that had to be there.

Was that a dark figure in the middle of the cloud? A sizzling fire bolt ripped down his side. Burning pain shot through his entire body. He screamed and jerked forward, still searching the darkness.

There she was! He lunged and grabbed her limp body. Now to get out, if he could.

He dove toward the edge of the storm, which multiplied its turmoil. The winds blew him head over heels, and his wings creaked and snapped. Lightning zapped him again and again until his muscles stuttered. The rolling thunder drowned out his cries of pain. The edge of the storm was right in front of him. He tightened his grip on Makana and swept his aching wings once more toward freedom.

As the lighting strikes homed in more accurately, his consciousness faded to fire-streaked gray.

24.ATTACK
(NORTH-WEST IOJ)

Do not press desperate foes too hard. If there is no escape, they will prefer death.

Beginning Battle Strategy

Ludik clenched his fists and watched the lightning double inside the storm. What was taking Ahjin so long?

Someone tumbled from the storm, crackling with lightning. After a moment, Ahjin flickered into view with his arms wrapped around the other figure, wings barely flapping. As they fell, Ahjin's wings collapsed, and the glide turned into a plummet.

Ludik swore and ran toward Ahjin, wishing for an intact net.

Just before the goddess and Ahjin hit the ground, Askari tackled them toward the stream. The three rolled down the muddy bank and splashed into the water. Askari yelped, but the other two were silent.

Nia dove for Ahjin while Askari grabbed the goddess' striped hair and lifted her head above water. Everyone fumbled across the mud and wet grass to drag the unconscious victims out of the stream.

Nia climbed easily from the water, but Askari struggled to exit with only one arm while the other hung limply.

Ahjin and Makanavailea did not move as they were carried a safe distance from the bank. Black scorch marks and vivid red burns covered both of them. Ahjin's wings bent in a dozen directions.

"Are you well, Askari?" Ludik asked.

"I think I broke my arm on a rock, but it can wait. What do you need?"

"I need my kit, and more blankets, and fresh water." Ludik laid the goddess on her back in the grass.

Sayaka did the same for Ahjin, carefully avoiding his fractured wings, while Askari and Nia ran for the supplies.

The goddess's pretty gown hung in shreds, and her long hair crackled as Ludik moved it to the side. The burns across her golden skin were a grisly mix of old and new, but she had fewer injuries than he'd expected. Maybe her power had protected her a little.

"Ludik," Sayaka said. "Ahjin is not breathing, and I cannot hear a heartbeat."

"Plague fleas!" Ludik flung himself over Makanavailea. "No, no, no," he roared. "Don't you dare." He pressed his hands in the middle of Ahjin's chest. Nothing. He did it again, then blew air down Ahjin's throat. "Sayaka, push on his chest right *here*. Press *hard* and fast while I breathe for him. Don't stop until I say."

Ludik inflated Ahjin's lungs again, then bellowed for Askari and Nia.

They ran, arms full of supplies, and skidded to a stop at his side. Nia wailed. Askari shook her shoulder until her howls faded to whimpers.

"We're here, Ludik," Askari said.

"I need you two..." Ludik paused to breathe for Ahjin, "to wash Makana with cool water... and cover her burns with my salve... If we haven't finished by then... you can start on Ahjin."

Not that Ahjin would need burn treatment if his heart and lungs didn't work.

After a few very long minutes, Ludik sat back on his heels. It was no use. He had failed his friend. He rubbed his burning eyes and tried to swallow the lump of guilt in his throat.

When he opened his eyes, Sayaka's mouth was agape. She stared as a dark brown hand withdrew from Ahjin's chest.

"I'm sorry," Darravani sighed. "That is all I can do now." She wavered into wolf shape and put her head on her paws.

Ahjin gasped for air.

Ludik placed a hand on Ahjin's chest and felt his own heart pounding in time to Ahjin's weak heartbeat. "Thank you," he whispered.

The wolf's ears flicked forward. The goddess reformed into a small, kneeling elephant, head hanging in exhaustion. If Ludik had a chance after he dealt with the others, he'd see if a restorative tea would help.

Askari and Nia finished treating Makana. Sayaka anointed Ahjin's burns, while Ludik splinted the major breaks in his wings. Bandages covered most of Ahjin's body, some tied in place with familiar ribbons.

Ludik glanced toward the lava pit. Zefra was still motionless, but Irajahan was awake, silver hair sticking out in all directions above his frantic eyes. He curled in a ball with his arms wrapped around his knees, squealing and mumbling.

Darravani didn't move except for her random transformations. Since she had crossed the stream by herself, he assumed she would recover. Ludik edged toward Irajahan and got within pouncing distance before the god screamed and grabbed rocks.

Ludik froze and held up his hands, keeping his voice low. "Good to see you. You're free now. Can I help?" He ducked a rock. "May I come closer?"

"Leave me alone, go away!" Irajahan scooted backward until his wings tangled under him. "I won't go back." He threw another rock, and his light gray eyes swirled with dark gray storms.

"He will be fine," Darravani croaked from her lynx's mouth. "If you get too close, he might pull himself together enough to hurt you." She shifted into an antelope without changing position.

Ludik carried Zefra across the stream, laying her by Ahjin and the two goddesses. She barely breathed, and her pulse was slow. Hopefully, she'd be safe farther from the sluggish volcano and its lightning storm. At the least, moving her from the field of steaming glass shards and smoking coals would make it easier to watch her.

"What's our plan to rescue Resef?" Nia asked.

"Makanavailea cannot help," Sayaka said.

"Nor Irajahan," Ludik added.

"Lady, I regret your distress, but can you help us save Resef?" Askari bowed graciously over his broken arm.

The ewe bowed her head. For a moment, a tall woman appeared. Her skin was a darker brown than Ludik's, and the ash blonde hair that waved halfway down her slender back was streaked with tawny brown. Subtly clawed hands flexed in her lap.

"As you can see, I am not yet recovered." Darravani's cat-slitted, hazel eyes were apologetic. "And, alas, when I do regain my strength, I have other things I *must* do." The earth trembled again, and she flickered into a colossal bear before reverting. "Where is Resef, that you think I can help?"

"At the bottom of the quicksand." Nia pointed. "We tried digging him out, but failed."

"I cannot go down there." Darravani blinked into horse form and back. "I can pull the earth to the sides of the pit, leaving just the water so you can dive for Resef. Be warned: the rush of water will not be good for him. You will have little time before it's too late for you both."

"Can you take a rope with you, Nia?" Ludik ran to retrieve it.

Nia and Sayaka half-carried Darravani to the quicksand. While the goddess drew her hands apart and pressed against an imaginary tunnel, Sayaka supported her shifting form.

"Hand me the rope, please." Nia slipped off her sandals and let Ludik loop the rope around her body. She tied a fancy knot and tested its hold.

"Be careful," Ludik said. "Pull twice when you're ready." He wrapped the other end of the rope around his waist and braced himself next to Askari.

Nia inhaled. "Courage," she murmured. "I can do this." She jumped feet first into the pool of now merely muddy water. She disappeared under the surface, and the rope pulled tight.

Ludik held his breath until he ran out of air. After three minutes, Nia was still underwater. He jiggled the rope. Still taut.

Darravani's eyes closed, and her shape varied rapidly again. At least she no longer shifted each limb separately.

After a few more minutes, the rope jerked twice. Ludik braced himself and pulled. Askari knelt by the quicksand, ready to help Nia.

Dark curls surfaced, dripping across desert-white skin. Resef dragged a hand from the pit to wipe muddy water from his face. His tilted eyes blinked open and revealed a mischievous amber gaze.

"Bright day, and my thanks." He pulled on Askari's outstretched hand until he could grip the long grass and haul himself free.

When the stocky god's feet emerged, a small fist was wrapped firmly around one ankle. Ludik shouted in relief and pulled Nia from the water.

Nia's hands and bare feet bled. She threw herself flat and patted the ground. "Good earth," she crooned. "I never thought I'd be happy to be out of the water." She coughed and closed her eyes, still clutching the grass.

Darravani collapsed despite Sayaka's support. Ludik considered the women, Askari's broken arm, and Resef, who sat on the ground with the sleeve of his plain, black robe pressed against a shallow cut on his cheek. Cuts and breaks could wait; he turned to help the goddess.

Resef snagged Ludik's robe. "I will take care of her, and I'm fine. You help your friends." He loped around the reconstituting quicksand and gathered Darravani into his arms.

Ludik turned back to Nia and brushed the hair from her face. "How are you?"

"I think my gills are clogged," she choked. "The farther down I went, the more sand was in the water. I couldn't see and could barely breathe."

Ludik brushed the largest chunks of mud from her gills. "You're so brave."

"I've swum in the dark before, but not in such *thick* water." Nia coughed again. "I thought I'd never reach bottom."

Ludik took a water gourd from Askari. As he washed off the sand, Nia's breathing gradually eased.

"I can bandage her cuts," Sayaka said, "while you fix Askari's arm." She moved the stream of water to Nia's hands and arms. "How did you do this, anyway, Nia?"

"I'm afraid it is my fault." Resef helped Darravani, now conscious, to sit. "I tried to boil away the water and dig myself out, but the sand melted into glass. She had to break it to free me."

Ludik stopped in the middle of arranging Askari flat on the ground. "You're awfully hard on your feet, Nia." He braced his foot against Askari's chest and pulled steadily on his arm until the bones slid together, then splinted the arm. "Try not to bump this." He helped Askari settle his arm in a scarf-sling.

"I couldn't leave him there," Nia continued. "I was sure if I came up to get a rock to break the glass, I'd never get down again. At least he was ready when I broke it. And we got the rope around him before the water weakened him too much." She hissed as Sayaka salved her cuts.

Movement in the forest caught Ludik's gaze. He squinted, and his heart sank at the shadows moving in the treetops. "The cleome make sense now. It wasn't their traditional meaning we needed, but their nickname, 'spider flowers.' It seems the Iojif legends are true. Those were webs, not vines, and we're out of time."

"I see nothing," Askari said.

"Neither do I, but Ludik has better eyesight." Nia shuddered and pushed her untied braids out of her face. "If there are real spiders like the ones in Ahjin's stories — ugh."

The earth shook hard, knocking everyone off their feet. The sky darkened. Irajahan bolted into the air.

"You'd better go after him," Darravani told Resef. "We need his help." She motioned to the storm crackling across the sky, clouds racing back and forth in front of the swollen sun.

"I cannot," Resef objected. "If I do not keep the sun from exploding, nothing else will matter. You must settle these earthquakes. What about Makana?"

"Your accidental glass protected you a little. She isn't conscious, and when she wakes, she must pacify the oceans. Besides, you're the only one who can catch Irajahan in the air."

Resef ran his fingers through his short hair. Red highlights shone in his rapidly drying black curls. "You win." His grimace turned into a sly grin. "Perhaps I can deal with three of our problems, instead of only two. Warmth to you."

He threw Makana's unconscious body over one strong shoulder and waved his free arm. A comet hurtled from the sky, heading straight toward them. Ludik's jaw dropped, and Nia squealed.

Just before impact, the horse-sized comet jerked to a stop by the Iskrin god of fire, searing the grass under it. Darravani cleared her throat, and the flames curled inward until they no longer touched the meadow.

Resef blew her a kiss and jumped aboard the fireball, which shot into the sky with a crackle. When the blaze of light crossed above the turbulent ocean, a body toppled from the sky and splashed into the tidal waves.

Ludik yelled and reached to the empty air.

"Don't worry, Makana will be fine," Darravani said. "She can't drown, and the ocean will heal her. I'm sure she'll discuss the delivery method with Resef later." Another tremor shook. "Please excuse me. I have work to do with the earth now."

"Wait," Ludik begged, "can't you help us with the spiders first?"

By now, the arachnids were close enough that the far end of the meadow was an acre of darkness.

"No, and I must ask you to protect me as well, for as long as you can." Darravani settled herself cross-legged, palms pressed to the earth, and closed her sad eyes.

"Plague fleas," Ludik swore. "Battle plans that *don't* include godly help?"

"Long-range weapons as long as possible." Sayaka had her bow strung already.

Ludik laid Ahjin's weapons beside the avian, though it was a useless gesture. After he strung his bow, the four warriors circled the wounded. Sayaka and Ludik fired arrows quickly. Whenever they hit, their target exploded, but the spiders were agile and frequently evaded the missiles.

The closer the enemy came, the more alarming they appeared. They skittered closer on hairy legs, standing knee-high to Ludik. The largest spiders came nearly to Nia's waist. They were various blacks, grays, and browns, and their black eyes reflected red from the dying sun. Their frenzied chittering, almost too high-pitched to hear, squealed painfully in Ludik's ears. Worst of all, their fangs glistened with drops of pale green.

"Try to stay away from their fangs," Ludik said.

"I wasn't *planning* to let them bite me." Nia rolled her eyes. She held her net as if to measure it against the attacking horde.

"Can you understand what they're saying?" Ludik asked. "Or estimate their intelligence?"

"Too many of them are speaking at once," Nia said, "but I think they're coordinating their attack."

"How lucky we are." Sayaka punctuated her sarcasm with another shot into the arachnids.

When the spiders got too close for the bows, Sayaka switched to her staff. Although less fatal than her sword, it was longer and smashed the arachnids at a distance. Askari wielded his long saif with his good hand. Nia used her harpoon as a deadly mix of spear and staff.

"You've been practicing, I see," Ludik praised, smashing half a dozen spiders with one swing of his ax.

"Sailing as a passenger was boring." Nia stabbed a spider. "I wanted to be dangerous if we met more scorpions."

"I suppose these are close enough." Ludik chopped through another batch of arachnids. Nemerra's hidden steel greaves were more handy than ever as he used his sturdy boots to kick any spiders that came too close.

The spiders ran across the corpses of their own companions in an endless stream.

"I don't think we can win this way," Nia panted. She swept away more monsters with her harpoon.

"We don't have to win," Ludik said. "We only have to stall long enough for Darravani to finish."

Nia stabbed another spider. "I don't think I like that plan."

There was no help in sight. Ludik wearily fought on, slowed by fatigue and injuries, hope buried under the constant onslaught.

"Ludik, watch out!" Nia yelled. "They're—"

A large cluster of spiders swarmed Ludik's ax and weighed it down. His rope-burned hands lost their grip. The arachnids dragged his weapon into the mountain of carrion.

"Mongrel curs!" Ludik dodged the next wave of spiders and transformed into a jaguar. His tunic ripped from neck to hem, and his abandoned boots fell against Zefra's arm. He charged the spiders with a roar.

Nia shouted warnings until a spider scurried under her guard and bit her sandaled foot. She screamed and fought on, slowing and stumbling. After a minute, she collapsed with ashen skin.

Askari flinched as a spider jumped in his face. He yelled and thrashed wildly. With one arm in the sling, he didn't regain his balance before more spiders attacked.

Ludik tried to reach him, but Askari fell under a river of the monsters.

Ludik headed for Sayaka, intending to fight back-to-back. He got less than halfway around the circle before she was rushed by the arachnids. She backed up and stumbled over Askari's body. That was the only mistake the spiders needed. Sayaka screamed as the writhing darkness buried her.

Ludik raced around the circle in a vain attempt to defend all sides. A sudden pain stung his flank. He raked off a spider and turned his fury on the rest of the monsters, but fire ran through his back. His legs fell limp. The spiders swarmed by the hundreds, hairy feet tickling and itching and stinging every inch of his body, until their sheer weight buried him.

His friends were dead. He was dying. The entire world was doomed if they had not bought enough time for Darravani to settle the earthquakes. Immobility crept up his body, dulling the searing pain. He forced his eyes open to stay awake until the very end of hope.

His sweetheart's face swam before his eyes, then faded. Ludik blinked, desperate to bring her back in focus. "Nemerra," he whispered with a paralyzed tongue. She would never know why he didn't return.

Her illusion disappeared. The lightning storm fizzled and died. The volcano stopped belching lava. Hairy legs rustled in the spider army, and the horde split from the meadow to the forest. A slight figure entered the corridor, carrying a spear and a bow.

Ludik's vision went black.

25.NOBODY

(NORTH-WEST IOJ)

Be as fast as the wind, as silent as a forest, as ferocious as fire, and as unstoppable as water.
Beginning Battle Strategy

A warm hand brushed Ahjin's ankle. Energy trickled through his veins, but not enough for him to move his stiffened limbs or open his eyes. What had happened? He remembered nothing after the lightning.

"Are you disappointed your little helpers failed?" The irate words echoed faintly above him. "If prison won't hold you, I have a more permanent solution."

Ahjin struggled to open his eyes despite overwhelming fatigue and blinding sunlight from an obviously recovering sun. Who was speaking?

If prison won't hold you. Chills ran up his spine. This must be the gods' enemy, the one the scroll and the scorpion called Nobody. If only Ahjin could see where — or who — he was.

"We need a better solution, but not that one," a woman's soft voice replied nearby. "Can't we talk?"

Was it her hand on his ankle? She'd escaped Nobody's prison; she must be Makana or Darravani. Darravani couldn't talk the last time he'd seen her. Had she recovered? Or had he rescued Makana?

He tried again to blink open his eyes and failed. His fingers barely twitched. Cool, flexible strands tickled his hand. Grass. The meadow.

Ahjin's nerves screamed into working order. His heart stuttered, and his skin stung worse than the time he'd crashed into a beehive. His entire body ached, and the familiar throb of broken bones laced all through his wings, not just the previously fractured ends.

Even with magic, breaks higher in the wing rarely healed well. Would he be flightless again, perhaps permanently?

But Nia said to hope, and despair could wait until after he talked to Ludik. Besides, the conversation between Nobody and the goddess continued above him. He had to know what was happening.

"Nothing you say can be trusted," Nobody scoffed. "You'd prefer I disappear. What if I don't want to?" Soft laughter followed, accompanied by a terrifying chittering and clicking.

"Would you be open to another way?" the goddess asked. "What if a neutral party mediated? I give my binding word to tell the truth and cooperate. If you believe we cannot avoid bias, we would allow the mediator to make decisions after our discussion."

Her hand tightened on Ahjin's ankle. Heat raced through his entire body. The largest breaks in his wings snapped together as his pain multiplied briefly from agony into torture, then dwindled to mere distress.

"I agree," another unfamiliar man rumbled over a sudden rushing static.

Ahjin's eyes finally opened, but his view of the meadow was blocked by a circle of living, giant spiders perched on heaps of dead ones. He shuddered. So much for telling his friends they were only legends.

"I also agree," said another woman's soothing voice.

Who were they? Where were his friends? Ahjin couldn't turn his head to see anything but the nightmarish spiders.

"I don't." Irajahan pressed inside Ahjin's head, his petulance unmistakable even through the haze of misery. "We should kill him now. Choose *that* solution. I'd be happy to carry out the sentence."

Ahjin forced his head to turn.

Irajahan posed with crossed arms a few feet away, hair and eyes much calmer than the last time Ahjin had seen him. His long satin robe was returned to its former orange glory, with yellow brocade suns cheerfully reflecting onto his mirror-bright wings.

At Irajahan's left, a brawny, dark-haired man in a black robe stepped off a comet as tall as Ludik. Desert-white skin meant he must be Resef. He removed his arm from the waist of the dazzling woman who had been riding with him and waved to dismiss his blazing fireball. Resef loosened the curved knife in his black leather belt and pulled a steel-capped staff from under his other arm.

The lavender-eyed woman with bare, webbed feet competently held a barbed harpoon, despite the flowing gown of iridescent pink and purple that clung to her generous curves. Pale scars covered her face and bare arms. Right before Ahjin's eyes, one blemish faded into unmarked golden skin. Harpoon plus lightning scars. Makana. Her hip-length fall of silken hair combined all the Nokai colors in a rainbow.

The hand on his foot belonged to a brown-skinned woman sitting cross-legged with wiry grace. She must be Darravani, settled into one form. Her long tunic idly shifted colors and patterns, and he saw a small crossbow hidden under one knee. She calmly watched a short, slight man standing between her and the other gods.

The man, Nobody, had tan skin; straight, dark brown hair cut above his ears; and unremarkably black eyes. While his plain green shirt and blue pants made him seem a common workman, the longbow pointed at Darravani's face gave a different impression.

Thanks to the battle above the ocean so many weeks ago, Ahjin identified his arrowhead as a razor-sharp bat tooth. The man had a net of vines slung over one shoulder — no, it was monstrous spider webbing, which also explained the sickly green gloss on the arrowhead. A jagged dagger hung from his belt, and a spear topped with a scorpion stinger lay at his feet. Ahjin bet the dagger was made from a kraken tooth.

All five of the figures had such sharp visual edges and bright colors that his eyes hurt.

"Well, if it isn't the brat, the slacker, and the rotten spy," Nobody gloated over his shoulder. "Did you come back to protect the poor little recluse? You've saved me the trouble of hunting you."

Ahjin closed his eyes to slits and hoped his friends were lying low. He didn't trust Nia's discretion.

Where *were* the others?

The three newly arrived gods lined up across from Darravani and Ahjin, with Nobody in the middle.

"I'm not feeling very lazy right now," Makana drawled sweetly.

"I can skip spying and move straight to action." Resef grinned and tightened his grip on his staff.

"We're here to *cause* you trouble," Irajahan blustered. "And *you're* the brat."

"Trouble?" Nobody smirked. "You don't even have a weapon."

"I *am* a weapon." Irajahan snapped out his wings and clenched his fists. "I'll blow you to the next star."

Nobody just laughed.

Darravani slid her other hand under her knee to touch her crossbow. "Excuse me, we're off-topic. Are you interested in impartial mediation?"

"There's no one neutral here. I'm partial to my side, and you to yours." He didn't sound disappointed.

"There must be some way to work it out." Makana smiled in their enemy's general direction.

Darravani squeezed Ahjin's ankle.

Ahjin recognized himself as the true target of Makana's charm. None of the gods had pointed him out yet, but they had obviously seen Darravani healing him and expected him to volunteer. At least she had acted in time for him to understand some of the situation. Ahjin sighed and pushed himself awkwardly into a sitting position.

Five sets of eyes turned in his direction. Nobody drew his bowstring tighter.

Ahjin quickly held his empty hands in front of him. To his surprise, bandages covered his hands and arms. A half-healed burn peeked from the edge of a dressing tied with a purple ribbon. His limbs quivered; his whole body stung. When he gingerly touched his face, he felt more bandages. Makana's still-fading scars were bad, but he must look even worse. Never mind, Ludik could help later. Right now, the gods — and Nobody — were watching him.

"Fair winds. We can be your mediators, if that's acceptable." Ahjin waved his arm to include his friends.

Makana scanned the area and sighed. Nobody raised both eyebrows.

Ahjin looked around. There were the splintered trees from Resef's vision, the smoking coals, the shards of glass. Those he remembered from before his flight into the storm. Zefra lay on the other side of Darravani, as still as ever since she'd battled the hurricane, but her chest no longer moved. The spiders were the black lumps he hadn't recognized in the vision.

And there were the rest of his friends, strewn across the grass like discarded toys. He had failed them.

The meadow spun in a dizzy circle, and his lungs refused to fill. They had rescued the gods. The others should have escaped if he did his part. What went wrong?

In the face of the enemy, his own death loomed nearly welcome. But what about Resef's second vision? Could he still save his family? He tugged on the purple ribbon and hid his shaking hands in the scarf around his waist.

"*I* can mediate," he wheezed, blinking back the tears that blurred his view of the scattered bodies.

The man Ahjin knew only as Nobody kept his bow trained on Darravani. "Oh, I wouldn't want to trouble you." He pulled back the bowstring and fired.

Just before the arrow hit her face, it burst into flame, and the ash blew away in a sudden gust of wind. Darravani whipped her little crossbow from under her leg and fired.

She was too late; Nobody had vanished. A second later, he was back again, behind the other three gods.

Ahjin threw himself on the ground to avoid the next fireball. His help was not wanted after all. He should worry about the fate of the world, but a blessed numbness crept over his heartache.

"You ruined everything!" Nobody shouted at the gods. "Why did you do it?"

"What do you mean?" Darravani yelled. "You started this war."

"You deserved it! You made the whole world forget about me." Nobody shot an arrow at Irajahan.

Darravani called a warning and scrambled to her feet. Irajahan flew out of range and imperiously raised his arms to summon the winds. Resef blasted fire at the spiders, enlarging the battle ground.

"Are you crazy?" Makana screeched. "What makes you think we did that?"

"This whole world was my idea. I put it in the heavens. I made your creations interact seamlessly. Now, nobody remembers me. They think you created everything. Why didn't I get any credit?" Nobody swung his spear at Makana. "You made people forget. They don't even remember I exist."

"Do not be ridiculous." Resef blocked the spear with his staff. "'Tis not our fault you do not have your own people to remember you."

"Your peoples should have remembered!" Nobody swung again. "You said you'd tell them. Why did you break your promises?"

Darravani shot at him, but her bolt was knocked off-target by the flurry of wind that buffeted Nobody. "I'm afraid I didn't monitor our oral traditions closely enough. I'm willing to correct them." She slapped another bolt in her crossbow.

"So am I," Makana said.

"What about my chronicles?" Nobody bellowed. "I spent decades recording our work. I left proof."

"I think I lost them, sorry." Makana tried to stab the man with her harpoon, but when he kicked her in the knee, she fell. She kicked back, and a flush crept up her cheeks.

"You're an idiot," Nobody roared, kicking her again.

"I'm smarter than you, and you know it!" She rolled away and sprang to her feet. "But the sun was shining, and waves were calling, and fish were singing." She stabbed again. "I thought worry would wait for another day." She shrugged her bare shoulders. "Today is that day."

"I kept my copies," Resef said. "Desert air is good for documents. I have not checked them in a long time, but I can if you come to your senses. I kept everything you gave me as well as my own records." He sidestepped a jab and ended next to Makana. The two of them blocked the furious spear attack.

"They aren't there," Nobody yelled. "I already checked."

Makana fought with Resef to repel their opponent until the fitful wind grabbed her hair and wrapped it around her face. She swore at Ira-jahan and swung her harpoon wildly.

Resef ducked frantically under her weapon, but failed to avoid their enemy's next spear thrust. He turned his fall into a frantic roll, but the scorpion spearhead tore through his sleeve, leaving an oozing scratch from shoulder to elbow. His injured arm convulsed and dropped his staff as he waved his good hand in the air. The little comet that had brought him to the meadow whirled from the sky and skidded to a halt beside him. With a roar, Resef leapt onto the comet and shot into the air. As he circled higher, he dragged a fireball across the gash until the flame cleaned and sealed the wound. Irajahan followed Resef into the air.

Darravani dug her hands into the grass. The earth trembled and knocked everyone off their feet. "I gave my copies to Irajahan to save in the Great Library of Vasi," she shouted over the noise. "He can show you."

"They aren't there, either," Nobody screamed. He dropped his staff and nocked an arrow in his bow.

Ahjin flattened himself into the grass. His view of the battle was not promising.

"Stop that!" Resef bellowed. "I know you were mad when you left, but I thought you were just cooling off. You should have come to us sooner. We could have solved this a long time ago."

Nobody vanished and reappeared to swing a punch at Resef's face. "I'll cool *you*. There are no copies anywhere, and I know what you think of me."

He fell through the sky and disappeared again. This time, he popped up behind Resef, who twisted around and threw a fireball.

Nobody didn't duck fast enough, and the flames zipped across his head. As he fell again, he brushed the sparks out of his hair. "I asked to talk. You refused. Irajahan quoted your insults when he relayed your replies."

"You're crazy. None of that happened." Makana threw her harpoon at his ankle before he vanished. "Oh, Darravani..." She waved her arms up and down like wings.

Darravani nodded. In moments, a mixed flock of birds darkened the horizon. They were met by such a large colony of bats rising from the forest that they shadowed the meadow. The air filled with tumbling fur and feathers and the cries of injured animals.

Thunderclouds rumbled, and the wind howled. Ahjin glimpsed the battle in the gaps between the clashing beasts and clouds. Irajahan tried to pin the flickering enemy in a hurricane. Makana directed torrential rains with expansive gestures that punctuated her cheerful battle chant. Resef lobbed sizzling fireballs and lightning at Nobody, who threw his net in return.

The purple ribbon wrinkled in Ahjin's clenched fingers. His friends had died for nothing. The gods would destroy the world themselves.

Ahjin turned away and found his weapons next to him. As he rearmed himself, gratitude and regret tied a knot in his chest. He couldn't even thank Ludik. He staggered to his feet, limbs twitching and half-healed wings dragging behind him, and struggled toward his friends. If he was going to die, he'd join them.

Askari was closest, long sword in one hand and his other arm in a sling. Ahjin pushed the dead spiders off his body and laid him out neatly, wondering how he'd broken his arm.

Sayaka was next. Her staff lay out of reach, but both hands clutched a dead spider. Ahjin straightened her body and tucked her staff against her arm. He threw the spider to the ground with a satisfying crunch.

Zefra lay in the middle of the circle beneath his shredded jacket, with no pulse under her unnaturally gray skin.

Ludik was the farthest, nearly invisible beneath a hill of living and dead spiders. When Ahjin tried to uncover the black jaguar, the arachnids hissed at him. They dodged stones from his slingshot and kept their guard.

Ahjin knelt in the mud by Nia to untangle her ribbonless braids from spider legs and smooth them over her arms. She'd never need that dye now. He left her harpoon on the ground. She was his merry companion in adventure, not a warrior.

A chill crept through him. It was his fault his friends had died. If he hadn't involved them in his selfishness, they'd be home, happy and alive. There wasn't even have a way to return their bodies. They'd stay here with the spiders that slaughtered them. It was a terrible reward for their valiance.

Ahjin struggled for breath through his cramped chest. Grief pressed him down, folding him over the hard knot of his stomach until his head hit the ground. He held Nia's cold hand and wept acid tears, blind to the gods battling overhead. The sobs racked his half-broken body until it ached as badly as his heart.

He didn't have enough tears in him to appease his grief. The rain poured as if to compensate.

When his eyes finally ran dry, he scrubbed his cheeks and looked for his pack. At least he could tell their families. If the ship wouldn't take him, he would swim. The trip wouldn't take long enough to be able to forgive himself.

Ahjin crawled upright, shivering, and wrapped his arms around himself. The earth shook again, collapsing his unsteady legs on the slick grass. The sun flickered, and the air grew thin. His friends were dead, and the world would still be destroyed. What had been the point of trying?

He hated the gods. Selfish, egotistical fools who wouldn't give up their petty quarrels even to save the world. Ahjin clenched his fists and howled until his throat burned.

When he stopped screaming, he was surprised by near silence. The sounds of battle had ceased. There were no more bird cries or bat squeaks from the animals still flying. Makana wasn't singing. The rain dwindled to a sprinkle. Only the occasional rumble of thunder broke the stillness.

Ahjin looked up to see four gods and their mysterious enemy staring at him instead of fighting. He gulped and hid his shaking fists behind his back, but he couldn't stop glowering.

Nobody, standing on the ground halfway between the two goddesses, transferred his glare from Ahjin to the tumultuous sky and the quaking earth. He pinched the bridge of his nose and grumbled. When he reached for his bow, the gods lifted their own weapons. He froze and growled softly.

Ahjin wrapped one hand around the slingshot tucked in the back of his scarf.

"You offered arbitration." Nobody spread his hands. "You have a point. Maybe things didn't happen the way I thought. I should let you explain. We worked too hard creating this earth to destroy it with a grudge."

He kicked his scorpion-tail spear away from him. When the gods neither advanced nor put down their weapons, he used two fingers to slide his bow to the ground.

Darravani removed the bolt from her crossbow, laid both at her feet, and spread her empty hands. Makana did the same with her harpoon. Resef dropped his staff behind him and showed his empty hands with a challenging grin. Irajahan crossed his arms and sulked.

Ahjin cleared his throat. "I've changed my mind, too." He struggled back to his feet and rubbed the purple ribbon, despite a stab of pain from the bandaged burn. "I won't help murderers and tyrants."

26.KASSIAN
(NORTH-WEST IOJ)

Keep your friends close and your enemies closer.
Darrendrakar Proverb

Perhaps it wasn't wise to insult the gods, but Ahjin didn't care. Makana's mouth fell open, and Darravani flinched. Irajahan hissed and lunged for Ahjin but ran into Resef's suddenly outstretched arm. He fell back choking as the burly god of fire twisted his arms behind his back.

Nobody looked at Ahjin. "I don't blame you. I've suffered insanity myself." He paused and muttered something that sounded like, "I'm still crazy," then continued. "We'd like to fix things now. Doesn't that matter? And we could use some impartial help to determine fair terms for peace." He glanced at the gods. "We don't trust each other enough to settle this ourselves."

Ahjin put a stone in his slingshot, hoping for one good shot before he died. "I don't trust you, either. And I don't care anymore." He might as well be as offensive as he liked before he was destroyed.

He ran his fingers across the new stitches in his scarf. At least he had written to his parents, though Nia could no longer make sure they got the letter.

"You shouldn't." Irajahan flinched as Resef twisted his arm tighter.

"We haven't given you much to trust. How can we convince you of our sincerity?" Nobody idly ran his hand up and down the hilt of his sheathed dagger. "Of course. We should have thought of that earlier."

"What?" Ahjin narrowed his eyes.

"How long has it been since the spiders' attack?" Nobody asked the gods.

Darravani checked the position of the flickering sun. "An hour or so."

"Then it's not too late." Nobody reached into a pouch on his belt and pulled out a vial of milky liquid. "I have an antidote." He wiggled the flask back and forth.

"They're *dead*," Ahjin shouted. "You killed them all!" He needed a god-killing sword instead of a slingshot and a measly dagger. Even his bow wouldn't help, not that he could draw it in his current condition.

"Not quite dead," Darravani said.

"Five of us and five of them," Resef said. "Divide and conquer?"

"I'm not interested," Irajahan said.

"And this will make it possible." Nobody waved the vial again.

Darravani snatched the cure. "We need to hurry, then."

"Get Ludik to help you," Makana said.

Ahjin grabbed his dagger and yelled, "What are you talking about?"

"It's simple," Nobody said. "Would your friends' lives be a sufficient reward for your help?"

"Yes, of course, but that's impossible." Ahjin's slingshot slipped from his hand. "Isn't it?"

"Great!" Makana pointed at Nobody. "Kassian, get rid of those spiders. Darravani, start with Ludik. Resef, go restart Zefra's heart and give her energy. Irajahan, you can help me with the antidote as soon as Darravani is finished."

She dragged Irajahan by the wing, and everyone scattered to obey her commands. Ahjin stood dazed. Nobody was Kassian? Who was that? And could they really save his friends?

Makana's bossy voice came again. "Ahjin, go help Darravani. Right now, little birdie."

Ahjin staggered to where Ludik lay buried under the spiders, wincing at the smell as Darravani opened Kassian's vial. The living spiders crept away amid a chorus of chitters.

He shoved aside enough carcasses to free Ludik's head and shoulders and awkwardly held up the panther while the goddess pried open his mouth and dribbled anti-venom down his throat.

Darravani threw the flask to Makana, then put her hands on Ludik's chest. "I know this is a lousy situation for you, Ahjin," she murmured, "but I cannot cure the venom by myself. That left you or Zefra to help, and she's so devout I do not think she'd argue with any of us, even if we need it. You, well." She chuckled. "You're different. Besides, you promised to free Irajahan, and he's not safe yet. Consider this an extension of your bargain, if you must. And you promised Kassian, too, before you knew about your friends."

"Hmm." Ahjin wasn't sure he made a promise, but he kept his mouth firmly closed and watched Ludik for signs of life. He was doing this for his friends, but if it completed his bargain and freed him of Irajahan, so much the better. The sooner he went home, the happier he'd be.

After a few minutes of no change, Ahjin looked at the others. Resef murmured to Zefra, with flaming hands on her head and chest. Gray faded from her face, and her chest slowly rose and fell. That was all, but breathing was an improvement. Did he dare hope for more?

Irajahan and Kassian followed Makana from one fallen friend to another. They took turns dripping the thick potion into limp mouths while another added energy, but there were no further signs of life.

Ahjin's heart sank.

Ludik coughed.

Ahjin jerked his gaze back as the panther shifted into a naked man and vomited on the dead spiders.

"What... what happened?" Ludik gasped.

"Welcome back, Ludik. It's good to see you again." Ahjin shifted his position to better support Ludik. He had never been happier to struggle with a dead — no, an *awkward* weight. Not dead!

Ludik coughed again. "I thought we were all dead." He pressed his trembling hand against his head.

"How technical did you want the diagnosis?" Darravani handed Ludik water. "If you're well, we need you to finish healing the others. I'm afraid we have another project." She prodded Ahjin's shoulder.

"I can't heal the dead," Ludik wheezed. "Not even the technically dead." He gulped the water and coughed.

"We've done the hardest part for you," Darravani said.

"If you say so." Ludik sat, spilling dead spiders in every direction. He started to rise, then sank again. "Throw my pack to me, please." His gaze flickered sideways to the two goddesses as red flowed across his cheeks and down his brown chest.

"Hurry, Ludik," Ahjin urged. "The others need you." He found the medical kit and brought it to Ludik triumphantly.

"I'm, um, not dressed."

"Oh." Ahjin escorted Darravani to check the other injured, then tossed Ludik his own desert robe from his pack.

"What is going on?" Ludik pulled the robe over his head and stared at the gods.

"I'll tell you later," Ahjin said, as Makana dragged him to where the gods had gathered in the meadow.

"Shall we sit like civilized people and try to get along?" Darravani's voice was tentative. She folded herself down and patted the ground next to her. "You can sit by me, brother."

Ahjin would have been surprised enough if either Resef or Irajahan accepted her invitation, but it was Kassian that knelt by her, empty hands laid palm upward on his knees. Resef pressed Irajahan down, and the other gods sat in a rough circle. Ahjin flopped between Resef and Makana and pulled his knees to his chest.

"I am sorry I did not have time to fix your wings or the lightning damage," Darravani said across the circle. "Please remind me afterward, as an apology for refusing when you first asked my help."

Ahjin waved forgiveness. "You're all siblings? Including Kassian?"

This would send shockwaves through the world. Five gods instead of four, and all of them related. But it did explain how Kassian was powerful enough to capture the gods. Irajahan wouldn't meet his eyes, but the other three nodded sheepishly.

"Kassian, may I introduce Ahjin, a brave young man from Ioj?" Darravani bowed from her cross-legged position. "Ahjin, this is our oldest brother, Kassian."

Kassian nodded to Ahjin.

"You nearly destroyed the world over some family squabble?" Ahjin winced. That was foolish.

"Kassian left a long time ago," Makana said. "We didn't know he was back. He snuck up on us."

"We did not know he was still angry, either," Resef said. "I had forgotten about our quarrel."

Ahjin tried harder to be diplomatic. "Your fight today was easy to overhear."

"I'm sure it was." Kassian sighed. "I'm glad to hear you remember at least one of my contributions, though."

Ahjin pressed his lips together and thought hard. "I'm sorry," he finally said. "Which one?"

"My language." Kassian smiled.

"Your... language."

Kassian's smile faded. "The one you're speaking?"

Ahjin flinched. "Trade tongue?"

"Trade — Are you joking?" Kassian glared at his siblings. "You lied about that, too?"

"And that brings us back to your problem," Ahjin said. "I know nothing about most of it, but one of Resef's priests read us a vague passage in the Iskrin legends that seems to apply."

"Will you explain what 'vague passage,' please?" Resef smiled at Ahjin with grim eyes.

"Something about 'Nobody' being jealous and promising vengeance."

"Are you still using that ludicrous old joke, Resef?" Kassian asked. "You even got my scorpions doing it."

"Sorry, big brother," Resef said. "You complained your name was too accurate." He whispered to Ahjin, "It means empty or lost," before turning back to Kassian. "I wish I had taken you seriously."

"Why, so you could kill me when I came back?" Kassian glanced at his spear.

"No, so I could apologize. Sometimes I take a joke too far." Resef stretched his arm across the circle.

Ahjin peered past the gods but couldn't tell if Ludik had revived the others yet. Why did he have to sit here when his friends' lives were at stake? Oh, yes. Because his friends' lives were at stake.

He swallowed a whimper and turned his attention back to the gods, though he was no help to them, either. How was he supposed to fix this?

While Kassian glared at Resef, Ahjin pleated his scarf, then smoothed it and traced Mother's embroidery.

After a long moment, Kassian glanced at Ahjin and then reached to clasp Resef's arm. "I should teach you how to be serious one of these days."

Irajahan snorted.

Resef turned toward him. "I noticed you said nothing during the battle. You were not much help, either. What is wrong with you?" He glared. "Why do the Iojif not remember Kassian? What happened to Darravani's records she lent to your library? Light our path of understanding, brother."

Irajahan sneered, his handsome face twisted into ugly derision.

Darravani leaned toward Irajahan. "Those are excellent questions. What happened to my records, little brother?" Her hazel eyes glowed cat-green in the artificial twilight of the unsteady sun.

Irajahan looked away.

"Kassian, you said Irajahan gave you our replies," Makana said, "but I got no message from you."

"I didn't, either," Darravani said.

"Neither did I," Resef said. "And I would have come to you, brother."

Kassian's frown lightened.

Makana hummed a few notes. "The flood of conclusions is rising. Irajahan withheld or altered messages between Kassian and the rest of us. He won't tell us why his people have no legends about Kassian. Darravani left her written records in his care and now they're missing. Those all have definite links to our dear, youngest brother." Her voice drawled the last three words for emphasis.

"My people are my fault, Darravani forgot to monitor the stories, and we don't know why Resef's chronicles vanished, but it sounds like Irajahan is responsible for much of this shipwreck."

Ahjin sat up straight. *The records vanished.* "Can you gods give abilities to your people that you do not possess?"

"No, why?" Resef asked.

"Well, I have this new talent for invisibility, and I've always had wings. If I want to steal something, I can leave no footprints *and* be unseen." Ahjin hoped someone would find a flaw in his logic.

Irajahan's face turned purple. "I did nothing wrong!"

The other gods jumped to their feet and shouted at him. Insults and accusations flew across the circle. It seemed the truce was ended.

Ahjin stood in disgust. If they wouldn't keep their promise to cooperate, he couldn't keep his own. Perhaps they'd remember how to behave in a while.

The gods reached for their weapons and shook their fists at each other. The birds and bats circled through the sky again. Clouds piled in front of the sun, and the earth shivered.

Perhaps they *wouldn't* remember how to behave. Did he have any way to persuade them? How could he get their attention without being obliterated? This would be easier if they'd act like adults.

A sudden weight rammed Ahjin's side and pinned his arms.

He struggled to reach his knife until the wonderful scent of salt water and too much perfume hit his nose.

"Ease up a little," he croaked, pulling one arm free to return Nia's hug. His arms shook, either from lightning damage or sheer relief.

"How do you feel?" Nia's question was muffled by a mouthful of broken feathers and choked-back sobs.

"I'm great." Ahjin brushed back her hair to see her face. "But I'd be better if you stopped cracking my ribs." Another broken rib would be worth it. Never flying again would still be worth it. "How are you?"

"Dying of curiosity." Nia let go slowly. "Everyone's waiting for you; hurry." She danced on her bandaged feet.

His heart flew at her familiar enthusiasm. Tears stung his eyes as he turned from the quarreling gods. They weren't paying attention to him, anyway. He used his free hand to rub at the tears before his eyes turned into rain clouds.

As Ahjin staggered with her, Nia frowned. Instead of slowing, she pulled one of his arms over her shoulders. Within a few steps, Sayaka joined them and used her greater height to better support him as they reached the others. He squeezed her shoulder harder than required, in place of a proper hug.

"I can walk, you know," Ahjin said. A slower pace might let him regain his composure and the shreds of his dignity. Then again, even walking home might not take long enough for that.

"I saw you walking," Ludik said dryly, rubbing his salve on Askari's arm. "I'm not impressed. Since you somehow didn't knock your bones loose again, Askari, I knitted them a little. It should hold for mild use now. Sword fighting and tackling don't count." He pulled down the warrior's sleeve and gave him a sling. "Wear this for at least two weeks.

Next victim, please." He rubbed his long-fingered hands in mock delight.

Ahjin's desert robe pulled across the shapeshifter's broad shoulders, and his brown back showed through the gaping wing slits. Its hemline ended at his shins and the sleeves long before his wrists. Ahjin made a mental note to help the poor man look for his baggage later. It was small thanks for everything he had done.

Askari clasped hands with Ahjin and murmured a welcome.

"It's good to see you all again." Ahjin blinked back pesky tears again. "I can wait. Zefra next." Evaporating the hurricane had drained her energy, though he couldn't scold her for saving them all with the dangerous feat.

Zefra was using her bandaged hands well enough, but she reclined against a pile of baggage, boots crossed at the ankle. Her fiery hair fell from its braided wreath and curled around her narrow face. Ahjin's jacket was folded by her side, and her dagger lay unsheathed in her lap.

"I already have my *lovely* concoction." Zefra shook a half-full water jug but kept her gaze on the squabbling gods across the meadow.

Ahjin looked from one of his crutches to the other. "Nia, your turn." Having her well might calm the stutter in his chest.

"He already fixed my sting, and my feet enough for now." Nia ducked from under his arm.

Sayaka copied her and swept Ahjin's feet from under him. They lowered him to his knees in front of Ludik.

"That antidote worked well against the spider venom," Sayaka said. "Where did you get it? And what in the sands happened here?"

"I'd like to know, too," Ahjin said. "Where did those spiders come from? What happened to you?" His stomach clenched again. They'd all died, and it was his fault.

Ludik ran one hand down Ahjin's spine. "The spiders happened, and the last thing I saw was them yielding to the one arguing with the gods. Who is he? I wasn't sure if I should help you or obey Darravani."

"That's Kassian's anti-venom." Ahjin winced as Ludik's gentle probing found a sore spot. "Zefra, you might like to know his name means 'empty.'"

Zefra flickered a confused glance at him before turning back to watch the gods. "Yes, I know. So?"

Ahjin gave her another hint. "Empty, like nothing, Nobody…"

Zefra choked and spit out a mouthful of tea. "Nobody from the scroll? Who captured the gods? The friend of the spiders and other monsters? Why would he undo his own work?"

Now he had his friends' full attention. "Your lives were a bribe for my cooperation. He seems to think I can broker peace between the gods." Ahjin tried not to laugh.

Nia gasped. "How are you supposed to do that?"

"I don't know, but I promised to try," Ahjin said. "If it isn't too late to save the world, I can't give up."

"This isn't time for one of your pranks," Ludik scolded. He listened to Ahjin's heartbeat and frowned.

"He's not joking," Makana said. She and the other gods walked up, weapons in hand.

Ahjin hid a sigh. If he hadn't distracted Zefra, she could have warned him they had stopped fighting. Another chance at this arbitration nonsense might be good, but when would the ordeal end? When could he claim Irajahan's bargain and go home?

Irajahan scowled up at Ludik and drew himself to his full height, four inches shorter than the barefoot shapeshifter. Then the difference shrank.

Ahjin blinked. Was the god growing?

Resef also noticed. With a wink at Ahjin, he snapped his fingers. A spark caught in Irajahan's hem and ran around and around until a foot of orange robe had turned to ash, revealing the god's feet in midair.

When Nia noticed the hovering god, she giggled. Irajahan turned red and thumped to the ground, level with Kassian and Ahjin. He threw a sour look at Ludik and a nastier one at Resef.

Ahjin pretended he hadn't seen anything. "Oh, good," he said. "We can continue."

He hoped a truce still had a chance, but if not, at least his friends were healed. Perhaps he could buy time for them to escape.

"Why do you always have to oppose me?" Irajahan howled.

Resef and Darravani grabbed his arms while Kassian and Makana pointed weapons at him.

Ahjin shrugged. "We can do it the hard way, if you prefer. It makes no difference to me." He nodded at the other gods and hoped his friends would run. "Go ahead, thrash it out of him."

Irajahan stopped struggling and glowered.

Ahjin glared back.

Irajahan thundered inside Ahjin's head. His voice pressed down. "Let me free."

Ahjin ignored him, thankful for the practice he'd gotten on their trip.

"Everything is Kassian's fault," Irajahan insisted. "*He* deserves to be punished. Obey me. As arbitrator, tell Kassian to leave and the other gods to return to their homes."

"No." Ahjin folded his arms and looked away.

Irajahan screamed.

The clamor squeezed Ahjin's brain. He cried out and clutched his head.

Irajahan's shrieks went on and on, louder and louder in Ahjin's mind, demanding his attention. "I am a god and will be treated as such. I demand respect and compliance. How dare you treat your god this way! Listen and obey! You promised to free me."

The pain multiplied until Ahjin's head threatened to explode. Ludik's strong grip kept him from falling. Zefra's warm hands wormed into his and stopped him from pulling his hair. Nia's arms circled his waist, and her voice whispered in his ears, singing "home again."

Ahjin thought of home and scraped up courage beyond hope. "No," he shouted in a wavering voice, "I won't. And you can't make me." His anger returned. "Why don't you GROW UP!" He pictured an iron door in his mind and slammed it shut. If it had any tangible effect, he hoped it smashed Irajahan's metaphorical nose.

27.PLANS
(NORTH-WEST IOJ)

We cannot enter alliances until we are acquainted with the designs of our neighbors.
Beginning Battle Strategy

V oices shouted, and a loud impact sounded overhead. The pain in his head dropped to a whisper. Ahjin drew a shuddering breath. When Nia tugged on his shoulder, he wiped his eyes and turned his head. Beyond Nia, Makana smiled and shook her reddened fist.

"Are you hurt?" Ahjin struggled to his feet with Ludik's help. "What happened to you?"

"Oh, nothing that wasn't worth it," Makana gloated, looking over her shoulder.

Ahjin looked past her. Irajahan stood between Resef and Darravani. His expression was surly, but he no longer struggled to escape. Claw marks ran down his arm, and one eye was bruised.

Ahjin bowed to Makana in heartfelt gratitude. "I owe you, my lady."

"It was my pleasure, but I only stopped his tantrum." She cradled her fist against her chest. "*You* beat his argument. That's twice you've gotten the better of him."

"Twice?"

"He told us about your bargain with him," Darravani said. "He was quite irate."

"I don't think that's a good gauge of my influence," Ahjin stammered. "I took advantage of his dilemma."

"Yes—" Irajahan started to protest. His teeth clacked shut when Resef yanked his elbow.

"And now you have discovered how to shut him out." Darravani nodded in approval. "It takes his priests weeks or months of training to learn that. You're the only one who has naturally out-stubborned him."

Nia giggled. "That's our Ahjin."

"I'm reasonable," Ahjin protested. He turned to Irajahan. "Are you ready to discuss a truce?"

Irajahan stared across the meadow at the tiny volcano that had been his prison, then glared at Kassian and Ahjin. "Why should I give in to thugs and mortals? Who are you to tell me what I should do?"

"You thought I was good enough to be your priest," Ahjin said, "whether I wanted it or not. You bargained with me for your freedom. You aren't free yet, and at this rate, you won't be. You agreed to arbitration."

"I am omnipotent," Irajahan said. "If Kassian hadn't tricked me, he never would have taken me. Now that I'm on guard, he won't succeed again." Lightning flashed in his eyes.

Even as a prisoner, Irajahan was intimidating. Ahjin swallowed hard. "The others have agreed to abide by my judgment. If I tell your siblings to thrash sense into you, how long do you think it will take? I'm willing to find out, if that's the way you want to do it." Sweat ran down his back as he stared at the god.

Clouds boiled in the sky, higher and darker. Lightning cracked into thunder.

Irajahan jerked his gaze to the storm, then looked at Ahjin. He shrugged his arms free of his brothers and crossed them defiantly. "I'm not worried."

"Do you really want to take on all four of us again?" Resef asked Irajahan. "How did that work for you before?"

Makana raised her harpoon and grinned at Irajahan.

Ahjin met Irajahan's eyes while he rubbed the lingering ache from his head. Darravani thought he could do this. He had to safeguard the world and free himself while he was at it.

"Look what you're doing. Is this what you want? If you destroy everything, what good will a little more power do you? How will the dead admire you? You started this mess. Now is the time for you to end it honorably."

Irajahan glared as the clouds darkened, and the thunder doubled. Lightning brightened the sky in place of the hidden sun. Ahjin held his breath and watched Irajahan's angry face during every flash. The air sparked and spat. Ahjin's skin crawled, and his ruined feathers crackled. His wings twitched with remembered agony.

At last, after Ahjin had almost given up hope, the god dropped his arms to his sides. The clouds flattened to pale wisps, and the lightning fizzled.

Irajahan rustled his wings and tried a lopsided smile. The expression sat oddly on his face. "I don't really want to destroy the world. I suppose if the others can make peace, so can I."

"Finally," Makana muttered.

Irajahan glared at her.

"Does that mean we finally get to find out what happened?" Nia flopped on the ground by Ahjin, propped her chin on her hands, and swung her bandaged feet in the air. "I love a good story."

Zefra settled cross-legged next to Nia. Resef pointedly sat next to Irajahan, and Makana laid her harpoon by her side. Everyone sat except for Ludik, who inched his healing hands across Ahjin's wings.

"Yes, I did all those things." Irajahan scowled. "I was jealous of Kassian." He looked at Ludik and fingered his burnt hem. "He did a great job planning this world. Too great. Everyone talked about how wonderful he was. His records would trumpet his success through the end of time. I did a good job, too, but the wind is invisible. No one cares about what they can't see."

He swallowed and looked down. "I thought if he was gone, and I destroyed the evidence, I could take credit for his work, too. Then I'd really be the All-Powerful. Darravani had no concern for anything but her own land. Makanavailea was too lazy to notice what I did. Resef was more interested in his own diversions than in power."

He raised his gaze to meet Kassian's. "You were the only one with any enthusiasm for global matters. You were my only obstacle. I didn't even have to harm you. If you left, I could have everything I wanted." Irajahan lowered his eyes again and picked at his hem.

"I suppose I should count myself lucky you only chased me away," Kassian grumbled.

"I thought about the alternative." Irajahan flickered a glance at the scorched tear in Resef's sleeve. "You're a little hard to pin down, though. I thought I was a hero, but it didn't turn out how I expected." He rolled his hem around his fingers.

"Real heroes do things for others, not for themselves." Darravani smiled at Ahjin.

Everyone followed her gaze.

"I'm no hero," Ahjin protested. "I fell into this accidentally, trying to save myself."

"We're lucky you're accident-prone." Ludik held down Ahjin's arms.

Ahjin knocked him head over heels with his wings instead. Ludik always forgot to account for his wings. The ache was worth it; it wasn't like he'd be able to fly again, anyway.

Sayaka shook her head. "You should know better by now, Ludik."

Ludik picked himself up and tugged on Ahjin's curls, then sat between Nia and Darravani, beyond Ahjin's reach. Sayaka reached to cuff him on the back of the head.

"Obviously," Resef winked at Ludik, "we all make mistakes. Life rarely turns out the way we plan." He smiled ruefully as everyone nodded, frowned, or grinned.

"Is it safe to assume the war is ended?" Ahjin glared at Irajahan and Kassian.

"Yes," Kassian agreed.

"Yes," Irajahan sighed.

"Then as arbitrator, I say it's time to plan for a better future. How can we make restitution to Kassian and encourage peace?" Ahjin looked at everyone for answers.

"An apology would be a good place to start," Kassian snapped, "and I mean from the creator of this mess." He glared at Irajahan.

"It's not my fault! Ow." Irajahan rubbed his shoulder and glared at Makana, who blew on her fist again. "Fine, I'm sorry. Are you happy now?"

"You should prepare yourself to repeat that in front of people," Ahjin said. "Public harm calls for public apology."

"You little—" Irajahan glanced at Makana's raised fist. "—Arbitrator. How long do I have?"

"You can travel to repeat your apology in every city personally," Darravani said, "or you can tell your Winds to relay it. As for my people, I will have my shamans correct the tales."

"Why would you do that?" Irajahan asked. "You aren't being forced to apologize."

"Some people do what is right of their own will," Resef said. "I will also talk to my priests."

Makana chuckled. "It'll be as easy as a dream for me. I'll handle it personally."

Kassian cleared his throat. "Thank you."

"What's next?" Ahjin asked.

"Perhaps Kassian needs something worthwhile to do," Zefra suggested.

"He already has a family, but he needs friends and people around him," Ludik added.

Nia smiled. "He needs to restore his legend."

"You need a home." Ahjin spoke directly to Kassian, more than ready to return to his own.

"That's a lot to deal with at once, isn't it?" But Kassian looked thoughtful instead of discouraged.

"Yes, but you need to travel a lot to tell your story," Sayaka said. "In the process, you can make friends and recruit followers. It would not be the first time something like that has worked." She wrapped one arm around Zefra.

Irajahan scoffed. "Does that mean he'll steal our people from us? Ow. Stop!" He rubbed his shoulder again.

"It's not stealing, stupid, if people want to go. You don't *own* them." Makana shook her fist at his nose.

"Yes, I do," he snarled.

"No. You don't." Ahjin folded his arms and glared.

Irajahan opened his mouth to argue, then looked around the circle and slumped. "Fine." After a moment, he smirked. "It won't matter. No one will switch allegiance. We've trained them well to keep to themselves."

"He might be right." Darravani sighed. "The Darrendrakar in particular are very..."

"Independent?" Resef asked.

"Secluded," Makana suggested.

"Detached?" Kassian shrugged.

"Prejudiced," Irajahan insisted smugly.

"I meant private," Darravani protested. "We are not fond of strangers."

"That's stupid," Nia said. "Strangers are fun."

Ahjin laughed. Nia stuck out her bottom lip, then howled in amusement over the crowd's quieter chuckles.

"That might be a good goal for you." Zefra glanced sideways at Kassian. "You should encourage everyone to talk and be friends. Think how good it would be to work together and learn from each other."

"Do you have any idea how long that would take?" Kassian paused and rubbed his chin for a moment. "Very well, I accept your challenge." He leaned forward in a sitting bow.

"If you'll be all over the world, we should call you Kassian the Omnipresent." Nia said the name like a gift.

"I'm sure he already has a title, Nia." Ludik patted her knee.

"Actually, I don't," Kassian said. "I like that, thank you."

"So we have a plan to find friends, share your story, and improve the world," Ahjin said, "and we've assigned you a new name as a bonus. What's left?"

"I like exploring," Zefra said. "I'm happy to help you look for a home." She hid her impressive blush with her hands. "Never mind. A god does not need my help to explore."

Kassian smiled at Zefra. "That's true, but if you helped, I'd have more time to talk to people and work on our other goals. I accept your offer. Now I need to find a place to live until then."

Resef bumped his shoulder against Kassian's. "You can stay with me."

"Done," Kassian said.

"Is that everything, then?" Ahjin exhaled in relief. "That was easier than I expected." He smiled his thanks at his friends for their help.

"But how will we keep this situation from happening again?" Kassian asked.

Irajahan smirked at his siblings. "I can keep you all under control."

"Not a chance," Kassian said.

"Kassian is oldest," Darravani said. "He could take charge."

Irajahan glared at Kassian. "Not a chance."

"Darravani?" Ahjin suggested.

Darravani blushed. "While I intend to be more involved in outside affairs now, I am busy with my own people."

"Do not look at me," Resef said. "Too boring. How about Makana?"

Makana grinned. "Telling all of you what to do could be fun."

Irajahan narrowed his eyes. "You will never tell me what to do."

Kassian sighed. "Makana, you know you'll get distracted, and then where will we be?"

"I think 'tis obvious we have enough history of bad feelings we cannot be trusted on our own," Resef said. "We need someone impartial to protect us from each other and guard the world from our misbehavior."

"It sounds like a job for a priest or shaman," Irajahan said. "Or a hero." He glared spitefully at Ahjin, who ignored him.

Darravani pinched his arm, right across one of the scratches she had given him.

All the gods looked at Ahjin again.

"Oh, no, I've done enough already." Ahjin waved his hands in denial. "Irajahan promised I wouldn't have to be a Wind if I rescued you. I'm going home. You need a priest or shaman from each land so you each have someone with whom you can communicate."

Even without flight, he wanted to be with his family. And perhaps he'd heal.

"But I have no one," Kassian said, "and committees are unwieldy."

"Priests are boring." Makana fluttered her eyelashes. "Dolphins and dreams are more fun."

"One messenger and arbitrator would be better," Darravani agreed. "All we need is someone who can talk to all of us."

"Well, that eliminates me," Ahjin said. "Only a freak accident landed me with Irajahan."

"Did you keep that a secret, too?" Resef nudged Irajahan, who covered his eyes. "Irajahan had a few favorites among the ladies, long ago. Several Iojif Houses are descended from his telepathic children."

Ahjin wrinkled his nose in disgust. "What does that have to do with anything?"

"They inherited my greatness, of course," Irajahan said.

Resef laughed. "If both your parents are descended from Irajahan, *and* they each pass the right trait in their blood, then you inherit the telepathy." Ahjin opened his mouth to protest, and Resef spoke faster. "It works even if your parents do not have the talent because they got only one portion from *their* parents."

Ahjin clamped his mouth shut and counted to ten. "I still can't communicate with the rest of you." He was torn between a frustrated growl and a relieved sigh.

"You can if we give you permission and a few drops of blood." Kassian beamed at Ahjin. A dimple in one cheek heightened his resemblance to Makana.

"If that's all it takes, you can choose someone else."

"We still want you," Resef insisted. "You're the best choice."

"I agree," Darravani said. "I already told you."

"I like the way you handle Irajahan," Makana said.

Irajahan shot her a nasty look. "I prefer to deal with one of my priests."

Kassian shrugged. "You have the telepathy already, Ahjin. It's easy to give you access to the rest of us, and I'm not worried about you favoring Irajahan."

Irajahan glowered at him.

"And then you'll all talk in my head?" Ahjin rubbed his forehead.

"It will work differently for all of us," Darravani admitted. "We will teach you later."

Ahjin clenched his fists. Home had filled his dreams for months. How could the gods ask him to give up everything when freedom was nearly within his grasp? There must be someone else who'd enjoy placating deities.

The gods were still watching him.

"Irajahan promised he'd set me free," Ahjin said.

"Then I take it back," Irajahan gloated.

"You can't do that," Makana said. "You can't break your word, even to one of your own people."

"I only promised he wouldn't be *my* priest. You want him to work for all of us." Irajahan grinned maliciously.

Ahjin tried to glare a hole through the god's head.

Kassian put a hand to block his line of sight. "We're sorry. Please, won't you continue to help us?" When Ahjin didn't answer, the god sighed. "Why don't you tell us what you wanted in life before this happened."

Ahjin crossed his arms. "I want to skydance with my parents' troupe."

"That does not help us," Resef grumbled.

"Why does that appeal to you?" Makana asked.

"I love flying. I can travel around the country and be outdoors." Ahjin sighed. "I'd be with my family." He shrugged and refused to look at Irajahan. "It seems avoiding a vexatious god should also be on my list."

Kassian elbowed Makana to make her stop snickering. "What if we arranged for you to still do most of those?"

"Aerobatics with my parents?" Ahjin's heart grew wings. He untied his scarf and smoothed the wrinkles. Perhaps he wouldn't explain the burns and mended slashes to his family.

"I'm afraid not," Darravani replied, "but you can travel the world. You and your friends can visit." A chorus of firm nods from her siblings ratified her offer.

How could they think that was enough? Ahjin pressed his lips together to hold in undiplomatic words. He carefully folded his scarf and slid it back in his pocket.

"Are you bribing me?" he finally asked.

"That depends," Makana demurred. "Is it working?"

Nia cleared her throat. "Does he have to answer now? Can he think about it while he travels home?"

Irajahan made a nasty face and opened his mouth.

"That is fair enough." Darravani cut off her brother. "We will support him whatever he chooses."

The other gods nodded.

"Ludik healed his wings well for a mortal," Darravani continued, "but I will make them fly. Now, there are things we need to discuss, if you will give us privacy?"

"We will get ready to go." Sayaka stood and bowed to everyone.

The others followed her to the other side of the meadow. Ahjin tried to match Ludik's long stride, but his legs refused to obey. When he stumbled, Askari hooked his good arm under Ahjin's elbow and helped Ludik carry him, toes dangling above the grassy meadow.

Ahjin's mind faltered as badly as his damaged body while the gods' request echoed in his head. *Someone to keep this mess from happening again.* But it could be someone else. The gods said they'd accept his decision.

Please, won't you continue to help us? No! Darravani had promised to heal his wings. He'd get his family and his flying back again. It had taken long enough and cost too much. Now the time had come to collect his reward.

He was going home. They could trick some other poor fool into helping the gods.

Who was that insane?

28.CHOICES
(NORTH-WEST IOJ)

All temptations are found in either hope or fear.
Iojif Proverb

Ahjin and his friends ate flatbread, jerky, and dried fruit while the gods cleaned the meadow. The innocuous-looking Kassian made the dead spiders vanish two at a time under his hands. Resef burned his share of the corpses, while Makana kicked hers into the stream where they dissolved as if in acid. Darravani made the ground swallow the lumps of coal, glass shards, and the entire miniature volcano, and Irajahan blew away the last of the lightning storm. Irajahan's robe had a fresh hem, but he'd given up his illusion of extra height.

"It's a start." Ludik nodded at the gods and took a strip of jerky from Zefra. "I'm impressed at what you accomplished, Ahjin."

Ahjin shook his head. "We worked together, and you rescued Resef. And fought giant spiders?"

Nia shuddered. "It was awful, and I don't want to talk about it." She gave Ahjin more bread.

"I wanted to say thank—" Ahjin started.

Nia shoved the bread in his mouth. "No talking about awfulness."

After he ate, Ahjin pulled his knees to his chest and rested his head on them. Everything had started just over four months ago. It felt like a lifetime since he thought running away would solve his problems. For a while, it *had* worked, especially after his deal with Irajahan. Their journey had been fun at first, despite the dangers. Until the desert, even the elemental upheavals had seemed more like a bad joke than an impending disaster.

He remembered Resef's visions with a shudder, matching them to the horrible events in this meadow. His shoulders tightened until his friends' living voices echoed behind him.

Everyone else was happily celebrating the end of their journey. It was over for them. They had rescued the gods and settled the enemy. The gods had stopped fighting, and his friends could go home whenever they liked.

It ought to be over for him, too.

Ahjin mentally rehearsed the aerobatic routine he had prepared to impress Father, going over every move until he was sure he could do it perfectly. If his wings healed. His dreams would be worth any amount of practicing to get back in shape. He felt Nia's gentle fingers stroking his feathers and realized his wings were twitching. Her touch reminded him of the way his little sister used to play with his wings when he was teaching her to flap her own.

Oh, no, he had missed Maili's birthday! She was a year old now and perhaps flying. Would she recognize him?

His worries were interrupted when the gods rejoined them. The meadow was restored to its original state, all evidence of the past horror gone.

"Now, if Kassian will let me communicate with my Winds again," Irajahan said, "the ones in Vasi can tell the rest of Ioj. They can send messengers to the other lands, too."

"Now I remember why I call it Vasi the Bossy," Makana murmured.

"You should recognize bossy," Irajahan hissed at her. "My priests, brother, *if* you don't mind?"

"I forgot." Kassian produced a bottle and uncorked it with a grin. "Drink this all at once, despite the taste."

Irajahan sniffed the jar, then flinched and almost dropped it. "Just free my priests. Please." He held it at arm's length.

"I did nothing to your priests." Kassian pushed it back. "I did it to you."

"I still spoke to Ahjin," Irajahan protested.

"I cut your established ties. You didn't have one with Ahjin yet." Kassian narrowed his eyes. "I should have eliminated your telepathy altogether."

Irajahan glared. "I'll get you for this."

He tossed the liquid down his throat. His face turned redder, and he coughed violently. Kassian grinned. When Irajahan recovered, he stuck out a vivid purple tongue and flounced off.

"This had better work," he croaked over his shoulder.

"I will eavesdrop on him," Resef said, "and send my own messages. Sisters, you should tell your people." He tweaked Darravani's nose and followed Irajahan.

Kassian trailed them both, while the goddesses wandered in different directions.

When they returned, Resef nodded to his sisters.

"Ahjin," Kassian said, "when you decide about being our arbitrator, write your answer on paper and say my name. I will expect it soon after you reach home, if not earlier."

At least Ahjin had time to think. "I will."

"Everyone ready?" Makana asked. "We'll meet you in Vasi in about a week and a half. Pleasant journey."

"Where are you going now?" Ahjin asked.

Resef grinned, snapping his fingers to summon his comet. "We will tell you about it later. Warmth to you."

"Good flight." Ahjin glimpsed Irajahan's still-bandaged arm when he raised his hands to call the winds. "Will you heal him, too?" he asked Darravani.

"I want him to remember what happened for a while yet. Keep well." The goddess wrapped her arms around Kassian's shoulders, and they vanished.

Irajahan sneered and flew off in lazy spirals, and Resef jumped aboard his comet with Makana in his arms.

"Are we ready to go?" Zefra asked.

"Do we need to drop anyone at home before Ioj?" Ahjin raised an eyebrow at Ludik, who was so close to his family and Nemerra now.

Ludik's face crumpled, and he crouched to brush off his boots. When he stood, his face was calm again. "I can get a ride home later."

"We will all go with you, Ahjin," Zefra declared.

Nia rolled her eyes and took Ahjin's hand. "Let's go, silly."

Ludik took one of Ahjin's arms and Sayaka the other, and they supported his stagger without comment.

Hiking downhill was easier, despite struggling through the underbrush, and they reached their last campsite by nightfall. Zefra pulled out a tiny lamp, and they kept going, too exhausted to speak.

At one point, Zefra hesitated before choosing the right-hand path. After a dozen paces, she screamed. Hundreds of eyes reflected the faint light of her lamp and a single moon. Spiders blocked the track.

One large spider stepped from the cluster and chittered softly, pointing at the path Zefra had declined. She shrank back through her friends and led the way to the left, lamplight quivering in her hand.

Ahjin watched behind, but no spiders followed. So far, Kassian honored the truce. What would it cost Ahjin to keep it that way? Would he lose his freedom, his skydancing, *and* his family?

Well after midnight, they stumbled down the last slope to the beach. The moon had set, and only Zefra's flickering lamp lit their way.

"Captain Fathi cannot risk the ship in the dark." Askari threw a blanket at Ahjin and wrapped one around himself. "We will light a signal fire in the morning."

No one had the energy to argue. Within minutes, they were asleep on the sand.

I n the morning, Ahjin awoke to the smell of breakfast. He opened his bleary eyes and groaned. Ludik handed him yet another cup of unsavory potion and a bowl of hot cereal.

"You did not have to do this, Ludik." Zefra inhaled the steam from her cereal. "We would have helped."

"Never mind," Ludik said between gulps. "You can wash the dishes."

The longboat beached before they finished. Koray jumped out first.

"Bright day. We saw your fire." The Rikatsu healer looked hard at their bandages, Askari's sling, and Ahjin's scorched and bloody feathers. "You did not take care of them well," he accused Ludik.

"We were dead earlier," Nia said, "so I think we look fine. Is there any cereal left?"

She held her bowl to Zefra, who scraped the remnants from the pot on her way to clean it.

"You cannot expect me to believe you," Koray protested.

Nia winked. "Ahjin has high-powered friends now."

Koray stared at Ahjin as everyone gathered their packs and climbed in the dinghy.

Ahjin remembered the reaction of his friend, Lee, in Vasi and sighed. Anyone who would have been wary of his supposed power or taken advantage of his position as a Wind priest would be a thousand times worse if he accepted the gods' proposal.

When they reached the ship, Captain Fathi resettled them in the barracks, and Koray helped Ludik treat everyone.

On the way to Ioj, Ahjin dreamed nightly of his friends' bodies in the meadow and woke panting when the winged corpse turned into his little sister. He found himself following his friends as if they'd disappear, not able to forget they *had* been dead.

His friends ignored his obsession for three days. On the fourth, Ludik politely asked him to stop, with an arm wrapped around Ahjin's neck. The fifth day, as soon as Ahjin came in view, Zefra walked away. On the sixth, Sayaka and Askari climbed the rigging in loose pants borrowed from the sailors. After a week, Nia threw him overboard with threats of more creative punishments if he didn't stop haunting them. By the time Ahjin pulled himself back on board, he decided to be more discreet.

Despite his efforts to forget it, Kassian's request ran through his mind frequently. It would have been easier to ignore four months ago, when Ahjin thought the gods were imaginary at best or superfluous nuisances at worst.

By the ninth day on board, Ahjin had something else to drive him crazy. Nia had taught the sailors her Nokai lullaby, and plaintive choruses of "Home again, go home again" tested his patience. He was close enough to home to see the damage to familiar landmarks. Gouges ran down the cliffs like giant claw marks, and crumbled rock covered the beaches. The cities at the top were likewise damaged.

Ahjin searched both sky and land in the vain hope his family would miraculously appear. The scarf in his pocket creased in his frequently clenched fists. His wings twitched so much with the burning need to fly that Ludik threatened to tie them down. Thanks to Ludik and Koray's daily healing sessions, Ahjin could walk by himself, though he still couldn't fly.

It was still morning when Ahjin finally saw white wings above the faint gleam of the city. When Captain Fathi aimed for the harbor, the distant figure looped toward the ship. Ahjin watched with hands clenched on the railing and wings twitching. His friends drifted near him. In a few long minutes, Ahjin saw Father's worried features.

Father thumped on deck and searched eagerly from face to face. "Fair winds. I was told to watch for a bronze and lavender flag. Do you have any news of my—" He spotted Ahjin and inhaled sharply, then stepped forward and threw his arms around him.

"You're here," he breathed. "I thought I'd never see you again. The letter you sent didn't help, either." He shook Ahjin a little before hugging him again.

"I know what you mean." Ahjin's laugh was like a sob. He stopped talking and just held Father.

Father took half a step backward to clutch Ahjin's shoulders. "I'm glad you're home. What happened to you?" He ran his fingers gently across the healing burn marks on Ahjin's face and hands.

"That's a long story." What had Father already been told? Obviously not everything. Ahjin was glad his wings were mostly hidden behind him. Did Father know about the gods' request?

"It will have to wait, then." Father frowned. "I have bad news for you. The earthquake two weeks ago — it destroyed our house." He paused. "Your mother and Maili..."

Ahjin's knees collapsed. Mother and Maili were dead, and his dreams were hopeless. He sat abruptly on the deck. Thundering in his ears blocked the rest of Father's words.

Zefra brought Ahjin cool water. "Your father has no tact," she said, "but listen." She shook his shoulder and pushed the cup into his hand.

Ahjin quelled his panic enough to hear Ludik swearing at Father.

"Quit yelling at me, you impudent whelp!" Father's face was red. "I admit I should have given him the good news first, so if you shut up, I'll apologize and take him to his mother now."

Hope grew wings in Ahjin's heart.

Father pulled him to his feet. "I'm sorry. They're fine; I'll take you to them."

Ahjin clambered to his feet and headed for the ramp to the dock. "Where are they?"

His heart pounded so hard he barely heard Father say their cousin's name. As soon as the ramp touched ground, he ran for the freight lift.

"Are you running the whole way?" Father's amused question came from above his head.

Ahjin saved his breath and snapped open his wings.

Father gasped. "What happened?"

Ahjin furled his tattered wings and kept running while Father swooped back toward the ship.

The narrow beach ended at the base of the cliff a few hundred feet from the dock. Ahjin pounded past the guard house and threw himself on the freight lift in front of an old friend.

"Up, Lee, quickly as you can," he begged, grabbing one pulley rope.

Lee's mouth hung open. As he finally reached for his own rope, a panther hurtled onto the lift and skidded across its length. The guard cursed and groped for his sword.

Ahjin flung his arm between Lee and the jaguar. "He's a friend!"

Ludik settled on his haunches and twitched one ear. His long lashes blinked slowly over his bright silver eyes. The soldier stretched for the rope while watching the cat. Ahjin glanced between Lee and Father, who was talking to Askari on the dock. Judging from the way Nia stomped around them, Father was being difficult.

Ahjin and Lee hauled the lift up the cliff and bumped to a stop in near-record time. Ahjin wrapped the cable around the anchor peg while Ludik waved his big paw at the gaping soldier. They bounded off the lift and headed into town at a pace that was a dead run for Ahjin and a lope for the giant cat. As they reached the first buildings, Father flew past them.

The road tilted across the cracked ground. Some houses had missing shingles or broken windows, and others had shattered walls and fallen roofs. Ahjin slowed at his house. It was nothing but rubble, with one crumbled wall showing traces of his bedroom mural.

He resumed his frantic race around the corner, heading for the low fence that had contained his cousin's goat until the earthquakes flattened half of it.

Father pulled Mother from the house. "Hurry, Aria, he's really here."

Behind them, Maili wobbled out the door, every other step a tiptoe flutter. Ahjin froze halfway through the wobbly gate, heart in his throat.

The panther hopped the fence and pressed his ear against Ahjin's chest, then nudged him and wriggled toward the tiny girl, waving his tail. She squealed and reached for him. Mother snatched her away with a cry of alarm.

"Never mind him," Father said. "He's a friend and a... person, not a wild animal." He turned her toward Ahjin.

Ludik twitched his whiskers.

"It's fine," Ahjin choked out. "Fair winds, Mother."

He stumbled to her and set Maili in front of Ludik, who promptly started a lazy game of tag with the delighted toddler. Mother touched Ahjin's face and wrapped her arms around him. Father embraced them both. It wasn't until their cousin, Charu, cleared her throat and offered refreshments that any of them moved.

"Where are my manners," Mother fretted. "Won't you invite your friend inside?" When she turned to look for Maili and Ludik, she kept a grip on Ahjin's hands.

At the sound of her voice, Ludik reappeared around the corner of the house with Maili on his back. Her fists were wound in his fur, and her heels pounded on his ribs. Ahjin rescued him despite Maili's protests. The panther shook his head at the repeated invitation and waved toward the sun. Ludik nuzzled Maili, then ran toward the cliff.

"He'll come tomorrow, Mother," Ahjin said, "and you can meet him when he's properly dressed. I'm sure he'll bring everyone else, too."

She blushed and drew Ahjin into the house. Maili stared at Ahjin before she smiled and threw her arms around his neck. "Ahja," she babbled.

Ahjin was never leaving home again.

Ahjin carried Maili while he greeted their cousin with Mother hovering by his shoulder. Charu's house, while still standing, was cracked from the foundation to the crooked roof.

His parents and Charu cooked lunch while Ahjin played with Maili. He described his new friends and the different lands he had visited but left out distressing details.

"It sounds like a grand adventure," Mother said.

"But what happened to your wings?" Father asked.

"And your face." Mother wiped her eyes.

"It's a long story. I'll tell you later."

For the rest of the day, Ahjin used that answer often. His parents seemed so ignorant of his experiences, he wondered what had been in Irajahan's message. When he had written his own letter, he thought only of apologizing. If he died, explanations wouldn't matter; if he survived, he'd elaborate. He hadn't realized it would be so hard to explain later.

Father interrupted his thoughts. "When the temple sent word of your return, they said to bring you there." He frowned. "At least we get today with you."

"Yes." Ahjin left it at that. Until he decided how to answer the gods, he didn't want to discuss it.

Father tightened his shoulders. "You're going tomorrow?"

"First thing in the morning." Ahjin kept his tone mild.

When Ahjin said nothing more, Father exchanged looks with Mother and changed the subject.

What would Ahjin's parents say when they learned the whole story? Would they be happy he was home or disappointed he still didn't want to be any sort of priest? Father had strong opinions about duty and obedience. Would he let Ahjin choose his own path?

Ahjin chuckled; if Irajahan gave his approval, no one could stop him. The Winds and temple guard would be helpless. With all five — *five!* — gods on his side, no one would contradict his choices. He could finally determine his own life.

If he gave in to the gods, he'd never be a skydancer, even after Darravani healed his wings. He wouldn't have time to improve his aerobatics. No mortal would dare order him around, but he'd be at the mercy of the gods. Arbitrating would be hard, boring work. He wouldn't be able to stay with his family, perhaps not even visit often. Ahjin picked up Maili and pressed his cheek against her wispy curls until she squirmed free.

But if he didn't help the gods, would the world stay safe for his sister? Would they squabble themselves into another disaster?

No, they'd find someone else. There was nothing special about him. It didn't have to be his responsibility.

He would be free.

Ahjin took a joyous breath. "Mother, Father, let me tell you about the deal I made with Irajahan." He omitted the deaths and the gods' last request. "And now Irajahan's free, and so am I," he finished.

"You defied your god." Father sounded horrified.

"Ahjin helped Irajahan in his time of need," Mother wrapped one arm around Ahjin and reached her other hand to Father.

"I thought you'd be happy I earned my freedom," Ahjin said. "I have Irajahan's permission to join the troupe."

"That's true." Father promptly began planning a tour across the country, with Ahjin as the newest skydancer.

Ahjin was so involved in the plans, he didn't notice what they ate or how late he finally retired to his pallet on the warped floor. All that mattered was the warmth of Maili sleeping next to him, the sound of Father whispering good night, and the feel of Mother's lips on his cheek.

Then the nightmares began.

29. DECISION

(VASI, IOJ)

And thus after a long absence did the eldest god return to this world, and all welcomed him joyfully.
A Comprehensive History of the Gods, vol. 6

First, Ahjin's old nightmare replayed incessantly. His friends broke and died in the meadow. He couldn't look away as his dream focused on each body, noting every wound received for Ahjin's doomed quest. The winged body was never him, but was Mother or Father or Maili. Gods fought above their corpses, destroying everything. Ahjin was helpless, and then the earth crumbled and the sun exploded, and he floated in the heavens, forever alone.

He shot upright, gasping.

After checking on Maili, he fell back asleep and dreamed of priestly misery. Each day, dawn to midnight, was buried in disputes. He made temporal treaties and arbitrated celestial arguments, then submitted petitions and studied religious tracts until his eyes crossed. Godly complaints banging inside his head woke him daily. Ahjin wore a path between his bedroom and his duty room without taking a step in the sunlight and wind. There was never time to fly or visit his family, except on the way to another land to repeat the entire tedious process. His wings withered, and he grew old and hunched.

Ahjin dragged himself awake and counted stars through a broken window until he fell asleep again. This time, he dreamed of flying. Sometimes he was alone in a vast open sky, spiraling through a cool breeze with the sun warming his wings. Often, he performed with his parents or their troupe. The wind whistled through his feathers as he pushed his healed wings through their tricks. He became as good as the best, and his parents smiled with pride. Years passed in his dream, until Maili was a young woman and performing with the family.

Ahjin woke smiling in the pure hope of morning light. He heard the roar of approving crowds, tasted Mother's cooking, felt his parents' love warmer than the sun. Everything he wanted was within reach.

It was time to decide. Sacrifice his dreams to help the gods, or fly in a lifetime of joy? He grabbed a pen and paper. All he needed to write was yes or no, but he had more to say.

This was Irajahan's fault. If he weren't a selfish, controlling brat, Ahjin would never have left home, and Kassian wouldn't have sought vengeance.

The gods had promised to uphold Ahjin's decision, so this was his chance to make a difference in the world. He raised his pen. "It isn't right to force people to be priests." He didn't care if Irajahan didn't like it.

The rest of his refusal went quickly. Ahjin slipped the paper under his pillow and whispered, "Kassian."

The sun was barely up, but his friends chattered outside. Ahjin covered Maili's ear and called out the window, "Shh, I'll come out in a minute." How did they drag Nia from bed so early?

Ahjin stopped by the kitchen and swapped Charu a hug for two hot cinnamon pastries. His parents were outside with his friends, all with pastries. Ludik had one in each hand and a very full mouth.

Mother looked at his travel-worn, Nokai-duplicated clothing and blinked back tears. "I'm sorry we didn't save any of your things from the house." She rearranged the drape of his scarf around his neck.

"You saved everything important." Ahjin ate a pastry in three bites, freeing an arm to hug Mother. "What's the plan today?"

Father handed him a napkin. "Are you still going to the temple?"

"Oh, yes," Nia said sweetly. "We can say pleasant journey to Ahjin there."

Ahjin glared at her until she shoved his other pastry into his mouth.

While he choked it down, Mother settled Maili in her carry-pack on Father's back. Askari set Ahjin's bag inside the house.

"Do you want your cloak?" Zefra asked.

"I'm warm enough," Ahjin said.

"But—" Zefra glanced at Nia. "Never mind."

"Didn't they feed you on the ship?" Ahjin asked Ludik, who savored his third sweet roll while they walked.

"Mm-hmm," Ludik purred, licking his fingers thoroughly.

Ahjin laughed and passed him a napkin.

Zefra murmured a polite stream of compliments about the damaged city. Nia looked everywhere while humming loudly. Sayaka and Askari hovered on the edges of the group, hands not quite near their weapons. Ludik teased Maili, who somehow recognized him without whiskers or fur and meowed at him between giggles.

The farther they went, the more neighbors leaned over their earth-shaken fences. A line of people noisily trailed them. Ahjin turned to see what caused the excitement, and the people cheered. He spun and gaped at his friends.

Nia waved her arms at the spectators and pointed to Ahjin.

"Spill it, Nia." Ahjin pulled her braid. "What did you do?"

"After Ludik came back yesterday, we went to see the temple." Nia grinned. "We visited the library, too, and the palace. Anyway, we heard Irajahan sent only a brief message, saying he had returned. Nobody knew you had rescued him, so... we told a few people?"

Ahjin smacked his forehead. "I could have been unnoticed?"

They turned into the city center. An aerial band played loud music. Skydancers flipped between the streets and roofs. Colorful birds flew bright streamers above the temple road.

Nia skipped. "Isn't this exciting? Look at that. Over there!"

When someone touched Ahjin's wing, he reached for his knife.

"'Tis me," Zefra murmured. "Here." She fastened her cloak around his shoulders and pulled up the hood. "I'm sorry."

"It's not your fault." Ahjin glared at the back of Nia's head and fell in step by Mother.

"Do not be angry," Zefra said. "She thought she was helping you. And the news would come out eventually."

"Speaking of news," Nia interrupted, walking backwards, "have you decided what you'll do?"

"I want to fly with my parents. I told you dozens of times." Ahjin didn't want to be a priest, or even a telepath. He didn't-want-it so badly his wings had ached with relief when he wrote "no" to Kassian.

"Oh, I know what you want." Nia winked, and he glared until she turned to walk properly.

The parade continued between damaged buildings. Nia waved cheerfully to everyone. Maili squealed with delight at the noise and colors. Ahjin strode across the cracked streets, daydreaming of skydancing.

The temple was missing several towers, and the stained-glass windows had shattered, but it otherwise showed so little damage that Ahjin suspected divine repairs.

A crowd of officially dressed Winds waited in the temple courtyard. Ahjin recognized the gray-haired man from his interview four months ago. His perpetual smile was a little strained as he hurried toward Ahjin.

"Come inside, please. Your friends and family can wait here." The old man motioned a priest to escort the others, then herded Ahjin to the temple. "Hurry," he urged, not quite dragging Ahjin.

They crossed through the tall doors, and the priest slammed them shut and leaned against them. He closed his eyes and sighed, then straightened. "This way, please."

The old priest led deep into the temple, moving so quickly Ahjin didn't get more than a glimpse of the murals. Stray sunbeams of white light sprayed through holes in the stained glass windows to illuminate the debris and shattered glass across the floor.

The priest noticed Ahjin's glance. "We're working on it," he said, "but we've had other problems. And here we are." He opened a gilded door and gestured inside.

Ahjin stepped into a large room. The door shut behind him, with the priest on the other side.

The room looked empty. Was he in the wrong place?

"How dare you," a voice howled from a dark corner.

Ahjin jiggled the door latch. Locked.

Irajahan stalked into the sunlight in the middle of the room. His oversized wings spread almost from wall to wall, and his face was purple.

"Your insulting little note arrived." He threw a wadded ball of paper at Ahjin's head. "How dare you encourage my siblings to clip my wings!" He flapped his wings, and dust puffed toward the walls.

"I didn't say that." Ahjin smoothed the note to see if Kassian had added rude words before delivering it.

"*It isn't right to force people to be priests,*" the note said. "*Not only do I decline your offer, but I insist you put an end to Irajahan's slavery. It can be part of the apologies you all promised to make. I wish you luck finding an arbitrator.*"

"I see nothing about clipping your wings," Ahjin said.

"You're stealing my priests," Irajahan screamed. "They are the manifestation of my power and glory!"

Ahjin tried not to laugh. "I'm not taking them. You can still ask people to be Winds. Some might accept, if you speak nicely."

Irajahan's nostrils flared. "I should have listened to Makana and sent you away! You don't deserve to serve me. Anyone else would be flattered to be my priest. Your stupid ban will make no difference. No one else will be so foolish to turn down the opportunity for greatness."

"I don't want greatness," Ahjin said. "All I want is my family."

He rubbed a finger across his scarf, and his heart soared on warm currents of joy. Tomorrow, he'd be skydancing with his family, and his life would be perfect.

"It's obvious you don't want to be glorious," Irajahan jeered. "I'm glad to see you go. Why don't you keep your mouth shut instead of giving my siblings unfair ideas?"

"Right is right." Ahjin frowned at the god. "It's wrong to enslave your priests or force out other gods. This world does not belong to you, and All-Powerful doesn't mean without moral limits."

A slow, nasty smile crept across Irajahan's face. "I created this world. I deserve to rule it. My siblings aren't allowed in my land, and they'll forget to watch me. I'll do whatever I want."

"I'll remind them to watch you," Ahjin said.

"You have no right." Irajahan grinned wider. "You lost your chance."

"They'll find an arbitrator who can keep you out of trouble."

Irajahan shrugged. "I'm not worried. I can be charming." He smiled at Ahjin very charmingly before resuming his dangerous grin.

Fear rippled across Ahjin's wings. Irajahan had almost succeeded against Kassian. If the sneaky, ambitious brat turned his sights on the gods again, would the world be safe? But who would keep him in line?

His siblings had failed to notice his treachery before. What if they *did* get too busy or forgot?

Kassian's request blew through his mind. *Please, won't you continue to help us?* Ahjin remembered his dreams from the night before. Freedom versus a lifetime of drudgery. Skydance with his parents or protect his family.

Was there another mortal who would recognize the dangerous truth about Irajahan? Ahjin squeezed his scarf until the silk creased. He could hold his course and be a skydancer, but at what cost?

If he let Irajahan go unchecked, thousands of innocents might suffer to satisfy the god's ego. More could die. His little sister might never grow old.

Were his dreams worth the price? Could he live with the potential consequences?

No. He couldn't risk it, couldn't trust anyone else. He had to keep Maili safe.

Ahjin clenched the scarf tighter. All his attempts to free himself had failed. He sucked in a shuddering breath and let his broken dreams vaporize on the exhale.

"I'm not charmed by you." Ahjin forced the words past the lump in his throat.

"You're nothing but a mite in my feathers," Irajahan said. "You'll be too busy skydancing with your parents to watch me. Enjoy your happiness." He smiled a real smile and turned his back to Ahjin.

Ahjin took another breath and flattened his note to Kassian against his raised knee. He didn't have ink, but he only needed to write a few words. He poked a finger with his knife, then plucked one of his scorched, broken feathers and dipped the quill in his blood.

Below his original note, he scrawled, "I accept." Ahjin signed his own life sentence with a shaking hand. A single tear smeared the words.

Ahjin held the note toward Irajahan. "Now I have the right to stop you. *I* will watch you."

He'd spend the rest of his life indoors, buried in paperwork and petitioners. It wouldn't matter if Darravani healed his wings or not, since he wouldn't have time to fly.

Irajahan turned around. "What do you mean?" He snatched at the note.

Ahjin said, "Kassian," and the note vanished.

Irajahan turned purple again. "Why give up your stubborn pursuit of skydancing now, just to take everything from me?"

Ahjin frowned. "I'm the one losing everything. You nearly destroyed the world with your foolishness, and someone has to stop you. I'd rather it not be me, but I can't take the chance no one else will see you for what you are. Even your siblings are too forgiving, considering what you did."

"Kassian deserved it," Irajahan howled.

"Your power-lust caused this," Ahjin retorted. "You need to fix it. Your siblings will make changes, too."

When Irajahan pressed into his mind again, Ahjin shut his mental doors. "I'm not your Wind. I don't have to listen to you except in performance of my duties, and I'm right in front of you. You can use your voice."

Lightning flashed in Irajahan's stormy gray eyes. "You might be in high currents now," he hissed, "but someday, I will rise again and blow you from the sky. I am All-Powerful. The other gods won't always protect you. You'll never even see me coming." He raised his hand and vanished.

Something struck Ahjin and threw him across the room. He hit the wall and collapsed. The door blew off its hinges, and the air rushed from the room in a gust. Glass tinkled from the windows.

Ahjin gasped for breath and failed to find it.

After a second, the air swept back in. Ahjin sucked in a lungful and pressed a hand to his aching ribs.

Actually, everything hurt. Ahjin carefully unfolded himself, one limb at a time, and struggled to a seated position. He eased his wings out of the way, unfastened Zefra's cloak from its twisted stranglehold around his neck, and leaned against the wall with a groan. Nothing seemed more broken than before, but he'd have new bruises. His finger still bled.

And he had a lifetime ahead of dealing with Irajahan. The other gods didn't seem as bad, but perhaps they had only been on their best behavior. Perhaps they'd be no better when annoyed.

How would he tell his parents he couldn't be with them after all? Father was excited about Ahjin finally joining the troupe, and Mother was overjoyed just to have him back. Would Ahjin get to see Maili while she grew, or would their visits be so rare she wouldn't recognize him?

Ahjin let his head bang against the wall and closed his eyes. He should stay here until the crowd left and he could break the bad news to his parents and friends privately.

The gray-haired priest skidded into the room. "Are you well? I'm so sorry about this. Let me help you."

"I'm fine," Ahjin said. "Hand me my cloak." He picked his scarf off the ground and tied it around his waist.

"It's not that cold." The priest dragged Ahjin to his feet and brushed off his clothing. When he got to Ahjin's tattered wings, he stopped abruptly. "Oh, I see." He shook the cloak and laid it over Ahjin's wings and shoulders. "Leave the hood down. Come."

They made their way through the temple and emerged in the courtyard behind the horde of priests. Irajahan waited, arms crossed, frowning at Ahjin, and the priests parted to allow the god to stand at the gilded marble podium. Ahjin hid among the priests when they closed ranks.

"Fair winds, my people." Irajahan raised his arms and wings dramatically. "I have returned!" He waited for the cheers to end. "Right now, all over the world, the other gods are telling their people the same thing. Thanks to me—"

The gray-haired Wind cleared his throat.

"—To one of my own," Irajahan rephrased, "the gods have returned. But all will not be the same."

The crowd murmured.

"It will be better! Yes, I — and the other gods, my sisters and brothers..." He emphasized the last plural and waited for the clamor to ebb. "We will bring a new era of world cooperation."

Ahjin had learned the hard way that the gods were vital to the world, but Irajahan sounded too optimistic. He wouldn't hold his breath.

The crowd cheered halfheartedly. Many whispered. "They're siblings?" "How many?" "Aren't there only four?"

Irajahan raised his hands for silence. "Now I present one of my priests, whose duties to me will be forgiven so he can serve the entire pantheon." His face dropped in feigned sacrifice, and he beckoned extravagantly to Ahjin.

Ahjin flinched. He had wanted a chance to tell his parents why he changed his decision.

The gray-winged priest pulled Ahjin next to Irajahan. Ahjin forced a bland smile and hid his clenched fists under Zefra's cloak. Wasn't everything bad enough without public humiliation? But of course, the All-Petty God of Air loved revenge.

"Meet Ahjin Machol, one of my most favored priests, now the mouthpiece of *all* the gods!" Irajahan proudly put one hand on Ahjin's shoulder and squeezed.

Ahjin cringed as his bones ground together.

"As one change in the new order, new adults will choose their professions with only the *advice* of my priests." Irajahan's face twisted. "No one will be assigned against their will, even my Winds." He muttered under his breath, "My way is better."

Irajahan raised his voice again. "My Winds will tell you the whole story. I apologize for my small part in the misunderstanding." He snapped his wings open and flew away.

What a coward, leaving the story of his betrayal of Kassian for his priests to tell. Ahjin would gladly share the true story. Later, after he escaped the horde streaming toward him.

The old priest stopped Ahjin from fleeing. "I'm sorry we weren't introduced." He escorted Ahjin toward his friends as the other Winds blocked the crowd. "My name is Amrafel. Your great-grandfather was my mentor when I was a mere Breeze. I intended to return the favor to you, but events have taken another current." He chuckled. "If there's ever anything I can do for you, I hope you'll ask."

They reached his family and friends. Amrafel said, "You have a remarkable son. I hope you're proud of him."

"Thank you, Your Supremacy," Mother said. "We are." She wrapped her arm around Ahjin, and Father bowed.

His Supremacy? Ahjin checked the priest's rank pin. His grandfather's Squall badge had three wind-curls, but this one showed the six of the Typhoon, the high priest who answered only to Irajahan himself. He was — or had been — the only priest who could even try to constrain the god. And he had wanted to be Ahjin's mentor.

"There is one thing you can do for me, Your Supremacy." Ahjin bowed his head. "Will you tell me how long my initiation will take?"

Perhaps his destroyed dreams would hurt less if he didn't dwell on what might have been.

"No time at all," Amrafel said. "It teaches new priests how to deal with Irajahan's... quirks. You already know. I hear you even learned how to shut him out, Your Supremacy." When Ahjin gaped at him, Amrafel laughed. "We need to choose a different title, to show your broader obligations. We'll talk later. Good flight." He clapped Ahjin on the back and left.

Broader obligations. Ahjin's shoulders sagged under the weight. And he still hadn't explained to his parents.

30. HOME

(EASTERN EDGE OF NOKAILANA)

And established they The House of the Gods on Arupa, created for that glorious purpose. And lived there His Holiness, Ahjin the Great, first of the Mouths of the Gods.
A Comprehensive History of the Gods, vol. 7

"Why aren't any of you surprised?" Ahjin watched the Typhoon instead of his friends.

"Don't be silly," Nia said. "I threw you overboard because you wouldn't stop fretting about *us*."

Ahjin crossed his eyes at her and turned to Ludik, who sat on the ground, gasping with laughter. "What's so funny?"

"Mouth of the Gods," Ludik choked. "That's what *I* said!"

Ahjin kicked his foot. "Get up, idiot. What do we do now?"

Sayaka held up a note. "The captain has directions to Ahjin's new home."

"I have a new home?" Ahjin missed his parents already.

Askari flicked the paper in Sayaka's hand. "When did you get that?"

"It appeared in my pocket. Like magic," Sayaka replied dryly. She turned the note to show Kassian's signature.

"This is our parting, then." Mother wiped at a tear. "We'll visit soon."

"Don't you want to come now? Or you can visit later." When their schedule allowed. If Ahjin wasn't gone. It was better than dead winds.

"Of course we'll come now." Father ruffled Ahjin's hair.

Captain Fathi sailed them southwest according to the instructions found in *his* pocket, and everyone but Maili stayed up much too late telling Ahjin's parents about their adventures.

By the time Ludik woke Ahjin long after sunrise, Zefra was meditating on deck, eyes closed and yawning. Nia dragged herself to the remnants of breakfast only after Ahjin pounded on the door for a solid five minutes. She ate slowly, then slumped on deck while Maili played with her braids.

"Me." Maili pulled on her own curls until Nia and Zefra plaited tiny tails across the toddler's head.

"There it is." Fathi lowered his spyglass and bellowed docking orders.

Nia climbed to the crow's nest. "Ahjin, this is where I found you." She clambered down the rigging and leaned over the bulwark. "It wasn't like this, though."

The ship bumped into a wharf on the east shore. Askari grabbed Nia before the jolt tipped her overboard.

A crowd of people stood across the dock, behind all five gods. Ahjin choked back his sigh. He'd hoped for a week or two with his family before his new job started.

The sailors anchored the ship and threw down the gangplank, but no one disembarked.

"The gods summoned you, Ahjin," Zefra said after a moment. "You lead the way."

Ahjin rolled his shoulders and walked down the ramp, followed by everyone but the sailors. When he had crashed on this island in spring, it was a rocky lump with no water or vegetation and barely enough room to pace. Now it was a mile or two across, with grass and trees, and buildings in the distance.

"Ahjin, thank you for agreeing to help us," Kassian said. "Greetings, family and friends. We thought about creating this new land in the middle of the ocean, an equal distance from each country."

"But that would have been too far away from everywhere and very inconvenient for your family," Makana interrupted. "This was a compromise."

"I enlarged the island for you, Ahjin." Darravani said. "We'll give you a tour soon, but first we have some gifts for you. Kassian helped me with something for Ludik." She stepped aside to reveal Ludik's twin supporting a rather sickly-green young lady with reddish hair.

"Gurryon. Nemerra!" Ludik took four long steps to embrace his beloved. "What is wrong?"

"I'll never travel like that again," Nemerra muttered. "I don't like falling through the air over and over."

Ludik kissed her. "I'm sorry I missed our wedding day," he murmured. "Will you still take me? I'll beg."

Nemerra put her fingers on his lips, wrapped her arms around his neck, and pulled him closer.

Ahjin gasped. The great oaf hadn't said anything about missing his wedding. Ahjin could never make this up to him. He looked away to hide his distress and give them a pretense of privacy.

"Stop that so you can hear the news, brother." Gurryon smirked. "Now that everyone knows about your healing magic, the village arranged for you to become our official healer."

Ludik let go of Nemerra to pounce on his brother. Their scuffle was ignored by the crowd in anticipation of the next gift.

"I just sent a message," Resef said to his Iskrins. "We hid their ship to surprise you."

He stepped aside, and a noisy horde boiled past the god. Zefra and Sayaka welcomed their families with hugs while Askari exchanged bows with Isvah, the Hotaru priest.

"So, where's my family?" Nia bounced on her toes.

"I'm sorry, Nia." Makana waved at the ocean. "Ya'eel is here, but everyone else is cleaning from the storms. They'll throw you a party later. Your mom sent two presents, and your family sent letters." She held out two floppy packages wrapped in plain canvas and tied with ribbons, as well as a string bag stuffed with letters.

Nia peeked inside one package with a chuckle and squealed at the second. "Is there somewhere to change clothes?"

"I'll show you later." Her goddess grinned, then turned. "Since we're all here, why don't we finalize our pact with Ahjin."

Ahjin clenched his fists and looked at Maili. It would be worth it. It had to be.

The gods arranged themselves at the end of the wharf. One side of the dock held the priests, with Gurryon between Resef's Isvah and Irajahan's Amrafel, and Makana's dolphin, Ya'eel, breaching in the ocean behind them.

Ahjin walked to the other side and reminded himself to breathe.

"There's one step left, Your Holiness," Kassian said. "We need to give you drops of blood so you can communicate with each of us."

Ahjin ignored the ridiculous honorific. "Will you tell me what to expect first?"

"You already know how I work," Irajahan whispered inside his head.

Ahjin tried not to flinch.

"I'll give you botanical knowledge," Darravani said, "and enough gardening skills to protect my garden. You can put blossoms on my shrine, or a written message with a flower to get my attention."

"You can send me a message with a dolphin." Makana motioned to Ya'eel. "There will always be one on duty. Or Nia can teach you how to scry in water. You may also hear from me in your dreams." She winked one lavender eye, and Ahjin blushed. "I'll also give you Nia's gift of languages," she said, "so you won't need interpreters."

Nia let out a muffled squeal.

Resef handed Ahjin a linen bag. "I made this set of obsidian runes myself." He waited for the impressed murmur to wane among the Iskrins. "I will place the dictionary in your head. You can lay them in a message or write a note with a rune for attention. You can also try prayer, if you like. I will listen for you."

Irajahan's threatening glare bounced off Resef's grin.

Kassian scowled at Irajahan. "I don't have a good history with verbal messages. I'll give you the ability to send me a letter directly." He motioned, and a paper appeared in Ahjin's hand.

"What exactly am I supposed to be doing?" Ahjin asked. "You were a little vague about my duties."

"I'm sure we'll work out the details later," Makana said.

Nightmare details. Ahjin shuddered.

"Any more questions?" Irajahan sounded bored.

Ahjin shook his head. He'd have many questions in the future, but none to change his fate.

The two priests and the apprentice drew small knives from their belts and approached their gods. Kassian and Makana drew their own blades.

"Ya'eel will witness, but he's no good with knives," Makana said mock-solemnly. She poked her finger and dripped golden blood into the bowl Amrafel held. Gurryon added Darravani's, and Isvah bled Resef.

When it was his turn, Irajahan protested. "Ahjin can already communicate with me."

"Do it for the formality, in case the next Mouth isn't one of yours." Amrafel jiggled the bowl until Irajahan scowled and held out a hand.

Kassian added his own blood last and dripped an elixir over everything. "It will help it absorb properly, instead of just digest. It might help the taste." He shrugged. "Or not."

Ahjin gingerly took the bowl with the tiny puddle of gold. How disgusting.

"You know what they say about people who drink blood?" Makana's macabre remark was overly cheerful.

"No, what do they say?" Kassian's grin grew until his dimple matched hers.

"Never mind, maybe I made it up." She grinned impishly at Ahjin. "It won't improve by staring at it."

Ahjin gulped it in one long swallow. It tasted a bit like fresh-picked summer berries, still warm from the sun. When it hit his stomach, the warmth exploded through his veins and burned up to his brain.

The next thing he knew, he lay on the dock while Zefra held a cold, wet cloth to his head.

"Don't worry." Ludik handed him a cup of the too-familiar painkilling tea. "You haven't been out long."

Ahjin tossed down the tea and hoped it would stop the pounding in his skull that seemed integral to godly gifts. He let Father pull him to his feet and turn him to face the gods.

"Would you like the tour before or after your parents leave?" Darravani asked.

Ahjin tried to speak, but his voice failed. He thought he'd have a little more time with his family.

"We'd love to see all the island," Father said. Mother rubbed Ahjin's arm and resettled Maili on her hip.

"Then hurry." Irajahan glared at Ahjin.

Makana elbowed her brother. "Whenever you're ready, Ahjin."

Ahjin shoved his hands in his pockets and strolled off the dock onto the narrow cobblestone road. In only a few minutes, he reached a small town square in the middle of the island. Empty buildings and market stalls ran down two sides, waiting for people to bring them to life.

A building on one corner dominated the plaza. While miniature compared to the Vasi temple, its elaborate architecture and marble columns suggested Irajahan's influence. As if Ahjin needed more reminders of Irajahan.

"I made this temple for you, Ahjin," Irajahan boasted. When the Typhoon, Amrafel, shook his head sadly, the god sniffed.

Darravani gestured west. "My garden is across the bridge. I'll introduce you to my plants later."

"If you look along the south road," Resef said, "you can see four houses to make petitioners feel at home."

The houses were a variety of styles, including a wooden replica of an Iskrin tent. Petitioners, too? Ahjin's island would have no family, no friends, just an endless flow of strangers. He reached for Mother's hand, but at the last second, pasted a makeshift smile on his face and took Maili from her arms instead.

Makana pointed to a colorful, two-story guest house with a domed roof, closest to a small pond. "Nia, you can change there. Want help with your hair?"

Nia and Makana ran to the Nokai house. Everyone else crowded through the temple's arched double doors for an inside look. Rainbows poured through stained-glass windows in the roof and walls. Each of the side walls had two shrines. The back had only one, with the sixth space occupied by a door to an inner sanctuary.

Ahjin easily identified each god's region. Darravani's shrine was dark wood, beautifully carved into a tree trunk, capped with a tray of dirt, miniature parchment scrolls, and a botany book. Irajahan's altar was jeweled marble with gold veins. Resef had a collapsible kiln of interlocking clay tiles, with candles and obsidian runes on the mantel. Maka-navailea's polished metal statue was a dolphin balancing a bowl of water on its head. Paper, ink, and quill sat on Kassian's pedestal, a clear glass block with white stars etched inside.

Darravani watched Ahjin with a frown, then took Maili from him and gave her to Mother. "You didn't remind me to fix your nerves and wings, did you?" she chided. "We need you in good health to keep up with our numerous demands." She ushered him into the sanctuary and closed the door.

If she hadn't been helping, the next hour could have counted as torture. Darravani had already healed the major broken bones, but rear-ranging the dozens of minor breaks in Ahjin's wings hurt more than breaking them in the first place. She mended his muscles with magic, but it felt like she sewed them with fire and thorns. Fixing his heart and internal damage was like drowning in lightning all over again. To avoid frightening Mother, he somehow didn't scream.

Ahjin thought that was the end, until Darravani tested his nerves with every possible sensation "to make sure they work." He didn't have words for that agony. When she offered to regrow his feathers, he declined. Healing major damage was worth the misery; feathers would fix themselves.

He fled the temple, missing Ludik's slower, gentler healing methods, even as he stretched his wings painlessly wide for the first time since the scorpions.

Zefra's sisters climbed up and down the temple steps with Maili while the adults chatted. Nia had a ready audience when she saun-tered up the road in a cloud of perfume. Her hair was braided for half its length, wrapped around her head into a lavender crown gemmed with flowers. The remaining tresses waved over her shoul-ders. The heavy silk gown flowed over her curves in an emerald color exactly matching her eyes. Her long skirt swirled above her sandals, revealing the different-colored paint on each nail of her webbed toes.

Zefra's brother stood to stare. "Incredible," Izo breathed. He glanced at Zefra and sank again.

"There's one more stop in the tour." Kassian led everyone north.

Izo worked his way to Nia's side. She danced down the road and waved her hands as she chattered at him. Ahjin watched sympathetically as Zefra's poor brother said only a few words the entire way.

Kassian pointed to four houses with small kitchen gardens behind them. "We saved the best for last. These are for the permanent residents, including your staff." He waved his hand at Ahjin's confusion. "You'll need staff."

It was nice of the gods to put so much thought into making him happy, though staff wasn't what he wanted.

"That one is for you and your family." Resef pointed to the largest house, closest to the temple and the stream.

"My family?" Ahjin grabbed his parents' hands. He knew he'd never perform with his family and had thought they'd get only the occasional visit at best. Living together was a lost dream.

"Oh, didn't we say your family can stay with you when they aren't performing?" Makana said. "Your parents have to get their things and tell their troupe, but they'll come back."

"I told you this would be his favorite part," Darravani said.

His parents stammered their thanks and hugged Ahjin.

Ahjin squeezed his family. They could stay with him. Joy rushed through his heart for the first time since he'd signed the note to the gods.

"Is that all?" Kassian asked. "Then it's time we left."

Resef snapped his fingers. Ahjin pulled his parents out of the way before the god's pet comet zoomed from the sky. "Anyone want a ride?" Resef reached toward his sisters.

"I'll swim home, but I still owe you for the last ride." Makana headed for the ocean.

"Farewell, brother, it was nice seeing you again before you die." Kassian bowed to Resef and laughed.

"I'll go with you, Kassian," Darravani said. "I want to talk to you."

Kassian and Darravani vanished while Resef and Irajahan flew in different directions.

That seemed to be the cue for everyone else to leave. Ahjin walked them to the wharf to delay farewells.

After boarding, Gurryon and Nemerra leaned on the ship's rail and watched Zefra's sisters ask the sailors a thousand questions. Askari boarded with Isvah and Sayaka's family.

"Will Captain Fathi take everyone home?" Ahjin asked.

"All the Iskrins," Ludik explained, "and he's meeting a Nokai trade ship to take us Darrendrakar home. Are you coming aboard to say farewell?"

Ahjin forced a smile. "You can't just disappear."

"We're going, too." Mother held one of Maili's hands while Father held the other.

Ahjin crouched to tickle Maili, hiding his disappointment. "How long will you be gone?"

"No more than a week, I think," Father said.

Ahjin's parents hugged him tightly before boarding. Maili waved until they went below deck.

"I'll make sure they get help," Amrafel said. "I'll visit you soon and give you some tips, Your Holiness."

Ahjin sighed. "Don't call me that, please, Your Supremacy. Will you go on the ship, too?"

Amrafel laughed. "I don't have a baby to carry, and I may be old, but I can fly myself home." The old priest bowed deeply to Ahjin. "Good flight, Your Holiness." A moment later, he spiraled in a warm updraft before turning for Ioj.

"Are you ready?" Zefra stood arm in arm with Nia. Izo hovered behind them.

Ahjin nodded, heart in his throat, and followed them up the gangplank.

"You're not far from Iskra," Zefra said, "and I must talk to Kassian about expeditions. If you forget to visit, I may have to shipwreck on your island. Warmth to you." Her bow did not hide the smile on her face.

Nia stepped up to kiss everyone on the cheek, Nokai-style. She started with Izo, who returned the favor. Ahjin stepped in for a hug from Zefra. To his shock, she pressed a quick kiss against his cheek. Nia kissed Ludik and embraced Nemerra, whispering something that made the tall girl giggle.

Nemerra turned to Ahjin. "Would you perform our wedding ceremony? It would mean a lot to Ludik."

"Am I allowed to do that?" Ahjin looked to see if Ludik was laughing, but he was waiting anxiously for the answer. "I'm honored. It's too little to repay you. Send word of the date."

He made a mental note to ask Darravani about Darrendrakar weddings, but his ribs suddenly cracked in a breath-stealing hug.

When Ludik let go, Nemerra clasped his hands in a warm but gentler farewell. "Keep well."

Ahjin took another deep breath and turned to Nia. "You're the last."

"Don't be ridiculous," Nia said. "I'll swim home with Ya'eel later. I'm not ready to end the adventure. I already put my things in the Nokai house." She picked up her long skirt and ran down the ramp, then waved at Captain Fathi.

Ahjin walked down the plank to the dock and watched as the ship raised sails and pulled out of the harbor. He turned to Nia and raised an eyebrow. "Now what?"

"You haven't seen my other package," she said. "It's Ludik and Nemerra's wedding present. You'll love it!" She ran into town, laughter trailing behind her.

Ahjin touched the scarf in his pocket. Summer was ending and the world had changed so much since spring. He had changed, too. Despite the bitter, life was sweet, and friendship was sweeter.

He laughed and strolled down the wharf toward his new home.

YAY! NOW OUR HEROES WILL LIVE HAPPILY EVER AFTER, AND LUDIK'S WEDDING WILL GO PERFECTLY!

Will it, dear reader?

DEAR AUTHOR, YOU ARE MAKING ME NERVOUS. EVERYTHING WILL BE PERFECT, RIGHT? RIGHT??

Well... Maybe not.
More surprises await our poor heroes.
Turn the page for info about **Seed of War**,
wherein Ludik is very excited to see his friends again
on his wedding day. Just before everything goes
very, very... wrong.

SEED OF WAR

Lies, suspicion, and a desperate trek.

In a world where no race trusts another, the shapeshifting jaguar Ludik became friends with the strangers who helped him save the world from feuding gods. Now a gilled translator, a fire mage, and the winged messenger of the Gods have come for his long-delayed wedding.

But before Ludik and his beloved can pledge their love, an accidental death threatens their happiness. Bad enough that a Fox trespassed into Cat territory, worse that he picked a fight with a bigger Leopard, but the true disaster is the witness who is running home to report that the Cats murdered his kin.

In a mad race to keep the misguided Dog from starting a civil war, Ludik must follow the trail through hostile territory and turn a fierce Wolf into an ally. If he can't root out the seeds of war before they sprout, how will he preserve the life of the woman he adores?

*Seed of War is a fantasy mystery that ponders justice, mercy, and vital choices when everything is at stake. It is the second book in the **Unexpected Heroes** series of clean YA secondary world fantasy and is best read in order for the most enjoyment.*

Check my website MCLeeBooks for links to buy the next story or get the entire series at once.

Still want more? Get free stories by joining my newsletter. Every two weeks, I chat about my current writing or my life & offer book news and deals. And did I mention free stories?

Sign up at https://dl.bookfunnel.com/3wwıak6pzb

Free Story #1: Nobody's Revenge

How in the world did Irajahan trick Kassian into leaving? Why did Kassian come back after so long? Why did he think kidnapping his siblings was a solution? How did he capture not just ONE god, but all four?!

Read Kassian's side of the story in Nobody's Revenge!

Free Story #2: The Cat's Fortune

On another world, so long ago that truth faded into legend, a cat and a boy seek their fortune together.

Orphaned and homeless, young Aktar travels to the city of Rapata for a better life.

But it seems the rumors of gold-paved streets are false. Can he find a home and a job before he starves? Maybe with the help of a foundling kitten.

A retelling of Puss in Boots and Dick Whittington, with timeless themes of belonging, courage, and self-discovery, set on the fantasy world of Kaiatan, home of the **Unexpected Heroes**.

If you liked this book, please leave an honest review on any retailer or reader site. Seriously, it would really help me. :)

If you found a typo, you're welcome to report it at mcleebooks.com/report-a-typo/

CHARACTER LIST AND PRONUNCIATION GUIDE

If you are interested in the meanings of the names, please visit MCLeeBooks.com

Name (Pronunciation) Identity

People

Ahjin Machol (AH-jzhin MACK-ole) Iojif, 16 years old, skydancer

Akamu (AH-kah-moo) Darrendrakar, Maon shaman

Amakualena (AH-ma-KUE-ah-LAIN-ah or KUE-ah) Nokai boy, Kala and Nia's friend

Amrafel (AHM-rah-fell) Iojif, chief priest in Vasi

Aria Machol (AH-ree-ah) Iojif, Ahjin's mother

Asad (Ah-SAHD) Darrendrakar, Maon headman

Asitha (Uh-SEETH-uh) Iskrin, apprentice priest

Askari (Uh-SCAR-ee) Iskrin, guard

Awakakama (Ah-wuh-kah-KAHM-uh) Nokai, one of Nia's twin far-brothers

Chalon (CHAY-lon) Darrendrakar, Asad's son & Kalliona's husband

Charu (CHAIR-oo) Iojif woman, Ahjin's cousin

Darravani the Omnifarious (DAR-uh-VAHN-ee) Darrendrakar Goddess of Earth

Fathi (FAHTH-ee) Iskrin, ship captain

Gurryon Moriko (GURR-yon) Darrendrakar, Ludik's brother

Haider Moriko (HAY-der) Darrendrakar, Ludik's brother
Haru Ashvakosha (HAHR-oo) Iskrin, Zefra's younger sister
Hesketh Ashvakosha (HESK-eth) Iskrin, Zefra's father
Heti (HET-ee) Iskrin, Hotaru healer
Hiranya Moriko (Her-AHN-yuh) Darrendrakar, Ludik's younger sister
Irajahan the Omnipotent (Ear-AH-jzhuh-han) Iojif God of Air
Isvah (ISS-vuh) Iskrin, Hotaru chief priest
Izo Ashvakosha (EYE-zoe) Iskrin, Zefra's older brother
Jayan Machol (JZHAY-an) Iojif, Ahjin's father
Kalalamoanani (Kah-LA-la-moe-uh-NAHN-ee or KAH-la) Nokai, Nia's older near-sister
Kamea(keikilani) (Kuh-MAY-ah-KAY-kee-lah-nee) Nokai, Nia's younger far-sister
Kassian (KASS-ee-an) Architect
Kalliona Moriko (Kal-ee-OH-nuh) Darrendrakar, Ludik's older sister
Koray (CORE-ay) Iskrin, Rikatsu healer
Lee (LEE) Iojif, city guard at lifts
Ludik Moriko (LUD-ick) Darrendrakar, 17/18 years old, hunter
Maili Machol (MAY-lee) Iojif, Ahjin's younger sister
Makanavailea the Omniscient (Mah-KAHN-uh-vie-LEE-uh) Nokai Goddess of Water
Narrasiman Moriko (Nah-RRAHS-ih-man) Darrendrakar, Ludik's older brother
Nemerra (Neh-MERR-uh) Darrendrakar, Ludik's betrothed
Niamolenulanami (NEE-ah-moe-LEN-noo-la-NAHM-ee) Nokai, 15 years old, singer
Prathap (PRATH-up) Iskrin, Hotaru chieftain
Risa Ashvakosha (REE-suh) Iskrin, Zefra's younger sister
Resef the Omnificent (RES-eff) Iskrin God of Fire
Sayaka Ruchi (Sae-YAHK-uh RUE-chee) Iskrin, guard
Shara Ashvakosha (SHAR-uh) Iskrin, Zefra's mother
Shri Okechuku (SHREE OH-keh-CHOO-koo) Iskrin, Tukiko healer
Usri Ashvakosha (OOS-ree) Iskrin, Zefra's younger sister
Ya'eel (YAH-eel, with click between syllables and a squeal-whistle) Nokai dolphin

Zefra Ashvakosha Kezhekori (ZEF-rah ASH-vah-KOASH-uh KEZ-eh-KORE-ee) Iskrin, 15 years old, Hotaru guide

Groups, Locations, Languages

Arupa (Uh-RUPE-uh) Island

Chiharu (Chi-HARE-oo) Iskrin clan, specialty: perfume

Darrendra (Duh-RREND-druh) Northern country

Darrendrakar (Duh-RREND-druh-car) People of Darrendra, shapeshifters

Darrendran (Duh-RREND-drun) Darrendrakar language

Devora (Dev-OH-ruh) Iskrin clan, specialty: grain

Hotaru (Hoe-TARE-oo) Iskrin tribe, specialty: maps

Ioj (EYE-ojze) Eastern country

Iojif (Eye-OH-jziff) People of Ioj, avians

Iojo (Eye-OH-jzo) Iojif language

Iskra (ISK-ruh) Southern country

Iskrin (ISK-ree) People of Iskra, desert-dwellers

Iskrit (ISK-rit) Iskrin language

Kanshi (KAHN-shee) Darrendra capital, in east

Kazuki (Kuh-ZOO-kee) Iskran clan, speciality: spices

Maon (MAY-on) Felid village

Nokai (NO-kie) People of Nokailana, aquastrians

Nokailana (NO-kie-LAHN-uh) Western islands

Noki (NO-kee) Nokai language

Ravisu (Rav-IH-soo) Iskrin clan, speciality: pottery, silk

Rikatsu (Rick-AT-soo) Iskrin clan, speciality: ships

Tukiko (Too-KEE-koe) Iskrin clan, speciality: healing

Vasi (VAHS-ee) Capital of Ioj

ACKNOWLEDGMENTS

Thanks to my extraordinary alpha and beta readers, Ammon Rasmussen, Autumn Gibelyou, Carol Malone, Cheree Myatt, Chris Cornetto, Donna Gonzales, Erin Lanham, Gail Porter, Hannah DeForest, Kyle Adams, Kylia Rasmussen, Laura Dotson, Liz, Mackenzie Bodily, Marion Boyd, Meg Grierson, Megan Hutchins, Naomi Rasmussen, Rebecca Keller, Robin Cranney, Ruth Morley, Shauna Watts, Tad Rasmussen, Victor Hatchet, Virginia Cummings, & Wendy Morkel

Special thanks to Shauna Watts and Laura Dotson, who turned my sketchy notes into real tunes,
and to my editor, Anna King, who saved my ending.

ABOUT THE AUTHOR

Marty C. Lee told stories for most of her life, but never took them seriously until her daughter asked her to write this one. Between writing and spending time with her family, she reads, embroiders, paints-by-number, and gardens.

She has lived in five states, seven cities, and ten houses so far. She currently lives in the West, but not in a tropical paradise. She doesn't like flying, even in an airplane. She wishes she could produce her own fire to warm her hands. She's glad she didn't have to wait a year to marry her sweetheart, who also wishes she could warm her hands.

You can find her at
MCLeeBooks.com and on Facebook and book sites

www.ingramcontent.com/pod-product-compliance
Lightning Source LLC
Chambersburg PA
CBHW031340020726
47499CB00005B/1343